Seeking Solace

A Novel

Kacy Cooney

For those who refuse to be victims

Acknowledgments

I have been blessed by support from many people.
My greatest thanks go to Gerald and Roxanne.
I would also like to express my gratitude to Byra Cooney Schworer
for permission to use the artwork of her son, Peter Schworer.
Also much appreciation goes to Karen Feldman, Karen Hammond,
John Steiger, Jessica Monte, Susan Garlock, and Amy Perina for
editing, encouragement, and writerly connections.

Also by Kacy Cooney:
In A Maze of Imaginations

Chapter One

"Are you a friend of Cindy's from Toronto, Solace?"

"No. I'm American. I don't know anyone here."

Mike Leahy was one of three men who had come to help us build a wooden storage box for Cindy's athletic gear. Because there wasn't enough for five people to do, he and I had wandered to the other side of the house. Brushing off sawdust, we found our way to the railing to look over the beach and beyond to the ocean. "I didn't think they printed the Carollons on your maps," he joked, flicking his sunglasses up to reveal his blue eyes.

"They use a secret ink that only special people can see."

"Special people like you?" Mike was a scrawny, blue-tongued, yet otherwise well-mannered rogue with short disheveled brown hair. He was friendly, but not someone I would have socialized with back in Virginia. As we talked, however, I stopped noticing his sun damaged skin and visible tattoos, things that would normally have caused me to assign him to some category of deadbeat.

"I might be the wrong kind of special."

"Sounds promising. What the hell brought you here then, heh? Job transfer? I hope you got a big raise."

"No. I came here on a well-planned whim. No job, no reason to come other than wanting to start fresh." There was a strong wind coming off the Atlantic, and I let it blow my long, golden brown hair in front of my face so I could hide from Mike's curiosity. I was unused to receiving as much attention I had gotten from the people I'd met since my arrival in Williamsport a few days earlier. "It's not a vacation." I hadn't intended to tell him all this, but I must have needed to say it. I was excited and proud of myself. This was the first time in my life I had done anything or gone anywhere by my own effort. I had done it all myself, refusing both discouragement and advice. "I'm here to figure out what I want and what my interests are without pressure. To experiment a little."

I had always depended too much on the people I trusted, especially my parents, whose protectiveness and generosity undermined my confidence nearly as much as had my ex-husband's constant and conflicting criticism. After my marriage ended, I had returned to my parents' home. In the first months my world began to expand. I poured my returning energy into my career and restarting friendships. Then just when I began to raise my expectations, it seemed my options were disappearing. I wasn't as lonely as I had been during most of my marriage, but I understood my situation better. I needed a new strategy, and I needed to stop looking to other people for approval.

"What did you do?"

"My work? I was a banker, a branch manager."

"You are in for a shitload of adjustments if you start hanging out with people like me. I mean, I doubt our bankers are as formal as yours." He leaned on the rail, studying me. "I'll bet you look really nice when you're all dressed up. You one of those small women who wear high heels all the time?" He noticed me recoil. "Sorry. Did I embarrass you? You are a beautiful woman, Solace, but I like you."

I relaxed. "What's wrong with beautiful women?"

"Probably nothing."

"So it's like the thing I have against tattoos?"

He held up his wrist, displaying a small tropical fish, which I might have liked if it had been drawn on paper. "Probably." Then he turned back to the ocean. "How'd you meet Cindy?"

I swallowed, relieved, and began to practice for explaining all of this to my parents. "I had dinner at the restaurant where Katie works, and she started talking to me about the house. Just dumb luck, I guess. I thought I'd live alone, but when she suggested I look at the house, I thought: why not? It'll make it easier for me to meet people, and it'll be a lot cheaper than renting a place on my own."

"And you get to look at the ocean from your bedroom window."

"Yeah. That's pretty good too."

"Are you going to take it easy for a while?"

"I think so. I really do need a vacation. Besides I don't know what I want to do."

"Really?" He sounded pleased. "Holy shit, we do have something in common."

"Is that unusual?"

"Well, yeah, sometimes I feel like I'm the only one who doesn't have a purpose. I even know people who are pursuing multiple careers. Not me though. I'm content to hang out on the beach."

"But you work?"

"Only on weekends. For now. I'm a Marine reservist. So are Liam and Tim." They were the other two men who were constructing Cindy's box. "Actually, I did want to be a Navy diver, but they wouldn't qualify me. So I joined the Marines instead. Fulfilled my mandatory service a long time ago, but I've stayed on. We've got a tight unit." He hung his head to one side.

I listened to him and watched the ocean. I was looking forward to settling into my room. Though the house was somewhat dilapidated, and the furnishings were rather shabby, the people I lived with were pleasant and considerate. The weathered grey, wooden house stood on stilts at the border of the sand and the land, the main body of the island where the soil is dark. The deck wrapped around three sides with a long stairway leading down to the lane called Grass Street. The view from this side of the house was gorgeous. My hair was a tangled mess.

"What was the problem with your bank, Solace?"

"Hmm? Oh, bad loans on the corporate side, but the part where I worked was good. I liked my job pretty well, but I just sort of fell into it. I think I might like to try something else."

"Must be tough, heh, to give up the big salary?"

"If I'd had one. The bank was cutting costs to survive. I was promoted when they let go of some more senior, more expensive managers about a year ago. I still hadn't gotten a raise when I left. I understand why they did it that way, but it feels like they took advantage of me."

With a sympathetic nod he turned and walked around the corner of the house to check on the work. I followed him. We were just in time to hold up a sheet of plywood while Tim screwed it into place. Cindy squatted inside caulking the seams. "We'll paint it later, eh, Solace. Let's have a beer while the caulk dries." The men strayed away. Cindy pushed her short blonde hair off her sweaty forehead, exposing dark roots. "I'll get them to help move the heavy stuff," she whispered.

Cindy Robinson had arrived from Toronto about a year and a half ahead of me. She had come on vacation and stayed. Because she'd had to wait about six months before she was cleared to work, she was still living on a tight budget a year after going to work in an antique shop in the Russian part of Williamsport. She was gregarious and athletic, about as different from me as a woman could be, except for the part about running away from home. While she went inside to fetch the beer, I sat at the table with Mike and Tim. Liam and Cindy opened and passed out the bottles. I already had a bottle of water.

"Has Cindy recruited you to one of her teams yet?" Tim asked.

"She won't want to do that," I assured him.

"Is that so? With those long legs," Tim said, eyeing them in a way I found unpleasant, but not in the same kind of sneering, unpleasant manner my ex-husband had used to suggest I needed to lose weight. "Bet you're fast."

"Dweeb," Mike said under his breath just loud enough to be sure we both heard him.

"I guess I'll go shake off the sawdust." Tim stood and walked away.

After he left, I asked Mike if they were friends.

"Not really. We used to be neighbors, when we were kids, but he's enough younger that we never hung out together. He's some kind of a throwback." Mike forced a laugh. "We're all on edge. You know, they might activate us. The Marines, I mean."

"Why?"

"Kuwait. The Iraqi invasion. It's getting more tense over there."

"I almost forgot about that. I haven't paid attention to the news since I got here."

"Yeah." He poured the rest of the bottle down his throat.

Not knowing what to say, I looked toward the ocean again. I spotted Tim wandering through the dunes toward the beach. He was barefoot, but he still had his beer. "I guess he left his shoes here."

Mike nodded. "The U.S. is involved too."

"When I went to the airport, my father wanted me to buy return tickets. He thought the airfare might go up with the price of crude."

"Did you?" His attention was reengaged.

"Nope. I don't want a deadline. I have a lot to do, and I've no idea how long it'll take. It would be humiliating if I went home before I worked out some of the things I came here to settle."

"Good. I think you're going to be a nice addition to our circle."

I wasn't sure I belonged in his circle, but I appreciated his friendly overtures. Cindy and Liam joined us at the table. She asked where Tim was, and Mike pointed to the beach. "What'd he do? Hit on Solace?"

The box was a success. Once all of Cindy's gear was moved outside, our room was pleasant. Our window looked out over the dunes and the beach, and we usually left it open to let in the fresh air. We found a good level of cooperation and intimacy, open and respectful.

I was busier than I expected to be, partly because Cindy took it upon herself to introduce me to the city and her friends. I got a bicycle and wandered on my own too. The house was out of the urban center that ran along the river from the harbor up past Little Russia toward the rainforest in the interior. I spent a few hours of most days at the beach swimming or wading or relaxing under my new umbrella, reading or cross-stitching, my needle moving in and out of the aida cloth to the rhythm of the surf. I had needed rest, but as my mind cleared my energy surged. I was ready to pursue my goals. It was time for me to go to work.

So what did I do? I went about looking for a job the way I always had. I went through the newspaper and picked everything that seemed to fit my basic criteria, and ended up working at a bank again mostly because the hours suited me. In addition to taking work, I had applied to the University of Williamsport. Thinking I might pursue full-time or advanced studies, I wanted to keep my work hours short, and the teller position was for twenty hours a week. The pay was enough to cover most of my living expenses.

That was acceptable. A young woman needs to be carefree sometimes. I was learning to focus on the present, though it meant going against both my cautious nature and my upbringing. In retrospect, I had wasted too much worry on what I might regret someday, and I did regret that more than I think I would have regretted many of the things that I might have chosen to do if I hadn't worried so much.

My work was familiar; even the currency was in dollars and cents. It made for a smooth transition. Too smooth perhaps, because I was supposed to be trying new things and all I had done from a professional standpoint was to take a voluntary demotion. I didn't let it bother me much, because my mind was opening. I could feel it. Each day, after I balanced, I could leave off thinking about my work until it was time to return the next day. I still had plenty of time to hang out on the beach and think about myself and my new surroundings, and to realize that I was not being selfish to try to find out what made me happy.

Given that Washington, D.C. must be one of the world's most uptight cities, it was no surprise that the Carollonians were a more relaxed group of people. They tended to be more polite too. Even in affluent North Beach, an American bank teller evoked curiosity, and many went out of their way to welcome me to their city.

One of these was Sean Donovan, a thirtyish charmer who showed up at my window several times a week. As usual he arrived with some trivia about the islands. "Good afternoon, Miss Murphy," he said with a smile. He poked his long nose and fingers into his wallet to retrieve his paperwork. When he handed me a check to cash, he asked, "Would you have moved to the Carollons if you had realized that there were no proper theatres in the entire nation?"

I took his check without looking away from his friendly face. "Probably, but…is that really true?"

"I don't make this stuff up, Solace." While I began to process his transaction, he nodded, continuing his diplomatic efforts. "You must not allow your wandering, Bohemian soul to despair, however. Williamsport is a hotbed for musicians. There are 78 clubs and pubs that offer live performances at least once a week."

I turned to the computer. "That's culturally lop-sided."

"I couldn't have said it better!"

"Drama isn't illegal, is it?"

He chuckled. "If it were, we'd have to build more jails." He stretched his hands on the countertop, adding, "There are some dinner theatres, but the movies are all imported, I'm afraid." Smiling, I slid my hand forward with his money beneath it. I froze when he spoke again, breaking my trust. "Would you like to go with me to listen to some music, Solace?"

As if from above I saw the counter, the money in my hands, even as I recoiled, pulling back behind the opening in the cabinetry. His hands were still flattened on the counter opposite me. My eyes locked, horrified, on the wedding band on his left hand. I felt my face grow hot. Collecting a shred of poise, I prepared to count the money out to him and brusquely wish him the life he deserved. I would leave him to infer to just what kind of hell I would assign him from what I hoped would be an atom-stopping cold, yet faultlessly polite tone.

He paled, unmoving, watching me. As I curled the money under my left thumb, ready to count, he stopped me by asking, "Are you alright? I didn't mean to startle you." His voice was placating. I'll credit him with persistence, for most men would have tried to step back to the friendly manners that had worked before, a pointless and insulting retreat.

This was no cultural misunderstanding, and I would do nothing to ease his discomfort. I stared at him, pushing him away with the venom in my gaze. I shoved the money at him. "Take it and go, Mr. Donovan," I hissed quietly. I did not want anyone else to know what had happened. Such an insult was too humiliating to share.

He finally accepted my rejection. "I'm sorry," he whispered in a shaky voice. Then he looked at the money on the counter. "That was just my excuse to see you, Sol—Miss Murphy."

"Well, you saw me," I said with exasperation, desperate for this scene to end. "Now, please take it. I've got other customers."

He swept his hand across the counter, taking the bills and shoving them into his pocket. He looked so miserable that I almost enjoyed it. Still pale, he straightened his posture as he turned to go and gave me one final look that was intended to confuse me into thinking I had hurt him. I knew better, and I wouldn't have cared if his lascivious pride had been wounded. Men like him were not owed explanations.

Finally he was gone, out of the door, and, if I had anything to say about it, out of my life. I did my best to regain my composure, though I still quivered, in the time it took to ring my bell for the next person in line.

Without taking another moment to consider the issue, I concluded that I needed to find a new job. I wanted no more of that kind of attention. I'd met men like him before, and I hated them. Married men who thought they didn't have to obey the rules. Men like my ex-husband who thought they were better than everyone else. Men like Sean Donovan who thought they had so much charm that they could spare some for women other than their wives. Damn him.

The Marines that Cindy knew began to tighten their social bonds as it became more apparent that the Carollons was likely to be drawn into any action the rest of the British Commonwealth took against Iraq. I would have stayed away from the frequent parties out of respect, but Cindy insisted that they wanted us both to be there. "They want to have women at their parties, Solace, and I think they should. Besides, the U.S. and Canada are in this thing too. It makes these guys feel good to see their North American allies, and it makes me feel good too. It's like I'm doing something for my country."

"Which one?" I teased.

She'd already persuaded me to go again. "Either one. Both. And yours too."

Later, on the bus, I asked her about Liam. They seemed to have some kind of special friendship. I didn't think that it was romantic, but I hadn't learned to read her yet. Though she shared her happiness readily, she was quiet about more serious subjects. "He's a huge bud, Solace. We like to do all the same stuff. And he's decent." I thought that Cindy, like me, had been through some bad relationships.

There was so much heavy drinking and raunchy behavior at the party that I debated leaving. Cindy had disappeared, and I hated to go without talking to her. Luckily I ran into Mike, who suggested that we go for a walk and circle back to the party to check in with Cindy. I agreed, and we walked a few blocks to the beach, and strolled along the ocean's edge. It was a lovely evening, moonlit and clear, and I was pleased neither us was the least bit tempted to take advantage of the romantic setting.

"How have you been keeping busy, Solace?"

"I got a job, but I should have looked more carefully. I went to work at a bank."

"Seriously?" He was clearly disappointed with me. "I thought you were all about trying new things."

"Yeah," I ducked, humiliated. "When I interview this time I'll say I wanted to have a job while I considered my options."

"That makes you sound very diligent."

"I've got enough faults of my own. I don't need to have people thinking I'm unreliable."

"At least you have money coming in while you look."

Suddenly I laughed, and he followed suit. "Aren't you surprised to hear yourself, Mike the beach bum?"

"Oh, yeah." His voice faded. "But I have another suggestion."

"I'm listening."

"Try my dad's company, Big Bob's Surf Shop."

I suspect I had a sour look of uncertainty on my face.

He saw it. With a stern expression, he went on. "My dad's always looking for good people, Solace. You seem real smart and responsible and all. Call the office. They could probably use a nice girl like you."

"Thanks, Mike. I appreciate the thought, but I don't know anything about surfing."

"You could work in the office, my girl. Dad needs people who can use computers and count all that lovely money. You were a bank manager in the States. You ought to be able to handle some books or something."

"Okay," I said nervously. Then I smiled. It wouldn't hurt me to look into it. "I'll check it out. Thanks for the tip."

"No sweat. I'm always ready to talk up Dad's business."

Big Bob's name was Ed. He had purchased the nearly bankrupt shack of a surf and head shop about twenty years earlier, and turned the business around within a week. The original Big Bob spent some time in jail later for tax fraud and selling drugs, but the name of the shop had some clout with the serious surfers in Williamsport, so it had been retained. Apparently, despite everything else, Bob had hired a sales clerk who really understood the sport. Ed Leahy kept him around and looked for others like him who could bring in repeat business. Then he began to add product lines, starting with diving gear, eventually turning it into a large-scale retail business with stores all around the tropical Atlantic.

I didn't call them right away, still held back by my image of a surf shop, which was somewhat mixed up with the completely unprofessional manners of the owner's son. When I did call, almost a week later, I was promptly brought in for an interview. I was offered a position as a staff bookkeeper, which though part-time paid as well as my job back home. My ego was delighted. I never mentioned knowing Mike, and he had never mentioned knowing me to his father or anyone else at the company.

Where my bank job had been too familiar, this job was nicely different. The cubicle I shared with another bookkeeper was the most private place I had ever worked, but the atmosphere around us was lively, energetic, and stimulating. I kept busy, but I was usually able to complete my work within my scheduled hours. This allowed me to feel like I was honoring my desire to take a break from commitments at the same time that I was developing a new set of professional skills.

"I'm psyched!" Mike yelled across the beach. He and Cindy hurried to my blanket after the volleyball game ended. He continued once he was close enough merely to speak loudly, "Cinderella just told me you took my advice, and you're working for my dad, and you like it? That is so fucking cool." He threw himself across the blanket and stretched his long legs.

"She didn't know you well enough to ignore your advice, Leah," Cindy jabbed. She sat down beside me and took a long drink of water.

"It was good advice, Cindy" he shot back.

"I'm going through a daring, experimental phase," I explained. "Who won?"

"We did, girlie girl" she said. "And I'm hungry. Let's get something to eat." Cindy pushed up from the sand and went to the bank of coolers shaded under a canopy.

"Me too. Bring any snacks?" Sitting up, Mike reached for my canvas bag. Before I could answer, he began to dig through it. "You brought a book? To a party?"

"It was in my bag already. I put my food over there," I added, pointing toward the canopy.

"Next game, you're on the team."

"I'd probably cause you to lose."

"Better to lose than have you start reading your book. My mates will think you are either a snob or sexually destitute."

I stiffened a little at Mike's frankness. "I know better than to read at a party."

He stood. "Let's go. I want a beer."

"You really shouldn't drink alcohol when it's this hot and sunny and you've been exercising." I tagged along.

He stopped briefly to stare at me. "I'm going to go into a war zone any day now, and you're afraid I might get, what, dehydrated?" He laughed. "That's really sweet, Solace, but I think I'll have a better chance of getting dehydrated when I'm in the desert." He opened a cooler at random. Cindy directed him to the keg. "Want one?"

"No. I'll get something else."

Cindy wandered away to join the crowd of shorthaired men.

Mike waited by the keg, watching me over his shoulder. "So my dad's a wicked boss?"

"I've barely met him. But the people I know seem nice. And there are happy hours sometimes. I've never had such a busy social life." I stopped, flustered, my attention snagged by the man drawing the drink ahead of Mike. For a second I thought he was that creep Sean Donovan from the bank, before I recognized the other creep Tim, who had helped build Cindy's box. He handed Mike a very well foamed cup. Tim and I ignored each other.

"Bastard," Mike said to him in a friendly manner as he spilled off the excess foam, elbowing him away so that he could top off the drink himself. "I want to know about the job, Solace."

"Okay. The company's not at all what I expected. It's huge. I wished you'd told me. I might have inquired there sooner if I'd known more." I picked up a can of cola.

He shrugged. "I'm used to people knowing."

We returned to my blanket. Mike stretched out looking ready for a nap, but still feeling talkative. "I can't help but wonder about you, Solace," he said slowly, thinking out loud. "The better I get to know you, the less you match up with the girl that crossed the equator for no good reason. You're so sensible and, and timid. Yet here you are, doing this fantastic thing."

I sat on the edge of my blanket, silently smoothing the sand in front of me with my feet. I was glad he had not asked me a question, though I suspected he expected some kind of response. My eyes on my feet, I waited for him to say more; perhaps he would even change the subject. I never liked talking about myself.

"Did your folks approve of your marriage?"

That was hardly the subject change I had hoped for. "They say they didn't."

"Now, you mean?"

"Right. Now. I don't remember them trying to stop me."

"So what happened?"

"I grew up, and he grew down." I saw Mike redden and smirk. "It's okay. It just means he tried to pull me down with him." I looked up again, and I saw that I could trust Mike. He wouldn't use my weaknesses against me. "He brought out the worst in me."

"Why did you let that happen?"

"How do you stop it from happening?" I saw that he really didn't understand. "I don't remember why I wanted to be with him at the beginning, but I did, and we were together for so long I thought we were meant to share our lives. I guess I was just trusting, or I didn't know that love could be better or should be better. But as time went on I realized that in his mind every problem was caused by someone other than himself. Nothing was ever *his* fault. And I guess I was pretty stupid, because it took me almost four years to see that I had married someone who wanted me to be something so useless."

"Did that son of a bitch hurt you?"

"Well, he never hit me or anything like that," I hedged. Suddenly I was thrust back in time to our honeymoon. I was floating in the motel swimming pool, tired from the activities of recent days and by swimming some uncounted number of laps. He didn't like to swim, and the last time I'd seen him he was reading a magazine. I had no idea he'd entered the water when, without warning, he lifted my ankles into the air, sending my head down under the water. I struggled to kick myself free. I backed away from him, still wild with terror and coughing water. He cradled his arm and yelled that I was impossible to please. I had apologized to him later. Even now, knowing how he had treated me later, I still discounted the possibility that he had intended me harm.

Mike must have read something on my face. "Motherfucker ate away at your spirit." My head spun around to meet his eyes. His assessment was too accurate to deny. He sat up, scooted forward to sit beside me, and put his hand over mine reassuringly. "So you really needed to get away from home?"

I nodded. "I like to think that I came here with some grand personal goals, but I wasn't doing very well back home. I'd become way too dependent on my parents. I've got to do some soul searching and figure out what I want out of life."

"Seeking solace, heh? Let me know when you find it."

I frowned at his word play. "I don't expect to find peace of mind, just a path that leads me somewhere decent. I feel I like I need to prove that I can take care of myself, because I'm almost twenty-eight and I've never really done it yet. I know I can, but the longer I wait, the harder it will be. I think."

"Probably."

"I want some good excitement and to shake up my preconceptions. I've always been practical, followed advice, and did what I was supposed to do. Everyone I knew was shocked when I decided to do this, and they all tried to discourage me. Besides feeling kind of guilty and selfish about doing it, I've felt like no one believes I can take care of myself."

"Well, I'm glad you got away from those people. If you start to believe them, you're screwed. I think what you're doing is great. And if I keep hanging out with you, I'm going to end up feeling like I've got to get off my bum too."

I laughed. "Well, if I screw up, at least I'll have more fun doing it than I would back home. Plus my witnesses will all be here."

"That's the spirit, my girl," he said, saluting me with his beer.

Chapter Two

For my birthday in November I decided to treat myself to tea and
dessert. I walked past my favorite hippie dress shop, then turned
back and went in. One can never have enough flowy, flowery dresses
and I had gotten a check from my parents in the mail yesterday. I
bought two. Cheery from a shopping high, I stepped into the tearoom
next door. The breeze was fresh and cool. I sat down at a table by an
open window with a cup of Russian tea and a caramel, gooey pastry
and pulled out one of the photocopies of the Sunday crossword
puzzles from home that had been enclosed in my birthday card.
Everything was perfect. I sipped my tea and licked caramel off of my
fingers as I deciphered the clues.

"Excuse me, Miss Murphy?" I felt myself slipping off the edge
of my cloud. I glared as I raised my eyes to see Sean Donovan. He
looked nervous. He ought to have. "May I speak to you? I wanted
to apologize."

"If you must," I said grumpily.

To my astonishment, he pulled out a chair and sat at my table.
He smelled of sunscreen. He tried to smile, and I was again tempted
to like him. "I won't keep you. I just felt so awful about upsetting
you, Solace. I wish," he paused and started over. "I didn't have the
nerve to come back to the bank for a long time."

"Then why do you have the nerve today?" I interrupted.

"When I did go in, finally, they said you'd gotten another job. I
hope you like it better."

I said nothing.

"Anyway, well, I hope you didn't leave because of me."

"I did."

"Oh. I am sorry," he looked sincerely dejected.

I tried to resist the passing urge to say something to make him
feel better. I failed. "I like my new job better."

"Good." He lifted his head and pushed up his eyeglasses. "Then
maybe someday you'll hate me a little less."

Scoffing, I lied, "Look, you're annoying, but hardly worth
hating." I attempted to dismiss him by pretending to return my
attention to my puzzle, half expecting the conceited busybody to offer

his help with it. After changing jobs, I had never expected to see him again, and I was not prepared for the strength of my reaction to him. He had no right to know my feelings, and I was angry at myself for not being able to hide them better. I wrote some letters into the puzzle grid, just to make it look like I was paying attention to it, then after a couple of minutes I looked up again with an expression that I hoped he would read as, "Are you still here?"

He rocked his paper cup, rolling it around on its circular base.

I gave in. "I suppose that in a twisted way you did me a favor."

He nodded and swallowed. His pale eyes were steady, but his lip was sweaty and quivered ever so slightly. He gazed at my table, tea, puzzle, and shopping bag. "I'll try to stay out of your way."

"I'd appreciate that."

He rose and stood by the table looking down at me. He had found his poise from knowing his position was futile. Instead of disappearing he remained a moment longer. "If I should see you, I won't speak to you, Solace Murphy, unless you tell me that I may. I swear to God." He held his hands in the shape of an "X" over his heart. "But I want you to know that I consider myself to be your friend, so if I should ever see that you need help, I'll do what I can. I would dive right into the river if I saw you drowning. I swear that too." Then he turned abruptly, not looking to see my reaction to his out of place vow, and he walked away with grace.

I watched him through the window as he turned onto the sidewalk. He wasn't as calm as he had tried to appear. Neither was I. I sat for a moment, reasoning that I should have felt threatened by his strange promises. I was irked by his intrusion. Struck by a wave of restlessness, I crumpled my puzzle, jumped to my feet, grabbed my bags, and stormed out of the café. I walked around the block twice before I could trust myself to return the dresses, which I felt no longer suited me.

When I got home I tore through my closet, taking all of my convergent anger out on my wardrobe, while I looked for something to wear that would cover my vulnerability. I moved all of my pretty dresses to the far end of the closet and dressed in something forgettable. I opened the door as quickly as I could so that my housemates wouldn't get curious. By the time Cindy was home, I was quiet, but I still felt disturbed.

Over the last few years, as I had brushed aside one hurt after another, my feelings had become raw, taut, and brittle. Though it came from a person whose opinion should have meant nothing to me, Sean Donovan's attention was the kind of insult I had hoped never to be subjected to again. Though I couldn't change the way I felt, I did have the power to alter the way other people perceived me. Maybe if I didn't seem weak, I would be treated better.

I had made a good start. Most of the people I met were impressed merely by my moving to the Carollons. They respected me for that alone. This fact made it easier than I ever expected for me to pretend to be the interesting, confident Solace Murphy I had left home to find. I hadn't really changed, but I worried less about dealing with other people.

In December, I bade farewell to Mike Leahy and his mates at a party before they shipped off to the Middle East. Except for Mike, who kissed my forehead with a loud smack, all the other Marines were sassy and kissed my lips as part of their demand for a proper American send off. I offered them the "cup" gracefully and immodestly, thankful that I didn't show the tears that would have been in my eyes before my birthday. Tears would have made their last night at home too serious, too sentimental, too memorable. They wanted one last bout of hard drinking and maybe the chance for some safe sex before they left for the desert. Perhaps I should have given that to one of them, but the offer would have had to come from me, and I'm not sure I could have made it even if I had thought to.

Liam Maloney and two other men I kissed that night never came home. In her sorrow for Liam, Cindy grounded herself by cooking, and I helped her to prepare baked dishes for dozens of families of service members. She made me go with her to the first funeral service, but after that, seeing how much it mattered to the survivors, I went by my own choice.

Mike was wounded. Ed Leahy turned an empty office into a chapel. Many of my coworkers found comfort there, but the crucifix reminded me of the boys who were gone. I didn't want to think about them. I was alert and watchful, but my emotions were restrained by the wall I had built to hide my vulnerability. The yellow ribbon I tied to the handlebars on my bicycle faded, frayed, and finally fell off without my noticing.

My classes started in March. I had always liked school. It wasn't hard to find reasons to spend extra time on campus. Even part-time students were permitted to use of the facilities. It must have been Cindy's influence that sent me to the gym to see what was there. When I learned that I could take free classes, I signed up for Yoga and soon discovered that its philosophy supported my new way of looking at life.

I took two accounting classes, and Bridget Murphy was in both of them. Though she was only a Murphy by marriage, it seemed natural for us to hang out together. She was a computer programmer taking business classes to further her career. Bridget was calm and practical, with shoulder length, soft chestnut hair. Because her husband, my "cousin" Rob, usually worked in the evening, she often invited me to their apartment for study, dinner, and girl talk. Rob was an actor and a writer, who had fairly regular work at a dinner theatre. He was fun to be around even though he often forgot to turn down his performing energy.

When Rob learned that I had revived my creative writing hobby, he pressured me to meet his other writer friends. They met weekly at a pub near the university for feedback and encouragement. Though I didn't expect to enjoy the experience, I changed my mind soon after meeting Steve and Karen. While I felt like I was a part of an exciting, arty circle, I wasn't intimidated by them. They were people like me who allowed themselves the luxury of making up another world in their spare time. They were the first friends I had ever made based solely upon a mutual interest. I warmed to the idea of sharing as my trust in Rob, Karen, and Steve grew. Our common pursuit brought us into an unusually intimate relationship. Talking about each other's stories encouraged me to begin to put on paper the stories I had always considered too private to pen. I began to keep a fiction journal for scribbling anything that came to my mind, assuring myself that no one would read it, and so I gradually found myself more willing to experiment.

I still drew interest as the American and the new girl. Many of the people I met went out of their way to include me. The positive attention bolstered my pretended confidence. I learned to enjoy social situations that would have made me uncomfortable before. This was my time to observe, explore, discover, and play the way most people do during their first freedom at the beginning of adulthood. I wasn't ready for commitments, but I didn't let that stop me. I didn't know what I wanted in my future, so I tried to find happiness in the present and rebuild my life in moments.

By nature and nurture I had always been cautious. For the time being my usually vocal conscience left me alone, and I didn't miss it. I may not have been able to hear it over the people around me, especially the men whose eyes and mouths told me that they found me attractive. It is also possible that my conscience was silent because I was not doing anything harmful. I wanted, probably even needed, physical relationships. In this my wish to prove wrong my ex-husband, who had complained that I was a cold lover, was secondary to my desire to know and find joy in my body. As long as I had been with him, I had been self-conscious about my figure. I had believed his possessive lies, my insecurities furthered by his intimation that I needed to diet, when in fact I was too thin and bony.

I was out on the beach early one Sunday morning in August with no design beyond watching the other morning people, mostly fishermen and elderly couples walking past me on the wet flats. I rolled my jeans high on my calves and waded at the water's edge, meandering down the beach slowly in a state of daydreaming. Imagining I heard my name on the wind I turned slowly toward the dunes. I looked twice before I realized that a man was bounding toward me, waving an arm over his head. "Solace," he called. "Shit, Solace! What the fuck are you up to, girl?"

I ran to meet him on the dry sand. "Mike! Oh, my God!" I screamed back, laughing. I jumped up to kiss his cheek, and before I knew it he was raking me into an exuberant hug.

"How are you, Solace?" he asked as if I had been the one off on a dangerous mission.

I was slow to answer him as I squinted up to see his face. "I'm fine."

"I'm so damn glad to see you! I just couldn't fucking believe it when I saw you out here. I blinked a few times to make sure it was you. Look how long your hair is!" He took my thick, golden brown braid into his fist, playing with it instead of looking at my face. "I've been home a while, you know. I just haven't been up to calling people."

"I didn't expect you to call me. And I, uh," I stopped. I had made enough excuses to myself during these last months for not attempting to welcome him home.

"Of course I was going to call you, Solace. You've been right at the top of my list, well, for months." His sincerity led me to picture a piece of paper stuck to his refrigerator door with my name at the top of a list of important people like dentists and insurance agents. My conscience twitched again for not making the effort. "Still work for my dad?"

"Sure do."

"Going well?"

I nodded. "I might even try surfing someday."

"Oh, girl, give me the word, and I'll give you a lesson. I ought to be able to get back on the board one of these days."

"So, when did you get home?" I knew the answer, as did everyone at Big Bob's, but I preferred to talk about him.

He started to walk, and I stayed at his side. He bounced a little with each step, not knowing how to put purpose with his returning physical energy. "Got back in June. Was in the hospital in London for a time. I even had a visit from the queen. Earned some medals to put on the uniform I don't wear anymore."

"You look better than I thought you would," I said looking at him carefully. He had a few little, red scars on his face. One of his eyebrows had been divided into two distinct sections. Underneath his clothing, there was surely more damage, but I would not ask about it. "I'm glad to see your smile."

"Broke a few teeth," he said. He pointed to the front teeth on the right side. "They built me some new ones, right on the roots. I was afraid they were going to give me dentures, but apparently dental science has made leaps since my granddad's days."

"You didn't need to tell me, Mike. I would never have known."

"Come up to the house," he said directing me with a hand on my shoulder toward an opening in the dunes. "I'm expecting some friends to come by, but no one has come yet. My brother's here now, 'cause my mum thinks I spend too much time alone."

I had never been to Mike's house before, and I'd had no idea that his was just a few blocks away from mine, an easy walk on land or sand. Small and ramshackle, it suited him and suggested that he mooched off his parents far less than he claimed.

At the top of the steps to his deck we stopped to brush the sand off our feet. When he slid the screen door open, the bones showed white beneath his pale skin. I could see that it still hurt to use his right hand. A jagged red scar ran up from the webbing between his index and middle fingers to his wrist beyond the cuff of his cotton shirt. The head of the tropical fish tattooed on the wrist was gone.

His brother was at the kitchen table, nibbling on the party food when we entered. "This is Jimmy," Mike said. "Jimmy, this is Solace. She works for Dad."

"Hi," Jimmy said expressionlessly.

"Nice to meet you." With no further communication from Jimmy, I turned back to Mike. "I really can't stay."

"Don't want to play with my mates today?"

"Not today."

"Well, you're probably smart. We're all desperately horny."

"That's a good reason to go," I said.

He smiled at that. We talked for a few minutes. As I got ready to go, he told me he would call me in a few days. "We can have lunch or a drink or something, and just be nice to each other. Would you like that?"

"Yes," I said. "I would like that."

We arranged to meet at my office for lunch that Tuesday. While he was waiting for me his father passed through the lobby and paused to find out why he was there. Ed Leahy seemed pleased to learn that Mike and I were friends. Knowing that his son needed to talk to someone, he pulled me aside for a moment to tell me to stay out as long as I was comfortable.

I wasn't comfortable for a minute, but I did owe it to Mike to listen. We sat over a half-eaten lunch for a long time. Instead of listening, I kept wondering why Mike would come to me to express his huge emptiness. Compared to his, my issues were puny, and I was a pathetic mess to be so hampered by them. The only thing he and I had in common was our inability to live as independent adults because our parents had helped us too much. It was hardly a promising connection. While it may have helped me to understand him better, it didn't give me any wisdom to help him find his way back home.

The experiences that weighed him down were so foreign. I couldn't relate to what the war had done to him and his friends. I had never had a serious injury or needed surgery. None of my friends had died. I'd never even been to a funeral until Cindy begged me to go with her to Liam's. I'd only begun to understand how the survivors appreciated that kind of gesture.

Mike was something between a victim and a survivor. Thinking my presence alone might be enough for him now, I worked harder at focusing on his voice and took in as many words as I could absorb. I reached my hand out and took one of his. It was sweaty and cold. I would try to help him in chips and slivers. "Have the Marines sent you to therapy?"

"Yeah. Couldn't talk."

"I'm sure it's difficult, but a professional would be best equipped to help you deal with these things. I don't know what to do but cry with you." Maybe not even that. I'd gotten quite good at closing off my emotions.

"God, Solace, that's what I need: a good cry with a friend."

I had never suspected that Mike had this kind of emotional depth. It's amazing what one can learn in just one tumultuous year. "I've never dealt with anything like this. Don't some of your mates have the same problems? Wouldn't it be more helpful to talk to one of them?"

"I don't know. Don't know if I could. It's easier to talk to you than my mates. They are all dealing with this same kind of shit."

"I thought it was supposed to help to talk to people who can relate to your problems. You can feel stronger knowing you are all miserable together, or something."

"I like that logic," he answered with a tired smile.

I took that as an opening to make another positive suggestion. "You ought to read a book or work puzzles. Occupy your mind with other things."

"That's good advice, Solace. I was afraid you'd tell me to get a job. I really don't have enough to do. The doctor won't let me dive yet, so I guess I can't be a beach bum anymore. I suppose old Saddam did me a little favor."

"I'm sure he didn't intend to."

That brought a bitter laugh, but it turned his thoughts elsewhere, and we ate some more and talked about simpler things.

Outside the corporate entrance to Big Bob's, Mike said, "Thanks, Solace. You continue to live up to your name. Maybe I'll try therapy again. It isn't fair of me to dump it all on you. But I can still cry with you sometimes, can't I?"

"I guess so," I said, not sure I was ready to take on the responsibility. "I guess you can't let go too much with your mates."

"Good lord, no! It's a sad day when the men start bawling. Most of them just wouldn't sit for it. Women are stronger. Look at you. I hardly recognized you; somehow you've kicked off that fragile look you had before."

"Mike, I," I began, but he put up a hand to stop me.

"I admire you, Solace."

There were no words I could use to reply to his simple statement. Arguing would have been wrong, but a word of thanks would have meant I accepted his admiration, and I wasn't inclined to believe that I'd done anything to earn it. He'd just laid another task before me, and that was to live up to his faith in me.

Cindy and I had the house to ourselves over Christmas, all the other girls having headed to their parents' homes as soon as they got off work for the holiday. We opened the gifts our families had sent us around a large potted plant on the deck. There had been plenty of parties before the holiday, and we were both content to relax quietly. We lay back in our chaises and sipped virgin pineapple daiquiris with barely the energy to get up and raid our "tree". The gifts were unimportant. We had each received plenty of warm clothing already.

I had gotten a new boyfriend for Christmas, a friend of a friend from work, and I had let him seduce me last night before we went to a midnight mass. It was our first time and only our second date, but I had invited him in afterwards for another go. I have always enjoyed unwrapping my gifts, and this one seemed worth repeated unveiling. It was Christmas after all, and the house was almost empty. We slept in one of the unused rooms, and he dragged himself off to his parents' house this morning early. I mused over whether I would see him again.

Cindy took the last present from under our plant. "Feels like another ski sweater," she said, rolling her deep green eyes. "Couldn't they just send me maple sugar?" She tore into her package. Flannel sheets. We both burst out laughing. "Look, little polar bears! I'll roast, but I love them." She plopped down on the chaise again. "So how was Mr. Gorgeous?"

"Peter? Fine."

She started massaging her feet. "I've always thought that a guy that handsome would probably be a dud."

"Like men with expensive sports cars?"

"Exactly. And I figured you'd go for someone who uses his hands well, like a musician."

"Peter might be a frustrated sculptor. I'll have to ask him."

She laughed, but then she blushed. "If you were still at home would you have so many boyfriends?"

"Would you?"

"I didn't live with my parents."

"Yeah. That didn't give me much room to experiment."

"Had you ever done it with anyone other than your ex before you got married?"

I shook my head. "But I'm not sure that what we did should count. It was always so forced. Almost every other guy I've dated has been more affectionate." I thought for a minute. "When I decided to leave home and come here, I didn't think, 'oh, I've got to have sex with more men,' yet, in a way it is something I needed to do. Part of figuring out what makes me happy." I smiled inwardly. "It's been such a discovery. I mean, it was always such a pressure thing with," I choked, "with him. Besides it would make him angry—even now, I think—if he knew how much enjoyment I was giving and receiving." I felt a smile come to my lips of its own volition. He would never know, but it still gave me pleasure to think of wounding him. There was no other reason to think of him.

"For you, it's probably just a phase. One of these days you'll be right back to monogamy." She sighed. "I don't know that I really like sex all that much. I feel like I should be getting more out of it than I do, like I'm missing something, so I try it with someone else."

"Maybe you should be more selective. Sex shouldn't just be physical. Not always. Not forever. There is a reason that we should be doing what they call 'making love'."

"I don't know," she began, her voice cracking. "I don't know that I've ever really made love, Solace. I've wanted it. I guess I've tried to force it." Cindy rarely let anyone see when she was upset. She jumped up and ran inside the house.

Rob was still home when I started making dinner. He and Bridget lounged against the kitchen counters watching me chop onions and herbs. "It already smells good," he observed.

Knowing that he was hoping for leftovers, I replied, "It always grows in the pot."

Bridget was a bit more suspicious. Her mother had taught her traditional Carollonian cooking, which for those with Irish surnames was the blandest cuisine anywhere near the equator. She seemed more concerned with nutrition than taste. Now that she was pregnant, I think that she was happier than ever to have Rob keeping house while she worked long hours at the office trying to increase her salary. Other than a little guilt on his part, because she wouldn't be able to stay home with the baby, he seemed content with the arrangement too. "Where did you find all these fresh greens?"

"This grocer near work. I should buy plants and grow my own herbs." I slid them into the hot olive oil in the skillet. "I enjoy cooking here. Your kitchen is so much nicer than ours, and you don't have six people trying to cook at once."

"Just three," Rob said.

"Should we move out of the way?"

"No. You're fine." I unwrapped the chicken. "How's your stomach doing, Bridget?"

"Better by far," she said. She'd just passed out of the first trimester. "It's good to be able to eat real food again."

I turned to stir my onions into the skillet on the stove. "This shouldn't be too spicy." A glance her way told me she didn't believe me, especially when I sprinkled some more herbs into the skillet. "Are you scared?"

"Of course." From the expression in her grey eyes I wasn't certain that she understood I was referring to procreation. She might have feared the meal I was preparing

"Just some more herbs. Don't they smell nice?"

"It smells wonderful, Solace." She wasn't afraid of the food.

"I shouldn't have asked you about that. I just wonder what it must be like."

She went to the sink and started rinsing some of the dishes and utensils I had used with her back to us. Rob and I exchanged a nervous glance. He tried to distract her. "Yeah, it's going to mean some big changes for us. But we'll manage. Bridget hasn't been around kids that much, you know, Solace. Sometimes all she remembers are soiled nappies and spit up. Already she's telling me she's going to work longer hours once the little booger arrives."

I forced a laugh, eyeing Bridget for a reaction. I wiped my hands and put one on her shoulder, trying to help her relax. Thinking statistics might help, I cheerfully offered, "Well, you know they say that having a baby is safer than walking down the street."

Rob gasped. Bridget dropped the spoon she had been rinsing. Her head fell forward until her chin hit her chest. Rob rushed to put his arms around her stiff body. He looked at me over her shoulder. "You couldn't have known this, Solace. I mean, it was years ago, back when I was still in the navy. We lost a friend, Megan, when she was pregnant. She was just walking down the street and got struck by a lorry." He kissed Bridget on her frozen cheek. "Solace didn't know."

Afraid to meet their eyes, I reached around them to turn off the tap.

"I'm not mad at Solace," she said at length. "I'm okay. I know she didn't know." She looked at me. "I'm sorry, Solace. Megan was a close friend. And I..."

I nodded. I thought it was better to remain silent. Rob coaxed her to a chair, and I followed with a glass of water. I patted her shoulder and went back to the stove. She was recovering, and she would do so faster alone with Rob. By the time he needed to go, her cheerful mood had mostly returned. After their farewells around the corner, she came back into the kitchen and shyly asked me, "Do you miss your friends from home?"

"I missed them more when I was married."

"Did you want to have kids when you were married?"

"I thought so. I'm so glad we didn't."

"You couldn't have moved here." She leaned backwards against the counter again, with her arms crossed under her bosom. She was trying to figure out how to direct the conversation away from her memories. "Have you got a special man?"

I thought about saying I didn't, but she needed me to share something with her, so I acknowledged my involvement with Peter. "Sort of. I do see this guy, but I don't think it'll ever be serious."

"Is he handsome?"

A big smile. "Very."

After a few minutes she joined me at the stove again to peek at my creation while I diced tomatoes. "Pray remind me what it's like to be single. It ought to make me feel better about this blooming belly of mine."

While I couldn't exactly call Peter my boyfriend, I might have been able to get away with describing him as my lover. We saw each other frequently, but irregularly, rarely making plans to meet, but doing so anyway because we went to the same places and knew some of the same people. Sometimes we just hung out with the group. More often we left together. Whatever we did, we did freely.

I enjoyed the feel of his hands and his gentle mouth. "Peter?" I whispered into his ear, running my finger along its rim. He turned toward me, his eyes opening slowly as he came back from some waking dream. "Why don't you ask me out more often?"

"Hmmm?" he blinked. His eyes focused. I knew he cared how I felt. "I didn't think you wanted me to, Solace. I thought you liked it to be spontaneous and *sans souci*." He kissed me on my laughing lips. "Is it working? I don't want you to grow bored of me. After all, you're a world traveler and adventurer." He rolled over on top of me, skin to skin.

"I thought you were the interesting one," I said. I admired Peter's sense of humor, tact, and the fact that he never spoke ill of others. I hoped to learn from him.

"Oh, now, that's not only untrue, but it's also far too much responsibility to place on a poor, old, local bloke like me. I'm a stockbroker. How dull is that?"

"Well, I'm only a bookkeeper," I returned. "The dullest of the dull."

"You can afford a boring job, because there is so much going on in your mind to keep you amused."

"It's not all in my mind, Peter." I moved my hands along his back.

"Most certainly not," he said, contentedly turning to make it easier for me to caress him. "You are generous enough to share your inspirations."

It was a relationship such as I had never imagined entering before. Just words and sex. I enjoyed both. I was in a transitional phase. Being with him was a way of looking after myself. My whole attitude toward him was related to how I could please myself with him. His was the same. It was selfish, and yet it was not hurtful or demanding. We were completely free with one another. There was no deception, and there might be no future. It was a form of masturbation, yet it was not a lonely act.

Part of the appeal of such a relationship was its impermanence. It was what I wanted at this stage, and I would probably never again wish for anything like it. Its strength came from its fragility. It gave me the illusion of rebelliousness. Yet the affection was genuine and unconditional. It helped to prepare me for the time in the future when I could commit to another person and accept him as a partner in my life. Because someday I would wish to share my life with a man to whom I would want to give more than I received. I would want to be with a man I was willing to support through any trial.

I began to wonder if it was possible for me to do it. Could I share selflessly and still be able to control my temper and tears? Would I be able to accept his values without giving up the independent me that I was working so hard to create? The prospect seemed more frighteningly challenging than I had ever before suspected. I knew I wasn't ready. I could only hope that I would be before I met him.

I took the bus to Little Russia late one afternoon when I had plans to meet my writer friends Karen and Steve. This was the part of the city created by the post-revolution Russian immigrants in the 1920s and 30s. It was uptown, to the northeast naturally, and upriver from the downtown where I worked. I took an express bus that made only a few stops at each end of the route. Reading a fast paced book at the stop, I barely looked up when I boarded. I dropped into an aisle seat, heedless of my surroundings until I realized the bus had stopped to let passengers on and off. I looked out the window to see where we were. Returning my eyes to my book, I caught those of my seatmate. He was Sean Donovan, the customer who had chased me away from banking.

I sensed that he had been watching me all along, cautious not to touch or speak to me. I didn't feel violated. After this much time it was probable that any interest he had in me had waned. For my part, I might not have recognized him if he had not so obviously been aware of me. He looked tired, like he'd had a very long, bad day at work.

I dropped my eyes quickly. I didn't want to read his thoughts or feelings. I didn't even want to see the names of the shops on the bags he held on his lap. I scrambled to my feet, shoving my book into my purse, and moved backward along the aisle. At the next stop, he rose and made his way forward to leave the bus, looking back at me with just a hint of a nod before he went down the steps.

I began to breathe again and realized that I was sweating as I clung to the overhead bar. I fought to put the image of his pale eyes out of my mind. Lucky for me, I was early and had time to settle down and force different ideas into my head before I saw Karen and Steve.

Little Russia was a good place for that. It was the liveliest, prettiest part of the city. As unlikely a pairing as Russian and tropical are, they came together here with a distinctive style: Edwardian houses and art deco commercial buildings, stacked with two or three stories of apartments over each store. Russian architectural forms were painted with coral and azure and glistening sandy shades. Far enough inland to have survived the German naval blockade during World War II, unlike what was now a very modern downtown, this district played up its cultural heritage.

I disembarked at the next stop, extending my walk. The day was fresh. It had rained harder than usual after lunch, and there were still a few puddles on the sidewalks reflecting the brightness. Officially, we were going to shop for a gift for the Murphys' baby, though a department store downtown would have been a more sensible place to look. The shopping was the warm up for our evening when Steve would lead us out for a Russian nightlife adventure, which he promised would involve no more vodka than we wished to drink.

There was no reason to pass the bakery on Tchaikovsky Street without going in, so I bought a bag of fancy pretzels to share while we shopped. I still had time, so I went through the alley to the next block. The antique shop where Cindy worked was on the next street. I didn't go see her, though the edginess I felt had passed. Instead I went to the right, to the art gallery, a place of solitude and calm. Most of the time.

Ever since I purchased a painting the owner Boris considered me a valued customer. My painting was of a pineapple harvest, like the one Cindy and I had seen when we went to Pentecost Island to climb the volcano in the first months after I came to the Carollons. At the time, the picture had seemed to be the perfect souvenir of the months I planned to spend in the islands.

Today Boris was busy measuring some paintings. He called to me when I entered. "Hi, Solace!"

"Would you like a pretzel?" I asked, holding out the open bag.

"Thank you," he shook his head. "I have lots of new things since you were here last. Enjoy my air conditioning as long as you like." To Boris I was something like an extension of Cindy. She was a business associate, but she didn't have the discretionary income for art, so I benefited in her stead. Of course, I sent my share of business his way, just as she did.

I left him to his work and looked around at the displays. Most of it was decorative, but some of it was art. I let my eyes go to whatever caught them. Mostly they didn't stay in one place long. Until I couldn't pull them away. For the second time today my attention was captured by intensely expressive eyes.

At the center, there was sorrow. As I pulled my focus back to take in the entire face, I saw the effort that held back the pain. My vision expanded again to see the man, the whole picture. In black ink faintly tinted by water colors, a Marine stood facing the grave of a comrade. His one hand was over his heart. His empty sleeve bore a black arm band. The face of this survivor was the focal point. He was a man who may have lost every friend who could truly understand the way he felt.

The Marine could have been Mike. There were times when he had pleaded with me for help. But it was the discipline, the control of the Marine, and the effort that Mike put in day after day to hold himself steady that wrenched my heart. This part of the man could help himself, and I knew that I needed to try again, harder, to reach out to Mike Leahy.

Chapter Three

I worked up the courage to drop in on Mike the next day. Part of me hoped he would be away from home. It was possible. His social network was back in service. His dad had given him a job at the store, which he didn't take seriously, but he did benefit from the structure that going to work imposed on him. He hadn't gotten permission to dive yet, but he was surfing again, which definitely brightened his outlook.

"Alô!" he said with a smile as he threw the door open wide. "Come in. You really don't need to knock, heh. I don't usually bother to lock up."

"I'm not about to just walk into your house, Mike. What if you are entertaining?"

"You're the only girl who's brave enough to come here. And this is the first time you've come here on purpose. Through the front door too! What's on your mind?"

I had come with the purpose of listening, not answering, so I didn't know how to begin. "I wanted to check out the front entrance. I thought that since you didn't use the door that often it might need some oil."

He threw his arm around me, laughing, and walked me into the lounge. "Want a drink or anything?"

I stopped at the threshold, taking in the disarray. "No thanks," I muttered. It was going to be difficult to find a positive way to approach him. It looked like Mike hadn't put anything away in months.

"I can get you a clean glass."

"Even if you have one, I don't think I could swallow anything. It stinks in here. I'm glad you take better care of yourself than you do of this place, because I'm more concerned about interrupting your bugs than something between you and a girl."

He opened some windows. Trying hard to act like he didn't care, he stated, "You're the only girl who might drop by."

"I've got five roommates, and I could arrange something with your mother," I threatened in a light tone that told him how unlikely it was that I would betray his secret. "A tidy house would be good for your morale. You've seemed more upbeat lately, Mike. I don't want you to go down again. Doing things, taking care of yourself will help."

"So you *did* come to save me?" He pretended to be clowning, trying to hide his despair.

"I'm here because I owe it to you to listen for a change," I answered with complete sincerity. "I've always been too worried about whether I could handle hearing your problems to really pay attention to what they are. You know I can't save you."

"I have to do it myself or with the help of Jesus Christ and all the saints in Heaven," he said with mock reverence. "I've heard that speech."

With a stern look of reprimand, I moved aside what I hoped was clean laundry and sat on his sofa. He lay down on top of the newspapers strewn over the rest of it, and casually put his bare feet on my lap. "I'm not a shrink, Mister," I said, lifting them down to the floor. I finally understood that the best thing I could do for him was to help him figure out how to carry his own burdens. "Seriously, Mike, help will come from Heaven or not as Heaven chooses. Are you going to wait on a miracle, or are you going to take things into your own hands? I know God is omnipotent, but he's also pretty busy, and he might have plans for you that you don't like."

"I take it you're not a Presbyterian." His hurt was easing.

"I like to think that I have some control over my destiny."

He laughed. "I think I like your religion, Sister Solace, even if it involves celibacy. It wouldn't put me at too much of a loss lately."

"Actually, I think you'd feel much better if you went out and got yourself laid. Sex might lift your spirits."

"You make it sound so easy."

"Nothing is ever as easy as it sounds, Mike. Do you have any idea how hard it was for me to let myself go the first time? It was hard, but I needed to do it so badly I forced myself to enjoy the moment. I made myself stop thinking about me and the future and just enjoy his kisses. Then, bingo, his hands went fishing."

"You got a fast one." He laughed.

"Yeah, I was lucky," I responded with a smile. "If he'd been too slow, I would have been so nervous that I'd probably still be waiting to lose my virginity again."

"I don't think anyone would want me, Solace," he whispered dejectedly.

"Why not, Mike? You're a good looking, intelligent man—a little lost, but so are most of the people I know. I know that I am. What the hell am I doing? I don't know, but I'm trying to find the right way. On my own. But you're waiting for a guide. You are thirty-two. Even your mom and dad know they can't hold your hand and walk you around any more."

"Why am I like this?"

"How should I know? Do you need a professional therapist? You should get one if you want answers to questions like that. Of course, he'll make you answer them for yourself."

"It didn't help to talk to my priest. And while I kind of like being at the store, I've been doing a shitty job, and I'm sure the people I work with are really pissed about having me there."

I agreed with that assessment. "What about your Marine mates?"

"I told you about that."

"Don't you have any old friends who were there? The kind that know you too well to hassle you? Wasn't someone your neighbor as a kid?"

"Terry? He's all back with his family like nothing ever happened. Donny might," he stopped. "You're thinking of Tim."

"Oh, that's right. I guess he wouldn't be much use."

"He's still in the hospital."

"Really? Still?"

"Yeah. He's in bad shape." He stretched. "But I might call Donny."

"Do that, Mike. It won't hurt, and it might help."

"Okay."

"One more thing. You should get another job doing something else somewhere else," I advised bluntly. "Do something that will make you hustle. Like waiting tables. You'd be great and make lots of tip money. Plus you wouldn't feel so bad about not having dates, because you'd have this great excuse that you're always busy at dinner time."

"That's hard work," he protested with an encouraging amount of spirit.

"Wasn't being in the Marines hard work? It would be good for you."

"I don't know, Solace." His voice trailed off, weakening again.

"The Marines let you out early because of your injuries, but is there any permanent disability, Mike? Is there any physical reason why you can't work?"

"Not really. I'm just a scratch and dent model now; I work just fine, though I ain't as pretty as I used to be."

"Nonsense. You are as attractive as ever."

"But you've never been attracted to me."

"I'm as attracted to you as you are to me."

He crossed his arms, pouting a little while he thought. "There are different kinds of attraction."

"Right, but this is always true: mean is ugly."

"And you would know."

"I do know," I said with a confirming nod. "Before I realized that my marriage was in trouble, I'd begun to wonder why I had thought my ex-husband was so good looking when we first met."

"Interesting," he mused. "So what's Peter do for you?"

"He fills a need."

"Don't you want to fall in love, Solace?"

"Of course I do. Someday."

"I think it would be nice."

"Probably." I sat back further on the seat of the couch. "You have someone in mind?"

"No. And I've been avoiding women because I don't think that the kind of girl I'd like to get close to would want to get close to me."

"Ah."

"You sound like a professional therapist, Solace."

I didn't reply.

"I guess I need to make a few home repairs."

I affirmed him by asking, "Where will you start?"

"Wash the dishes?"

"That seems like a good choice, Mike."

He was pleased to receive my approval.

"Stick with the things you can control. Don't worry about what you can't."

"Is that what you do?"

"Me? No, I worry about everything. But I know that I shouldn't."

He leaned over to kiss my cheek. "You are wonderful."

I sighed. "What's next after you clean up the kitchen?"

"Clever girl, I only said I was going to wash the dishes."

"But how will you wash them when there's stuff everywhere on the counters?"

"Hire a cleaning lady."

"You need to do this yourself."

"Damn, you just nixed my best idea."

"That's my specialty."

"Guess I should start before you get out your famous whip."

I stood up. "I'll get out of your way."

"Deserting me?" Despite his seeming agreement, Mike had not moved yet. Slumped on the couch with his feet on the coffee table, he was the very picture of youthful, athletic sloth.

"Hardly. This is a rite of passage, Mike, for you to complete on your own."

Straightening and stretching forward, he began to collect a pile of tableware. Already he seemed to have forgotten my presence. He carried the dishes to the kitchen in the corner and placed them on the counter. On his way back to the couch for a second load, he turned aside, distracted by a pile of dusty diving equipment sitting on the floor in front of the salt-filmed glass door.

"Bye," I called from the door.

His arm moved in what must have been intended as a wave.

I fought the temptation to go back inside to help him as I closed the front door behind me. Now that he was ready to begin helping himself the best thing I could do was allow him to go forth independently.

Bridget went into labor at her office and delivered a son, Patrick, the same afternoon. She begged me to visit and bring a sandwich, so I went to the hospital straight from work. There was a man waiting for the elevator when I stepped out onto the maternity floor. My attention was drawn to him because he looked down as soon as he saw me. It was Sean Donovan. He looked happy, and I wondered, frowning, if his wife had just given birth. He hightailed it into the elevator. I stopped in the middle of the corridor to settle my nerves, unable to resist watching the elevator locator board that showed it going up. I was disappointed that he wasn't leaving the building. When I saw it on the way down again, I fled away to Bridget's room.

She was practicing different ways of holding Patrick, but when she saw me she didn't waste much time exchanging him for the sandwich. Rob moved from her shoulder to mine. I forgot about everyone else who was in the hospital building, laughing with my friends and admiring their beautiful new son.

Mike did more than clean his house and bring it back into order. He began a complete overhaul with paint, sandpaper, and whatever else it took. He took pleasure in his work. He shared his pleasure with me by asking me to come over to talk to him while he worked or to inspect and encourage his progress. While we used plenty of words on soul-searching issues, we probably spent more time discussing such practical topics as the virtues of vinegar. In the process we became best friends.

"This place looks so totally bitching now, Solace, I could show it to my mother."

I tilted my head, and he stopped to listen to the wisdom he expected me to bestow. "Can you cook?" I asked. He had only ever offered me purchased refreshments during my visits.

"Well enough, especially over charcoal."

"You *should* have your folks over, Mike. Grill some chops or something."

"That's damned ingenious."

"Pick a date."

"I'll have a dinner party when you get your permanent residency."

"That could take years."

He flashed a smile. "I'm counting on it."

It was my turn to smile. "But then, it could be only weeks."

"Really? That soon?" he stammered. "I mean, that's great."

I shrugged. "They told me that they had all the paperwork they needed. I assume that means they will review it and figure out if I'm a potential threat or drain on society."

He laughed. "I will attest that you are definitely not a drain on society. In fact, this society," he pointed at his chest, "considers you to be an asset worth far more than your weight in platinum."

"Well," I said blushing. "Flattery will keep your therapy rates low. You need me to plunge your toilet or something?"

"I couldn't live with myself if I asked you to do such a nasty job," he replied laughing, but he was serious. "You may not have meant to save me, but you did anyway. Telling me to get a job as a waiter was brilliant. Mr. Sikorsky even complimented me the other day on how well I was fitting in."

I beamed at him. "I'm proud of you."

My residency status was updated in September, and Mike invited his parents and me to his home for dinner on a midweek night when he was not working. They may not have realized how much work he had put into his house, but they complimented him generously about how nice it looked. Mrs. Leahy kissed his cheek. His father wandered around leaving them the opportunity to talk alone. I was in the kitchen corner shaking the excess dressing from the salad. I didn't think that I should have been included in this family event, but Mike had insisted, saying that his father wanted to celebrate my permanent residency status. There had been reports of him skipping for joy when he learned that he no longer had to purchase private health insurance for me, since I was now qualified to receive care through the national medical system.

Mike was a skilled host. Even with my boss sitting beside me, I relaxed and enjoyed getting to know the elegant Laura Leahy better. It was she who delivered the evening's biggest surprise, which was just a little more surprising due to the fact that I was the recipient.

"Solace," she said after we had drunk to Ed's toast welcoming me to my "true" homeland. "Ed and I would like to thank you for all of the kindness you have shown to Michael. It has convinced us that your own family must miss you terribly." She handed an envelope to Ed, who passed it along to me with a serious expression on his face.

"You're welcome. I'm Mike's friend. He helps me too," I stammered.

All three of them nodded. Laura continued, "We know that, my dear, and we are very glad that he has a friend like you. This gift is something we are delighted to give."

Curious, but nervous, I struggled to open the envelope with shaking hands. I dropped it, and Ed picked it up and handed it back to me. I pulled a pretty card out of the envelope, which also enclosed some folded papers. I sensed all three of them watching me eagerly to see my reaction to the gift, so I skimmed over the kind words of thanks Mrs. Leahy had written inside, to read better later, and unfolded the papers, my hands still trembling. They were airline tickets for a roundtrip to Washington, DC, for ten days around the Christmas holiday. For a long moment even my lungs froze from shock while I stared at the tickets.

Ed Leahy waited until I took a breath. Then he spoke in a fatherly manner. "Now, Solace, I spoke to your folks to make sure that this was a good time for them, and I put your holiday on the calendar at work. We'll have someone drive you to and from the airfield, and so you don't have to worry about anything but packing your bags."

"That's the hardest part," I squeaked truthfully.

They took it as a joke.

"I'll pack for you," Mike offered.

That threat brought me back to reality. "Cindy will help me."

"Your parents are lovely people, Solace," Mrs. Leahy said.

"I think your dad would love an excuse to visit," Ed added.

"I haven't encouraged them to come. I'm not sure they would approve of the way I've been living," I confessed.

"Well, you've obviously made choices that suit you, Solace. It's hard to imagine they wouldn't notice the blossoming you have done over the last couple of years. Your parents must be very proud of you."

"What am I going to do? I have more than two months to think about packing. I'll go crazy," I moaned. Cindy laughed again. "What am I going to take to wear? Oh, I guess, I really don't need to pack much, do I? My winter clothes are in boxes at home."

"Hope you haven't changed sizes," Cindy teased. She knew I had gained at least ten pounds since I arrived in the islands, and I looked better than I had at my previous weight. The swimming, biking, walking, and yoga were paying off.

"They should fit. I just hope they haven't gotten mildewed in the basement."

"Are you going to take some of those frilly things you used to wear?"

"I don't know. I might go as myself, but then again I could go as myself."

"It's a costume vacation, is it, eh?"

"All the world's a stage," I quoted, hoping I'd gotten it right.

"You ought to try out for one of your friend's plays," she said.

"Me? Lord, no. I could barely handle singing in public the few times I did it."

"You are such a hoot, girl. I could talk, but sing? No way."

"That's understandable, Cindy."

She threw a pillow at me. "It's true. See why we get along so well? We don't compete. We couldn't compete. We aren't good at any of the same things."

"My frillies are mostly for hot weather. I think they will stay here. I've got lots of sweaters at home. I'll just need my jeans and leggings. My dressy winter stuff is there. I'll be okay then, unless the styles have changed too dramatically."

"You have your own style. You don't need to worry about what the ghosts in Paris and Milan are tripping down the runway in."

"Then I guess packing ought to be easy."

"Good. I was afraid you'd toss and turn and keep me up every night for the next three months. Then I'd feel like I needed to visit my family, eh, just to get some sleep."

"And you couldn't do that."

"I'm looking forward to having the house to myself for a few days, Solace. Last Christmas I had to deal with you and Peter humping in the other room. All that moaning. What did you do to the poor boy?"

I didn't remember any moaning. "Uh-oh," I cried in panic, almost grateful that I remembered another problem so that I could change the subject. "I've got to get gifts for everyone!"

"It's Christmas. Of course you're going to get gifts for everyone."

"Well, no, normally, we draw names."

"Now you know why Mr. Leahy gave you so much time to prepare. But there's lots of great stuff to choose from. I could take you shopping, eh, and we could find gems at bargains."

"Don't think I have the endurance to properly shop with you, Cindy."

"I won't run you all over the place. You can even buy things the first time you see them, if you're dead set on wasting your money."

"I consider my time as having some monetary value."

"Just come to the shop then. We got in some beautiful icons the other day. That's very Carollonian," Cindy said, still finding humor in my situation.

"Saints on surfboards?"

"Now that's an idea. No, these are the real thing. From old Mother Russia."

"I doubt icons would go over very well with my family. I think they'd rather have St. Mary's Bay tee-shirts."

"I saw a great print at Boris's shop. Had the volcano on it. Erupting." Her eyes lit as she emphasized the last word, trying to tempt me.

"The volcano is dormant," I reminded her, cautiously taking the bait.

"So? It's really great. You should go see it. Then get tees for your sibs."

Cindy had a good eye, and she had learned to evaluate my tastes well. "I'll check it out," I said.

"Let's go."

"Now?"

"Sure, it will be fun."

"Are you looking for anything?"

"Just presents for your family. I saw some shell jewelry your nieces might like. What about football jerseys for your nephews? They all play soccer, right? I think you can get the Carollons national team jerseys. That would be a rarity back home, eh. Plus it would support the Olympic team."

I smiled. Despite my lack of interest in competitive sports, I knew the children would love receiving such a gift. "That's a great idea."

We biked the few miles from our house to Little Russia using the pedestrian-bike path along the river for most of the distance. It was a major commuter route from the harbor to the Uplands suburbs. Within the city, sections of the path were crowded with shops and restaurants, but much of it was a park, with plenty of green areas on both sides of the river, a few old mills to explore, and access to each of the automobile bridges.

We left our bikes in the rack behind the bakery. We went through the alley to the art gallery, where I paused at the window, hoping I could see the print from the sidewalk. Cindy said, "It was inside," as she opened the door.

"You didn't check the price, did you?" I asked under my breath.

"No, I didn't think to. Wasn't thinking of buying when I saw it. What would I do with a nice litho?"

"Hang it up in your Toronto home someday, to remind you of your tumultuous years in Williamsport."

"That's way too far into the future for me to think about now," she said.

"Hi, ladies," Boris called from his worktable in the back corner.

"Hi, Boris," she returned casually as she sashayed through the maze of easels with me trailing her a little more slowly and warily. "This is it, Solace. Shit! It's like two hundred dollars. Sorry."

I moved into position behind her. The print was stunning. The rainforest was represented abstractly in the foreground, ringing the mountain, as it did in reality, with deep greens and browns while the sky above completed a broken circle with lapis swirls. The volcano towered majestically over the green and living wood, threatening it with a red and black explosion, while orange sparks shot upward, breaking through the peaceful arc of sky. I was rendered speechless by the power of the piece.

"Great, isn't it?" she said breathlessly. "Worth the trip, even if it's out of budget."

I moved in close. I backed away, studying it. "I think my mom would hate it."

"So would mine," she giggled. "Maybe I'll save up and buy it for her."

Boris approached us. "You like this one, ladies?" he asked. "It's a great print. It's the artist's first lithograph. His originals have fetched very good prices. This one is an investment." He emphasized his statement with a firm, downward nod of his head. "This one you buy. If you change your mind, you'll be able to sell it for a nice profit. See? Only one hundred fifty prints made. See?" He pointed to a Cyrillic signature in the lower right hand corner, printed on the lithograph and signed again in pencil on the surrounding paper. "Only a Russian could make you believe the volcano will blow."

"Only a Russian would think of it," I responded. "Drink some vodka and watch the lava flow."

Boris laughed. "That's good. I can use the line with my customers."

"You can knock fifty dollars off the price then," I countered. I hadn't even considered bartering when I bought my first painting, and if I had, I probably wouldn't have dared to do it.

His eyes flickered over me, instantly evaluating me. Nodding, he asked, "Do you want it framed?"

I arranged for him to ship it and asked him to time it so that it would arrive in the U.S. at about the same time that I would, envious all the while that I had no place to hang it myself.

Cindy couldn't believe I had handed over that much money with so little thought, but it didn't seem like that much to me. I had been earning a good income at Big Bob's, and I was living very cheaply. I could well afford it, and I enjoyed being able to partially return the generosity my parents had offered me all my life.

"You look like you need a change of scenery. Would you like to join me for dinner?" Peter whispered. I hadn't realized he was in the bar until he was at my side, putting his arm around me. "There's a Chinese place nearby where they barely speak English." He smiled tenderly. I agreed and bid my coworkers goodnight.

As we walked along, he kept his arm around my shoulders protectively. I felt restless. "Why aren't I in love with you, Peter?"

"You have to be open to it, I guess."

"And you? Are you content?"

"In some ways. I like to be with you any way I can, and this is the way you seem to want it. Would you be open to having more of a relationship with me?"

"I don't know," I said. "I think that part of me wants you to mistreat me." I didn't really want that, did I? There had to be something more that was holding me back. "It's not that I think you would."

"I guess I met you before you were ready to have what I might want with you. In some ways I really don't feel like I know you."

I found his clarity and logic comforting. We entered the restaurant, and ordered our supper at the cash register before we settled into one of the empty tables around the corner, nearly hidden by a refrigerator holding bottled drinks. Peter reassured me that the food would be good, and it certainly smelled appetizing, though the place appeared to meet his description as a "Health Ministry special".

"I really care about you very much, Solace," he said, bringing us back to our conversation just as I was hoping we might just discuss our dinner prospects for a while.

"I know," I swallowed.

"Can you talk about it?"

"Part of me," I began slowly, afraid to find out what I might say, "wants permanence: you know, marriage, family, house. Part of me wants none of those things." As I spoke, my words began to flow more quickly. "Since I came to the Carollons—actually, since I decided to come here—I've been happier than I can remember.

Learning to relax and put myself first. Why should I want to change that?"

"You were a happy child, right?" He waited for me to nod. "Then your body and the people around you started telling you that you were changing, and so you did, even if you weren't completely ready. You did what you were supposed to do. Then you cast aside all that adult crap that you took on too early and let yourself have the fun that you should have been having all along. Only now you're starting to realize there are some nice things about being an adult and you are missing out on a lot of them."

"I want a place to hang my print," I blurted out.

"Your print? I thought you bought it as a gift."

I went on rapidly. "I love living in the house, but if Cindy would get an apartment with me, it might be even better. I could have my furniture shipped here."

"You're planning to stay that long?"

I smiled. "I guess I am. I could arrange everything while I'm home. I still have a lot of work to do on myself before I will be ready to face my old way of living."

"Oh, don't do that!" he cried. "If you go back, promise you won't throw yourself back to the wolves." Suddenly a genuine look of horror swept over his well-proportioned face as a new thought occurred to him. "Solace, you can't move back to the States. Don't they have winter there?"

I laughed, truly amused by his concern. "I like winter."

"But sex in a cold room?" An involuntary shiver punctuated his question.

"I can't remember doing it." I paused. "Maybe I liked winter because I took a break from sex."

"You were definitely married to the wrong bloke. You should have slept around more before you married him."

"I don't think I could have done that." I caught a hint of understanding in the way he shrugged his shoulders. I was explaining it more to me than to Peter. "I didn't want to make mistakes. I thought that it was important to be a virgin when I got married." Nervously, I worked at breaking apart a set of disposable wooden chopsticks. "He'd've killed me, or dumped me at least, if I went out with someone else."

He was quiet for a minute as he tried to think of a tactful way to move on. "I'm glad you are able to be more adventurous now. You're smart enough to be careful."

The cashier came to our table with our supper. It looked and smelled delightful, and we eagerly pinched up some tasty tidbits with our chopsticks. Before he took his first bite Peter said, "Is your writing becoming more adventurous too?"

I cocked my head, pretending I hadn't heard his question.

He understood not to pursue the topic. He took a few bites. "It will come to you, Solace," he said in a soothing and confident tone. "You have been blessed with a longing to communicate from your soul. Someday you will feel safe enough to write your thoughts, and eventually you will be able to share what you write." He patted my hand encouragingly. "Now let's eat before it gets cold."

As uncomfortable as I felt about bringing up the subject of moving to Cindy, I knew I needed to settle my plans before I traveled home. I was studying in our room when she came in to change to go out.

"Where are you going?" I asked.

"Meeting Melissa." Melissa Maloney was Liam's sister. She had played on some of her brother's teams, and so she and Cindy had been friends for a few years. Since his death they had spent a lot of time together. "Might go to the movies, eh. Want to come?"

"Test tomorrow." I lowered my book. "I've been thinking about moving out of this house. Would you like to look for a place together? Maybe with two bedrooms? It would make sense for me to arrange to have my things shipped while I'm home."

She stopped what she was doing and sat heavily on her bed. She seemed upset, and I felt selfish. She stared at the floor, her face flushed. She looked like she was ready to cry. "Come here," she said in a low voice. I sat beside her. "Melissa and I..." her voice trailed off.

I waited a moment for her to continue. "Have you two been talking about sharing?" Were we both afraid of hurting the other's feelings?

"No." Her voice melted into silence. She seemed to shrink with it.

My imagination began to fill in the missing words. We were caught in a sort of silent, prolonged gasp. "Cindy," I said as a new thought dawned. Eventually, I realized that she was more uncomfortable telling me than I was afraid of her reaction if I guessed incorrectly. I forced a normal breath. "Are you and Melissa in love?" She burst into tears and threw herself around me. I couldn't move. She was crying loudly and my mouth was embedded in the midst of her bosom. Slowly, I wriggled out. "I should have known. You've been so happy lately. I just didn't think." I was able to sit back and see her face again. "Why are you crying?"

"Solace, I never ever thought I'd fall in love with a woman. When things started happening, you know, after the way things have been with men, I thought, 'Okay, I'll try this.' But I never thought it could be so wonderful."

"You're happy, aren't you, Cindy?"

"I've never been happier, but I'm a little scared and sometimes it seems like too much to deal with. I've never felt so strongly about anyone in my life before. But I'm not quite sure," her voice trailed off. "It changes a lot of things. If we stay together, I might have to give up a lot of things that I always thought I wanted."

I waited. Though I hadn't expected this, I was pleased that she had found someone who mattered so much to her. All I wanted was to find a way to let her know that I cared and would try to support her.

"I think she's my soul mate." She looked dejected. "But I have always wanted children." Cindy would be a good mother; she was kind and patient and fun. We do not always know what life will bring us, but we resist having to reject outright its possible blessings.

"You don't have to decide your whole future now, Cindy. You have time."

"I suppose." She shrugged. "I know I should have said something to you before now. With us sharing a room and all. I was afraid you'd be uncomfortable, and I just wasn't sure how to bring it up. And I didn't want things to change between us. Well...I mean," she stumbled, embarrassed.

I nodded to let her know she need offer no further explanation. "I trust you. It doesn't bother me, and I'm not worried. Nothing between us has changed."

"You're so accepting, Solace," she said. "I'm having more trouble with it myself."

"Of course you are, Cindy. Just don't let yourself get hurt while you are figuring out who you are and what you want. If you've found someone who makes you happy, you're way ahead of me."

She hugged me again, cheerfully thanking me for my encouragement before she breezed out of the room, somehow having transferred some of the weight of her burden to me. I didn't mind.

On my next day off, I went to Cindy's shop. I bought my parents another Christmas gift, some Russian tea glasses I thought they would both like, so that I could keep the volcano print. Boris was very excited when I returned to pick out a frame. He urged me on in my bold choice of a red matte, which drew out the intensity of the fires atop the mountain.

Chapter Four

The day of the Murphy family picnic, in early December, Bridget swapped Patrick to her parents for the use of their car. She and Rob picked me up in the late morning, and we reached the sheep farm in the interior mountains that belonged to some of Rob's relatives before lunch. A meadow had been cleaned out for the picnic and we were fenced safely away from the cattle and sheep. A few hundred people came and went throughout the sunny day. We stayed until nearly sunset. I had had a wonderful time, but I was ready to take my Murphy hugs and climb back into the car. I felt ready to fade away in the back seat, but Bridget insisted Rob sit in back this time.

"So, who was he, that big guy?" she asked. "He's American, right?"

"Yeah. His name is Ken Williams."

"Does he come from Washington too?" Rob called from the back.

"No. He's from Pittsburgh."

"So tell us about him, then," Bridget urged. "How did you start talking?"

"Someone brought him over. You know how everyone thinks that I know every other American in the Carollons." I tried to melt into the seat, but Bridget obviously wanted to hear more. "He works with Paul Murphy. That's who brought him. Anyway, he's an engineer, and he's here on a contract to work on the Hydro project upriver. I didn't realize it, but they are going to renovate the dam and the power plant. He just arrived and expects to be here for a few years."

"My company is working on the dam project too," Bridget said. "The improvements are supposed to make it more enviro-friendly."

From the backseat, Rob redirected the conversation. "So, Solace, will you be giving yourself an early Christmas present this year?"

"Rob!" Bridget cried. She had a panicked looked on her face. "Oh, Solace, I didn't mean to tell him."

I buried my face in my hands, knowing I should be embarrassed, but just laughing instead. These many months with Peter had been better in most ways than my playful prior year. I had real feelings for him, and though I did not quite know what they were, I regretted nothing.

"I think that I should meet and approve all of your boyfriends," grumped Rob. "This Ken chap, for instance. I could never get near him, as if he were trying to avoid me. I want to meet Peter."

"Peter and I aren't really..." I grimaced.

"Well, of course not. You can't *be* until you've introduced him to your friends. It doesn't count for much if you're afraid to do that."

Back at my house alone, I found myself aroused by the prospect of a new relationship. A just right tipsy from drinking a little beer all day had relaxed me, I suppose. I thought about calling Peter, but knew it would be wrong. Instead, I changed into one of the flowered sundresses I had not worn since my twenty-eighth birthday nearly two years ago. I pulled down my hair, and it fell in waves from the braiding over my shoulders and down my back past my waist. I looked very sexy and vulnerable.

I took a bottle of beer from the refrigerator and walked down the beach barefoot without a plan, sauntering in time with the waves, the unopened bottle in my hand. I stayed away from the water, recognizing its danger. I was teetering on irresponsible. If it felt right, I wanted to go over the edge.

I walked past Mike's house. He was having a party. He'd invited me, but I had told him I couldn't make it. I knew that he wouldn't mind if I went anyway, and I suppose that was where I had intended to go all along. I circled back and watched. The deck was lit and full of people, and a few couples had found privacy in the darkness on the beach, and as I became aware of one couple near me, my body responded with a touch of envy.

I relaxed, and my shyness eased. I started toward the circle of light around the deck. Coming out of the darkness, I nearly collided with a man and a woman coming around from the front of the house, their night vision, like mine, disrupted by the brightness. I smelled my favorite sunscreen, and turned, backing away from them while I formed an apology.

"Excuse me. Sorry, we didn't see," he stopped the instant he recognized me. I blinked to test my vision. It was Sean Donovan remembering his promise.

"Sorry, dear," the woman said. "We didn't see you."

"No problem," I stammered. I looked past her, over her shoulder to him. I did not want her to know that I knew him. It seemed terribly important that our acquaintance remain a secret, though I couldn't understand why I felt this need to protect him. Though I was surprised to see him at Mike's, and I didn't wish to socialize with him, I found myself ready to follow his guidance. He smiled and tilted his head in a friendly enough manner toward the house. I quickly flicked my eyes back to her. Though my dislike for him was rooted in distrust, I found that I did trust him to ignore me, even if he had been there alone. He had kept his promise before. As time went on, it was surely less tempting for him to break it.

She grabbed my arm and led me up the steps. "I'm Betsy. This is Sean."

I didn't say anything, though I knew she was waiting for me to. I had been living too thoroughly inside my head during my beer bottle clinging beach stroll. I felt the need to remind myself that I was Mike's friend and always welcome in his home. I did not even know how they knew him

.

He went into the house ahead of us and disappeared into the crowd. Betsy still led me by the arm and only tightened her hold when I tried to shake loose. "Let's see if we can find you a bottle opener, um?"

"My name is Solace." I was blushing and hot and no longer the least bit horny.

Just as I was saying this, I heard Mike calling my name as he bounded across the room. "You made it! My mates were wondering if they would get to see the prettiest American in the Southern Hemisphere, and here you are!" He embraced me, laughing like the drunkard he was not. "Betsy, how've you been? Been a while."

"I'm good, Mike, but it looks like Sean is trying to leave already. I'd better stop him. We can't leave the kids with a sitter long enough to suit me," she said, forcing a laugh to make it seem like a joke. "I'd better stop him. Get him to drink something."

"Yeah. He needs to do that. I'll be over to help you in a bit," said Mike with a grand gesture. Once she left us, he turned all of his attention to me, whispering in my ear, "My God, you look gorgeous! I almost didn't recognize you with this new look. You'd better be careful or my mates will get out of control."

"I can handle them," I whispered back.

"I know you can, but what will we do about all those broken hearts?" He laughed as he walked me around the room offering hospitality and introducing me to some people I didn't know.

Sean Donovan kept out of my way, but each time I caught a glimpse of him, he was watching me. Betsy noticed, and she was soon trying to get him to go outside or perhaps to leave the party altogether. The ice of her scowl nearly brought pity to my heart, much as I also thought that he deserved whatever she gave him.

Mike wouldn't let me walk home alone. He gave me his room and must have slept on the couch. He had already gone out by the time I was up.

The lounge was neater than I imagined it would be, but I found some litter to toss before I helped myself to a cup of dry cereal and settled onto a deckchair to await his appearance. Soon he came up from the beach, dripping in his swim trunks and carrying a surfboard. I wondered how he could be so chipper on the morning after a late party. I wouldn't ask. He apparently just had the metabolism for it. "Day!" he called cheerily.

"Thanks for the lodging," I said. "I helped myself to breakfast."

He looked into my cup. "That's breakfast? Not even milk?"

"It's a breakfast snack. I'll eat again after I get home. I just didn't want to leave without seeing you. Your sheets are in the wash."

"Shit. I was looking forward to having my bed smell like a sexy woman," he teased me good-naturedly.

"You'll have to do that on your own, Mate," I returned.

"And don't you think I can't!" He smiled. "Things seem to be improving for me. And you?"

"Met someone yesterday. We'll see," I said shrugging.

"At my party?"

"No. At the other one."

"Damn...oh, well..." He leaned the surfboard against the side of the house and went inside. Reappearing a moment later with the open cereal box, he sat in another chair. He took a handful and stuffed his mouth while he tilted the open end of the box toward me. I took it and refilled my cup. "Want to go to Mass with me?"

"Sure. Can I go to confession?"

"Oh, boy! You must have had an interesting yesterday," he exclaimed.

"It's all in my head."

"Then you can't confess it," he decreed. Laughing, he took another handful of cereal.

"I need to go home to shower and change."

"I like that dress, Solace. Is it new? It really suits you. I noticed you drawing lots of attention."

"Great," I said glumly. I had only noticed the attention I drew from one man.

"That's an odd response, girl. Don't you want the boys to turn their heads? You know, I hand pick all my male party guests just for you. If I wouldn't want you to date 'em, they can't come."

"Yeah, right," I said in a leaden tone.

"Okay, nobody meets the standards I have set for you, but I keep trying. It forces me to hang out with a better class of people." He was enjoying this conversation far more than I was. I kept thinking that perhaps he did not know some of his friends as well as he ought to. "What's the matter? Did someone say or do something that was out of line?" He bristled.

"No." My calm reassured him, and he settled back in his seat and dipped his hand into the cereal box again. "I ought to go, if we're gonna get to church," I said, rising to make my exit.

"Yeah. I'll come by your house in about half an hour?"

"Perfect." I picked up my still sealed bottle from the doorway where I'd left it earlier. I ran down the beach to my house, wondering how much shaking a beer could take. It seemed terribly important that I return the bottle to the refrigerator at home without any of my housemates realizing it had ever been gone. There was no worry on that end; the house was empty. If even one of them had come home, she had already gone out again.

"So, you're all ready for your trip home, then, heh?" Mike asked as he hoisted some oxygen tanks and other diving gear from his front porch to the trailer for his motorcycle.

"I guess I'm ready. Why do you need so much stuff?" I was trying not to act disappointed about learning he had plans with someone else. I'd gotten used to being able to drop in on him anytime, just assuming that if he wasn't scheduled to work that he would be available to hang out with me.

"I'm taking friends. We'll probably just snorkel, but I figured I might as well bring the scuba gear too."

"They don't have their own stuff?"

He shrugged.

"Can I help?"

"I have to pack it just so to make everything fit. I don't think I could explain it." He shifted something and slid in a bag of masks and air tubes. "Today should be fun. Since the war Donny's turned artist, and he said he was thinking of painting the reef. He knows I know my way around."

"I bet you do."

"And Cara's just tagging along for fun." I almost invited myself along then, but I knew Mike would have asked me if he wanted me. Besides, I wouldn't have wanted to leave the boat.

He fussed with arranging the trailer for a minute. "There. All set." He pulled the lid over the trailer and latched it. Turning back to the house, he asked what I was planning to do with my afternoon. "Seeing that American dude today?"

I shrugged. "Sometimes he just turns up. But I'm planning to study. It's almost time for finals."

"Maybe that bastard will take you out for dinner." He picked up his helmet from a chair near the front door and circled back outside, pulling the door closed behind him.

"Really, Mike, can't you just use his name?"

"I keep forgetting it." He put on his helmet. "Do you want a ride home?"

"I'll walk."

"Say, why don't you come with me up to the hospital? I was going to visit Tim before I meet Donny and Cara."

I tried not to show my cowardice, but I think I failed. "How is he?" I managed to ask.

"Better, but he still looks pretty damned awful."

"What is wrong with him?"

"Well," he said thoughtfully, "I'll try to explain what I understand." He took his helmet off again and walked with me to a spot of shade. It wasn't going to be a short answer. "His body was hit, and there was a lot of damage. He'd be dead if the medics hadn't gotten him choppered out to the American hospital ship. Then they sent him to Germany to the American hospital. Your people are the best doctors in the world." Mike crossed himself. I didn't dare to ask any questions. "The thing is: no one can totally predict how a drug will affect someone, especially with all that internal damage. He'd had a shitload of surgeries, started to heal, and then some of his organs started shutting down. Different drugs, more surgery. He was in a coma for more than a month. He's wasted and weak as a kitten." He shifted his helmet in his hands. "Now that he's home, man, it's just so good that he can finally have his family near him."

I began feeling the old guilt pangs. My chest tightened until I spoke. "I should have paid better attention to things when they were happening. I was barely touched by the war, and I should have been. It made such a difference in the lives of so many people I know. I ought to have done something, praying or making care packages. And I still don't know if anyone I knew from home was over there. I didn't have any close friends in the military, but there could have been school friends or customers. At least I should have been reading about it in the newspaper."

"It's old news now, Solace. Seriously, I think you can stop feeling guilty about it." He wasn't chastising me as I thought he should. "You had plenty going on in your life, and when it mattered, you were there to help me and stand by Cindy. And if you had other people who asked for help, you'd have done your best for them too."

"I wouldn't be so sure, Mike. I ignored you until I couldn't ignore you any more."

I sat on the wooden steps to the house, in the shade, feeling the breeze off the ocean and waiting for my ride to the airport. As usual, I was slathered in sunscreen, the only truly essential cosmetic in the tropics. I loved the smell. I bought my Big Bob's special blend at work. I had an employee discount, but I bought it because it had the best scent of all. I decided I would wear it while I was on my visit home. Home? I would wear it while I was visiting my family. My Big Bob's Burn Blocker would be an intimate reminder of this home.

I was ready for my ten-day return to my previous existence. I had even packed my bags without too much trouble, and I was beginning to look forward to getting there. I still hated leaving, but I knew that, though it may be strained, seeing everyone would be wonderful. I also understood that the longer I stayed away, the harder going home would be once I did it.

On the way out I had looked around the crowded, messy, little room that Cindy and I shared. She and Melissa were dating more openly now, and I was happy for her. We got along well, like sisters do. We had learned how to share our space, we were caring toward each other, and we had grown close, but we were also thrown together by chance more than choice. Our success as roommates came from our differences more than anything we had in common, other than just being two nice, if slightly misguided girls who had run away from home.

I had already dragged one of my bags down the stairs. The other, the one that was filled with gifts, rested beside me. After only a few minutes Mike arrived, driving his mother's British sedan. "I like your mom's car," I called to him when he got out. I was half way down the steps before he started up the flight, but he took the bag from me and carried it the rest of the way. "Do you really know how to drive a car?"

He answered with an impish shrug, "Do you think Dad would let me take you in a car if I wasn't a good driver?"

"He's sending me away, isn't he? Maybe he will cancel my return trip ticket, and I won't be able to come back."

"That's it. It's all a plot to get you out of the Carollons," he said with a hint of annoyance. "You're turning paranoid. Don't you want to see you family?"

"Yes. I just wish I didn't have to."

"Get in. You can sit in the back, if it'll make you feel safer." He opened the rear door. I got in the front on the passenger's side. When he slid in, he said, "So you really are afraid to go?"

"Yeah. It took a lot of nerve for me to come here, Mike, and I'm not sure I've accomplished any of the things that I meant to before my first visit home."

He shook his head. "Guess it's good to know that you haven't picked up my bad habits."

I looked out the window as we drove away, watching the street across from the ocean. "How's the restaurant?"

"It's alright. I'm making good tips now."

"Good."

"I like working hard, Solace. It's scary. It's like the Marines in a way, only this is full-time and the explosions and fires are usually smaller and unintentional." I laughed. He joined me. "You knew I would like it, didn't you?"

"It feels good to take care of yourself," was my only answer.

"I'm learning about that, Sol," his voice cracked. "You know that even after the doctor said I could dive I was still nervous about really doing it. I was afraid that my bones might break again and that my stitches might come open. It can't happen, I know, but I wouldn't really go down and stay. But since I started going out with Donny, I've found out that I could do it, and that I still love it."

"What's it like?"

"Fucking glorious." He made a goofy face and patted my hand where it rested on the center console. "I know you're all set on me being a waiter, and I like it and all, but I've applied for a job as a diver at St. Andrew's University as an assistant to the marine biologists."

"That would be great, Mike," I said enthusiastically. "I hope you get it."

"Me too," he muttered feebly. "I didn't tell my folks. Don't mention it, okay? Donny's tried to coach me a little on the interview, but that's where I know I'll fall apart."

"Nonsense, Mate. You've got a nice way with people." He looked surprised and turned to look at me for longer than I wished considering he was driving a car, so I added, "Keep practicing with your friend. It sounds like he's giving you the right kind of support."

We were nearing the airport, and our conversation turned to the logistics of parking and carrying bags. "Don't know if it will be me to pick you up when you come home. If it's someone you don't know they will have a sign."

Chapter Five

Mike was waiting for me outside of Customs, jumping up and down and making sure I couldn't miss him. I suddenly felt very lonely for my friend and yet as if I had just said good-bye. He raced forward, dodging other travelers, and hugged me. "I've been dying to talk to you! I almost called you."

"Oh, I wish you had. Did you get the job? Have you heard yet?"

His smile grew, and he nodded deeply, slowly. "They offered me the job the next day after the interview."

"Oh, Mike, I'm so happy for you!" I squealed. On my tiptoes, I gave him a loud kiss on the cheek. "I'll bet your folks are so proud!"

"Well, that's it, Solace, I wanted to tell you first. And I've been so fucking bursting! Now, tell me about your trip. Was it nice? Did they spoil you?"

"Of course. But I got busy making arrangements to have my things shipped here anyway."

"No shit!"

"Oh, yes. Lots and lots of it, but I weeded it down a bit."

"Your folks must be freaking." His voice shook with excitement.

I shrugged. "Half freaking. They took turns both making me feel guilty and proud. It was weird. And nice. It was good to see them. I owe your mom and dad a huge thank you. What could I do for them?"

"Write a note."

"Done. It's not enough."

"Then wash their cars. No, don't. If you did that, Mum would start trying to marry you into the family, so I'd have to marry you, because I couldn't let my best friend go to Jimmy. I love you too much to do that to you."

"I can say no."

"Don't count on it."

I rolled my eyes. "When do you start the new job?"

"Next Monday. And get this: Mr. Sikorsky wants me to stay in touch, in case I ever want to pick up extra money." As we walked out of the airport to the car and all the way back to my house, he continued going on excitedly, often repeating himself. I hoped he was not over-glorifying the position. I would hate it if he were disappointed with the work once he started doing it. I was not sure that Mike could have handled that. While many of our problems had the same roots, I was sure that I was stronger than he was. I knew from experience that handling disappointment was difficult even under the best of circumstances, yet I didn't have the heart to dampen his enthusiasm. It was extraordinary to be with a person who could truly go that close to the edge of his emotions, and I wondered if I was ready to give that gift to my friends.

Arriving at the house marked my return to reality in an odd twist of my usual perception of my real life being in Washington and my fantasy life being in the Carollons. This time I was going back to work, rent, school, friends, and my new boyfriend. A few weeks later, Cindy and I moved to our new apartment two buildings away from the Murphys, in the same complex. Except for my bicycle, all of my belongings easily fit into the trunk of Ken's car, but Cindy needed to borrow a truck to lug along everything from the big box on the deck. I slept on the floor, and we ate off paper plates for over a month.

Cindy and I took the day off work to unpack when my shipment was delivered. We had finished in the kitchen before Ken dropped in offering help. He hadn't told us that he was going to leave work early; he liked to show up without prior arrangement. I was setting up my room when he knocked. At the door Ken touched his lips to mine. "I thought you might like me to do some of the heavy work for you."

"You timed it perfectly," I replied cheerfully. "We're all done."

He looked around the living room. "I thought you said you had a lot of stuff."

"I do, but we are efficient. Like a drink?"

"Sure." Once we were in the kitchen he started looking around in the cabinets. "You aren't planning to do much cooking."

"Sure we are. Why do you say that?"

"I've got more pans and utensils than you do, and I don't cook much."

"Really? I think we've got what we need to do most things, but I'm sure that eventually, we'll pick up more and end up with too much stuff."

"Seriously, Solace, you don't have to do without. I'll buy you whatever you need."

I was getting ready to pour his drink, but I put the pitcher down on the counter and turned to look at him. He was still nosing through the cabinets. "Thanks, Ken. I'll get what I want myself. And I don't want a bunch of junk I won't use." I turned my attention back to pouring.

He took the glass when I offered it, frowning. "You don't have to bite my head off. I was trying to be nice."

"I know." I got out a glass for myself to give me a reason to look away. "I'm sorry. I'm not exactly impoverished."

"Then why did you let her move in with you?" He glanced over his shoulder to where Cindy was breaking down a box in the living room.

"Why wouldn't I?" I settled my fists onto my hips defensively.

He opened the refrigerator. He didn't want to answer or knew I didn't want to hear his answer. He wasn't comfortable with Cindy's sexuality. I couldn't understand why it would matter to him or why he even needed to acknowledge it. "Want me to move the couch for you?"

"No." I leaned against the counter and took a sip. "Why don't we just relax and enjoy our iced tea? I've done enough work for today."

"Fine." His feelings were hurt. "Where am I allowed to sit?"

"Look, Ken, I've moved all of this stuff a few times before. I know that you'll help me if I need something, but right now everything is fine. Would you want me to start rearranging your things?"

"I took off from work early to come help you."

"But you didn't even tell us you were coming or I might have saved something for you to do. We've done everything we are going to do for now."

"Of course you knew I'd come to help you."

"I guess I should have," I mumbled. I went into the living room and flopped onto the couch. "I've missed this couch. I've had some great naps on it."

He sat beside me. "You are tired. I'll take care of you tonight."

Cindy and I enjoyed cooking our meals together. We also frequented the pool, visited the Murphys and other friendly neighbors, and watched Patrick so that Rob could have some time to concentrate on editing a newly completed play. I still had Fridays off, so I was able to keep up with chores and errands despite the demands of an ever busier schedule.

Ken came over most days, using his nearby gymnasium as an excuse for not calling ahead. We learned to expect him before dinner, and I always cooked enough for him to join us, though he usually wanted to take me to a restaurant. Cindy and I learned to manage the leftovers and ate much better lunches than we had before this time.

Between Mike's new job and my new location, I saw a lot less of him. Getting together became something we had to plan to do, and neither of us was very good at planning. We often missed opportunities because of prior commitments. I hoped he knew I missed him.

Early in March, Rob invited me to join a group of friends, writers and actors, to read his new play aloud. Each of us was assigned a part, and asked to read it over to ourselves ahead of time to help us prepare. I lay on my stomach across my bed reading it when Ken knocked at the door. I heard Cindy going to answer it before I began to move, so I stole a few more moments with the story while I waited for him to join me in my room.

"What are you doing?" He came in and sat next to me on the bed.

"I'm reading Rob's new play." I arched my back, raising my face to kiss him.

"Yeah?"

"It's called *Tropical Heat*, and it's really good. I'm glad I have a chance to read it to myself before I'm asked to read it with the group, especially because Rob gave me a really big part. I'm Ludmilla," I said, pointing to the script.

He looked up at the volcano print on the wall in front of him. It was in my room, because it clashed with the living room furniture. "How can you sleep with that thing in here?"

"Spend the night sometime and find out." I closed my notebook and rolled over to my side, touching his thigh invitingly. "I made spinach lasagna for dinner." Seeing the look on his face, I reassured him, "It's good. Everything I make is good."

"But aren't you tired of all this Catholic food? I mean, it's not even Friday. Well, if you really want me to, I'll try it." He ignored my touch, remaining tense. I didn't really mind; it was exciting to maintain the mystery, and I felt like waiting was a mature choice. "Is this play thing going to take a lot of your time?"

"I don't know. I imagine we will need to meet several times. Why?" I asked.

"Well, you always seem so busy. Do you think you'll get a reprieve from babysitting while you're helping him?"

I shrugged. "Maybe I'll hold Patrick on my lap while I read." Seeing his frown, I added, "It's okay. You always say you wish you could play more golf. Think of this as an opportunity."

He took a deep breath. "So where should I take you to rescue you from that meatless thing you said you made?"

"I could fix you something else," I offered, trying to hide my hurt feelings.

"Oh, no. I don't want to make you do extra work. What would you like? I'll take you out."

Rob arranged for us to read in a vacant classroom at the University of Williamsport on Friday afternoon. Afterwards, I decided to visit Cindy at work, too excited by my star turn to go to the market or do anything else so mundane. She would be ready to leave work half an hour or so after I got there, so we could bike home together. I dropped into the antique shop, visited and browsed for a little while, and agreed to meet her outside the shop at quarter past five. When I walked past the gallery, Boris, who was cleaning the windows out front, flagged me down. "Miss Solace! I have something I've been saving for you."

"Oh, hi, Boris," I said warily. "I'm really not in the market for temptation right now."

"I won't tell your boyfriend you said that," he said slyly. "Come see."

"Alright," I agreed. Feeling trapped, I followed him into the shop. I muttered under my breath, "I'll bet I can't even afford to look."

He bounded to the stockroom door behind his framing table. "Wait there, Miss Solace," he commanded, pointing to the table cluttered with sample mattes and frame corners. He was out again before I had time to wait. "Close your eyes." I obeyed. "Now open them."

"Oh," I gasped in amazement at the simple, pastel sketch. It was of a mermaid with a fancifully colored tail and a frame of golden brown hair floating all around her head and covering critical areas of the human half of her body. "She looks like me."

"Da. She is beautiful enough to make women interesting, even to me—almost," he said with a playful wink. "Perhaps with such a tail."

I put out my hands silently to take the drawing. I rotated it to study the mix and texture of the colors.

"A while back we had a show of his work, and I told him how much my prettiest customer loved his volcano. Then recently he brings this in. Voila! For you, a gift from the artist." He puffed his chest proudly. From my trance, I barely noticed him speaking. It was hard to believe that this picture had been drawn by someone who did not know me, much less that he had not asked me to pose for it.

"Boris," I protested, "you can't give it away!"

"Donny gave it to me to give to you. It's just a little sketch he did—five minutes work. Perhaps she will be in a painting he does someday." He shrugged. "The frame is nothing." This was not true; the piscine texture and aqua hue that brought out the variety of colors in her tail without overwhelming the delicate tints of her face made this frame perfect for the piece. "I couldn't let her get smeared, so I let him choose a frame from the scraps. Does that make you feel better?" He looked at me studying the picture. "So? Don't you want to take her home with you?"

Accepting it made me feel guilty, but I knew that I would feel guiltier if I did not accept it. "You could sell this for a fortune, couldn't you?" I asked.

He shrugged.

Returning my eyes to the drawing, I realized there was more to the composition than just a pretty mermaid swimming in the water. Very subtly, so that it took those five minutes of studying it to become aware of it, a net had been drawn around her. She did not seem to have realized yet that the fishermen above had captured her.

"Boris, I couldn't." My voice cracked. "It is too great a gift."

"You want it. The artist wants to give it to you. What is the problem?"

"Why does he want to give it to me?" I asked skeptically.

"I don't know. But I can guess. I told him you admired his work, not only the volcano, but that watercolor of the Marine. Maybe he had already drawn the picture and thought of you after I told him about your vodka joke. He's a decent chap. I don't think that he has any harmful inten—"

"But how?" I began. "Did you show him my picture or something?"

"Nyet. He didn't even ask what you looked like. He seemed know who you were."

"Donny?" I said remembering Mike's friend. That must be it. He probably did know who I was, though Mike had never even pointed him out to me.

"Da. Sean Donovan."

"Sean Donovan?" I squeaked. I felt sick. "Is Donny?"

"Da. You do know him!"

"We've met," I said coolly.

He paused for a moment, his composure disrupted as he realized that I was not pleased by the artist's attention. "Just a moment. I have a picture." He pulled a file from under his framing table, and took a photograph from it to show me. It must have been taken at the show here at the shop; there was Boris standing with the very same Sean Donovan I always tried to avoid. What the hell was he doing giving me sketches? And how could I have come to admire his art so much?

"No," I said to Boris, handing back the sketch. I ran out of the shop with my hand over my mouth, afraid that I would vomit on his carpet or on the sketch, because despite everything, I did not want to destroy anything so lovely.

I ran down the sidewalk, too agitated to go to Cindy. I had to calm down before I saw anyone I knew. I didn't pay attention to where I was going, and even crossed a few streets, just running wildly, without looking out for traffic. My thoughts raced faster than my feet. After all this time, why couldn't the man just leave me alone? After all this time, why would he break the promise he had heretofore kept so faithfully? After all this time, why did it upset me so much to be contacted by him?

I slowed to a walk as I neared the river. Seeing the water reminded me that Sean Donovan had also promised to rescue me if he saw me drowning. I walked up the slope to the top of the bridge's arch and looked down into the water while I tried to put my thoughts in order. For a moment my anger shifted to my best friend. But it wouldn't stay there. Without even asking him, I knew that Mike had done nothing but mind his own business. He would not suspect Sean of doing anything wrong, because Mike was kind and he would believe Sean was too, just as I had when I first met him. If Mike had spoken to him about me, it was only because I was so important to Mike. He wouldn't have shared anything he thought was private. Sean may have used Mike, but even now I did not believe that. Though I wasn't ready to heed his warning, I could accept that Sean Donovan was trying to keep his promises.

The breeze over the water dried my tears and cooled the remnants of my temper. When I returned to his shop, Boris was helping a customer, but he excused himself long enough to remove the sketch, now wrapped in heavy brown paper, silently from the place he had stowed it under the work table and hand it to me. I bowed my head in gratitude.

"What did you buy?" Cindy asked when she came out of her shop.

"Nothing. I'll show you when we get home."

"What is it?"

"A gift," I said choking. "A gift from my favorite artist."

We sat side by side on my bed while I removed the brown paper. "This is wonderful, Solace," she said after a few moments of silent admiration. Wordlessly, she watched me bury it in a dresser drawer. "I won't tell anyone," she whispered.

Then I rather successfully put it out of my mind. I left the volcano print hanging in my bedroom. I still loved it, and Ken hated it, and it hadn't been custom-made for me. I could forget the mermaid while I thought of the artist as a good friend to Mike, while I tried not to admit that somehow that busybody stalker lowlife cheating scumbag Sean Donovan had earned some kind of position of trust.

I kept busy over the weekend. Ken's insensitivity to my moods gave me the freedom to think more than I wanted. He was grouchy because Cindy and Melissa stuck around the whole time. Cindy wouldn't have told Melissa about the mermaid; she didn't need to, because neither of them liked or trusted Ken anyway. I found it amusing that my mother would have been disturbed if she realized I was living with a lesbian, yet this lesbian couple had taken over her job as my bodyguard with nearly as much thoroughness and considerably more muscle, if it came to that.

If I had seen Bridget, I might have talked things out. She understood me better than anyone, except perhaps Sean Donovan, and she listened well. I only saw her from a distance though, and Rob not at all. She had a couple of extra kids around on Saturday, red headed girls like herself who must have been nieces, and I didn't want to interrupt.

On Monday evening, the night the dinner theatres were closed, I read with Rob's group again. I was now deep into the story and my character Ludmilla as she learned that her husband had taken a lover. As we were leaving, Steve suggested going for a drink. When I hesitated, Rob put an arm around my shoulders and guided me along the sidewalk. "Pray tell me you don't have to rush home for a date."

"Well, no," I said slowly, thinking. "I don't have a date, but Ken might call or drop by, and he'll bug Cindy if I'm not there."

"Then we'll find a phone box, and you can ring his home and let him know that you will be out too late to see or talk to him tonight, and that I will make sure you get home safely. Or you can let Cindy deal with him. She's quite capable. And you can just forget about it, as you ought to, and not call."

"Can I really do that?" I didn't realize I had actually spoken.

"Of course, you can. And you should. If seeing your boyfriend worries you so much then you should stop seeing him." I could hear the irritation in his voice. "Solace, he doesn't give you enough space or time on your own. Granted, you are his only friend, but even then you should be able to balance seeing each other with time apart. You have to be able to live separate lives to bring something into your life together, and I'm not just talking about spending the day at work." After we were seated in the pub, Rob slid up right next to me so that he could continue our conversation, while Karen and Steve gave us privacy, somehow aware of the nature of our discussion. "Are you writing at all?"

"No. I'm way too busy."

"That's why you're so down. You've got to tell the man to give you a night off every now and then."

That would have been the answer for Rob, but for me it was more complicated. "I'm not down. I'm just busy—doing. When I'm ready, I'll find a way to fit writing in," I said, shaking my head and wishing I was as dedicated to my art as he.

"Fit writing in?" Rob's voice was shrill with shock. Karen and Steve looked up at us. "Solace, you need to write. That's the thing that you want to do, remember? Don't get used to a fast pace. You'll dump everything that's important to you all over again, and be as miserable as you were back home. You came to the Carollons to get away from your old life, right? So, now you meet an American and you go right back to it. What's wrong with you? Why are you allowing yourself to be trapped in another controlling relationship?"

"Rob," I said in a low growl, warning him away.

"I'm your friend, Solace. I have to speak up for you when you won't take care of yourself. We're worried about you. Doesn't this remind you of something? Or was that memory so bad that you've repressed it completely and don't recognize that it's happening again?"

"You're exaggerating," I said. I felt my breath tighten. I was angry, at myself, but I was still afraid that I might punish Rob for so clearly delivering the very message I had been trying to ignore.

"Shit!" Rob hissed.

I looked up, following his gaze, to see Ken entering the pub. "Dear God, no!"

Ken squinted as he looked around, spotted me, and headed directly to our table. Rob and I pretended we hadn't seen him, and forced our faces into neutral expressions. My dear friend covered for me, millimetering himself away from me until he reached a more socially acceptable distance, smoothly beginning a story mid-narrative. Karen and Steve played along, laughed at the right times, and gave Ken no reason to be suspicious of what he had interrupted.

Rob went on with his story after Ken arrived at our table, leaving him standing there like an eavesdropper until he suddenly stopped, pretending he had just noticed him. "Olá, Ken," he said. "This is unexpected, heh. What brings you here?"

"Solace, my magnet," he answered. Ignoring my friends, he turned to speak to me. "I knew you came here sometimes, so I thought I might find you here, you know, when you didn't come home."

"How sweet of you to worry about me, Ken." I smiled politely, beginning to boil with rage.

"I wasn't worried," he stumbled. "I just wanted to be with you. I wasn't busy, and I haven't seen you all day." Ken stood looking at me and the table, trying to figure out how to sit by me. Finally, he took an unused chair from another table, and Karen and Steve made room for him as far away from me as possible. He offered to buy another pitcher of beer, but everyone sighed and said it was time to go home.

Just outside the door I said in the kind of dismissive tone a hostess uses with an over-staying guest, "Well, good night, Ken." Rob and I stepped away together, beginning our walk to the bus stop.

"I'll give you a ride, Solace," Ken said, clearly not extending the offer to my neighbor. He smiled confidently.

"No need. Rob will make sure I get home safely. Good night again." Eager to go, my tone became less tolerant.

"What?" he cried. He thrust his face close to mine. "Why?"

"I don't have to go with you, Ken," I explained.

His face grew redder. "But I came to get you," he began.

"Do you think that you can just follow me around town even when I'm doing something that doesn't involve you? That you have the right to pull me away from other friends and other activities to suit your whims? You never ask me if I want to see you. Now you've come down here. Like this. Don't you trust me?"

"What the hell? You're my girlfriend, Solace. I want to be with you."

"All the time? Don't you have any friends of your own?"

"Of course I do."

"Then why don't you spend time with them sometimes? And why haven't you introduced me to them? And why are my friends suspicious of you? And why did I make myself believe I was in love?" My voice began to crack. "What is wrong with me?" I burst into tears. I balled my hands into tight fists and pressed them against my thighs.

Rob stood close enough to monitor our exchange. Steve waited behind Ken, and Karen stayed by the door, ready to run inside for help. I didn't notice them at the time. My eyes and thoughts were on Ken only.

"But, Solace," he pleaded. "We don't need anyone else."

"I do," I said. "It should trouble me that people who care about me don't want to have anything to do with you."

"I thought you liked being with me," Ken said. He sounded reasonable enough.

"Not all the time." I stopped crying and shaking as I regained control. With a steady voice, I continued, my certainty growing, "Not any more. You have invaded my space, my existence too completely. You're smothering me. And...well...you just proved it."

"Solace," he croaked.

"Are you trying to isolate me?" I asked, staring unblinking at his face for a reaction. His body was frozen, his face livid. His jaw hung grotesquely as he tried to stammer something. I could not or would not allow it to be comprehensible. I had seen enough to be terrified of learning more. Unwilling to listen, I screamed, "Then thank God it went no further! It's over, whatever it was. Stay away from me forever!"

Then I turned my back on him and walked away.

Chapter Six

Steve and Karen stayed behind to watch Ken until he stopped flexing his fists and stomped off to his car. Rob scurried after me, catching up before we got to the bus stop. We sat in silence, though I let my head fall on his shoulder. I was upset, but I didn't need the consolation he was prepared to offer me.

I was angry and tense, but calm. I was able to examine events and recall things I had held back so long without reopening the wounds. The familiarity that had led me to feel secure in my relationship with Ken was the result of so many similarities to my former marriage. I could see the parallels: the undermining, the isolation, the shutting out of my fantasies, the depression, and the self-doubt. In the instant that I saw how it had happened again, I lost my naivety. I had let it happen.

"Don't be so hard on yourself, Solace," Rob said, breaking the silence. "It is impossible to see this kind of thing coming. You can't be sure it's going bad until it's gone too far."

"Shouldn't I have learned something from the past, like you said?" I asked.

"I'm sorry, Solace. I shouldn't have yelled at you. I was angry, and I took it out on the wrong person."

"You were right. I didn't want to hear it," I said shaking my head. "You were trying to help. Thank you."

He laid his arm over my shoulders and rocked us slightly to remind me of his support. "I didn't like watching you get hurt. And I kept thinking about how you met Ken at the family party."

I burst into nervous laughter. It was such a Rob thing to say, and it was the kind of thing that would have worried me. "You didn't know him or even that he would be there," I sniffled.

"I was afraid for a minute tonight that you were going to kill him," he joked, encouraging me to see the miniscule amount of humor in my dilemma.

I pulled away and met his brown eyes. "I was ready to beat myself up, Rob. That's more my style."

"How do you expect to find happiness when you add to your own suffering?"

"I don't know, Rob. I mean about finding happiness."

"You've done pretty well, my girl, until recently."

"But am I doomed to live out my days alone, because I am such a poor judge of people?"

He huddled slightly as he thought. "No," he said at last. I looked at him, waiting to hear more. "First of all, you don't misjudge everyone. You've made good friends with decent people. Even that bloke Peter—once I finally met him—is decent. The problem's that you hold your boyfriends to different standards than you hold your other friends."

"I suppose," I stammered.

"So, you are capable of making good character determinations."

"Except with boyfriends," I frowned. "I get too serious, and I want it to work so badly that I forgive too much."

"That's mostly a good thing, Solace. Even Mr. Right will need you to forgive him periodically."

"But how will I know that he is the right one?"

"Not sure." Then he chuckled. "You could always hook up with someone you hate and hope that you were wrong about *him*."

I gave him a tolerant smile, swallowed, and deemed, "That's not much of a plan."

"See? You do have good judgment, you little she-beast. You were impressive tonight. Your instincts pricked up, and you put on quite a show. But then, you were headed that way at the reading. You know you are quite a good actress. It's hard to believe you've had no training."

"Just life, Rob. Life provides lots and lots of training."

Rob made sure I made it safely into my apartment. As I went about my bedtime ritual, I was jittery at noises, especially the sound of the building's outer door. Cindy was asleep, so I didn't have a chance to learn if Ken had disturbed her earlier. My mind remained active through my exhausted sleep, yet somehow when my radio alarm went off in the morning I awoke refreshed, upbeat, and energetic.

"Hey, Solace," Cindy said over the top of her cereal box. "How'd your acting thing go?"

"Fine. We went out after, and Ken popped in, so I broke up with him," I said briskly.

Her spoon clanged into her bowl, and she pushed the box over so she could see me. "You did what?" She was smiling. She wanted to hear it again.

"I told him to leave me alone, that I never wanted to see him again."

She clapped her hands together. "Just for showing up uninvited?" Her tone was delighted. I nodded. I didn't need to explain. She jumped up and ran over to hug me. Then she stopped. "You won't make up with him, will you?"

Some kind of wicked smile dawned on my face. "No. I definitely won't make up with him. I had not realized what was happening, but now that I have," I stopped, shook my head, and started over again. "It was all wrong. I just wanted someone too badly. Maybe it was that visit home. I kept thinking my parents would like him. I came here to prove that I could make decisions for myself, and what do I do? Try to guess what my folks would want for me! What a silly, stupid fool I am."

"It's engrained in us, Solace. I've been trying to figure out how to deal with telling my parents that I'm dating another woman. It's not the lesbian thing so much, eh. I really think they can handle that, but they disapprove of promiscuity, and I have been quite promiscuous. So how do I tell them that I prefer a woman without them knowing that I tried it with several men? They never needed to know before."

I moved toward the kitchen and started getting my breakfast ready. "Do you and Melissa want to live together?"

"Solace, I don't—"

I interrupted. "Yes or no or maybe sometime, Cindy. I don't need an explanation."

"We've talked about it. We might want to."

"I was just thinking that I might like to get my own place. I'm sure we could have the lease amended. I don't know when I could move, and you probably don't know when Melissa could move, but probably sometime in the next few months. I think I'd like to be back by the ocean and have a proper place to hang my art."

"Don't move too far away, girlie girl. I will miss having you around."

"Well, across the hall is not close enough to the ocean. I still want to hang out with you and Melissa too. I like her. You're good for each other. How did you find that? How did Bridget and Rob? Or my parents?"

"When you do, you'll understand, Solace."

"I don't think I can trust myself."

"Well, then don't get into anything serious. Go out and party like in year one. Just have fun. You were happier then."

"That was the experiment with freedom. I've done it. I don't think I'm seeking freedom for freedom's sake anymore."

I waved good-bye to her on my way out the door. She was still at the table with cereal and newspaper, but she was looking out the window. "When you meet him, Solace," she said, "it will feel different than it did with Ken or the ex-hub. You won't hear your stupid head saying anything because your heart will be crying for joy. Trust me."

After I got to work, I jotted a note of thanks to Sean Donovan for the sketch. I addressed it in care of Boris at his shop, and posted it over my lunch break.

Early in the afternoon, Ken suddenly appeared at my desk. I was working with a pair of trainees so I didn't see him right away, but my cubicle-mate, who worked facing out, did. Upon her recognizing my cheery mood in the morning, I had explained that I had broken up with him. She was still staring daggers at him when I turned to see what was going on behind me.

"Hi, Solace," he began in a thin voice. His manner was self-deprecating and uncomfortable, as well it should have been. His shoulders turned in; his hands were hidden behind his back.

"Excuse me," I said to the trainees, making a point of being polite to them because I was so very angry about seeing Ken. I rose and stepped toward Ken, on the attack, the she-beast coming out at the very sight of him. "What are you doing here? I told you to leave me alone."

"I thought about what you said. And I can see that you might want more time apart. I'm so crazy about you that I—"

"Crazy? Oh, that's a good word for it. I told you I never wanted to see you again. Don't you think I meant it?"

"You couldn't just decide something like that so quickly," he declared. "Let's make up." Suddenly he thrust forward a bouquet of flowers he clutched in his fist and shook them at my face.

Seeking Solace

I hate to be given flowers as a peace offering. They are reminders of the fight and the reasons for it, and also of my having given in to everything that my ex-husband had supposedly apologized for doing and promised never to do again. Flowers are for funerals and celebrations, sickness and no reason at all. They were proof that I had made the correct decision last night. Without counting, I knew there were twelve of them, making it a completely unimaginative one dozen red roses.

"Here. Take them. They are for you. I love you, Solace." He wiggled them closer to me. The stems were already bending under the weight of the flower heads. A couple of broken leaves drifted to the floor.

"No you don't. I don't know what your motivation is, but I'm not about to open the door to you again. Go away and take those stinky things with you. I told you I never wanted to see you again." I took a deep breath, but calm was beyond my reach. "I meant it."

"You're delusional, Solace," he chided, his neck swelling as his stance became defensive.

"I am not. I was slow to grasp it, but you're bad for me, Ken. I don't care what you think, what you want, or if you have genuine affection for me. It doesn't matter. I will never be happy if I keep seeing you."

"What? Have you gone lesbo, like your queer room-mate?"

"Let's pretend you did *not* say that," I seethed between clenched teeth. "This is between you and me." Was it possible that he realized he had gone out of bounds? His hand dropped, his head sagged a little, and the flowers hung heads down at his side as he displayed the first signs of contrition I had ever seen in him. "Be glad it went no further," I said calmly, without venom. "I am."

He had no dignity. He fed on my anger. Exploding, he pounced with both hands outstretched. He knocked me over, pinned me under his weight, and pounded my body with his fists. My head hit the base of one of the chairs, then thudded to the floor. I don't know if he meant to use the flowers as a weapon or if he forgot he held them, but the thorns caught on my skin and the smell of the iron in my blood mingled with the sickening sweet scent of the crushed petals and broken stems. He sat straddled over my belly with his shins on my wrists preventing me from covering my face. I could do nothing to protect myself.

It seemed to go on forever. In reality, the beating lasted only moments, but the blows were hard and receiving them was a shock to me. I had never been beaten before. Even my ex-husband had maintained that much pride and self-control. In my stupor, I thought I should write to him and thank him for his past restraint.

I heard screaming, but it wasn't mine. I had retained enough sense to hold my mouth closed. Ken's body rocked and his blows, less forceful, went wide as he was pulled away from me. He kicked me as he was hauled away, still flailing the air with bare stems. At last my hands could cover my face, and I lay still, using every bit of my remaining strength to shut out the noise and commotion. Time, which had moved so slowly while I was being beaten, now sped forward as if trying to make up for the inertia of those other dread-filled moments.

Before it seemed possible, the police and the ambulance crew arrived. I reserved my short attention span for dealing with them. "We're going to take you to the hospital, Miss," one of them told me. "We are going to lift you up onto the stretcher. No, don't lift your head. We've got you. It's over. You'll be fine. Just got to have a doctor check over you before you can go home."

The personnel administrator from my office followed me to the hospital to support me during treatment, and she drove me home after I was released. My facial injuries were much less severe than I feared while my imagination was being stimulated by my shock. My cuts were cleaned and some broken off thorn tips were extracted. The doctor's primary concern was the concussion I received when my head slammed onto the concrete floor, and he ordered me to rest for a few days. I was dizzy enough not to argue when both my physician and employer instructed me not to return to work for the remainder of the week.

Cindy took charge of my home care. With Melissa's help, she coddled me until bedtime. I was to worry about nothing, especially not about advising my parents. Ed Leahy had already taken care of that, and they had telephoned while I was still at the hospital. "They know what happened," Cindy explained. "They said to tell you they love you, and that your mum will phone you in the morning."

She woke me several times during the night to test my brain function, and got me up in the morning so that she could help me wash and dress before she left for work. She left as soon as Rob arrived. Alone because he had left Patrick at home with Bridget's mother, Rob settled down to work quietly at the dining table, seeming to forget my presence, while I rested on the couch watching TV. I envied his ability to concentrate, and I wished my television had a remote control so I could try the other channel. I turned it off and the radio on when I had a reason to rise. After Rob and I shared a can of vegetable soup, I napped.

When I woke, Bridget was with me. She sat, rocking in time with the music on the radio, watching me. She had closed some of the curtains, shutting out much of the afternoon's brightness. I felt more alert and less dizzy, and the ringing in my ears had finally subsided. I pushed myself to a seated position, touched my face, and felt the crisscrossed lines of raised scabs on my cheeks and a bump where one of the thorn tips had been removed. I was tempted to ask Bridget to bring a mirror so that I could fling it against the wall. Would I even notice another seven years?

She came to me and touched my hand, restraining my fingers with her nearly imperceptible healing, painless, and calming mother's touch. "Now, Sweet, leave it be and let it heal." She shook her head and clicked her tongue. "What won't you do to make a fashion statement?"

I whispered, "I have a reputation to maintain."

With a smile, she patted my knee and said, "You know, Solace, tattoos take longer, but if you go to a good shop, you shouldn't need to visit the hospital after."

The throbbing in my cheeks checked my urge to laugh. "I think I'll get a really thorny, long-stemmed red rose to wrap around my guts to remind me to be more careful."

"Not a dozen?"

"No. One is enough. I have to leave room for the next ex-boyfriend."

She knitted her brows together, leaning over to examine my face. "I imagine it feels worse than it looks. None of the cuts are deep. I doubt you'll have scars, except where the thorns broke off. There are…" she counted, "five, maybe six places where you might have a little mark. If you don't touch them, they'll turn out better than pox."

She moved back to the rocker and said, "Your mum rang earlier—when Rob was here. She said not to wake you. She'll try again later. She's at Faith's house, watching the kids. Your sister was getting ready to go to the hospital. Might have the baby today. But guess what? Your dad is coming here! Mrs. Leahy will bring him in from the airport tomorrow afternoon. Isn't that lovely?"

"My dad?" As pleased as I was by the news, I couldn't help wondering if it meant I'd been hurt worse than I'd been told.

Bridget saw my concern, and immediately changed the subject. "Want a creamy?" She was already heading toward the kitchen. "Made one for you earlier. It should be thick frozen by now." I heard the freezer door close, and she reappeared holding a stadium cup brimming with a very thick chocolate milkshake. My mouth watered as I sat up straighter and took the cup from her. I skimmed the frozen spoon across the top, put it in my mouth, and felt the cold of it.

She sat again, thinking. "Your life must be exhilarating," she remarked. I looked askance at her. "You live closer to the surface than most people, Solace, like your windscreen's got no glass, but it doesn't seem to slow you down."

"Maybe that's why I keep running into ditches."

"But you don't," she objected. "You never get stuck anyway. And think how much richer your life is. I'd love to read one of your stories, if only to see life from your perspective."

"But, Bridget, I can't write about this kind of thing."

"Why not? You should make use of your experiences. You have so much to share."

"Would you?" I asked.

"Me? No." She blushed. "But I don't have your gifts."

"So, you are no braver than I am?"

"Now that," she said leaning back and starting to rock again, "is an interesting question from a girl who moved to a foreign country thousands of miles from anyone she knew, without even a job. Then you moved in with the waitress who served you your first meal in this country and went out with Michael Leahy!"

"I never dated Mike." The cold in my mouth was pleasantly numbing. I held the side of the cup against my swollen cheek.

"But he became one of your best friends," she protested. "He always used to be such a pest. But he's ever so much better than that rose basher Ken," she added shaking her head.

I thought I had introduced her to Mike. Suddenly tired, I loaded creamy into my cheeks.

She crossed herself hurriedly. "Thank God Rosie doesn't pack a bone crushing punch. You know, Solace, it's in the news. I've got the paper if you want to see it."

"Later," I said. "Don't want to spoil my creamy." I only wanted to think about the cold: ice, snow, even a drizzling, dampening, misty rain. Damn, I was hot. I held the cup to my forehead and let its perspiration drip down my face.

It was easy to be quiet with Bridget, and we let the afternoon slide toward evening until Mike and his father arrived nearly simultaneously. Ed's visit was brief. He informed me of his call to my parents and explained my father's arrival plans. He also explained that Ken had been arrested for trespassing as well as assault. "I will pursue him legally, Solace, even if you choose not to. I hope you will. If you choose to forgive him, that should be a private matter. He needs to receive society's punishment."

I swallowed. I had not known Ken was dangerous when I decided to stand up to him, yet despite the uncomfortable results I didn't regret doing it.

"You have complete vindication that you made the right choice," Mr. Leahy added.

"I might have incited him." I bit my lip. Bridget stretched her fingers up to my mouth to stop me from gnawing.

"Even if you provoked him, his reaction was excessive. You had already told him to leave." Mr. Leahy gave me a comforting smile. "Now, I need to get home. I told Laura to sup, but I know she'll wait for me." He stood. "Take care of yourself, Solace." He put his hand on Mike's shoulder as he turned to leave, kissed him on the top of his head, and rumpled his hair affectionately. "Give me a call later, Son."

"Right, Dad," Mike responded in a monotone without taking his eyes off me.

Bridget remained in the rocking chair, and Mike sat on the floor beside me. After a long while he spoke again, and I sensed his determination. "We will take care of you, Solace. We'll watch out for you. Dad has already talked to some people about improving security at the office. Rosie should never have gotten in the door without your permission. Lucky thing you were training that bruiser Mulligan. The stupid asshole obviously didn't scout the territory very carefully to attack you in front of him. What impotent balls he's got!" He turned to Bridget, "You should see the body on young Mulligan. Puts me and Shakespeare to shame."

Bridget slapped at his arm playfully, saying, "Oh, Leah!" in her light way. How could I have not known they were old friends?

"He's been working out at the Big Bob's warehouse, Mike. I don't think it's your kind of place," I whispered. "Too much purpose."

"I'll remember that," Mike whispered back.

The next day I was mostly left on my own, with Rob only looking in every few hours. The police came by to interview me in the morning. They explained that Ken had been released from jail on bond into the custody of his employer. The judge had forbidden him from making any kind of contact with me. Understandably, he was not permitted to leave James Island, the very place from which I most wished he would vanish.

I napped again after I ate some of the lunch that Cindy had left for me in the refrigerator, then I read for about an hour until my father arrived. As difficult as the circumstances made our meeting, I was happy to see him. We hugged at the door, disregarding my bruises. "It's good to see you, baby," he said. "You're okay here alone?"

"Yeah. Rob's been stopping in every now and then, but I've enjoyed the quiet."

He settled into the armchair, and I sat on the couch with my feet tucked under me. "And how are you doing? You must be tired."

"Yeah," he admitted, trying not to let it show. "You look better than Ed said you would. They must be treating you well. How on Earth did this happen?"

I shook my head, wondering that myself. "I let the wrong guy get too close, and then I told him off."

"He hit you with a bouquet of flowers? Roses with thorns?"

I nodded.

"What an ass," he muttered, making a rare use of color in his speech. I could see that healthy men had absolutely no sympathy for a man who would hit a woman, but I also understood that every one of them had even more difficulty accepting that it had not been done cleanly. My father, if ever driven to violence, would have fought fairly, subduing his enemy without inflicting unnecessary injuries. I was coming to understand the disparaging remarks and the nickname of "Rosie" with increased perceptiveness.

"I wish I'd seen it sooner, Dad." It was too early to broach this topic, so I turned the conversation to him. "How was your trip?"

"It was long, but I'm glad I finally did it. I'm relieved to see that you are already recovering. Youth is on your side." He breathed deeply, relaxing and settling deeper into the chair. "I can't stay long. Laura took my bags to the hotel, but I'm nervous about leaving them at the front desk."

"They'll put them in your room."

"Is it that small an island?" he asked, relaxing a little.

"Yeah," I said, shrugging. "I guess it is." I had forgotten my wonderment about the small kindnesses that had become routine to me over the last couple of years. For a guest of Laura Leahy, the hotel would make a greater than usual effort. "Are you staying at the Royal Carollonian? That's where they usually house their guests."

"Yes. I didn't have time to look around to find a place, but just let Ed—oh, I guess it was probably Laura—handle making the reservations. I hope I can afford it," he said without sounding at all concerned about the price. I held back a chuckle. I imagined that Ed's secretary would have arranged for my father to receive the room at the corporate rate. "So, this company really is okay? Despite everything you've told me, I can't help picturing you working in a crowded, dirty, little back room surrounded by standing surfboards and oxygen tanks." Meeting the refined Laura Leahy must have brought it home to him that I worked for a real corporation where people knew as much about business trends as they did about riding waves.

I nodded. "In a couple of days I'll show you around town and take you to the store. You'll get a kick out of it."

"It sounds like you really like your job. I'm glad. Since you seem to be a career girl, it's nice that you have finally found a career that suits you."

"I do like it," I paused. "How long are you planning to stay?"

"Through next weekend to get the airline deal. I hope you can handle having me around all that time."

I nodded. "There are so many things I've wanted to show you and Mom." I paused, too excited to continue without another breath. "I still can't believe you're here."

He smiled a patient, fatherly smile. I knew he was thinking about how much he and my mother wished I would come home, but wisely, he said nothing.

However, I decided to make my thoughts known to him. "I don't think I will ever go back permanently, Dad. I've always told myself, until now, that this was temporary, just about finding myself amidst the mess I've made of my life. But now I've realized that this place has become my home."

"Your boyfriend beat you up, and you were sent to the hospital." His voice was commanding, but it shook with emotion.

"It might have been worse, Dad. In the past, the most I would have done was run and hide, but this time I stood my ground. I didn't see this coming. I misjudged him. Well, I guess I misjudged him all along. Who'd have thought he would turn violent when if anything I'd thought he was dull? I may have some scars, but I'll be fine."

"A good florist will remove the thorns," he muttered.

"In the end I won, if that's the right word."

"It's close enough." He accepted my arguments more quickly than I had. He looked around the room, then turned his wrist to check the time. "It will be nice to have some time alone with you, Solace."

"Why don't you go check into the hotel and get a little rest? Come back here for dinner. Cindy will be making something easy to chew. Do you want me to call a cab for you?"

"Sure. That would be nice," he said, trying not to appear to jump at the offer. His shoulders sagged a little. If he had slept at all en route, it had been cut short by the time change.

At the time the cab was expected, I rose again. He trembled slightly while he embraced me. He looked lonely as he left and gave me one last look over his shoulder from the top of the stairs. Playfully, I blew him a kiss.

He returned to join us for dinner, quickly taking in the nature of Cindy's relationship with Melissa. He questioned me the next day, "You chose to live with this girl when you knew she was a lesbian? Is there something else I should know?"

"No. Cindy and I get along very well. She's not attracted to me—and I'm not attracted to her, if that's your worry. She's a good, good friend, and this has been a difficult time for her. I like to think I've helped her by not changing the way I act around her. And why should I?"

"I guess if nothing happened in the first two years it's unlikely to start now," he said slowly, still thinking about the situation, not comfortable, but understanding my reasoning. Then he moved on.

"They seem like nice girls. They have obviously put a lot of energy into taking care of you."

I nodded my agreement. "Do you like it here?"

"I can see why you do. Once you get used to the heat, I imagine that it is very nice. Your view is wonderful." He took a sip of his iced tea, and surveyed the ocean in the distance from the shade of the balcony.

"I'm going to get my own place soon," I informed him. "Closer to the beach. I miss the sound and the smell of it, and I can afford to live alone. I think that Melissa will move in with Cindy."

"Have you arranged the new place?"

"Not yet. But think I'll look for a nice condo, in a building with a good security system."

"Do you need help, Solace?" he asked. When he realized what he had said, he added, "I know that you don't need it, but I always like to offer it. You don't even seem to need help now, but I'm glad I came. I'm glad to see where you live and meet your friends."

"Me too. Perhaps now that you have come and seen what I'm up to, Mom will be more comfortable too."

"I'm sure she will be." He took a few long sips and pulled out the lemon half that was buried in the ice. He took a big bite of the rind and devoured it. "She reminds me sometimes that I suggested you travel. I was thinking you might spend a week in London, but she still can't quite let it go."

"Sorry, Dad. It was a great idea to travel, but I was already itching to move, to do what I have done, although I wasn't thinking of going quite this far until you suggested Europe."

My healing moved forward rapidly. Each day I noticed improvements, but as the incident became more distant, the terror of it became more real to me. That fear pushed me out of my door so I could be with people.

I showed my father around the city, and we even went over to St. Mary's Bay for an overnight stay at the resort, where we gorged on seafood and Russian pastries. We also let go of our modern inhibitions and tried taking the healing waters. The mineral springs brought up a warm water with a distinctive taste. It was not strong, and we both decided we liked it and luxuriating amongst the wealthy English patrons who came every year to indulge in this healthful custom. It was an odd connection with the past, something that I had never considered doing until the concierge came by to make sure that we had a reservation. Something about the place, the luxury, or the waters surely was healthful, because we both came away saying that we felt invigorated.

I also took him into Little Russia to look through the shops for gifts to send home, and on Thursday evening we went to the dinner theatre to see Rob and some of the other actors I was getting to know in their current play.

"I'm impressed by your friends," Dad told me later. "That Rob is very talented. I wonder why he doesn't move to London or New York so he could develop his career better. And you didn't tell me that Steve was really an historian. I gave him some names of people I know who might be able to help him find publishers and other sources." Dad could not resist giving advice and assistance.

"What do you think of Mike?" I asked.

He hesitated, then spoke a little grudgingly. "He has forced me to look at my own prejudices. I would not have given him the time of day from the way he dresses, that mop of hair, and the tattoos. He's too skinny. If I didn't know he was your friend, I might have guessed he used drugs. But by looking past his appearance, I can see that he is a decent young man. He's been very kind to you. I can see why you feel close to him."

I smiled at his comments.

"I'll prepare your mother," he added. "I want to plan a trip back with her soon. She needs to see this place and you in it. I think a few days over at St. Mary's Bay would seal the deal."

"Good plan, Dad," I agreed. "Offers to stay at five-star resorts tend to appeal to her."

The next Sunday he left, looking tanned and rested. I shared a taxi with him to the airport, and helped him manage the bulky load of gifts for the family, mostly beach toys for his grandchildren he had been unable to resist once I got him inside Big Bob's. The load of worrying about the way I had been living for the last two and a half years had been lifted from him, and most important of all, he had finally accepted my adult ability to manage my life.

Chapter Seven

"That's it then, heh, Miss Murphy," the property manager said, closing his file. "Here are your keys. If you need anything, have any questions, just call me. I'll be around. As you know, I've got grandkids here in the building, up in 311."

"Thanks, Mr. Reilly."

Bridget had recommended Kevin Reilly, a family neighbor, when I said that I was going to look for a place to live on my own. He had made simple the task of finding a home that met all of my criteria. I was back in mid-town, just blocks from the university and a quick trip to the beach or Mike's house. In this seemingly secure, high-rise condominium building there was a front desk, an underground garage, a pool, a fitness room, and bright, clean halls. For the first time in my life, I was going to live alone, and I was elated about attaining this goal. After signing the lease that last Friday in April, I walked from room to room, touching the walls, digging my toes into the carpet, and cleaning every surface to my own nutty sanitation standards despite Mr. Reilly's assurances that a professional cleaning crew had done a thorough job.

After bringing my things from the U.S. at a considerable cost, I had sold my living room furniture to a grateful Cindy, and was only moving the furniture from my bedroom and dining room, along with smaller household items like dishes. The second bedroom was to be my study and would hold only my desk and computer. My living room would be empty, save for my Boston rocker, television, and stereo.

I slept at the apartment that one last night, and was up early in the morning to close the last few boxes and wait for Peter to arrive with the rental truck. He had called after he heard about the incident, and we began seeing each other again. Steve met us at the new place to help unload and unpack. They had set aside the day to help me, and having two tall, strong men made the move much easier. Steve gracefully excused himself when Peter offered to order dinner delivered, and Peter left just after we finished eating, because he had to catch an early flight to London in the morning. As much as a romantic evening would have been a nice way to celebrate my move, I preferred being alone. I made some popcorn and sat on the floor watching television, contentment lapping in gentle wavelets all around me, until I retired early to nestle in my familiar bed.

I was up early again the following morning to meet Mike at his church followed by breakfast at a little place with tables overlooking the beach. The patio was nearly empty, it being a cooler than usual autumn day. We were actually wearing sweaters, but that was not about to send us inside. The day was beautiful, like springtime in Virginia.

"What are you doing today?" I asked.

"I'm going out to the reef."

"Again? After working all day yesterday, I thought you'd want a break."

"Sorry, Solace, I can't hang out today. This was the best time for me and Donny to get together."

"That's okay, Mike. I have plenty to do."

"Good," he said, either not catching on or choosing to ignore my disappointment. "We've been having a blast, but he doesn't seem to be finding his muse down there."

"He isn't?" I started. Then trying to cover my interest, I said, "Sometimes, if you look too hard, you can't find it."

He looked up at me then, narrowing his eyes to scrutinize me. "Are you looking hard enough?"

"Michael Leahy! You, of all people?" I bristled.

"Hey, Solace Murphy, I happen to be in a very good groove. I'm motivated. I'm working, studying. What are you doing? Moving from place to place? Getting beat up?"

"That's not fair. I admit that so far 1993 has been a waste, but I think I'm absorbing something. I feel the presence of one of the nine. She's hanging around, but hasn't introduced herself to me yet. I think she's trying to decide if I'm worthy."

"Then you'd better fucking damn well get off your ass and show her that you are worthy, Solace. Shit! Just sit yourself down and mark the page. I know the words, the sentences, the ideas will just come flowing out of you once you start. I can feel that bitch hovering around you too." He took a deep breath. "There. I said it. I've got to go home and get ready. You go home and see if Erato or Calliope or whoever the fuck is making your lunch."

I stiffened back into my chair blinking my eyes, stunned by the force of Mike's instructions. With Mike, one could always measure his earnestness by the number of expletives he used in his speech. This time he was dead serious. "It's not quite that easy, Mike. I don't know what to write about."

"Why don't you write about a girl who figured out her boyfriend was a regular blighter and how she handled the situation?"

I thought about it. "I suppose it would be a good place to start."

He jumped up and kissed my cheek. "Love you, Solace. I gotta go." He threw down double the amount needed to pay our combined bill and wove his way away through the maze of tables.

I tucked the bills under an unused dish, and settled back to finish my meal and watch the waves. I would not go straight home. Despite the explicit nature of his instructions, I had no interest in eating lunch that day. This late breakfast would hold me well until tea. I started my walk home along the beach, dawdling to wade occasionally, carrying my shoes in one hand. The simple acts of living—breathing, walking, feeling the sand in the wind—were too exhilarating for me to worry about monumental activities like taming a muse. I had waited for her for years; she could wait an hour for me. Yet as I walked I felt an increasing eagerness to see whether it would be the writing muse or the decorating muse who would grab me at my door.

It was the decorating muse, but I knew she wasn't the only inspiring presence nearby. While I adjusted items on my shelves and made shopping lists, I thought over my experiences with Ken and my ex-husband and some ideas emerged. Perhaps if I did what Mike said and just put pen to paper, my ideas would take on verbal form. With my afternoon tea I meant to test his theory.

My plans were interrupted, however, by the hospitality muses knocking on my door. Through the peephole, I was surprised to see two giggling, redheaded girls. "Hello," I greeted them.

"Hello, Miss Murphy," they said together. "Our grandfather asked us to see if you were settled in," continued the elder girl.

"Is your grandfather Mr. Reilly?"

"Yes," the younger sister replied. "We baked these biscuits for you." She held out a cookie tin. "I am Irina, and this is my sister Maureen." Maureen nodded politely. Their wide eyes were pale blue and radiant, bright as the Arctic summer sky. The girls were as Irish and Russian as their names, and purely Carollonian.

"Would you like to come in? Are you allowed?" I asked. The Carollonians were less cautious than we Americans, but I always hesitated to make offers to children that broke the safety rules I grew up following. In this case, I hoped they would be permitted to come in for a visit, because I was curious about them beyond neighborly friendliness. I had a feeling that I had met them somewhere before and hoped to place the memory.

"Yes, Miss Murphy. Our dad said we could," Maureen replied. I was glad to hear a parent had been consulted. They entered the apartment, elbowing each other playfully and looking around.

"I just put a kettle on. Would like to join me for tea?" I opened the tin. "Your cookies, biscuits look delicious."

"We do hope you like them," chimed Irina. She looked around, obviously disapproving of my lack of decorating. "Your flat is empty! Granddad said you'd moved your things in yesterday. Don't you have furniture?"

"Sh!" her sister said. "We used to live in this flat, Miss Murphy. Our new one is bigger."

"Really? This was your place? How long did y'all live here?" I asked.

"Since we were little. We moved here after our mother died." Looking uneasy, Maureen changed the subject. "I like it like this."

Still bothered, Irina asked, "Are you going to get some things, Miss Murphy?"

"When I find just what I want, and not before," I answered, half grateful for the change of subject, yet still curious to learn more about their situation. "But don't worry; I've got a nice table in the kitchen for us to sit around while we have our treats."

I ushered them into the kitchen. The kettle began to whistle and I made sure to fill the milk pitcher as I pulled out all the things we would need for our tea party. The cookies looked good, but I also cut up some fruit, which was what I had planned to have with my tea before my guests arrived.

Irina was pleased when she came into the kitchen. She tried out all four of my chairs, and declared, "I like your table, Miss Murphy. May I help?" Maureen was still wandering about surveying my partially arranged space.

"Thank you, yes, Irina. Could you put those on the table?" I pointed to some placemats stacked on the counter. Maureen rejoined us then, and began to help her sister set the table. Without a question to me, everything was laid out properly.

That was the first of many visits from my young neighbors.

Monday after school, they returned bringing another housewarming gift: two tins of loose tea and a strainer neatly wrapped in royal blue, floral tea towels. The colorful towels reminded me of the flowered dresses I used to wear so frequently, making them an eerily perfect choice for me, as if the girls knew me better than they could possibly have known me after our hour together the day before. I guessed that they had done their shopping on the way home from school by their eagerness to give what seemed to me to be an overly generous gift.

When they arrived, I had just gotten home from work and was not planning to have tea. In their excitement, however, they forgot to ask before they frolicked into my kitchen to begin preparing it for me with the new things and the cookies they had brought the day before. I had no reason to object to their hospitality, however unconventional their manners, and I was a happy guest at my own table.

I enjoyed their company, and I chose to ignore their role in their grandfather's apparent matchmaking scheme. Being friendly with the girls didn't require me to meet their father, and they had the good sense not to offer an introduction. I held a bias against dating men with children, even previously married men without them. I guess I still thought of myself as the innocent, young girl, untested and wanting to experience things for the first time with someone else who was experiencing them for the first time. I wanted a man who came without the kind of baggage that my experience forced me to carry.

Though sex was still an important part of my relationship with Peter, we tried to find other ways for our lives to connect. We went out, we stayed in, we planned, and we were spontaneous, mixing our styles so that there was some amount of comforting routine and exciting variety. I couldn't understand why I had felt that I couldn't have a future with him when I saw how easy it was for us to get along in a more mature and respectful manner. I felt free and refreshed. I even joked with him about Kevin Reilly's matchmaking schemes and my frequent visits from his granddaughters.

"You have tea with these girls all the time?" he asked. "Does this infamous son, or is it son-in-law, like heavy women? Is that the plan?"

"It must be his son. What man would be trying to find a girl for his son-in-law? But I haven't been putting on weight."

"I know, but it could be their goal," he persisted.

"The way you're eating tonight, I think it's you we need to worry about!"

"I can always do a few extra pretend miles on the stationary bike," he laughed. "You're such a good cook."

Irina chattered about whatever came to her active mind, including intimate details about her home. Maureen would say, "Rina, Miss Murphy doesn't want to know about that family stuff," when she ventured into stories that she didn't understand. Irina was thoroughly caught up in details of domestic life and couldn't comprehend why one should not share every detail of home with others. She freely asked me about mine.

"Is your dad strict?" I asked.

"Not really," Maureen answered. "He lets us do most of the things we want to do. He just likes to know what we're doing and where we're going and who we're with."

"And we have to stay together most of the time," Irina added.

"Right," Maureen said, her face revealing a longing to have more independence from her sister. "Dad says we have good sense, so he trusts us to stay out of trouble."

"I think he knows everything about getting into trouble too," Irina said laughing. "He probably did everything that he won't let us do. I bet he was fun. Now he's just like everyone else's dad."

Obviously disagreeing, Maureen shook her head while she decided how to explain. "Dad's a lot younger than any of our friends' dads. Our mother died when Irina was born, when they were just twenty-one."

Maureen was thirteen, Irina eleven. I could do the math. As Maureen had said, their father probably didn't have much in common with the parents of their friends. Most likely Irina was also wrong about his days of mischief all being behind him. I didn't need to meet the man to see that having been forced into maturity at such a young age, now that his children were more independent and he was hitting his prime, he was probably more ready to cut loose than I was when I arrived in the Carollons.

Maureen spoke again, "I don't remember her."

"I almost wasn't born," Irina informed me.

"Yes. She was walking with me along by a park," Maureen explained. "A lorry hit a parked car and pushed it up onto the sidewalk where we were. Our mother was pinned between the car and a tree."

"You were with her? You were hurt too?" I think I squeaked. My heart went out to the young man who nearly lost his wife and two children all in one day. Just losing his wife must have been difficult enough.

"No, I wasn't hurt, Miss Murphy. I was all belted into my pram, and Mother let go of it, so I just rolled off into some bushes. When they got her to the hospital they decided that it would be better to deliver Irina. It was the only chance they had to save either of them. They operated on our mother, but she was just too badly injured. She lived for a few days. At least she got to know that Irina was doing pretty well. My sister was tiny, you know, because she was born early."

I stood agape, listening and fascinated. When Rob told me this story, I had been guilt-ridden for upsetting Bridget, caught up in trying to console her. He had spoken briefly about their friend Megan's death without detail, and we had never mentioned it again. I had supposed that the baby had been killed with the mother. Yet here was that child, now a beautiful and lively eleven year old girl. I felt crushed. It seemed so sad that these girls couldn't remember their mother and that they could tell this story so calmly. They missed her, of course, but in ways they would never be able to understand.

"They baptized me right after I was born."

"It worked out that everyone in the family was there, so our mother asked for it. She wanted to be sure to be there for it."

It was the last thing she could do for her child. I hoped it brought her some comfort.

"Miss Murphy? You're crying." Irina popped out of her seat and threw her arms around my neck. "Do you still hurt from that man beating you up?"

"No," I both choked on tears and smiled at her reaction. I hadn't realized that they knew that part of my history. "I was thinking about your mom." I wiped my eyes. "Did you realize that we had some of the same friends?"

"The other Murphys. Yes. Bridget told us about you," Maureen said. "She was one of our mother's best friends."

I nodded. "They told me about your mother once. And I knew I'd seen you before. But I didn't realize where until just now."

"I've taken a daring risk," Peter said about halfway through our dinner. It was Thursday evening, and the restaurant was quiet. "I hope it won't be a problem for you to go away this weekend."

"This weekend!" My eyes popped open wide.

"I know how you hate to prepare for travel," he explained with a smile.

I nodded my agreement enthusiastically. "I don't have too much that I have to do this weekend. Just a date on Sunday with my realtor's son," I added, teasing.

"I guess I could have you back in time for church on Sunday," he said in stride. "You may want to go to confession."

"I don't have to be back that early. Especially, if I'm going to need to confess. I've been told I'll want to postpone that as long as possible."

"Well, this is what I was planning. Tomorrow after work, I will pick you up and we will take the ferry over to St. Mary's Bay. Dinner on the ferry followed by two nights at the old inn. We'll come home whenever we feel like it on Sunday—in plenty of time for your other date."

"Peter! That sounds wonderful. Wow! What a wonderful surprise. Thank you."

"Two wonderfuls and a thank you," he said with a Clark Gable style smirk. "I think this is going to be fun."

"Definitely. Oh, Peter, it sounds so romantic."

He reached over the tabletop to hold my hand. "I'm so glad to be back with you, Solace. I wish things hadn't turned out quite the way they did, but I'm glad you figured out that Rosie was wrong for you. I want you to find a happy situation. Of course, I hope you will want me to be a part of it too, because you bring something to life in me that isn't alive when you're not there."

"Thank you, Peter." I couldn't imagine him ever doing anything that was meant to harm me. Then I began to understand what had held me back from him. It was hard to imagine being so close, like married close, without tensions stirring anger. My thoughts escaped my lips. "I've never seen you angry."

"I don't get angry often, Solace, but I was angry about what Ken Williams did to you. Most of the time, however, I can understand how the other person feels and turn what might be anger or irritation to making the situation non-confrontational."

"Do you end up with what you want or do you always compromise and settle for less?"

"I don't feel like I cheat myself, if that answers your question." He studied me.

"I don't know how to control my anger, Peter. It rules me in many ways. Knowing that I might lose my temper or break down emotionally from the futility of expressing myself, I often just try to avoid situations that frustrate me. I usually don't get what I want."

From across the table I could see him trying to figure out how to offer me comfort and hope. He squeezed my hand, then wrapped his other around them both. "We have to find our balance. I need to be more passionate sometimes, and you need to learn to express your passions productively. I feel for you. I know you second-guess yourself. Yet at other times, you are so vividly confident and controlled that you intimidate me. Usually I feel like we are on equal footing though, and I think that is important in a relationship such as the one I want to have with you." He lifted my hand to his lips and held it there without kissing it.

I smiled across at him, relaxing. An emotion had been building, threatening me with a flow of unbidden, gentle tears, but they evaporated like shy sisters relieved to be returning to their convent refuge. "I wish I felt like I could help you too, but you seem so self-sufficient. I wouldn't know what I have to offer you." I shrugged.

He shook his head slightly. "You have plenty to offer. You don't need to change as much as you think you do, Solace. Just be yourself. You are stronger than you realize."

He walked me home, but left me at my door. "We should rest tonight, so we can be up late tomorrow. I'll see you around four then, heh? Good night."

I raised myself to my tiptoes and kissed him like it was a first date. "Good night, Peter."

Chapter Eight

In the morning, I awoke filled with anticipation about the trip with Peter. Dinner in the candlelit dining room on the ferry over to St. Mary's Bay would be romantic enough to keep me happy for a weekend of camping in the rain forest. Knowing that we were going to share two nights at the old inn was almost too exciting to bear. Though less plush than the hotel where I had stayed with my father, the old inn was far more charming and private.

I had plenty to do to get ready, however, so I couldn't afford to spend my morning reflecting on my expectations. That was just as well, because I did not want to over-anticipate the luxury and sensuality of our excursion. I ate my breakfast quickly and got ready to rush off, list in hand, to the supermarket before nine o'clock.

I was lighthearted and looked forward to being alone with Peter. He had always been supportive, impatient physically, perhaps too patient emotionally, and I had wandered around not ready for him. That was it, wasn't it? I was not ready to commit to someone yet. Peter knew that, and so he waited for me to slip into his arms without hesitation. The question was when, if ever, would I be ready. Well, the time had come for me to do more than merely react. And, for once, I did not fear to be the one who made the effort to advance our relationship.

On the way back from the market, I passed a lingerie shop just as it was opening for business. I decided I had time to browse. Hoping to find a new sexy something, I tried on a simple, delicate nightgown. Picturing Peter's reaction, I became aroused. I changed back to my jeans and took the nightie to the counter to pay. Then I hurried home. I had a bag to pack, some cleaning to do, a dishwasher to unload, and a lunch to prepare and eat before I spent my afternoon at my studies and daydreams.

I was glad that it was a school day, because this would be just the moment when my young friends would decide to invite themselves in for a visit. The thought of them wandering into my bedroom while I packed for a romantic weekend almost made me laugh. They were a delightful duo, and I realized that I would be unhappy if they learned something about me that lowered me in their esteem.

The carpet outside of my door was wet enough for me to feel the suction and squish of it through my shoes as I juggled my bags and dug through my purse for my keys. When I finally managed to get my key into the lock, I pushed the door open with one foot and stared across the floor to the kitchen. I tiptoed through the carpet-bog, dropped my purse and purchases on the counter, and opened the cabinet under the sink. I squatted, trying to keep my jeans dry, and began pulling out bottles and soggy sponges until I could reach the handle to the water shut off. The flow stopped. My first reaction was to feel relief that I was a renter and could pass this problem along to someone else.

Next, I carried my table and chairs to the empty, dry dining room, wiping off the water and checking for damage. It was only when I called Mr. Reilly's office that I began to worry. Kevin Reilly was on vacation, and the receptionist was useless. She put me into another realtor's voicemail, but that was as much help as it seemed I was going to get. The frustration only served to increase my determination to have this problem handled immediately, so after a moment's consideration I decided to test one further option. On the off chance that my friends' father was at home, I raced up one flight of stairs and down the hall to their door without even bothering to close my own.

I knocked and waited, and knocked again, pounding too hard in my impatience and growing hysteria. I reddened, almost hoping now that he was not there. I knocked again immediately, harder than the first time, but more politely than the second, almost as an apology. Picturing the flood looters invading my home, planning to steal my old TV and tinny stereo, but throwing them through the window instead, when they recognized their age and quality, I found myself wishing I had closed and locked my door. Dejected, I turned away, heading home to get out my mop and wait until the other realtor called me. I watched my feet as I trod to the stairwell, ready to cry and not caring if I did.

The fire door moved away from me just as I reached for it. Stunned by the sudden evidence of another human, I stopped awkwardly, staring at the knob and waiting for my turn to pass through the door. The man exiting the stairwell held the door for me. I looked up to acknowledge his courtesy and met the eyes—so like those of his daughters—of Sean Donovan.

"Oh!" I gasped. "It's you."

He nodded in response, his clear blue eyes searching my face. He remained silent, as he had promised, but I could tell that he was wondering if he had been freed of his vow. I was too stunned to be considerate; I just stood still while he politely held the door open. He tilted his head toward the stairs, and I took a step, then stopped. I forced myself to speak again. "Do you know how to reach Kevin?"

"No. He's away," he said softly, shaking his head.

I did not have the strength to cover my disappointment. "There's a water leak. I think it's coming from the dishwasher."

"Would you like me to help, Solace?" he asked.

"I was looking for you. Oh, could you? No, no. I don't deserve your help. Thank you. You've been kind when I have only been...no. I can take care of it." I was close to ranting, very much wanting his help and afraid to accept it.

He smiled then, the kind of smile I suspected he used with his daughters when he needed to coax them through some adolescent trauma. "I know you can handle this yourself, Solace, but it might be easier if we worked together. You don't not deserve my help." He rolled his eyes with mock impatience. "I am happy to give it if you want it."

"Why would you want to have anything to do with me?"

He shrugged. "For some reason, I just can't bring myself to dislike you." My view of him moved from his sky blue eyes to his face and the rest of him. For once, he looked a God-awful mess. His clothes were disheveled and paint-spattered, and his hair, which was longer than I remembered, was green. It stood out in clumps around his face. My attention returned to his eyes. "Besides, I'm your landlord, and I have an interest in the condition of the property." His face was sober, defying its whimsical frame of hair.

My plumbing woes forgotten, I tried to address a much more important issue. "Your wife?" I started. I had to try again to complete my question. "You were widowed when we met?" The pitch of my voice was too high. He nodded solemnly. "I-I-I'm s-so sorry," I stammered. "I thought you were married."

I expected to collapse without the crutch of hating him, but though I felt weak and shaky, I had not set aside all of my unnecessary burdens. I still bore the one I had not admitted to myself. I had not hated him so much as I had hated to see him. And I had hated to see him, because underneath my confident act, I had always understood that I should have said something more to him when I saw the hurt in his eyes. Instead, I had sent him away in the same manner I would shoo away a disobedient dog. I had not believed he deserved an apology, but perhaps one kind word would have changed my mind. Even if he was as terrible as I had believed, I could have given him a chance to redeem himself. I could have been kinder, but I had not known how.

"That explains a good deal," he responded after he was sure my attention had returned to him. "I have always found it difficult to tell people that Megan is dead." His eyes were liquid, his emotions churned his melodic voice so that it stumbled and tumbled on his words as he said them, yet his face was calm. I realized that the green in his fair hair was only paint, where he had pushed his hair out of his eyes with his hand. "I could tell you all about her, even about how she died, but uttering that cold fact is still difficult."

I wanted to say I understood, but there was no way that I could understand. That was not today's issue anyway. I had something else to say that was more important than my sympathy. I had to tell him the rest, and I had to do it now, because I might never again have the courage to say it. In a low, hoarse whisper, I confessed, "I almost said yes to you anyway."

If he had not already known it, he understood it retroactively, and his reaction was slow and imperceptible. His eyes narrowed to slits as he studied me. "Well, I guess that explains the rest," he whispered as he lowered them. When he raised them again, they were full of questions and tenderness. Their clear blue shone in the magical way that had nearly made me willing to be a partner to adultery, but this time they looked upon me directly, kindly, and with tears hovering above the lower lid. If he had looked at me this way back at the bank, I would have said something more. That is, if I were me as I was at this moment.

I began to crumple, the weight of my guilt dragging the tears down from my eyes. This secret of mine had weighed on my conscience for so long that I felt unbalanced now that I had laid it aside. He put a hand under my elbow in a supportive gesture, not explicitly holding me, but ready to catch me should I need it, crooning, "Now that I know what I suspect is your darkest secret, Solace, can we try to be friends? May I talk with you?"

I nodded my assent. My tears were flowing hard now, and I dared not speak. My lips and throat pulsated as if they too were sobbing.

"Let's make it easy," he said. He smiled at me the way he would smile at one of his daughters if she were hurt. "We don't have to start with the past. Let's just talk about the present. Okay? You came to find me. Well, not me, I guess, judging by your reaction." Then he began to play with me, teasing me into a place of comfort. "You really didn't know it was me? I suppose my girls never bothered to tell you their surname. I'll have to speak to them about their manners. And you, I thought you kept a watch out for me all the time. Don't you have a special sensor that goes off when I'm around? I thought it was just broken that night at Leah's party or that you'd forgotten to turn it on that day you sat by me on the bus. Your mind was obviously occupied." His smile changed from fatherly and comforting. "My mind was rather occupied then too. A number of ideas raced through my brain when you plopped down next to me, let me tell you! Would she forgive me or would I just wake up in a sweat in my lonely bed?" He was trying to get me to laugh. It worked.

It was only a nervous, little laugh, but I stopped sobbing and brought my attention to the present. In a childish voice, I said, "Yes, I went to see you about reaching your father. I mean, I guess he's your father-in-law."

"Have you spoken to Nancy?"

"She isn't in."

"Nancy will ring you back, but I'd be happy to help. May I inspect the damage?"

We started down the stairs. "The kitchen is flooded, and the water's gone all the way out the front door, but I did shut it off."

"Good," he said, nodding approvingly. "I'll get someone out to get the carpet dried. That's probably the worst of it. Was any of your furniture damaged?"

"I don't think so. I moved my table and chairs out of the kitchen. They looked alright. I wasn't gone even two hours, so the water shouldn't have been standing for very long." Trying to seem at ease, I asked, "What were you painting?"

"You like my hair gel?" he asked with a little laugh. "I'm painting our house." Then he added, "We'll be moving in a few months."

"Oh," I said. Then to cover my sudden disappointment, I added, "Thank you for helping me, Mr. Donovan. After the way I've treated you, I deserve a kick not a helping hand."

"Please call me Sean."

"Sorry. Awkward circumstances bring out the best and the worst in my manners."

"Then let's get past awkward, Solace. And one way to do that is for you to get it straight that you do not, under any circumstance, deserve a kick. Don't even think it, and if you say it again, I will get so angry with you that I will send the girls downstairs to have tea with you every day." He put a gentle hand on my forearm to stop me. "You believed I was married, and a married man should not be looking to spend time with other women. Not the kind of time I wanted to spend with you. So your reaction was justified."

"I could have asked you."

His brow wrinkled sadly. "I could have told you about Megan. We could have cleared things up. But you had no reason to do anything other than what you did. You owed me nothing."

"I didn't think so. I harbored an unreasonable amount of hatred toward you. I think I aimed the anger toward every bank customer who ever abused my professional courtesy right at you." Then I added, "I thought Betsy was your wife."

His nostrils flared as he shook his head. Then with an expression so full of sincerity that I found him more attractive than ever, he confessed, "I still have a killer crush on you. If you don't like me, please be nice to me this time when you tell me where to get off."

When we stepped out onto my floor, my opposite-door neighbor was standing on her threshold studying the seepage. She looked up when she heard us. Ignoring me, she said, "Oh, good, Mr. Donovan. You'll get this taken care of, I hope, before it comes through my door?"

"I sure hope so, Mrs. Dean. Miss Murphy has already shut off the water." He turned to me. "Solace, have you a directory?"

When we went into my place, I pulled out my telephone book and set it on the counter that ran between the kitchen and the living room. He inspected the damage and even gave my furniture a careful examination. Before he opened the phonebook, he called the real estate office to ask if any arrangements had yet been made to clean and repair my unit.

I had not fully assimilated the knowledge that he was my landlord until I was faced with the evidence. Seeing my reaction, he whispered, "I don't keep a key. Does that help?" Back into the telephone, he said, "I'm sorry, Miss, but I'm hard of hearing and I'm not using my amplified telephone. I must ask you to speak up." As he listened, he slid down the wall to the floor and buried his head between his knees. His hand went to his telephone ear to adjust the volume on one of the hearing aids I had not previously noticed him wearing. He looked up at me and pointed at the sliding glass door to the balcony and mouthed, "Open it." I obeyed. He dropped his head again, only lifting it to speak into the telephone.

After he explained that he would contact the insurance company to begin the process, he sat quietly for a few minutes, head down on his knees, holding the phone in the on the hook position with his thumb. Instead of looking discouraged, as I had expected, when he finally raised his head, he looked amused. With a hint of a chuckle, he said, "Well, having a property manager is a bit of a disappointment. I'm not supposed to have to handle situations like this."

"I'm sorry," I said.

"It's okay, since it's you," he said cheerily. "When I heard you were moving in here, I thought about coming to your door and handing you a note that explained how I just couldn't promise to never bump into you. Then Kevin started trying to find ways of bringing us together, with the girls doing their best to help him. They adore you, by the way, if you hadn't noticed."

"I had thought they might be trying to introduce us," I said, understating my impression of the situation and giving him a soft smile.

"Well, yes…and I couldn't tell them that I was avoiding you. They would have gotten their feelings hurt and been confused. Maureen would have felt that she should stay away from you, and Irina would have started asking you all kinds of questions about things that are not her business. Whatever. There are some things parents don't need to share with their children. So I just found ways to make sure I didn't run into you, like using the stairs instead of the elevator. I guess it was foolish, because as hard as I've tried to keep my distance from you, we just keep meeting."

"I usually use the stairs," I said. I decided it was time to take the edge off my curiosity. "I guess you've heard about me from Mike Leahy? Or was it Bridget who told you I needed a rescue?"

He tilted his head to one side. "Your cousin Rob."

"Bridget was a friend of your wife's, right?"

He nodded. "We all grew up together, Solace, in the same neighborhood. Mike, Rob, Bridget, Megan, me. We went to the same church and school. Rob and I have been best friends since grade seven."

"Good Lord," I cried. "So if you really had been a stalker, you would have had an easy job of it."

He screwed his face and studied me again. "Yeah."

"But how did they know we knew each other? Other than Mike's party?"

"That's when Leah learned that we knew each other, but he doesn't gab, Solace. He's mentioned you over the years, just to say 'I did this or that with Solace'. And since that party, he's said even less. He's protective of you, and he's astute.

"Rob, on the other hand, has this idea that I want to know all about you, even when I tell him that I don't. It slipped out once that I had had this thing for an American girl, so when he met you, he started telling me how he'd met this American girl who was so nice and pretty. Had to be nicer and prettier than that one I'd been mooning over. I told him to leave me alone, but he kept talking about you, and I had to tell him you were the same girl and that you really didn't like me. Bridget got him to hold his tongue most of the time after that, but sometimes they couldn't help it. Like with Leah, you were just around so much that every now and again you would rear your pretty head. Over time, it got easier for me to hear about you, that is, until they started going on about this rotter you were seeing, and how he was isolating you, and they were worried. For good or ill, I couldn't just tell them to be quiet when I was hearing that kind of thing.

"Then Boris mentioned you bought one of my pieces." He blushed. "I guess I'd spent too much time trying to draw fish." A nervous laugh. "I hope you like the picture and that she won't be a reminder of bad times."

"Oh, I love it!" I exclaimed. Then, thinking that I should restrain my enthusiasm, I added, "She could be being returned to the water, right?"

He stood, not answering me. "I ought to ring the insurance company."

I watched him, unable to control my urge to stare at the soaked seat of his blue jeans. They had already been intriguing, with an array of colors dripped and smeared on them. "From the war?" I asked as he began to readjust the hearing aid on his telephone ear.

He nodded. Then his eyes came to rest upon my bags where they lay forgotten on the kitchen counter. "Does any of your food need to be cooled?" Though he only mentioned the food, I sensed him reading "Lacy's" on the bag containing my new nightgown. I waded across the tile floor and began sorting the food, putting the cold things away first. Pointless as I knew it to be, I tucked the bag from the lingerie shop under my arm before I carried it to my bedroom.

With the flood and meeting Sean, I had completely forgotten about my weekend trip with Peter. In fact, I had completely forgotten about Peter. That answered one big question, didn't it? I was able to put Peter aside for three months to suffer with Ken. Now, I had forgotten his existence entirely as I freed myself of my old guilt and felt the pull of the attraction that had nearly made me break one of the ten biggest rules. What might develop with Sean was not the issue; I couldn't be what I had hoped to be for Peter. It would be wrong and it would be completely dishonest for me to continue to pursue a future with him, no matter how I felt when we were together.

Sean must have felt something. I can't explain why I thought so. It was a change in his posture or a relaxation in his face. Perhaps he knew that I had a habit of returning clothes I purchased just before encounters with him. It wouldn't have bothered me if he had laughed at me. I knew with certainty that he had picked out the tea towels to be a part of his daughters' gift to me.

When I returned to his side with my mop, he tried to smile, but he was a touch too nervous to hold it steady. "So, after the cleanup crew arrives, would you like to have a more organized conversation? May I take you out for lunch?"

Alone again, I went straight to the far end of my closet where I kept my old dresses. I picked out a yellow jumper with periwinkle flowers, then fished through my bottom drawer for the shirt I wanted to wear with it. A corner of the shirt caught on the mermaid's frame, and I brought it out too. I unwrapped it and smiled at the scene, but decided to wait to display it until the workmen were gone. Not knowing how much time I had, I raced to dress and apply some make up. With a careful addition of jewelry, just something playful, I was ready.

I figured Sean and I would spend some time talking while we waited for the cleaning crew, but their arrival was unexpectedly quick. After assuring me that a plumber was expected, they revved up their water sucking machines. Shortly thereafter Sean, now showered and wearing the green on his shirt instead of his hair, and I left the wet and noise behind.

"Are you ready to eat yet, Solace?" he asked. "It's earlier than I thought it would be. Would you like to take a walk or go someplace where we can just relax for a while?"

"Oh, no, I couldn't eat yet."

"Thirsty?" He was toying with me, because I had declared my lack of hunger so emphatically.

"Yeah?"

"Are you sure?"

"I am. I just didn't realize it until I said it."

"Would you like something cold from the machine or tea at Higginbotham's?"

"Water would do."

"Haven't you had enough water already today?" he joked. Then decisively he said, "Let's go to Higgie's." He grabbed my hand and pulled me swiftly along the sidewalk. When I managed to keep up with him, he accelerated, and we were running and laughing at our silliness by the time we got to the tearoom. "Would you like to sit outside, Solace?"

"Yes, please."

He pulled out a chair for me at a clear table in speckled shade. "Then you sit here, and I shall get you some water." He went inside the dark paneled café and returned within three minutes carrying a tray with a glass of water, two mugs of tea, and a small dish of mango and pineapple chunks. "Can you get this stuff in the States?" he asked, pointing to the fruit as he unloaded the tray.

"Yes, but it isn't this nice."

"What about tea?"

"I don't think there are many Americans who know how to make tea." I tried to think of something to say, feeling as I'm sure he did too the strain of keeping the conversation going now that we could no longer rely upon the flood for fuel. Forcing myself to speak, I blurted out, "Did you mind going to the war?" Then I backpedalled, "Oh, I guess, that's a stupid question."

"No." He shook his head. "It's not. I can't say that I wanted to go, but I wouldn't have missed it for any reason. You know we are required to serve in the military, so it's not like the American all volunteer force, but I didn't know anyone who was not serving willingly"

"I take it you reenlisted like Mike did."

"I felt I belonged in the Marines." He looked like he was going to say something else, so I waited. "I liked the camaraderie."

"Is painting what you do for a living? I mean, like full-time?"

"Still the banker, heh? Painting's a sideline. Mainly I'm a piano teacher."

"Really?"

"I used to teach music, back when I met you. I taught at North Beach High School, but I haven't gone back to it." He pointed at his ears.

"Do you have trouble hearing people talk? Should I try to speak louder?"

He shook his head. "The aids work quite well, and I've learned to read lips. It's fine," he said, clearly not wanting to discuss his disability. "Just look at me when you talk, and I'll be fine. It's my problem, not yours."

"So, how many students do you have?"

"Around forty. I like to keep a few evenings open, so on days like today, I have them lined up."

"Kids?"

"Mostly. I like working with kids best, but if you are interested in learning, I could squeeze in another adult."

"I wish I could play, but my fingers aren't that dexterous," I said.

"You type, don't you?"

"Yes, but it's not at all the same. I used to play the guitar, and as much as I practiced I never really could move my fingers around on the strings."

"That's easy to fix, Solace. You need to cut your nails."

"I know that." I made a clawing motion in the air. "I sold my guitar when I moved. I haven't played in ages."

"You always focused on singing, didn't you?"

"Yes, but I worked much harder on the guitar."

"What you need is an accompanist. Once you learned to sing in front of him," he pointed at himself, "then you might be able to handle standing up in front of the whole congregation for a solo."

"You move fast, mister," I said laughing. More seriously, I added, "You must be a great teacher."

"I think I was a good teacher." He made a face. "I loved it."

"When are you moving?" I asked.

"In December, when school lets out."

"But you've already started working on the house? Does it need a lot of work?"

He shook his head. "Not any more. Most of it is done. I bought the house way back when the girls were little. I received a sizable sum of money when Megan died. I bought your condo for us to live in, and then Kevin helped me find a bargain house to improve and let until we wanted more space. Only we liked it here, and my plans for the house got more complicated."

"Oh?"

"It's an older house, from the twenties. Structurally it was in great shape, but over the years some very bad things had been done to it. So I did a little work, got a tenant, did a little more work, and got another tenant. It's been empty for most of the past year, and I've been spending most of my daylight hours and money up there." He laughed. "When I got back from the war, I had a lot to think about. You know, like what to do for a living and how to get the ghosts out of my head. I also realized that my girls were getting ready to turn into women, and I still hadn't gotten around to living in the house I bought to raise them in. So, I went for it. Hired an architect and a contractor to do some major renovations. I'm very excited and pleased about it."

"It shows."

"So, how about tea and water for neighbors who are overdue to become friends? I offer a toast to you, Solace Murphy! Thank God the cut I made in your pipe wore through before I moved out of the building!" He raised his mug, and I clinked mine against it. He emptied his in one gulp and hurled the cup against the brick exterior wall of the restaurant, shattering it in a noisy burst.

"I can't believe you just did that!" I screamed, laughing.

"Go on, Solace," he said. "Drink up or throw it full, but the toast is not complete if you don't smash the cup."

"I can't," I choked. I tried to take a bigger drink. When I put the cup down, he whisked it off the table and threatened to throw it himself. "Don't, Sean. It's delicious."

"I'll get you another. I've got to pay them for the cups anyway. Why not another full one, even if they serve it in a paper cup?"

"I want to drink it," I said firmly. He handed me the cup, and I tried to enjoy it.

"It would be best if you threw it," he advised in a solemn tone.

"I'll break the window too," I mumbled.

"What the hell," he said. "I'll pay for that too."

"Then I would really feel guilty."

"Today is a no guilt day."

Though it still held tea, I began to weigh the cup in my hand, wondering if I could throw it with grace and accuracy. I closed my eyes. The next thing I knew, Sean was lifting me up, his front to my back, holding me close. I could smell tea and pineapple on his breath. His whiskers, which I had already learned from Irina he only shaved on Sunday mornings before church, were soft against my cheek. My right hand was in his right hand, as if one of us was the other's shadow. I opened my eyes. "Just let go when I let go of your hand. It won't hurt, I promise." He swung my arm around, quickly but without jerking me, and he let go of my hand. I let go of the cup and it flew away and crashed, smashing into sticky, sweet chunks of pottery. I felt giddy. It was such a harmlessly naughty thing to do.

"Now, I must go and confess," he said. "There are lots of Russians in this town. They must have a policy to cover this sort of vandalism." With a wink, he added, "Run for it if I'm not back out in a few minutes." He went inside again, and returned with a broom and a dustpan. "They've got lots of cups." He swept up the broken pottery and tossed the shards into the waste bin. "But we should go."

Today may have been a no guilt day, but it was definitely an uneven one.

We went to a seafood shack down on the beach for a lunch of broiled "fresh catch", a mixture of fish and shellfish that had come in on the morning's boat, chips, crunchers, and raw vegetables dressed with a cucumber sauce. We washed it all down with limewater, and we talked. Once he got going, Sean's quiet manners became animated as he balanced between fearing to reveal too much and wanting to tell me everything. I suppose I did the same.

"Why did you come to the Carollons in the first place?" he asked. He sprinkled vinegar over his french fries.

Repulsed by the smell, I asked, "How can you do that?"

"Do what?" He waved a particularly drippy chip under my nose and I moved my head back, attempting to close my nostrils. "You have to develop a taste for spoiled food, Solace. In the old country, they had to eat whatever they could get, even if it was rotten. Now it's part of the culture."

"Which old country?"

"Both. And even the rotten stuff was scarce, I've been told."

"Your tsarist ancestors were starving?"

He shrugged. "I asked you a question."

"I ran away from home."

"Is there an angry husband I need to worry about?"

I laughed. "No. I was disposable. That prize found another victim. I am divorced."

"How long were you married?"

"About four years."

"Were you always unhappy?"

"No." I thought about my answer. "No, I wasn't, but it's what I remember best."

When I looked up, I could see that he was deep in thought. He felt me looking at him, and he lifted his eyes, blinking. "Sometimes it's hard to remember what was important to Megan. I try to take her wishes for the girls into account, but I don't know what they are most of the time. So, what the hell, I'm the one who has to handle everything day by day. I can't go blaming my bad decisions on her now, can I?"

"Did you plan to have children?" I asked even as I thought I shouldn't. Awkwardly, I tried to apologize by explaining, "I mean you must have been very young."

"Yeah," he said, shaking his head, seeming amused. "Yeah, we were young and foolish and careless and confident. Megan wanted to have children early; I thought we should wait, but, well, you can imagine—I hope you can imagine—how a couple of lovebird kids will spend their time. Hell, we couldn't afford to go to the movies!"

"So you had a baby?"

"Right. The whole process provided a great deal of free entertainment."

"Except for all the stuff babies need."

"Actually, they don't need much. And since we both came from big families there were plenty of hand-me-downs and gifts. And, of course, with us coming from large families, we couldn't let our baby be an only child. Then we were going to wait until we were better established to have any others." He took a drink of water, and I wondered if I should ask him more about it. I didn't need to. "Megan and her mother didn't get on well, so we ran off and got married just after we finished high school. That's why I joined the Reserves instead of doing the two-year sailor thing like Rob. It was weird. It's a little hard to remember why we felt it was so important, but it was, and we were happy."

I fiddled with my silverware. "How did your big families feel about you eloping?"

He laughed as he answered, nodding his head rhythmically. "Every reaction possible, I'd say. Her mum freaked. She was so disappointed. Her dad thought it was lovely that he didn't have to pay for a wedding. My dad was fine with everything except that we got married at our church. Anglican. He's still a little funny about it, though I don't think he believes much differently than I do. My mother was happy for us about everything, except that she was afraid I was giving up my future because I felt sorry for Megan."

"Really?"

"I didn't." He straightened in his seat and pushed his plate away about an inch or so, demonstrating that he had finished his meal, an unnecessary act since his plate was empty. "I was crazy about her, and I wanted to be with her, and I wanted her to be happy. It didn't change much that we were married, in some big ways, I mean. She got a job, clerical work. I started University, very part-time, played in a band, worked as a carpenter's apprentice, and worked at Big Bob's during the holidays."

"And you were a weekend Marine."

"Knowing how my mother felt gave me initiative to work harder."

"I guess anyone who is anyone works a Big Bob's."

"Amen." He tilted his head. "I had a lot of energy."

"You were an eighteen year old b—man." I pushed my plate away too. "How many are in your big family?"

"Eleven kids. You?"

"There are four of us."

"Where do you fit in?"

"I'm the youngest."

"You had your own bedroom, didn't you?"

"Was that what you always wanted?"

"Hell, no! It was way too much fun sharing with my brothers. And seeing how my parents managed to fit everyone into a three-bedroom house. You do understand we never all lived in the house at the same time? My oldest brother is forty-two, and he's not the only one with kids older than my youngest brother, who's sixteen. Anyway, my apartment is almost as big as my folks' house. Isn't that a kick in the arse? One loo too. How my sisters griped about that!" He looked at his watch. "I hate to say it, Solace, but it's nearly time for the kids to be out of school. I need to go home."

I smiled. "I've enjoyed this, Sean."

We got up and began to walk home. "I wonder how things are going at your place. If the plumber didn't come, you'll be in a mess all weekend." When I gasped, he gave me a puzzled look. "What's wrong? You won't have to turn off your water completely. And you are welcome to use my kitchen."

"I have plans to go away this weekend. I've got to rush when I get back. I haven't packed yet."

"Oh," he said, instinctively understanding that my plans involved another man. He sounded dejected. I didn't know what to say, so I said nothing, and we walked in silence the rest of the way home.

After we got back, I found the old water line in the trashcan. I picked it up and twirled it around in a few slow circles as I said, "It doesn't look like it was cut."

"Even an expert can't tell when I've done a proper job of it." He winked. He took a step closer to me. "I was wondering if I could spend more time with you. I had heard you had a boyfriend, and I conveniently forgot about him today. Are you? What would the right word be?"

"We aren't." I blushed. "I conveniently forgot about him today too."

"All weekend?" He looked sympathetic.

"Yes. He planned a little getaway to St. Mary's Bay." I groaned.

Sean's manners were so good that I wondered if he had studied acting with Rob when they were younger. "That sounds nice."

"It did last night."

"You're in a tight spot now, aren't you?"

"What should I do?"

"Steal his tickets and take me."

"I don't think I could do that," I said with a laugh. His comedic response was reassuring. "Thank you for everything, Sean."

"You're welcome. I had a wonderful day."

"Me too. Except for the flood."

"It was a good flood. It brought us together. May I see you again?"

"I would like that."

He beckoned me with his index finger, and I stepped forward obediently. "Here's something to think about this weekend," he whispered. The next thing I knew he put his arms around me and drew me into a kiss. It was sweet and gentle, but then the embrace tightened and he pulled me into another long, wet, passionate kiss. Peter had never kissed me like this. But some time would pass before I would think about Peter again.

"Hello, Darling. Are you packed? Are you ready?" Peter bustled in, charming as ever. He paused to look around at the mess as he walked through the door. "Good Lord, what happened here?"

"A pipe burst under the kitchen sink while I was out this morning."

"What a mess. Were any of your things damaged?"

"No. It pays to keep a nearly empty apartment."

"Can you leave?"

"Yes. In truth, I'm glad to leave it. The landlord is taking care of everything."

"Then I'll get your bag. Don't mean to rush you, but the taxi is waiting. Traffic was heavy. That's why I'm a little late." He was in a hurry. If he noticed my jittery mood, I am sure he ascribed it to the flood. "By the way, you look stunning. Love your dress, Solace. It really suits you." I was still wearing the yellow jumper that I put on for lunch with Sean. He put his arm around me and drew me into a familiar kiss. Then he grabbed my suitcase. Once again, I left without closing my door.

The St. Mary's Bay resort ran an elegant dining room on the ferry. The service was perfect. The food was incredibly delicious. It was probably the best meal I have ever eaten. The wine Peter ordered was very nice, and it went down easily. It occurred to me that one way I could get through tonight was to drink plenty of it.

I was silent, and Peter watched me without saying much. "You don't want to go away for the weekend, do you, Solace?" he asked over dessert.

"I'm," I hesitated.

"You're very distracted. We don't have to go."

"I'm sorry, Peter. We can still have a good time."

"Are you worried about your apartment? We can reschedule. We can just take the ferry back tonight."

"It's not that exactly," I said.

He tensed and straightened as his eyes sharpened their focus on me. "You met the realtor's son today, didn't you?" It was not really framed as a question.

"He's my landlord, it turns out," I said, trying not to reveal any emotion.

"You like him?"

"Yes."

"All this time we've joked about the realtor and the daughters." He shook his head. "I don't stand a chance, do I?"

"A few years ago we met and didn't get on, but we talked it out. It seems that the matchmaker knew what he was doing."

"He's the one," he said, dropping his gaze.

"I'm very sorry, Peter." I clammed up, unsure what I could say that would not hurt this kind man.

"I'm glad you're happy, Solace." He paused. I was too distracted at the time to realize that he showed no surprise. "I hope you will stay that way."

Relieved and thankful, I gasped, "Oh, Peter, I love you!"

Calmly, his emotions safely tucked away, he asked, "Did you realize that this is the first time you have ever said that?"

Chapter Nine

My apartment was still a disaster zone when I got home on Sunday night. I ignored all of it and just unpacked and went to bed. By the time I got home from work on Monday, I had adjusted to the bare concrete floor, rolled up and hopefully dry carpeting, noisy dehumidifiers, and a few stray tools.

I set to work on the homework I should have begun days ago, wondering if Maureen and Irina would visit me. I hoped that my meeting their father would not put a damper on our friendship. I forced my head down into my books and worked steadily for nearly an hour before I heard Irina's knock. She was not shy, but she wouldn't come without Maureen. I smiled and braced myself. I heard the usual laughter as I walked to the door.

"Hello, Miss Murphy," they said in unison as I began to open the door.

"Hello, Misses Donovan."

"What a mess," Irina declared, stepping carefully, as if the room was still flooded. "We should have our tea on the balcony."

"Would you like to join me for tea, Irina?" I asked.

Maureen, looking ill at ease, blushed and said, "Dad spoke to us about our manners, Miss Murphy. I do apologize for not being more correct. I guess, I, we just assumed that you knew our last name from Granddad."

I shook my head, smiling. "No problem. Your manners are much better than mine were when I was your age."

She followed me into the kitchen. "I don't imagine you would invite yourself over for tea." She looked at her sister who was bravely investigating the damage by pressing on the rolled carpet with the toe of her shoe.

"I probably wouldn't, but I was always shy. It's good that Irina is so comfortable. If she didn't ask, I might forget to offer. It works out well, because I like having you come to visit. I hope that you feel welcome here."

She didn't say anything, but she remained thoughtful as she helped me get things ready. When I turned the water off after filling the kettle, she said, "Dad asked me to ask you to have supper with us tonight. Can you come?"

"Do you want me to?"

"Yes, it would be lovely." Her manner was very polite, but sincere.

"I would like to accept your invitation, but I have plans for the evening. Do you think that will cause a problem?"

"I don't think so, Miss Murphy," she said. "May I use your telephone?"

"Sure. But, Maureen, should we let him cook?"

"I beg your pardon?" She froze with the receiver in her hand.

"You've told me so many cooking disaster stories I have to wonder if it's safe to let your father cook." I tried to maintain a serious expression. Maureen's eyes brightened, and she proceeded to make her call.

Testing her balance by walking along the rolled up carpet, Irina proclaimed, "He's got a chicken in the oven already, Miss Murphy. If he burns it, we'll just have eggs." She came into the kitchen while I dug through my cabinet for some granola bars to eat with our tea, asking, "Will we be able to do our homework here? Your table is a mess."

I nodded. "I'll shift my junk. I left it until today to start my assignment. Remind me not to do that again, Rina."

"Me? Not Dad? He's very good at reminding me to do my work."

"I'd prefer having you remind me."

Maureen pulled her aside and whispered something into her ear, to which Irina responded in a loud whisper, "But doesn't she want excuses to talk to him?"

Sean was far from helpless in the kitchen, and he had the girls firmly under his tutelage as all three of them busied their way through this every evening routine. They chatted candidly while he supervised them, especially Irina, who was handling a sharp knife to cut vegetables.

"Is there anything you don't like, Miss Murphy?" she called out, displaying the crisper drawer.

"Cucumbers," I said.

"You ate cucumber sandwiches," she protested. "Are you sure?"

Maureen rolled her eyes. Sean looked ready to speak, but never did.

"Yes, I'm sure," I said. "I like cucumber sandwiches, but not cucumbers."

"Okay," she hollered back, digging around the cucumbers in the drawer.

"I can pick around them," I offered.

"No, no. We won't put them in," she insisted as she began unloading fresh vegetables into the sink.

"What would you like to drink, Miss Murphy?" Maureen asked. She opened a cabinet and began pulling down glasses. "Milk, juice, water? Was any of the apple juice left, Dad?"

"Water is fine."

"Do you like ice? I heard Americans drink everything cold. We have ice made." I got the impression they had made it especially for me.

"I'll go native today, thank you."

The girls were busy with their jobs. With a flirtatious wiggle, Sean met my gaze and stepped away. "Reen, watch your sister with the knife, heh? I need a private word with Miss Murphy." He led me away from the happy domestic scene. The girls exchanged a glance behind his back.

His manner was that odd mixture of shy and confident I had found so appealing and had contributed to my belief that he was a philanderer when we first met. His eyes twinkled in the reflection of the dining table chandelier. "Let's sit for a minute. Dinner is under control."

"Y'all make quite a team," I observed. "It's nice to see such a flagrant display of good parenting."

"Thank you. I am proud of the way they are turning out. Some of it must be a reflection upon me." We had walked to the window, and we stood there, despite his invitation to sit. He didn't touch me; I wished he would.

"Did you have a nice trip this weekend?"

"Yes, I did."

"St. Mary's Bay can be delightful. Did you take the waters?"

"Yes."

"Did you find them healing?"

"I don't know." I shrugged. "When I was there in March with my dad, it seemed to help. If I could have stayed longer, I might have healed completely."

"Let me see. I didn't think to look over your injuries on Friday." He put a finger on my cheek to guide it as he turned my face to catch the light. "You look great. It must have been the waters. You must have bathed in them too."

I smiled. I still had little pink scars all over my face from the thorns, but the scratches had mostly faded to nothing. The worst of them had become thin white lines. For some reason my eyes started to water. I had not been feeling emotional until they did, but once I realized that I was going to cry, I felt a surge of emotions: happy and sad, tired and excited, brave and frightened all mixed together. The tears spilled over. He continued to study my face, still controlling my movements with his one finger. His wide eyes drew in with concern. "I'm sorry, Solace."

I shook my head. "It's not you."

He wrapped me in his arms, stroking my hair and patting my back. I buried my face in his chest, finding comfort in his strength and the steady beat of his heart. "Would you like a tissue?"

"Yes, please," I said with a nod.

"Let me show you around," he said in a normal conversational tone. He guided me with one hand on my lower spine, as we walked from the dining room, through the cluttered living room, to the hall and the bathroom. "The girls use this one," he said. He grabbed the box of tissues from the sink counter and held it out for me, making no offer of privacy from himself, despite his care not to expose me to the girls' eyes and ears. I was relieved that he seemed comfortable around my bouts of tears. Most people like to escape, and the ensuing embarrassment makes it harder to control them.

As my tears dried, I wetted a second tissue to dab away smears of mascara. I threw the tissues into the wastebasket and asked, "Aren't you going to continue the tour?"

"Why not?" We stepped across the hall to the door of the girls' room. It was tidier than the living room, with twin beds covered by matching blue spreads and kitten posters on the wall around their desk. It reminded me of my room when my sister Faith and I had shared.

A few feet down was the spare room. Sean's art supplies, including an easel with its back to the door, dominated a third of the room, but there were a few bean bag chairs and zabutons on the floor around a small table holding an in-progress jigsaw puzzle. Other puzzles and games were stacked on a bookcase. The electronic devices, stereo, television, and personal computer, were in this room too.

"Video games?" I said with surprise. "I can't picture the girls playing them."

"Oh, they do! They're rather skilled. I don't like to encourage it, but it's," he blushed. "Actually, it's mine."

"Yours?"

"Yeah. My folks got it for me when I lived home after I left hospital, for something to do while I got things going again. That's why I decided to get contacts."

"You had to get contact lenses so you could play video games better?" I failed to keep laughter from bubbling through my words.

"That's the official version," he said with a shake of his head. "Truth is: it was vanity. You see, when I first got home I couldn't hear a blessed thing. I knew that after surgery I would still need hearing aids, and I was afraid no one would be able to see my face anymore behind all those accessories."

"It's okay, Artificial Boy," I said cheerfully. "It's nice that you are treating yourself to a few things."

"Artificial b-b-boy?" He laughed. He had a melodic laugh. Now that I had gotten to know him, I could see that music was definitely a part of his make up. "Make that Bionic Bloke, Lady. You're hurting my feelings."

"I like being able to see your eyes," I said.

"Oh? Yes, contacts are better for a few things."

"Really?"

"Really." He leaned in close. "I don't have to worry about bumping pretty ladies when I try to kiss them. My glasses used to slide down my nose at the most awkward moments."

"Your nose looks like it could hold up a pair of glasses pretty securely."

"Yes, well, but gravity is gravity, and my nose itself can be somewhat of an obstacle." He ran his finger down the center of his long nose. "You have such a nice little nose that it may not be quite such an interference as, um, mine can be." He smiled and reddened again.

"I've been bonked by smaller noses than yours, Bionic Bloke."

"Perhaps we should test it again to make sure we fit."

"We seemed to fit pretty well on Friday," I whispered, watching his eyes.

"What? Don't you want to kiss me again?" He made a pouty face. "I thought that maybe." He tilted his head, finishing the question with his eyes.

I put my hand to his cheek and pulled his face toward mine. We kissed, and barely pulled away after. "You didn't ask permission on Friday," I said.

"Well, you remember, Friday was a tumultuous day. I can't be held completely accountable." He turned his head toward the living room. "I suspect dinner is ready. Let's move on with the tour." We left the playroom and walked another ten feet to his bedroom.

I hesitated outside of the door. "Have you looked in my room?" I asked.

"It used to be mine, remember?" His tone told me he had respected my privacy. "But I promise I will ask you to let me visit you there soon." In response to my embarrassment, he said, "I enjoy being with you so much, Solace. You're so much fun." I had to let this latest remark sink in; no one had ever used that particular adjective to describe me before. "Go ahead, Solace. No need to be nervous. Dinner is ready, so I don't have time to ravish you." When I didn't move, he grabbed both of my wrists and pulled me in with a gentle amount of force that brought me, as planned, right into his arms. "Now you have to pay the toll," he said playfully, and he kissed me again. I melted into it, loving the taste of him. The kiss ended and he gradually let me go. I wobbled slightly and felt that I needed to straighten my clothing. He had not let his hands wander, but that didn't matter. I felt as if he had. He moved out of the way, and I shyly looked around.

He had told me Megan had been an expert at shopping the thrift stores and had completely furnished their first little apartment for less than one hundred dollars. It seemed that he was still using that furniture, which, though worn, had nice lines and appeared to be well made. The room was very plain, except for the quilt on his bed. I stepped forward to take a closer look at it. The colors were vibrant; the pattern was eastern. "Baba made that," he said.

"Your grandmother? It's beautiful." My eyes lifted slightly, and I saw the table on the far side of his bed. With the lamp and alarm clock were photographs of his daughters and his wife. Megan's photo was too small for me to see well. Instead of going closer, I kept my eyes moving, sweeping around the room as I prepared to leave. He watched me for a reaction, but I didn't show one. Those photographs belonged there. I wanted to see Megan's face, but I could wait. If Sean and I grew close enough, I would come to know it well.

"Does it pass muster, Sergeant?" he asked.

There was a pile of books on his dresser beside a basket with scissors, a pincushion, and a couple items of clothing. A guitar leaned against the solitary chair, which was stacked with music books. "Probably not, but I like it. Your home seems a happy place."

He looked relieved. When we returned to the dining room, the girls were pointedly waiting for us in their seats with the food laid out on the table. I sat opposite Sean, and after we sat the girls each offered me a hand to hold during the blessing. It was Irina's turn, and she ran through the prayer quickly enough to get a reproving look from her father.

"I hope you don't mind, Solace," Sean said as we began to pass the serving bowls. "Rob called me earlier to ask me to fill in for Mick Gallagher tonight. I agreed to go."

"Oh," I blinked. "Okay."

"May I walk with you?"

"Sure."

"We'll wash up supper," Irina volunteered.

Gone were all my illusions of privacy. It occurred to me that if I didn't get along with Sean Donovan after I got to know him better that I might not be able to continue to live in the Carollons. But I didn't need to worry about that today. On our walk to campus, Sean asked me if I would like to go out with him on Saturday. After I agreed, he took my hand and squeezed it.

A few minutes later I broke the silence again. "With such a large family, do you have a lot of obligations? Or do you get off easy by sharing duties?"

He shrugged. "We do stuff together. The only obligation I can think of is seeing Tim. He was in the Marines too, but he's been sick since the war. I visit him most days."

"That Tim? He's your brother?"

Sean nodded and slowly admitted, "Yeah."

"Do you know every person I know?"

"Sorry. I know it must seem that way."

"How is he?"

"He's been improving, but he's still in rotten shape. He doesn't have much to show for his life, and he's bitter and depressed, and he's got every right to be. He likes to give people hell." Sean let go of my hand to press the button for the walk signal. "My mum keeps a fire lit under the doctors. She fusses at Tim to treat his caregivers better. And Dad is kind of withdrawn. He has trouble dealing with the reality of it. He went through most of the Second World War without a scratch. He hasn't quite accepted that two of his sons were so badly injured in such a small war. Tanya and I are the ones who try to keep Tim informed on what's going on in the world."

"Tanya is your sister? Is it Tatiana?"

"Right. One older than me."

"And you're half Russian?"

"Correct again. My mother's family is Russian, Dad's is Irish. Long time Carollonian."

"Since the potato famine?"

"You know your history. Is that when your family left Ireland?"

"The Murphys did, but most of the rest were already in America. I'm more English than Irish."

"So is Solace an old family name? It sounds Puritan."

"It is."

"Well, it's beautiful. Like you."

I felt my skin flush and whispered my thanks. "Is Tim at St. Andrews? That's quite a trip to take every day."

"No, he was moved to a nursing center in Little Russia a long time ago. He was only at the hospital while they evaluated him and worked out a treatment routine." He picked up my hand again and swung it easily as we walked. "It's pretty easy to get there. I bet Tim would love it if you dropped in on him someday."

Horrified, I admitted, "I never really even tried to like Tim, Sean."

"He's not easy to like." He chuckled. "Honestly, I don't think Tim cares who visits. He's bored out of his mind."

"That's not terribly persuasive."

Still laughing, Sean let go of my hand and put his arm around my shoulders, pulling me close enough to kiss my cheek. "I place you under no obligation. And I am certain that Tim would enjoy your visit more than you would." He took his arm away as we approached the building where we were to meet the others. "Is school going well? Are you working on a degree?"

"Yes. I'm doing okay, but I've been slacking lately. I ought to work harder."

"You've had a rough year. Maybe you should take a break and get your focus back."

"Is that what you're doing, Sean?"

He paused and blinked. As if it were a revelation, he said, "I suppose I am."

Sean had been on Rob's team a few times in the past, so he not only knew the process but he knew more of the people than I did. I sat by Karen, who restrained her bursting curiosity and merely commented, "He's sweet on you." Sean sat with a group of actors across from me, which meant we could look at each other. I fumbled with the new pages, trying to get them sorted into my binder before we began, while Sean was man-joking and stewing up God only knows what kind of trouble.

Afterwards, Rob asked if we could go out. Sean looked at me, and I might have said yes, but I was frightened of going out with a group of people before I had gotten to know him better. "You still have homework to do tonight?"

I nodded. "I'm afraid I've had a lot of distractions in the last couple of days."

"Is your place still a mess, Solace?" Rob asked.

"Kind of."

"It should be much better soon," Sean told us. "If the carpet's okay, they're going to re-lay it tomorrow."

"If you have to replace it, can I help pick the new one?"

"I don't know how it's supposed to work."

Rob laughed and teased us. "Small wonder it took three years for you to get along with each other."

We dawdled on the walk home. There was a refreshing drizzle, and I wasn't ready to say goodnight. There were so many reasons not to invite Sean in, including my strong desire to be alone with him. I hesitated, but he followed me inside and reached to embrace me as soon as the door began to close behind us.

We kissed over and over again. Once we slowed enough to speak, Sean laughed lightly and said, "I've been dying to do that all evening." I kissed his chin and the tip of his nose. In turn, he kissed me on the part in my hair. "I like your place, Solace. I like all this empty space. But where do you sit?"

"On the floor," I said. "Or at the table, on the balcony, or my bed."

"Do you prefer the floor or the bed?" he said with an innuendo confirming smile.

"Depends."

He stared at me for a moment. "May I go back there?" he asked pointing his thumb like a hitchhiker down the hall.

"Fair is fair," I said with a little bow.

He poked his head into my study, and then he looked into the bathroom. "You have a nice sense of color, Solace. Did you notice that I re-grouted the tile for you?"

"Yes, thank you. It was a pleasant surprise."

Outside my bedroom door, he stopped snooping and looked at me. "Coming?" He put his hand through the door and flipped on the light. "Good Lord, there's furniture in here!" he exclaimed as he ran his hand over my Virginia-made dresser. "Impressive. And what are all these trinkets. Crystal perfume bottles?" He looked up at me with a question on his face.

"Gifts," I shrugged. "They're pretty."

"They're empty."

"I don't wear perfume."

"You smell nice. You don't need perfume," he said softly as he came over to me. He put his arms around me and began to sway.

"You can dance?" This was like the maraschino cherry atop a perfect boyfriend sundae, and certainly a novelty among my suitors.

"My mother believes in certain courtesies," he replied. "It wasn't so bad to learn, especially once I started to get interested in girls. Not an expert, mind you, but I can lead you into fun or trouble."

"What a fine example you must have set for your students."

"Criticizing my teaching methods?"

"Is this a lesson?"

"Perhaps, but I have a feeling there isn't much for me to teach you." Suddenly, he looked tired.

"You need to go home, Sean. See to the girls and get some rest."

"And I should let you finish your assignment."

I nodded. "The romantic moment is officially ended."

"You've got a knack for deflating a man's ego," he said lightheartedly. The skin around his eyes crinkled in a smile.

"I'm just teasing," I said apologetically.

"It's okay, Solace. I'm glad you feel that you can play with me. You don't have to apologize all the time."

"Old habit."

"At least you didn't apologize for apologizing."

"I think I've done that."

"May I read something you've written?"

I was so startled that I jumped. "I don't know. It's hard enough to share with my group."

He put his hand on my shoulder reassuringly. "When you're ready."

"Now I feel guilty for not wanting to show you."

"Did I forget to tell you that today was a no guilt day?"

"That was Friday."

"They come up rather often. I guess I'll have to ring you every morning and advise you, like a weather report."

"Clever boy."

"I've had a long time to practice what to say to you," he confessed.

"I don't think I'm ready to show you my writing, Sean."

"Don't wait too long, dear; it will only get more difficult," he advised. He looked around at my walls. "I like your room. May I sleep here sometime?"

Both stunned and relieved by his directness, I managed to say, "You are mighty forward."

"You seem to need to warm up to ideas, especially when they involve intimacy."

"I do? I'm not so sure about that. I've been bedded by a few men, you know."

"I'm glad you have something to be proud of, Solace," he said with complete sincerity, understanding that pride itself was an important achievement for me.

I closed my eyes, and dared to prove I had other, better reasons to be proud. I went into the computer's bedroom and grabbed a file from the drawer where I kept the small group of stories I had bothered to polish. Carrying it in front of me, I walked to where he stood waiting in the hall. I shoved the folder into his hands.

"You sure?"

"Don't give me the chance to back out," I quavered, already weakening.

He took the folder gravely with both hands. "I'll bring it back tomorrow, and leave it right there by your computer."

"That's fine." I smiled bravely.

He stepped forward and kissed me on the cheek. "Good night, Solace. Now, go do your work. Don't flunk out." Then he took my hand again and led me to the door.

"Good night, Sean. Thank you for dinner, and everything." I opened the door, and I was alone again.

Chapter Ten

I crossed the hot sand to the oasis of shade Mike had made over his blanket. He started to get up when he saw me, so I removed one of my flip-flops and hurled it in his direction, causing him to duck back down.

"If you're mad at your boss, don't take it out on his family!" he cried.

In good humor, I dropped my towel and bag, which contained my mostly completed homework, onto the blanket, commenting, "This *is* a nice way to end the work day."

He dug through my bag, looking for snacks. "Is this all you brought?" he asked, holding up a bottle of grape soda. I nodded, and he tossed me the sunscreen. "How's it going? What did you do this weekend?"

"I went to St. Mary's Bay with Peter."

"Holy shit, girl, you must have been in fucking heaven."

"Well, that's usually where I am when I'm with Peter," I said, unable to control a little, recurring smile.

He laughed. He also noticed the smile. "What, did he propose or something?"

I shook my head. "We decided not to see each other anymore."

"You went there to break up?"

"No. That's not why we went there."

He sifted through the many jokes that might be appropriate for the occasion, but when he looked at me again, he merely said, "You look happy. I take it *you* broke it off."

"In a way." I nodded.

He scanned my blushing face. Then with sudden energy, he cried out, "You've got someone new!" He sat straighter, more from pride at having reached this conclusion than out of interest in the circumstances. "You must have it bad for this new bloke to dump The Pump."

Ignoring his vulgarity, I explained, "Well, the truth is, Mike, I forgot Peter even existed."

Mike's jaw dropped, and he evaluated me with concern and suspicion, but he said nothing.

I opened the sunscreen and began to apply it. The smell reminded me of Sean. "I had a flood in my kitchen Friday morning, and when I tried to reach the property manager, I found out that he was out of town, so I ended up dealing directly with the landlord."

"And you forgot all about Peter?"

"Do you know who my landlord is?"

"Should I?"

I shrugged. "Just thought you might. You know him. His name is Sean Donovan."

Interrupting, he screeched, "Donny? Holy shit! I thought you loathed him." Sean had been right about Mike. He was more perceptive than I had realized.

"I was wrong. We talked. A lot."

Mike nodded along as I spoke, agreeing and just listening. "Yeah, Donny can talk. So how did you hook up with him? And what made you decide to give him the time of day?"

"Didn't I mention the hospitality muses?"

"Huh?" He gave me a blank look.

"The day you ragged on me, Kevin Reilly sent them to my door with freshly baked cookies. He's my property manager, and they are his grandchildren. There was a little matchmaking conspiracy."

"Sean's kids? Reenie and Renee?"

"Reen and Rina. Maureen and Irina."

"So? I still don't get it."

"I like them. They come over after school sometimes, and we have tea together while we do our homework."

Mike started laughing. "Donny's been using you as a babysitter!" He stretched and asked if I wanted to swim. We walked down to the water. I tried to change the subject by asking what he had done over the weekend. Half attentively, he told me he'd been working all weekend and had a great time. He was still thinking about Sean and me. We jumped waves for a while and then rested, dripping and bedraggled, in knee deep breakers before he spoke again. "So, you like hanging out with the girls. They talk about their dad, and you decide he might be okay? It seems weird, Solace. Are they troublesome? I mean, Megan was a spitfire."

"They're full of energy, alright, but I don't think you need to worry about them," I said, shaking my head. "They are well-behaved and Sean seems very involved with them." I tried unsuccessfully not to think any further into the future than Saturday's date. "It could be interesting to go out with a man who has children," I commented. It was strange how my feelings for the man could change the way I felt about that circumstance.

"Indeed," he agreed, looking relieved that it would be me not him gaining the experience. Gently, he added, "You took a shine to him, heh?" Shrugging, I admitted that I had. "He's a good man, Solace. You're right. I've known him for a long time, though we haven't always been close. I didn't know how to act around him when he got married and had kids. That kind of blew me away. Then when Megan died, I really didn't know what to do. I don't know how he took it, and I don't know how he got by. I was too scared to ask, get involved, or even offer condolences. Now you know what kind of irresponsible ass I am."

I didn't want Mike to feel badly about himself. There was so much time between then and now, and I believed that Mike had been supportive of his friend after they returned from the war. I ignored the confession. "I'd say they've managed pretty well."

He nodded. "He's a survivor, Solace."

I snatched Sean's note off of the folder beside my computer and fled the room. I was too terrified to read it, but I knew that I would squirm until I did. I skimmed it first then reread it more slowly. Joy mingled with relief rained down over my cheeks.

He wrote: "Solace, What a lovely story. Did you write it after you met my girls? Jennifer reminded me of Maureen and Susan of Irina. We've spent many hours at the Art Museum. They love that painting of the lady with the pearls in her hair and of course they're fascinated by the nude statues. You understand so much. Thank you for sharing this with me. I hope you will wish to share again. Sean"

After the previous night, my dinner seemed very quiet. I washed the dishes by hand, half-fearful of flooding the apartment again, but also because I found it relaxing to play with the bubbly water. After I got home from school, I got ready for bed. As I went around the apartment turning things off and neatening, the telephone rang. I jumped at the sudden sound.

"Hello, Solace. It's Sean, uh, Donovan. Do I need to use my last name or might you confuse me with every third bloke on this island?"

"Hi, Sean," I answered, delighted by his reference to a remark I had made in my story. "How are you?"

"Well enough, thank you, and yourself?"

"I'm fine."

"I hope I'm not calling too late. I lost track of the time."

"I was still awake," I said.

"Good. I won't keep you. I just wondered if you want your key back."

I considered demanding that he return it immediately. I smiled. "There's no hurry."

"I've made copies for my entire family," he said. "So I can just slip this one under your door if you aren't dressed for company."

"As a matter of fact...."

"Oh, Solace, don't. My dirty mind was just trying to imagine you in whatever was in that bag you tried to hide from me on Friday. Tell me you're in your old gardening clothes or something."

"I didn't move any old things, remember?"

"You're a flirt."

"So are you."

"Must I bring the key down immediately and slide it under the door?"

"Next time I see a Donovan would be fine," I said, hoping he would come, but not wanting to reveal my desires.

"Oh?" Then he tried to cover his disappointment. "No preference which Donovan?"

"To bring me my key? Actually, no. Any one will do. For other reasons, I might have my preferences."

"I think that's good," he said in an uncertain tone.

"You'd be safe to take it that way," I answered. I braced myself. As kind as his note had been, I was still shy about mentioning my story. "Hey, Sean? Thank you for what you wrote."

"You're thanking me? Why? I should thank you for letting me read it."

"You already did. Your note was nice. Your comments didn't scare me away from writing ever again. I was kicking myself all day for choosing that story. It's one of my favorites, but when I remembered how much the girls reminded me of your girls, I thought maybe I should have chosen something else."

"You made me think." There was a short silence which I wondered if I should try to fill. "Well, I won't keep you. Good night, Solace. I hope you find yourself in your dreams."

Sensing some joke on Sean's part, I put out my hand to accept the key that Maureen dropped from her fingers. She quickly vanished, and I did not see a Donovan again for a long enough time that I began to wonder about my plans with Sean for the upcoming weekend.

I spent nearly an hour on the telephone with my parents on Thursday evening while my mother pelted me with prickly questions about living alone and my pretrial meetings with the prosecutor. Her concerns awoke mine. Tired, I was considering resorting to television for noise and escape when there was a knock at my door.

It was Sean with his glasses askew, his clothing rumpled, and his hair standing on end. I wondered if he was trying to impress me with his ability to look sexy in any circumstance.

"Girls do your hair?" I asked in lieu of a greeting. He beamed a smile at me, transferring energy and lifting my mood. I invited him inside with a gesture. The touch of his hand felt like a secret kiss.

"Yeah," he said ducking sheepishly. "They attacked me with mousse or something when I went to the kitchen to ring you. I hope you don't mind that I just stopped by. The line has been busy for a while and, frankly, I needed to escape."

I touched his hair. It was still damp and sticky. "It's okay for you to knock on my door."

"I wanted to make our plans for Saturday. May I stop by at half past three? I'd like to take you to tea, then somewhere else for fun before supper."

"Okay."

"Could you do me a favor, Solace? Could you wear one of those pretty dresses that you stopped wearing a while back? You looked so beautiful on Friday, and it would be just right for where we are going." He pretended to beg.

"Where are we going?" I asked. I probably would have worn one of my old dresses, but I resented the request.

"I must still decide." His manner told me that he had everything planned.

Fighting annoyance, I asked, "And how should I wear my hair?"

"I'll send the girls over if you like," he joked, melting my irritation. "They can be quite creative."

"Are you modeling?"

He ducked his head and blushed. "Wear your hair any way you like."

"It's cute." I pushed the door closed.

"Thanks." Sensing the need to appease me, he leaned in shyly to offer me a peck. I demanded a full smooch, and pulled him in closer with both arms, wrapping a leg around one of his to secure him to me, though he offered no resistance. We kissed. We paused for breath. I thought he was going to say something, but he dove in again and enclosed me in his arms. Though the captivity of a lover's embrace often makes me nervous, I felt safe wrapped in his strength.

His lips strayed to my ear, nibbling and licking me like a cat, quick and dry. His beard was soft by Thursday, so it didn't scratch as it had on Monday. I leaned my head over to make a larger area for him to nuzzle, and he ran his tongue along the side of my neck until he reached my collar. It was wet now, more of a dog lick. He slid his hands down to my bottom to feel my shape through my blue jeans. He stopped nibbling my neck and said, "I can't stay. I must make sure they don't destroy anything better than my appearance. They were in a dangerous mood."

"They seem so sweet and harmless," I said trying not to make it hard for him to go, but I must have looked disappointed.

"Would you feel better if I told you that I wish I could stay longer? And how's this? The girls are going to spend the night with their grandparents on Saturday night, so I will have no curfew."

"Yes. You want to spend the night?"

"Oh my God, Solace." He laughed, but looked ill at ease. "On second thought, I might be safer at home. I can usually maintain some level of discipline with the girls, but I fear that you will challenge me in perpetuity."

"Isn't that one of my attractions, Sean Donovan?" I hooked a finger around one of his belt loops.

"I didn't want to believe the rumors."

"All exaggerations," I said separating myself from him. "I should let you go back to protect your belongings from your offspring. Are they really thrashing and trashing?"

"Maureen was using the sprayer from the kitchen sink to squirt Irina. It goes on from there. If I wasn't having such a hard time saying good night, I would invite you up to witness. It has been so lovely to see you."

I looked up at him, eyes aglow with naked warmth. I opened the door, preparing to push him gently out of it. He slammed it back against the wall and plastered me to it with his full body. "I think I love you," he said rapidly. Then he kissed me on the mouth, and let me go all in less time than it took me to take in what he had said. Already out of the door, he called back, "Goodnight, Serenity." He threw me a quick salute as he disappeared into the stairwell. Shaking myself back to reality, I heard the thudding echoes as he took the steps two or three at a time.

I spent Friday evening with friends. Karen, Steve, and I went to dinner at a new place up in Little Russia, and Rob and Bridget joined us at a bar on the riverfront later. Bridget was curious about how Sean and I had managed a truce, but she didn't pester me. "And don't worry that Sean was going around bragging. It only came out because Rob had been trying to call him during the time he was off helping you."

"Good. Okay," I muttered from under my hair, which hung over my face, my fingers splayed through it at the top of my head and the heels of my hands holding up my forehead. "I might not have talked to him last week if I knew how much excitement this was going to cause."

"Sorry." Bridget patted my elbow. "It's because we love you both. You do understand?"

"Yeah," still grousing.

"And now that we've seen you and know that you're okay, we won't ask you any more questions than we would ask anyone else." I'm not sure how gentle that sounded at the time. "We trust Sean not to abuse you."

I did, too.

At this time, as I was choosing to be with Sean, I knew that I could trust him, and he trusted me, though I had yet to understand why he did. I remembered why I had avoided him and thought I hated him, and though all of those reasons had turned out to be false, they had not melted away. I would remember them as long as I remembered him. I had hated myself. He had never given up his faith in me.

If this was merely a passing relationship, he would be worth remembering, but it was already more than that. Though this phase of it might not endure, we had already known each other for several years. He was one of my earliest acquaintances after my move to the Carollons, and though we had spent most of that time in avoidance, he had always aroused strong feelings in me. Hate was the mask of lust, lust was a cover for attraction—I could not state love, but the word hung out there. It was waiting to be used by me as he had already used it, and as fast and lightly as he had said it, I knew he meant it.

Chapter Eleven

I spent my morning on the beach alone. I had stopped in to see if Mike wanted to join me, but he hadn't been there. His brother Jimmy, looking very suburban, professional, and uncomfortable in his brother's permanent vacation home, was at the kitchen table. I asked him to tell Mike that I was out on the beach and left, glad to be away from him though I knew it was unlikely that he would relay my invitation to his brother. Something about Jimmy reminded me of my ex-husband; he was a lump and a grump, bitter and ignored because he hadn't made a positive comment within anyone's memory.

As I waited for the warm breeze to dry away the excess sand from my feet, I wondered what had gone wrong. The rest of the Leahy family was so pleasant. Oh well, I suppose there were people who said things like that about the Murphy family. What had made that girl run off to another country?

As I shook the sand from my blanket, I wondered how anything could be wrong with the world on such a beautiful day. I certainly had no complaints. I had picnicked, played, and managed to finish an assignment, all while being so eager for my date with Sean that I almost hated for it to begin. With all that activity, I was still ready early, so I settled down at home with a book and tried not to look at the clock. At 3:32 I heard a knock. I opened the door, and Sean stepped inside. He took me in his arms and kissed me. "Sorry I'm late," he said.

"Do come in," I offered belatedly.

He kicked the door closed, still holding me in his arms, and kissed me again, this time using his tongue. It lasted a long time, and I wished it would never end. "You look so beautiful," he said. "I shouldn't muss you." He looked sharp himself in tropical light fabrics that fit just tightly and just loosely enough in all the right places. He had gotten a haircut, which gave him a neater appearance, though it was still longer than he had worn it before the war.

"I can fix myself."

"Oh!" The single syllable was stretched out over the space of a sentence. He reached his hand out to touch me, then he pulled me closer, and we kissed again. When we resurfaced, he chimed, "Let's go."

Thinking I had been wise to skip the lipstick, I struggled to regain my balance in the hall on the way to the elevator. When I saw Sean press the button for the garage level, I asked, "You have a car?"

"Sort of," he blushed.

"I'm not exactly dressed for riding a motorcycle," I protested.

"Sorry, Solace," he said as the elevator doors opened. "It's worse than that." He led me by the hand, and we turned between two vehicles. "It's a minivan." Shrugging modestly, he opened the passenger side door. "I rarely need it unless I need to carry lots of stuff or people." He helped me up and closed the door. When he climbed in on the other side, he added, "It's American."

"Oh, that's right," I said, suddenly realizing that I was sitting to his right. "This seems so natural I didn't notice. Where are we going?"

He backed out and headed to the ramp and daylight. "To my house."

"Cool!"

"It's a bit like your place, Solace. Empty, I mean."

We went west across town along Harbour Boulevard to the Williamsport Bridge, the grand suspension bridge over the river as it widens into the harbor. After we crossed, I was quickly lost on the side streets. Driving around a bend in the road, he gestured to the right. "That's where the girls will go to school next year."

All I could see was the sign: Uplands Secondary School. The building itself was hidden by trees and speed. A few turns later we pulled up at a stop sign, and he said, "This is my street." I looked both ways down the tree-lined street. Sean turned the minivan and soon stopped in front of his house, a charming, white-shingled, arts and crafts bungalow, trimmed in the same sea green paint I had seen in his hair last week. "I usually park behind in the alley, but I'll take you through the front today." He came around to open my door, but I was so busy studying the house that I was slow to move.

Still transfixed, I followed him through the gate. "This is gorgeous, Sean. And you've already planted the garden?" I turned to him, amazed.

"This has been my job since I came home from the Gulf, Solace. I mean, once I felt well enough and had begun to paint away some of the images that haunted me, I have worked here. You are here." He waved his arm toward a wall of tall, colorful annuals that grew along the white picket fence while I tried to assimilate his giving me personal credit for my name's attributes. "The girls enjoy gardening too. We eat quite well from this little vegetable patch. Including cucumbers." He gestured to the side yard as he spoke.

Guiding me to the porch, he pointed up. "The roof needed to be replaced, so instead of just finishing a few rooms, like I'd planned to do, in the attic, we added a second story. The architect drew up this plan, and I loved it," he effused. "I ended up with a lot more space than we need, but unused rooms don't require much maintenance, heh. And if I ever sell, it will pay off." He took a deep breath. "I guess you can tell I'm proud of the way it has turned out." He reached into his pocket for his keys. Opening the door, he added, "Welcome to my real home, Solace."

My eyes explored ahead of me as I stepped inside. I knew that he had spent a lot of money on it, but what impressed me even more was the quality of the work that I knew he had done himself. The woodwork was beautiful. A careful restoration had been made in the front rooms, but the back of the house was completely modern, open, and tropically cool.

"You must have put in hours month after month to do this, Sean."

He nodded. "It's been a big job. You like it?" My approval seemed very important to him.

"I love it, Sean. It's like a dream home."

"So now I'll have to wonder if it's me or my house you like, won't I?"

"Not today," I sighed. "You brought me here, remember? To see the house for the first time. Tomorrow, if I ask to come back, well, then you might have to worry."

He gave me a quick tour of the first floor on the way to the kitchen. He filled the kettle and took a plate from the refrigerator. "Cucumber sandwiches." I placed them in the basket, which was already packed with tableware, soda bread, cookies and fruit.

"Can I do anything?"

"Look pretty and kiss me until the kettle sings?"

"I can do that." I hung my arms around his shoulders and reached my face up to his. We gave each other pleasant kisses, appetizer kisses, not the passionate type we had exchanged earlier at my place. The teakettle whistled, and I let go. "I'll carry the basket.

Where are we going to sit?" I eyed the patio, but did not see any furniture.

"The front porch."

We took a walk around the yard again after we ate. He pointed out plants, naming ones I had only seen in the Carollons. "I feel like I live here already, yet I've been afraid almost to actually move in. Does that seem too strange to you?" Timid again, he looked at me for reassurance.

"When I left my marriage, I moved back to my parents' home. The thing that was hardest for me was leaving mine and returning to theirs. I had to. I mean, I could have lived on my own, but I would have spent everything I earned on rent and never gotten ahead, because I wasn't prepared to go back to group homes. I wanted to get my own place. And I saved everything that I could reasonably, so that I would be able to buy my own home. Then things piled up on me, and the closer I got to being able to buy that home, the more I realized that I wanted to be somewhere else, doing something else, only I didn't know what to do or where to do it. I don't think it was the house or condo that scared me. I think I still want it, but I guess I—I guess I don't know. But it's kind of like you coming here and making it ready but not moving in."

"You realized that you had just ended up where you were. You were working hard and outwardly doing well, but you weren't directing yourself."

"That's it, Sean," I exclaimed, lighting at his understanding. "I just rode on the currents, but that seemed all I could do when I didn't know where I wanted to go."

"Do you know where you want to go now, Solace?"

"Haven't a clue," I replied with unemotional honesty. "But I've taken a more active role in steering myself."

"I think you should embrace your fictional world."

"I think that's a bad idea," I argued, feeling defensive.

"I'm not suggesting you lose touch with reality, just that you should create life stories for your imaginary people and let them interact. You can write. You just need something to write about. Now, me, for example: I would make a splendid romantic hero. I save the girl from a lifetime of drudgery as a banker and help her make the transition to working at a totally rad company where she learns to surf or bungee jump."

I started laughing hard. It was close enough to reality, yet twisted. "Right. She quits her job because she doesn't want to see him again? That's very courageous."

"You are courageous, Solace," he said seriously. "I admire you. You grab at life; you don't hide or pour your energy into gardens and refinishing wood floors. Did you notice they were mahogany?"

"I guess it makes sense with the insects."

"You hide more from yourself than you do from the world."

"You aren't hiding, Sean. You've made this place beautiful. You've done something constructive with your transition time. You had to make some big changes when you lost your hearing. It took your livelihood away from you. And you risked your savings to build this home for your children."

"I'm not exacting scraping bottom, Solace," he said. "I could have afforded to do this years ago, and my kids could have lived here since they were little. The schools are better here too. But I liked my apartment in the city. It seemed better for a single person."

"Surely there are other single people and single parents living in this neighborhood."

He shrugged, ducking his head to divert my attention from some emotion he didn't want me to see. With a hard swallow, he was calm again. Men can do that. I don't know how they do it, but though I admit it would often be a blessing to have that skill, I still think that a good cry can wash away much of a person's pain.

"Megan must be very pleased with the way you've handled everything," I stated.

He raised his head to meet my eyes. "I guess I figured I'd have settled down more before I moved into the house. When I bought it, I still felt married. I feel younger now and more carefree than ever."

"I've felt the same way, Sean. Yet I didn't think you would. Not with children. I thought kids might age you more than even a bad marriage."

Amused, he said, "They make you younger too. Some days they make me feel so old and responsible, and sometimes they make me feel infantile."

"You seem to have a good balance."

"You haven't known us very long!" He bent down to pull a weed. "Do you carry your experiences around with you all the time, Solace?"

"I guess," I replied somewhat puzzled by the question. "How can I not?"

"Well, I'm being really nosy, I guess. I can't help but wondering about how you got messed up with Ken Williams when you had the marital experience that you had. Did things feel okay while you were going through it?"

I couldn't answer that question without a good deal of thought. I stood still watching the breeze move the leaves and the bees among the flowers. I heard him apologize for prying. Eventually, unemotionally, I tried to answer. "I think that I picked up on a lot of things that I wasn't willing to admit to myself. I said something once. I just remembered. I said this to Peter, that part of me wanted him to mistreat me. I've never wanted to believe it, but it must be true. Peter's a good man. He never promised me anything. And I guess I trusted him enough to say that. And I don't know quite what I meant. I think I just meant the way we left our dating thing up in the air, the mystery. But Ken was different. He seemed solid. Always sure of how things would be. I thought he was dull, if anything. I guess I mixed dull and safe up in my head."

"You are trusting."

"Not always. I don't think I am very good at figuring out who I should trust. I've learned to trust you under the most negative circumstances, and that confirms why I shouldn't always trust myself. My judgment needs lots of testing. My track record is pathetic." I looked up into his pale eyes. "I also have a feeling that I will learn that you have a few imperfections of your own."

He grimaced and nodded. "I try not to let them get in my way."

"It's okay to let them show. I do." I smiled uneasily. "If you were one of those people who'd led a charmed existence, you probably wouldn't be as interesting or comforting as you are. Even when I thought I hated you, I could see that you were giving. It'll sound really weird, but I thought of you as a guardian angel or guardian devil or something. Do you remember what you said about being there to rescue me if I fell in the river? I took it literally. Even though I've learned you are a regular interactive human, I feel like a very weak fool, compared to you, to be so hobbled and aimless."

"It's just a matter of perspective, Solace. Sometimes problems are more difficult to face if you know there is something you can do about them. For you, deciding what to do is difficult. You lived through things for too long before you decided you needed to make changes, so you had a big hole to dig your way out of. You are too strong and too patient, or you were, for your own good. I understand that, though I handle my problems differently. When I met you, I could see that you felt things deeply and were amazingly easy to move. I've never been sure why I wanted to be with you so badly, when you wanted me to leave you alone, but perhaps that was it: the empathy you radiate. When you finally let me speak with you, I knew that my life as I knew it had ended one way or another." He gave me a thorough visual assessment, and cut me off before I felt the need to respond. "Well, Miss Murphy, are you ready to go have some fun?"

"I thought we were having fun," I answered brightly.

"We are, I guess, but I think it's time to move on to stage two."

"And what is stage two?"

"We are going to see the fishies."

I cringed. "Fish?"

He nodded, grinning broadly. Then to my relief, he added, "At the Aquarium."

What an excellent choice for a first date! It was a just-right mixture of busy and private, calm and public for us to relax and chat and get to know one another in a less intimate setting. On the way out, we both made stops, and agreed to meet up again at the shark model in the main lobby. I was there a minute before he appeared suddenly at my side, looking a bit smug, and handed me a small bag bearing the gift shop logo. "I found something for you." Curiously, I reached inside to retrieve a tiny parcel of folded tissue paper containing a small silver charm of a mermaid. "If you don't have a bracelet…"

"I do. Thanks, Sean. She's sweet. You shouldn't have."

"Sounds like a good reason to do it," he said, putting his arm around me and starting to guide me out of the building. He let go long enough to open the door, then picked up my hand so we could walk more easily. "What would you like for supper?" he asked as he helped me into the van.

"I thought you had everything planned."

"Well, yes, I had planned to take you to Sikorsky's, but after being at the big fish tank, I don't think I could eat any of the little buggers tonight. What about O'Brien's Pub? They make a tasty shepherd's pie."

An easy walk from home, O'Brien's was a cozy, noisy place where the floors were sticky from spilled beer. We ate and drank lightly, our tongues flowing faster than the tap at the bar.

"Are you ever lonely, Sean?"

He mused for a moment. "I don't think I've ever had much chance to be lonely. You?"

"Sometimes," I confessed. "Sometimes I think it's easier to be alone here."

"Easier to be lonely or easier to handle being alone?"

"Easier to handle. Mostly, I like to be alone, except when I want to be with people and can't."

"You like having your own place, don't you?"

"Very much, but I do miss Cindy."

"I haven't seen her in ages. How's she doing?"

"She's alright. Of course, she almost never complains about anything!"

He nodded in agreement, smiling. "I was going to invite you to church tomorrow until I remembered that I have to pick up the girls from the Reillys in the morning."

"If you don't go to church, do you have to shave?"

His face lit with a humorous expression. "You like Mr. Scruffy? My mother says she's ready to petition the Marines to take me back so that I will have to start grooming again."

It should have been funny, but for me it rang too true to find humor in it. "Mothers." I stabbed a chunk of carrot and dropped my fork into the bowl. "I'm thirty years old, and my mother lives thousands of miles away, but she still manages to control me in many ways." His eyes narrowed, studying me. "Does your mother check on your social calendar?"

"Heavens, no!" he cried, working hard to restrain a laugh. "The younger kids give her enough to worry about."

"Sometimes my parents are still too involved in my life. They worry about me living alone. And they remind me that there's no one watching out for me."

"I will," he offered.

"You already do," I said solemnly. "They would never understand."

"I met your dad when he was here. I was at Rob's," he explained, "and you were at work or something. We chatted a bit. He's cool."

"Oh, yeah, well," I stammered, stunned. "He might treat you differently if he met you now."

He shrugged as if their approval was of little consequence. "So?"

"You might scare them."

"I promise I turned in all my weapons when I was discharged from the Marines."

"I don't think so," I said, watching his charming smile appear in response. "No. You are definitely still armed."

I had no plans at all for Sunday. I considered trying to get ahead on my schoolwork, but I was too restless to sit still for very long. I went downstairs to the swimming pool. It was beautiful, with a large patio around it, enough chairs and tables, shade around the patio and sun shining into the water keeping it warm. The exercise room was on the other side of a sliding glass wall, and the life guard was also the fitness trainer. I decided that the hospitality muses and I should have some of our tea and homework parties there.

I grew hungry early, and decided to go upstairs to make a lunch to bring back down. In the stairwell, I met all three of the Donovans. "Miss Murphy! Are you all done swimming?" Maureen asked. "Would you like to go back after lunch?"

"Actually, I was just going to get my lunch and bring it down with me."

"Dad, can we eat at the pool too?" asked Irina.

Sean looked at me with questions and sympathy both. I smiled. "If it's is okay with Miss Murphy."

"It is."

"Then we're ready," Sean said. "All this stuff we're carrying is left over from my mother-in-law's bridge party on Friday." He turned around and started down again. "Lunch."

"Do we need anything else?" I asked.

"How hungry are you?" He shot me a big smile. "We can just get some pop from the machine. Or is that not healthy enough?"

"Me? I thought you were the health food guy. I could carry something."

"We're good. You can go ahead and reserve a table if you'd like."

"I'll see what I can do." All of the tables were available. I chose one with access to shade and breeze, away from the gym, where there were a few people working out.

When they joined me, Sean handed change to Irina for the soda machine, and she sprinted away. "She's got a play rehearsal at church this afternoon."

"Can I stay at the pool, Dad?"

"Sure. But you can't bug Solace and you can't swim if Yuri isn't paying attention to the pool." Then to me, "That happens a lot. He's in the training room more than the pool."

"I won't bug you," she said. She was busy opening aluminum foil packets so that we could see what was inside. Sean and I began making sandwiches. Irina returned with four bottles and dropped the change on the metal table with a maximum amount of noise. Some of it rolled to the deck, and she went chasing after it. Sean and I suppressed laughter, while Maureen looked annoyed. "I thought it was going to go into the salad."

After a better lunch than I usually made at home, they went upstairs. Maureen was back in about fifteen minutes in a cute two piece suit. She dove right into the water, still a kid, while I continued reading my book until I reached a good stopping place. She interrupted me a few times before I placed my marker and got back into the water. After we swam for a while, we both got out and pulled out our books, but we didn't do any reading.

"Did you like our house?"

"It's very nice. Have you decided which room will be yours yet?"

She shrugged. "Maybe. We keep changing our minds. Sometimes we think we'll still share. Sometimes we want to be as far away from each other as possible. Opposite ends of the house. I've even wanted the old bedroom downstairs, but Dad says 'no way.' It's to be the guestroom."

"I think it will make a good guestroom, since it's separated from the other rooms."

"That's why I'd like it to be my room." She smiled.

"You think your dad wouldn't find out if you snuck out of the house?"

Her head shot up, revealing a surprised or possibly angry expression, before she forced her gaze down again. "If Irina didn't know to tell on me, Dad would never know."

"Unless you had a problem. If you didn't get home, he'd miss you."

"I wouldn't."

I wasn't sure what her precise meaning was. She could have only meant that she wouldn't have a problem, though even her sister would have known I wanted her assurance that she wouldn't sneak away. "I hope you wouldn't. I hope you wouldn't take that kind of a risk."

"Are you sure you don't have kids?"

"Absolutely."

"Do you want kids? I mean, if you and Dad got married, and you already had us, would you want to have your own kids too?"

I'm sure I made a face. "Gee, Maureen," I tried to say calmly. What should I say? "Your dad and I have just met. We don't know each other very well. I mean," time for a little honestly, "if I was thinking about having a serious relationship with your father, then I probably wouldn't have even gone out with him because he has children. It's not personal. I like you and your sister very much, but I'm not at all ready to think about moving in with you."

She laughed nervously as she realized she had broken a taboo.

"People have to grow together. There's probably even more growing required when there are more people involved."

She nodded. "That makes sense." She didn't say anything else or look at me for a long time.

Apparently the only thing that had kept Mike from shanghaiing me off to the Charles II Reef was my abhorrence of Sean Donovan. As soon as that obstacle was removed, a boat trip was arranged. Sean was still studying the reef for artistic reasons, and Mike was more interested than ever in the scientific aspects. I was relieved Sean had already seen me in a swimsuit and that Cindy, who joined us, had never done any snorkeling before either.

The day was clear, the water calm, and the wildlife ignored us. There was more excitement on deck, during lunch, when Cindy asserted that Mike couldn't get a reunion organized for the surviving Gulf War veterans before Tim Donovan was able to attend one. While they argued, Sean and I pulled closer and whispered about more personal things. By the time we were ready for one last dip into the ocean, Mike was talking about dates and what type of entertainment should be arranged. My only comment on the entire matter was, "I am not popping out of a cake."

On Monday when the girls came to see me after school, they brought samples of several sugar-free cakes for me to try. Never fear, they brought enough for themselves too, along with rating questionnaires. "This is very scientific," I commented. "Why are you trying so hard to perfect a sugar-free cake recipe?"

"For Uncle Tim," Irina stated. "For his birthday. He can't eat sugar."

"And he pretty much missed his last two birthdays," Maureen explained more seriously.

"And he loves cake."

"I see," I said with a nod. "This is important. What are we going to drink with the cake?"

"For the party, we'll have to ask Granny. For now, water. It shouldn't influence our results," Maureen answered.

After we tested the samples, finding a clear winner, I asked the girls if they had considered using their research for a science project. Irina looked at me like I was crazy, and Maureen quietly said, "Oh, I should ask my teacher about it."

Irina's mind was occupied with another concern which was much more important to her than her uncle's birthday: her own. "I've always wanted to have a pajama party, Miss Murphy. Dad has never let me, because he's afraid to be the only grown up in a house full of girls. Do you think you could stay over with us? He might let me have the party if there's a woman in the house."

"Possibly, Rina. When do you want to have your party?"

"The last weekend in July. Friday, preferably, or Saturday. My birthday is the Monday. I hope you can come over for our family party too."

"I'll talk to your dad."

Tim's birthday came before Irina's and I was recruited one more time to taste-test icings. Then Sean asked me if I could come with them to deliver the cake. "Tim keeps asking when I'm going to bring you. I thought this might be good, since it will be such a short visit. You are, of course, invited to the party." When I agreed to go with him, Sean kissed my cheek. "Tim will be stoked. You'll be over the first, probably easiest hurdle of meeting my family."

"You were lucky you met my dad when we weren't together."

"I know. But don't worry about Tim. He gripes a lot, but he doesn't bite. His condition isn't contagious, and I'll be there."

The four of us took the cake up to the nursing home the morning of the party. The girls unveiled the cake in the kitchen before we left home. It was an amazing creation, decorated with tropical reef fish and a seaweed edging that looked inedibly real. Proclaiming that the wrong person was trying to paint the reef in the spare room, Sean rattled his keys and urged us to move along.

The girls took the cake to be stored in the facility's kitchen while Sean and I went to Tim's room. He was staring at the ceiling, ignoring a television by his bed when we entered. Sean didn't bother getting permission before he turned it off. "Where's your roommate?"

"Physical therapy," Tim replied, his eyes still on the ceiling. No one had mentioned that he had lost his vision, but I couldn't help but wonder if he had until he suddenly turned. "Holy shit, it's Solace Murphy! I forgot how frigging quiet you were." He was so pale and drawn that I wouldn't have known him.

"Hello again," I said.

"Sean, go away. Come on. I want to steal your girlfriend. I didn't get a kiss before I went to war. What about one now?"

Sean frowned. With a smirk, I replied, "Too late, Tim. You missed your chance a long time ago."

Tim glared at Sean for a moment. "Can't I talk to her alone?"

Sean looked from Tim to me. "Good luck." I'm not sure for which of us the comment was intended. "Back in a few minutes."

"Make sure to put a pretty bow on my present."

I stared at Tim for a moment. I was tempted to walk out behind Sean, but before I took a step, Tim turned his full attention on me. "You aren't going to break his heart are you?"

"None of your business," I returned frigidly.

"It is my business. You were quite the little enchantress back in the day, and I wouldn't have thought you had the class to draw his attention. So, have you cleaned up your act? Are you honest with him about sharing your attentions?"

"You think you have the right to insult me just because you can't get up and walk out of the room behind me?" I stiffened. "First of all, being sick doesn't mean you have the right to pry into things that aren't your concern, even if they worry you. And secondly, you aren't that sick anymore. Get it straight right now. You may ask Sean if we get along, but not what we fight about. You may know we are close, but not how we show it. Do I need to be any clearer?"

"You are a wicked, little bitch." He chuckled. "Here I was worried about your safety. You've had a streak of abusers, haven't you? Do you let Sean hurt you?"

"You know damn well," I seethed, "that your brother wouldn't intentionally hurt anyone."

"You probably thought the same thing about your ex-husband too. Once."

"What is the matter with you?"

"Lots of things. But mostly I've spent way too much time staring at the ceiling."

"Don't you get to go to physical therapy too?"

"The ceiling in there doesn't look all that different from this one."

"Then turn on your side as often as you can." I was disgusted by the man. It was sad to see someone who resembled Sean so much showing so little of his quality. "I'm going to find Sean now. Good-bye."

"Solace!"

"What?" sharply.

"Come back soon. Okay?"

"I don't think so." I walked out into the hall.

I saw Sean walking back to the room with the girls. I didn't have the heart to tell him how unpleasant my experience with Tim had been. I smiled and waved, and when they got close enough I told them that I was going to the washroom. I took my time, and stayed in the background for the rest of the brief visit. Tim had the decency to say he was tired and needed a nap if he was going to make it through the party in the afternoon. The girls kissed him and wished him sweet dreams, but I don't think Sean believed him. He knew his brother better than we knew each other, and as we walked to the car, he put his arm around me and thanked me.

"You were wrong, Sean." Before he could ask what I meant, I added, "I would like to meet the entire rest of your family before I see *him* again."

He nodded, slowing his steps. "That long?"

"At least."

With Irina and her friends supposedly bedded down for the night in the bedroom, Maureen and I opened out the sofa where we would sleep. Sean, at loose ends, wandered around the lounge, grumbling, "I'm a prisoner in my own home."

"You've always wanted to say that, haven't you?" I asked, flinging a sheet open over the sofa bed.

"Not really." He sat on the mattress. "Especially not when it's true."

"Hey, Dad," Maureen began fussing at him. "You're in the way."

He stood up again and looked around for another place to plop his bottom.

"Sean, you are not a prisoner. You can leave. I can handle this sleeping crowd," I said. "If you aren't ready to settle down for the night, go down to O'Brien's and listen to some music."

"They are not asleep," he said in a spooky voice. "And I can't leave. I am the parent. This is my home. I must remain."

I shrugged. He was right. "Could you hand me that blanket?"

"What blanket?" he asked.

"The one you're sitting on, Dad," Maureen said as she tried to pull it out from under him. "You really ought to go to bed, Dad," she admonished in a softer tone.

He tilted to one side in his chair, and pulled the blanket from beneath him. When he handed it to her, he said, "I'm getting the feeling you don't want me around."

"Sorry," she said, and kissed him as she took the blanket.

"I know it is more socially acceptable to be a single mother," he began. "No one ever objects to sons sleeping over when the only parent home is a female."

"It's just what people are used to," I said.

"And men are more likely to be accused of something improper."

"You need to be more careful," I agreed.

We looked up to see Irina and a few of her friends, dressed for sleep but looking wide awake, dawdling at the end of the hall. They fled, trailing giggles.

"I wonder what they want. I've never seen girls eat so much," Sean said. They had devoured all of the food and drink we had laid in, except what Sean had hidden away for breakfast. Thinking that we had stocked up generously, Sean and I were astounded by the quantities these little girls had consumed. Maureen was disgusted by it.

"They're growing," I suggested.

"Sideways," grumbled Maureen. "Come on, now, Dad. You need to go to bed."

"Alright, I'm going. Good night, ladies." He kissed us both and started down the hall. He still looked sad, so I left Maureen to finish making the bed.

"Sean?" I whispered as I tapped his shoulder. "What's the matter?"

"Nothing really, Solace," he said mournfully.

"It's Irina's birthday, Sean. Be happy. Forget everything else, at least until Tuesday. You've always told me that you consider her birth to be a miracle. Please remember that."

He screwed up his face, thinking. "I usually make it along fine while the party lasts."

"The party is still going."

He was quiet for a little while. "How many years are they going to want to do this sleeping together thing?"

"Until they want to start sleeping with boys."

"Oh no," he corrected me. "I happen to know there is an overlap. At least for some girls."

"Oh? Well, most of my friends didn't want to sleep on floors any more after they went away to college."

"That's a long time." He paused. "I do remember that—as a kid—it was fun. We used to camp out together in the back yard, Rob and some other boys from the neighborhood."

"Just the boys?"

"Yes. When we were older, we'd really go camping, you know, away from home. That was partly to keep the girls away." He laughed, and then slapped his hand over his mouth to suppress the noise. With his eyes shifting guiltily to make sure none of his young charges were within earshot, he whispered, "When we wanted to be with the girls, we wanted to be alone with them."

I rose on my tiptoes and gently kissed his cheek. "You have so many good memories. As brief as your time was, it was happy."

"You're right, Solace. Thanks. You have lived up to your name, once again. On Thursday, I'll spend a little special time at Megan's grave. I have this gardening tradition, on that day. Then I'll take the girls down with me after school to plant something special for her too."

"You can plant things at her grave? How nice."

"It's an old cemetery. They don't do much to maintain the graves, so we can fix it however we want. I have kept Megan's covered with wildflowers. It suits her, because she was a bit of a wildflower. It's very pretty. I'll take you some other time."

Quietly, I said, "I won't expect to see you, but if you need to talk or anything, just let me know, okay?"

He nodded. "Okay."

"I should go back to Maureen."

I felt awkward, but not because we were talking about Megan; I was already getting used to that. There were times, like this one, when his memories of her were more important than what we were doing in the present, but he never excluded me or made me feel that I could not grow to understand how he felt. I wondered how other women he had dated had felt about her lingering presence. It could have been daunting, I suppose, for some of them, yet I never found it to be so. Perhaps it was because it had taken my knowing about her to accept him as my friend. Perhaps she, not her father or her daughters, was the matchmaker who had brought us together. Perhaps I just hoped that if I were her that I would be remembered the way he remembered her, not as a threat or source of competition to the next great love of his life. He had already told me that she had loved him enough to tell him she hoped he would find happiness with another woman after she had gone. I knew by instinct that in life and death I could get along with Megan Reilly Donovan.

"I won't be mourning all day on Thursday," he said. I looked up, reminded of his living presence. "I'm not canceling lessons. You can come over for the evening, if you want."

"Why don't we see how we feel later? I might let you and the girls have a night off from me, and go out with friends, or something."

"Well, stay out of trouble," he said laughing. "I get the point, though. You need a night off from me."

"Sometimes. But you are pretty good about giving me space." I smiled.

"Well, should you decide to hang out with Peter, be sure to bring along some you-know-whats. I'll get some for your handbag," he said turning toward his bedroom.

I grabbed his arm. "Don't be silly, Sean. Peter always has plenty."

He whispered, "I trust you," into my ear.

"I know."

I was assigned to keep Irina busy on Monday while Sean and Maureen got everything ready for the family party. Irina and I were the last to arrive. Her enthusiasm served its purpose; I was so ready to share her attentions that I wasn't shy about meeting Sean's parents and two youngest brothers. George was a quiet and grey, balding man. He was scrappy and looked small next to his sons. Olga was gracious, and I could tell from Sean's expression when he saw us getting along that her apparent affection for me was genuine. The kids played loudly together, giving us more time to talk than I would have wished for going into the evening. Before I thought it possible they were refusing Sean's offer to drive them home, saying the bus was easier.

I chose to hang out with Bridget that Thursday evening, something we girls had rarely managed to do. We met in a bar after work. Basking in the irresponsibility of it all, she swirled the wine in her glass, daring it to slosh over to the top, but maintaining control over its motion. "Drink up, cousin. I can't play darts with you if you are sober and I'm all fuddled."

I took a sip of my beer. "That might even the odds. You know I can't hit the target even dead sober." I picked up a piece of toast and began to spread bruschetta on it. "You'll have to slow down, Mrs. Murphy."

"Now you've ruined my chances of getting picked up by one of those lily-white hunks," she said with a disdainful nod toward the bar where some English tourists were shouting at the television.

"I doubt they care if you are Mrs., Miss, or Sister Purity."

"I wish they'd make them have a thorough physical examination before they let them onto our island," she said with a sour look on her face. Bringing her eyes back to our table, she began to fidget with a piece of toast before she finally picked it up and nibbled at it. I reminded her that she usually voted for the pro-tourism Liberal Party. Instead of responding, she put a miniscule amount of the bruschetta onto the rest of her toast and smiled at her first nibble. "I hate it that I have to raise my child in this global community. There are just so many problems in the world."

"It's frightening, but what can we do? Once Pandora opened the box...."

"You know, Solace, that is strangely comforting," she said. "Even the ancients had some of the same worries we have. They survived them, and we're still here. Most of us manage to stay safe." She loaded another piece of toast so heavily that, soaked by the sauce, it fell apart and dropped onto her plate. She used her fork to get all the tidbits to her mouth. "So, have you posed for Sean?"

I shook my head.

"Don't you want to?"

"I might do it if he asked, but he hasn't asked."

"These boys of ours," she began dreamily. "Some people feel sorry for me, you know, because they think Rob doesn't take care of me. But he does, you know. He takes care of both of us. I don't mind being the one who goes out and gets the regular paycheck. I like my job, and I love my family. I probably love them more because I get to be away from them for ten hours a day."

"And is Rob happy being at home?" I asked.

She nodded and drained her wine glass. The server appeared instantaneously; Bridget just pointed straight down into the glass. He whisked it away and disappeared. "It works well for him. He's writing more than ever. He's content."

"Is he too content?"

She avoided answering my question directly. I suppose I shouldn't have asked it; some thoughts are best left unstated. She made a fuss over spreading some more bruschetta on a piece of toast, and looked up with a smile when her wine arrived. "His ambitions center on writing, not performing. If acting was his goal, I'd encourage him to move to London or New York, but I don't see why he can't write from here. He can always visit those places to promote his work, if he needs to, but there are so many reasons to stay here."

I agreed.

Chapter Twelve

The girls were in their room doing their homework. I was trying to do mine in the lounge, but it was ever so much easier to focus my attention on Sean as he moved around the room with graceful ease doing some light housework than on the textbook in my lap. I set the book on the coffee table, my elbows on my knees and my chin propped by my fists.

"Don't let me distract you," he said dusting his metronome.

"I'd have to leave, and then I'd distract myself," I responded.

"Which behavior should I encourage, Solace? Good studying or good relations?"

"I'll study later, at home, alone, when I'm tired enough to sit still for it."

Partly to hide his amusement, he stepped outside and shook his dust rag. "You'll manage to stay awake, then?" he asked when he came back inside.

"I might. You might have to join me, to prod me to stay awake while I read."

"I thought you needed to be alone."

"I'll pose for you. You draw; I'll read. How about that?"

"I don't need you to pose for me. I can remember every frigging inch of your body well enough, but I wouldn't want to draw when I can look at or touch the real Solace. I'd want to do other things."

I patted the seat of the sofa next to me. He accepted my invitation and slid his body against mine like a heat seeking cat. We kissed for a long time, and then we chatted for a while about us, the house, the girls, and more about us. When we started kissing more intensely, we needed more space, so we moved to the floor between the couch and the table. He peaked into my shirt quickly, laughing as if it were a forbidden joke. I imitated him just for fun.

"Do you want to go to my room?" he asked, but I could tell he didn't care.

"Nah," I said lazily. "Probably should."

"You're just hoping the girls will catch us doing something."

"That's right. I'm an exhibitionist, you know."

"Now, that doesn't surprise me. I hear you offered to pose for an erotic painting," he teased.

"I did? Oh, yeah, well, if you put it that way."

"Just trying to start a scandalous rumor."

"Like the one about me having sex with every guy in Mike's unit?"

"Except Leah himself."

"Details," I chided.

"I never believed it." He walked his fingers up my arm with a pleasurable amount of pressure.

"No? Then why did you ask me about it?"

He blushed. "I thought you might have done more than you did. You were rather lost for a while there. I hope you feel better about yourself inside now. You seem to, but you were always such a good actress. I used to think that you were doing fine sometimes, and then I'd realize you were still having trouble. It would be some little thing that someone would say. You know, someone you would let talk to you. It is so hard for me to believe you have been a victim of abuse, and yet it is your history."

"I can't either. I feel gutsy, sometimes."

"And you are. You don't let your fears paralyze you."

"Nope. Just take 'em with me wherever I go. Keep them in my purse when I'm not using them."

He laughed. "Are they friendly?"

"Some of them are. I can inflate them and use them as a life preserver if I fall in the river when you aren't around."

"You'll never fall in, Solace. You won't get close enough to the edge."

"I might stand there, mesmerized, and drop in face first."

"You get distracted too easily." He snuggled down against me again, with his head on my shoulder and breast, cocked so that he could see my face. His arm went around me. I combed his hair with my fingers, content, and I felt him relax. "I'm never moving again," he whispered.

"For a few minutes anyhow."

"I don't worry about you that way anymore, Solace," he said. "I know now that you love life more than you fear death."

"And you, Sean?"

"I love life, but I don't fear death so much. It's dying that scares me. Once I'm dead, I'll be fine."

"You have your reward in the afterlife."

"I hope you'll join me there."

"None too soon, I hope," I said, becoming uneasy.

"Time doesn't exist in Heaven, my dear. We shall all arrive there together, with all our own memories to share with one another."

"Megan will be there."

"Yes," he said with a nod and a little smile. "It won't matter in Heaven, Solace. Don't worry about eternal jealousy. God would not permit it. He has a plan. For thousands of years, there have been people like us who are starting over with new partners. Do you think you'll have to hang out with your ex-husband just because he was first?"

"I guess I never figured he'd be in Heaven, but then again, I could go to Hell and have to be with him and Rosie for all eternity." It was a twist that I couldn't believe.

"Oh, no, Solace. That won't happen. You will be in Heaven with me. Megan's there, so I have to go there too, and if I'm there then you have to come along. I won't be parted from either of you in the next life. I love you too much to spend eternity without you. Believe with me. Have faith. Trust in God. That is all He really asks of you." He craned his neck to kiss me.

"That's the hardest thing to do."

"But you do it every day, though your mind may deny it."

From the time Sean and I first met, we had been pulled by a powerful attraction. It had made him speak too early, before I knew his situation. It had made my rejection of him more painful, for both of us, than it should have been given our perceived circumstances. My views toward him had softened through the contact we had had over the silent times. Yet I know that my heart was warmed to him by knowing his daughters and getting to know him through them. The facts made a difference, yes, but the insight I gained through them helped me to open my eyes to the kind interior of the man. We grew together quickly. All four of us did. Sometimes it was complicated. Often we lacked privacy. We broke many parenting rules. Sean said it was fair for us to break half of them since my half of our couple was not a parent. At least the girls were old enough to understand when we explained that there were things a thirty-year-old can do because she has the maturity to handle the consequences that a fourteen-year-old should definitely not even consider. I certainly felt more mature than I ever had before, or maybe it was that I didn't feel the constant need to justify my thoughts and actions. Our homes and our lives blended together, sometimes so smoothly that I didn't always catch on until some massive change had become the new normal for us. Though Sean was, as expected, better at setting boundaries and answering all of those questions that began with 'why,' the girls accepted my reasoning well.

I soon learned about living in an extensive family. Though the various siblings and cousins did not often plan social events, we did encounter them frequently in the course of our daily life. I had always liked my anonymity; at first the constant requirement to be socially adept was a strain. As I adjusted, I learned to fall back on my natural, quiet friendliness. I found that most people appreciated a listener, and because I listened, they were more inclined to return the courtesy when I had something to say.

I always felt a little guilty when Sean found something for the girls to do in order for us to be alone. As a single parent and former weekend Marine, he had routinely shipped the girls away to various family members for a night or a weekend. No one in the family wanted to end these arrangements just because he was around more often now and the girls were old enough to stay home by themselves. They didn't ask him to reciprocate either. "Some of them think they owe me because I visit Tim and they don't. Others are just waiting until payback is really inconvenient, but at least they aren't asking for discounted piano lessons."

The first whole weekend that we had came in September when their aunt Cara invited her sister Grace to bring the girls with her to Hibernia Beach. We saw them off at the bus station on Friday afternoon. Because Sean's send-off included a good number of warnings, I couldn't help asking, "Aren't their aunts responsible?"

"Not really," he said with no sign of worry. "They won't do anything terrible."

He had told me that Megan had gotten into some things she didn't know how to handle as a teen, and I couldn't help wondering if her sisters had had some of the same problems. Megan had attended a teen mentoring program at St. Anne's Anglican Church, the church Sean still attended, but as far as Sean knew neither of her sisters had ever looked for professional guidance.

"You didn't let them go just so you could be alone with me, did you?"

"No." He shook his head. "No. I'd have let them go anyway. They love to play with the big girls. Besides they put their aunts on their best behavior."

We joked that we would spend the whole weekend in bed, but though we did spend a good deal of it indoors and unclad, we made it to the beach and to a restaurant both nights for dinner. On Saturday night, we met Mike and some of his Marine mates at a nightclub to hear the most recent incarnation of the Punk Monks, Sean's band from his university years. Their name was now Solar Flair. Around our table there was unanimous agreement that they had noticeably improved after Sean stopped playing with them.

Mike showed more interest in what the girls were doing than I expected until I remembered that he had seen Cara Reilly for the first time in years not that long ago. "Will you sail your boat around the island to visit her sometime?"

"My boat? Not bloody likely. It'd be a hell of a trip. If I were going there, I'd take the bus or the ferry. Why do you think I'd go see Cara anyway? I barely know her."

"She went out on your boat."

From behind his pint glass, he said, "So?" His eagerness to deny interest answered the question I hadn't asked.

"Oh, don't tell me she's too pretty."

With a nod, "Alright then."

"Right. Forgot. That can be a problem."

Late on Sunday morning, Sean and I were cuddled together in my bed. This was the second time that we had been able to spend the whole night together in my room, the first being the preceding night. I liked waking up next to Sean.

"You want to cook your own birthday dinner?" Sean looked surprised, but pleased. "Would you like to have your birthday party at my house?"

"Really? No. I want it at my place." My blood had adjusted to the tropics. The room seemed chill. "Can I borrow your table?" I rolled over on my side and ran my fingers through the hair on his chest. It was nearly the same color as his skin. Sean was made up of the colors of the beach, hair and skin like sand, eyes like the sky.

"Anything you want. What I have is yours." He moved my hand to a particularly sensitive part of his body.

"I've always thought you were a bit too generous."

"There are even days when I would give you my children."

"There are days when you *do* give me your children."

"Don't you want us to treat you for your big day?"

"Maybe. I'll have my party on the weekend so that everyone can come," I replied. With more energy, I explained my idea. "Sean, this is something I've meant to do for a long time now, and my birthday just gives me a good excuse to do it. I'd like to have all of my best friends together at one time. Plus, I promised the girls a long time ago that I'd feed y'all my hometown cuisine. That's how I want to celebrate."

"It sounds terrific, Solace," he said. He moved his hand up from my thigh to my bosom. "I'll be glad to provide a table or chairs or whatever you require." He kissed me. "I'm sure," again, "it will be," and again, "delicious."

"And you're still enjoying motherhood?" Mike asked, chuckling. He was treating me to lunch in honor of my up-coming birthday. He leaned back in his chair, studying my face as he lifted his glass and took a long drink. I picked through my potatoes to find the crispest ones. I was getting full and didn't want to waste the calories or the remaining space in my stomach on them if they were soft or soggy. "Don't like your chips? Was my question a tough one?"

I took a mouthful of warm, spicy applesauce. It was worth finishing. "You're right, Mike. It isn't an easy question. I can tell you things were simpler when we were just friends. I enjoy the girls. I like playing house with them. You know, baking and shopping, that kind of thing. I'm even pretty good about helping them with their homework. But our relationship keeps advancing." I shrugged, trying to think of a way to explain. "Sean calls it the Mother Courtship."

"I think you like it." He reached over to my plate and took a handful of potatoes. He ate them. I said nothing. Leaning back, he continued more energetically. "Yeah, Solace, you fucking like it."

I had to laugh. "Yes, sir, Mike. I fucking like it."

"You need to develop your cursing style, Solace. Use more finesse."

"I've improved a lot, Mike. Remember when we first met? I never ever used such language."

He dipped his bread in his vinegar. I cringed. He was very hungry today, but he always had an appetite. Mike was a skinny guy, sinewy and toughening with age and too much sun, and he burned off every calorie he consumed.

"I'm glad that I've been getting to know Sean better again. He's always been around, but we never did much together. Other than the Marines, we didn't have anything in common." He paused and played with the empty vinegar cup, looking into it sadly. "I get pissed at myself sometimes when I see what he's been able to do with the odds against him like they were. I had all the resources that he didn't have, except character and drive. Hell, he's got a master's degree and I'm practically illiterate. He's got two kids that are turning out well. He lost his livelihood, but then he found a second calling, and he's like a better painter than piano player, so it didn't really hurt him."

"Yeah, Mike," I said, patting his hand. "Sean's alright. He's made do. He hates to admit it when he can't hear something. And he really hates to admit how much he misses teaching school."

"You mean he really wanted to be a teacher?" He made the kind of face I would have made had I eaten food dipped in vinegar. "I always thought that that's what he did to make steady money for his kids." He shook his head in quiet amazement. "I guess it's been harder on him than I thought."

"He won't allow himself to flounder."

"There's nothing like necessity," he mused. "I've never needed to look after anyone but myself, and I barely do that."

"But you do take care of yourself?"

He shrugged. "Are you self-sufficient, Solace?"

"Yes." I chose to overlook grey areas, such as gifts, advice, and favors.

He pushed his plate away, and looked up at the paraphernalia on the walls of the dining room. "I'm the last child. All my friends have grown up. They have careers and dreams, education and partners, even kids." He wiped the condensation off the side of his glass, and then rubbed his fingers on the paper napkin so hard that it ripped. "Somehow, I just can't make myself do the things everyone else does, though I see they are happier than I am."

"I know how it is, Mike," I began, leaning forward over the edge of the table so that I could speak to him more privately. "I've been frozen, trying to figure out what I should do. But sometimes, Mike, sometimes you just have to do something, any action you choose, because not choosing is a choice to have others choose for you, and not acting is still an action. The world goes on, and you could be left behind."

Pale and doubtful, he looked up at me.

"You have done a lot already, Bro. Your job is good. You did that. Be proud."

I had been honest with Sean about my first meeting with Tim. He was sympathetic, but he hoped that we could improve our relations so he invited me to go with him occasionally. For Sean, I accepted some of his invitations. Though Tim never repeated his ugly behavior, I still didn't care to be around him, mostly because, among other things, he played on Sean's survivor guilt.

One day I had the inexplicable urge to confront him. I took the bus from work to Little Russia and went to his nursing home. I found his room, but stopped outside, regretting the impulse that had brought me there. I nearly turned to leave by the nearest exit, but before I could someone spoke to me, and Tim heard my reply.

"Solace?" he called. "Are you coming to see me?" His voice sounded cheerful, very much like Sean's yet lacking the musical quality.

I squared my shoulders, swallowed hard, and then meekly poked my head through the doorway. "Tim? Hey, yeah."

"Is Sean with you or did you pluck up to see me on your own? I'll try to be nice today."

"Good." I found a chair. "I came by myself."

"That was brave. I have *so* wished you would come alone." So far, he wasn't behaving much better than the last time we spoke alone.

"I don't need to hang out with creeps, Tim Donovan."

"You sure?" When I stood in response, ready to leave, he reached out his hand. I wasn't close enough for him to touch me, but I stopped to give him a second chance. "You know I have to make sure. You've got that history. I have to make sure you're good enough for Sean."

"While that would be a noble rationale, it has nothing to do with why you say such nasty things. I don't even think your bitterness over being sick so long is the reason. I think you like to irritate people."

He laughed. "And you rile so easily." He pointed to the chair. "Please stay, Solace."

"Only if you remain civil."

"That's fair." He scooted up so that he could sit when he raised the back of the bed. "Sean helps me get to a chair. I won't ask you to do that. It's the best part of my day."

"I know you're bored. Can't you do anything?"

"Out of my mind. And out of my manners too, I guess, though I never picked up my mother's teaching like the other kids did."

"I guess there's got to be an odd one in every family."

"Are you it in yours? Oh, yeah, I can see it. Only you're quiet and smart, and I'm loud and stupid."

"But aren't you stupid by choice?"

He didn't say anything for a long time. I hoped I could come up with more conversation stopping conversation when I had a reason to speak again. Meanwhile I was content to examine my fingernails.

"What would you have me do?" he asked.

"What can you do?"

"What do you mean?"

"You are here in this facility. You have time, but not necessarily resources. Can you read? Can you draw? Write? Carve wood? Sew?"

"You mean what am I capable of physically?"

"And mentally."

"I've never liked doing those things."

"What did you like to do?"

"Hang out."

"And?"

"I don't know."

"What do you miss?"

"Everything, Solace. I miss being able to move around. I wish I could eat a good meal and wash it down with a pint. I'd like to go outdoors. I did like being outside. I liked working out in the sunshine, helping my dad in the garden, and volleyball on the beach."

"Are you allowed to go out of doors here? I thought there was a garden."

"I guess."

"Do you want to go outside now?" I started to get up. His response was a grunt. I left to ask the nurse, and returned telling him that he had permission. "She said you could walk there. Where's your walker?"

"Oh?" He looked bemused. He pushed himself up, though, and slid his feet off the top of the bed. "Thanks, Solace."

"You're welcome. Don't Sean and Tanya take you out?"

"Never wanted to go."

He moved slowly. I walked ahead, then waited every few feet. He was nearly exhausted by the time we got to the nearest bench, and I had to help him lower himself because that took more effort than standing. He didn't feel like talking either. I thought I may have provoked him enough for one day, so I didn't talk to him either. After about half an hour, I asked him if he was ready to walk back inside, because I thought I should start toward home. He only shrugged, so I went to ask the nurse about taking him back inside. She said she would see him in, and I went back to him to tell him and say good-bye.

"This was better than I expected, Solace," he said softly. "Will you come again?"

"Maybe."

Chapter Thirteen

My party was on the Saturday before my birthday. I spent my whole day preparing for a Chesapeake-style crab feast. In the morning, Sean brought sawhorses and plywood from his house and helped me to set them up as a table. Soon after, I went to the fish market to buy several kilos of shrimp and live crabs. I would steam the local shellfish in the spices I'd had sent from D.C. Cindy arrived at lunchtime, and after we ate we began to prepare everything together. I mixed coleslaw and two cornbread batters, one for the hush puppies, the other to coat the onion rings, while she sliced onions and potatoes. I set out wooden mallets and picks. "Do you think it's too early to put out the cocktail sauce?"

"No," she said. There was a knock at the door. "That's probably the cake, eh, Solace. I'll answer it." Sure enough, the hospitality muses entered. Irina bubbled. Maureen carried the cake in a paper grocery sack on its side. As Cindy followed Maureen into the kitchen, I heard her say, "You girls gonna start a bakery, eh, one of these days?"

"You can't look, Solace," Irina told me. She began to inspect the table with its newspaper covering. "Wouldn't it be better to leave the table bare, since you don't have the right sized tablecloth?"

"This is how you eat crabs and shrimp, Irina," I explained. "It's very messy. When we're done, we just roll up the paper and throw it in the trash. Have you never eaten them from the shell before?"

"Don't we need silver?"

"Forks! I forgot the forks. Thank you." I started toward the kitchen. Maureen handed a box of plastic forks to me over the divider and asked if I needed plates. I pointed at the stack of paper plates on the table.

"I'll help with the dishes tonight," Irina offered.

"That's very generous," said Cindy. "The pots will be a mess. I'll be glad to have your help." Irina made a face. It was obvious that she disapproved of the meal already.

"Do you want to see the crabs?" I asked. "They're still alive."

"Would you like help steaming them, Solace?" Maureen asked. "I've helped my granny with it before. Sometimes they try to crawl away."

"I'm ready to leave," Irina announced.

"Go on back then, Rina," Maureen instructed. "Make sure that Dad dresses nicely, heh. He was looking at some strange colors when we left. I don't want him to spoil our appetites." Irina opened the door, and Maureen shouted one last instruction. "Bring the camera!" The door slammed.

Cindy and Maureen were lifesavers. With so much last minute cooking, it was a huge help to have competent, calm hands and heads working in my kitchen. Just as I started to get nervous about pulling it all together, they set to work and the moment passed. It wasn't long before Irina returned, barging in without knocking, hollering, "Miss Murphy, your boyfriend is at the door."

I poked my head over the divider and smiled. He smiled back and blew a kiss. He had something hidden behind his back, so I dried my hands, removed my apron, and went to greet him. He took me in a big hug and swung me backwards gracefully to give me a kiss, while bringing his free arm around in a smooth arc to present a bouquet of flowers. When our kiss ended, he lifted me and presented the flowers. "From our garden."

"Thank you, Sean. They are beautiful."

"I'll vase them for you," he said. He stepped out of the door again and bent to pick up a tall glass pitcher. "Where would you like me to put them?"

"On top of the TV," I called over my shoulder as I returned to the kitchen.

He followed me in a few moments later, and began poking around the sorted ingredients. "Need help?" he asked with such an air of incompetence that Cindy practically chased him out of the room. I had been in the kitchen too long already, and wouldn't have minded if Cindy had banished me.

Sean stood in the living room looking at the pillows I had tossed around the floor. I went up to him and wrapped an arm around his waist. Silently, he mirrored me. I leaned my head against his upper arm. "I like the pillows," he whispered.

"I needed something like furniture for my guests to lean upon after they eat and drink too much. Irina can use the chair."

He laughed. "She told me about the table with a rather sour look on her face." Over our shoulders we saw her placing a dish on the table, then walking around it, slowly examining it and shaking her head. "I guess I've raised a snob."

Mike came in through the open front door, toting a case of beer because he thought mine would be too cold for the average Carollonian. Karen and Steve were right behind him, and helped him distribute drinks. Melissa rode with the Murphys, who were predictably the last to arrive, and she helped them haul up the equipment they needed to take Patrick out for an evening before strapping on her apron to help Cindy.

"Flowers, Sean?" Mike remarked.

"Roses!" Rob screeched. "Are you feeling alright, Mate?" Rob and Mike teased him and bumped him around roughly the way men do to turn such a conversation into a sporting activity.

"I saw Rosie," said Bridget. The room silenced. "You know we are doing a lot of the computer work for the dam project? Well, we had a presentation up at his company offices, and he was there. He looked awful. It was quite scary to see him again. He kept looking at me. I guess he's really lonely."

"As he should be," Cindy said vigorously. "I hope you reacted appropriately."

"Gave him the bird at the very least," urged Mike.

"I looked away. I didn't want to make eye contact. But I felt sorry for him. No one talked to him, not even the people with his company." Bridget looked sad.

There was a stubborn silence until Sean smacked a kiss on my cheek. Then I took a deep, delayed breath and said, "I knew that he was still here. Life goes on, thank God. And I like the flowers."

My friends began to move and make noise again. Cindy asked for help to get the food to the table, and everyone except Bridget, who was settling the baby, volunteered. Maureen and I steamed the crabs without incident, and while they were still trying to get away from the heat, I began the first batch of shrimp. When all the little critters had turned red, Cindy waved us on to the table while she and Irina turned a big batch of fried potatoes out into a paper lined bowl.

Sean remained behind with me after everyone else went home. He whispered in my ear. "Can you stay with me tonight?" We lay on the floor, propped against some pillows. I smiled at Sean's suggestion. While rising seemed beyond my ability, I only needed to scoot over a little to reach him. I traced the side of his face with a finger following a row of tiny scars that ran from his temple to his jaw. Normally they were barely visible, but in this light, this close, with his skin pale from fatigue, they stood out.

We leaned in to kiss, and he wrapped his arms around me, pulling me to him. I would be one body with him if it were possible. That is the reason we have sex: to be physically one, even for just a moment. I wrapped a leg around him. He rolled us both over, flattening me underneath him.

"Can't let you take over yet, Solace," he said. "I want to make this last a while."

"I'm not in a hurry, Sean."

He uncovered my belly and delicately nibbled at it. "Having a happy birthday?"

I stretched lazily and reached out to comb his wavy hair with my fingers. Not really meaning to speak aloud, I whispered, "Sometimes I wish that I had known you when you were younger, and sometimes I think it is probably good that I didn't. It sounds like you were very interesting."

"What? When I dyed my hair blue and spiked it?"

Shaking my head, I remarked, "I never thought I'd date a punker."

"My best friend was an actor." He shrugged as if that explained everything. "I didn't do anything harmful. No permanent damage."

"No." I studied his face, his hair, his body. "You seem rather a perfect container for this really nice man I met."

He blushed. "I have to try to live up to being your partner, Solace."

"I think it's the other way around."

He kissed me. "I have a little present for you tonight. And don't worry. I've got more for the big day."

We continued kissing while we thumped and bumped our way from my unit to his. It was late enough that we didn't worry about embarrassing encounters, but we kept our clothing intact until we fell on top of his bed. He kissed and nibbled the underside of my arm down to my wrist, then lifted his lips away to whisper, "I've got to lock the door."

While he was out of the room I rolled across the bed to the nightstand and opened the drawer to get a condom. I couldn't feel the box, so I switched on the light and found it under a framed photo that had been placed upside down in the drawer. "So that's where she went," I exclaimed as I turned the frame over and saw Megan's face. "Why did you put her away?"

He came around to sit on the bed beside me, took the photo from me. His head was bent, but he was gazing off into space. I touched his arm. "Why was Megan's photo in the drawer, Sean? I don't mind her. She's part of you."

He turned his gaze to me and quietly said, "I thought it was time for me to ease away from her."

Shaking my head, I took the photo from where it lay in his lap. As much as I had meant what I said, I also liked his idea of adding some distance, so I rose, walked to his dresser, and stood it there. "If I thought it was painful for you to be reminded of her, then I might feel differently, but I know that you like to see her. I like seeing her. It isn't morbid. She helped make you into the man that I love."

His eyes smiled, while the rest of his face remained neutral. "I like that spot, Solace. I can still see it there, but it's less intimate." He relaxed as I crawled onto the bed from the other side and ran my hands over his bosom. "I feel her presence sometimes, like a whisper saying, 'do this or that thing to make Solace happy'."

I faked a Carollonian accent and said, "Solace wants to get laid."

He laughed. Shaking his head, he said, "That was almost eerie, Solace."

I waved a condom in front of his face. "Let's get naked and play."

"You two do have much in common, but you are also very different."

"It makes sense you would find the same attributes attractive in different women."

"You are like molasses; Megan was rum." He lifted his hands to caress my embracing arms, concluding, "Strong in different ways."

"I'm not intoxicating?" I asked, wishing I were the rum, but knowing he had it the right way around.

"Oh! You are very intoxicating."

I waved the little square packet in front of him again. He snatched at it with his fingers a few times before he got it from me. I ran my hand down his thigh, and he stroked my hair. "Now, I've got to get your gift." Backing away so that he could watch me, he added, "You undress while I find it."

"I wanted you to undress me," I pouted.

He assessed my clothing. "I, um." Hating to admit his lack of confidence with women's garments, he continued backing away until he reached the closet, watching me unbutton my shirt. I threw it across the room and flung my bra at his head. He never took his eyes from me, even as he felt around in his closet for my gift. As I dropped my skirt, he returned holding the box in front of him.

The store's name, Lacy's, was embossed on the top of the bone white box, which was embellished with only a pink, lace ribbon tied in a pretty bow. I smiled and took it from him. I slid the ribbons off to the side so that I would not destroy the bow before I lifted the lid. Inside folds of pale lavender silk and lace were neatly arranged. I hesitated to mar the presentation. I could feel his impatience, however, and I raked my fingers inside. I held the soft silk against my cheek before I looked at the nightgown made from it. Beneath was lavender robe of a heavier, more practical fabric and styling. It was one I could wear for breakfast with the girls. "It's beautiful, Sean. Thank you." I stood up and kissed him.

"You can try it on in the morning," he said. "I'm afraid I don't want to risk having you put it on now, in case you won't take it off."

I wrapped my arms around his neck again and our mouths came together. We kissed, and lowered ourselves to the bed. All of our business, save one most important project, was completed. When we were done, I cried, "I want to throw a glass, Sean!"

"Now?"

"Da!"

"Okay. I'll get you a cup of water. A paper cup."

"You must be feeling Irish tonight," I said.

"I am. I'm famished." He grabbed my arm and put his lips around my wrist. I giggled and wiped his saliva on the sheets. "I'll just get your water now," he said, rolling off the bed. "You look pooped. Guess you'll sleep well tonight."

I drank all the water in the cup, then let it roll from my fingers to the floor. "Don't wake me in the morning. I was on my feet too much today. I want to be horizontal for a long while."

He pulled up the covers and wrapped himself around me, kissing first my neck and my ear before coming to rest with his chin on the top of my head. His hands touched my thighs, and some tiny, distant part of me that thought I could move reacted and wanted to begin our lovemaking anew. His hand settled onto my belly, warming me through, and we slept like this all that night.

My plan to sleep straight through the last church service did not come to fruition. I awoke early, around five o'clock, and slipped from Sean's arms without waking him. He could sleep so soundly that I often wondered how safe his small children had been living with him as the only adult in the household. It was a selective skill, he had told me, acquired in childhood by sharing a room with his brothers, improved upon while in the Marines, and finally perfected with his hearing loss.

I showered and slipped back into the bed next to him wearing my new silk negligee. Now that I had freshened, I could smell the night and the beer on Sean. He was still attractive, but I much preferred his usual mix of soap, Big Bob's Burn Blocker, and manliness. He stirred when I slipped between the sheets, and he woke when he realized that I had moved. Shy now, knowing he had not brushed his teeth since before a highly spiced dinner, he just rubbed his nose on my earlobe and stroked my side through the sheet. I settled deeper into my pillow. "You probably taste good again," he mumbled, trying to sound sleepy. "Think I'll bath too."

I dozed until he slid under the covers on the other side of the bed. He pulled up close to me, and we talked quietly about what we might do with our day as the sky brightened. It was special for us to have such a peaceful time together alone, and we were slow to let go of it even as we heard the girls stirring. Gradually their voices gained volume. "Another day begins in the Donovan household," Sean announced. "Suppose we ought to rise and shine too?"

"Yes," I answered. Neither of us moved.

"Do you want to go to church today?"

"No."

"Would you like to go to the beach?"

"Yeah," I said stretching. "Going to the beach is almost as good as sleeping."

"You don't seem sleepy."

"Last night might catch up with me later."

Maureen knocked on the door and softly called, "Dad?" Then, as the door opened, Irina asked if they could enter.

"Reality sees itself in," Sean whispered, before he called out a cheerful greeting to his daughters. "Good morning, darlings! How are you this day?"

"Good morning, Dad." They entered, each carrying a breakfast tray. "Oh, good morning, Solace," Maureen added, pretending to be surprised.

"You're up early," Irina began, adding misery to Maureen's embarrassment, "to be here already."

"I gave her an early wake up call," Sean said. "So she could join us for breakfast." No one mentioned that they had already prepared breakfast for four. After their second trip to the kitchen, they climbed up onto the bed too, fully dressed, and began munching and chatting as if we were at tea in the dining room. Sean and I exchanged a glance that somehow acknowledged the nuances of the situation. It was certainly not a scene I could have imagined when I moved into my apartment six months earlier.

Before I went home, Sean led me into the spare room to show me his progress on the reef painting. To my surprise and pleasure, he had begun a new painting. Though it was still in a crude state, it was more complete than the first, which he had cast haphazardly into a corner. His long silent muse was now singing like a siren, and the new work immediately captured my attention and imagination.

With the reef in the distant background, a mermaid created the focus the other piece had been missing. As in the sketch, she was created in my image, but this time she was free and strong. The painting showed her saving a man, protecting him within a magical sphere of oxygen and love. There was no way of knowing how or why the man had entered her world, but his face, Sean's face shown in profile, gazed at her in wonder, lit by the aura which made her clearly visible, though there was no source of light. With hands clasped and his arm encircling her waist, they rose toward the surface in an aquatic waltz. Sure as the truth of nature that forbade his lingering in the depths with her, she would see that this memory would be exiled from his waking thoughts so that he would embrace his life above and not attempt to return. She could not do the same for herself, and amid the joy of ensuring his survival was sorrow, because allowing him to live meant saying good-bye.

I stood silent and staring long, wondering if he was leaving me, and my eyes shed tears without my realizing it. He took me in his arms. How did he know what it was that worried me? It was uncanny sometimes, but he did know, and he whispered, "We will only be parted for a short time, Solace."

I blinked at him and asked, "Where are you going?"

"On holiday with the girls. When school lets out, I'm going to take them sightseeing in the States. Then we will meet you at your parents' home for Christmas." He kissed my wet cheek. "If you didn't have to go to court, you could join us. Yet perhaps, it is right for me to take them alone this last time."

I didn't notice his voice faltering, because I was busy preparing my protest. "I want to have Christmas here, with you and your family." I wiped my cheeks with the back of my hand. I knew there was no point in arguing. He needed to occupy himself while I completed my business with Rosie and put an end to my sordid past. I had requested that Sean remain apart from it; I had pushed him to go.

He did not speak of the past, but kept his reasoning reasonable. "It's time that you introduced me to your family, Solace. You know that I should go to them. It's more respectful and proper. I'd like to meet them without the kids the first time, but, well, your folks might as well get to know me as I am."

"They won't appreciate you."

"Will I shock them?" He liked the idea.

"I've told them about you, but they don't seem to have listened. It's going to be uncomfortable."

"So they will be relieved that I'm going to spend some time away from you?"

"They will be the only ones." I moped.

"Despondency. You are good, Solace. You could almost make me feel as guilty as you feel for trying to make me feel guilty about going. Then when I'm gone, you'll have this party going every night. You'll be spreading out in your bed, going 'it's all mine!' You'll get your assignments done on time, and you'll go diving with Leah."

"I might enjoy a quieter schedule," I admitted.

"Do you want to see less of me?"

"No."

He leaned over and kissed me. "Thank you, my love, for your undimmed honesty."

Chapter Fourteen

As spring progressed toward summer, Sean began to prepare for moving into his house. Finally, he seemed to welcome it. Perhaps all it took was his teacher's biological clock to tell him that the end of the school year was at hand, or maybe he was eager to settle in there so that he could go off on his American adventure. It could have been that he was simply ready. Suddenly decorating took on an urgency for him, and he dragged me off to the hardware store time and again to pick out closet hooks, window shades, and every other little item he could think of to complete the house.

He also engaged an interior decorator, and knowing I would be available to join them and help him with ordering curtains for the parlor and other things that seemed of rather low priority to me, he scheduled a meeting with her on a Friday in late November. The morning before, he called me at work. "Solace, can you leave work early today? The decorator has an emergency and has to go to Ireland tomorrow, but she can see us today."

"Why don't we just see her when she comes back?" I asked in return. Sean had never interrupted my work before, but I liked to keep my schedule and I felt that the decorator's time would be better spent packing her suitcase. Why couldn't he just hang sea green curtains in the shape of surfboards or starfish? That was what I pictured being his choice. I asked him to hold.

"What's wrong?" asked my cubicle mate.

"Sean wants me to leave work early today to see some woman about curtains for his house. It feels like an invasion, but I don't think he means it that way."

"Doesn't sound like a last minute thing," she said sympathetically.

"It wasn't. We were supposed to see her tomorrow, but she has an emergency and has to leave town."

"That's not an invasion, Solace," she said. "The poor bloke is afraid to see a decorator alone. Most men are. He needs you. If you don't ask to go, I'll ask for you."

"You're sure?"

"Absolutely. My husband would be waiting at the front desk for me already. Go on now."

After a visit to my supervisor, who confirmed her opinion, I arranged for Sean to pick me up a few hours later. On my way to the elevator, I saw Ed Leahy coming in from the store. He smiled and nodded, and put out an arm to stop me. "Where are you going?" he asked. But as I started to redden, he began to laugh quietly, a twinkle in his eye. "I heard. Have fun. Stay out for the day. It's beautiful outside."

"I've got lots of work, Mr. Leahy," I stammered.

"Yes, I'll make sure to keep it that way too. That's my job: keep Solace busy and productive." I sensed that he was mildly annoyed by my dedication. "Enjoy your day. We'll see you on Monday."

"Thank you, Sir. Have a nice weekend."

"I plan to," he said. "Laura and I are having dinner with Michael tonight. That's a good start, if early, don't you think?" He continued on his way, looking chipper and making me wonder if seeing his son made him so happy or if Mrs. Leahy had just ordered new carpet for their house without involving him.

Sean made a bumbling apology when we met. As we crossed town, he asked me about my day, and let me talk. As I left work behind, I began to feel silly to have been irked. After all, I work to support my life, not the other way around, and Sean was certainly an important part of my life.

When we walked into his house, I was greeted by wonderful kitchen aromas. "What's going on?" I asked inhaling deeply, tasting the air. "If you had a tree up, I'd swear you were cooking Christmas dinner."

"Good," he responded with a huge grin. "Didn't you look at the calendar?"

"Why?"

"I believe that today is a very special day in the United States." He evaluated me as he would one of his students.

"Oh my God, Sean! You tricked me!" I had been away from home so long I had forgotten one of our most important holidays.

He nodded, looking wise and somber. "I'm afraid I did, my love. We are going to have a traditional American Thanksgiving dinner this afternoon, surrounded by family and friends. Sorry I lied to you, but I wanted to surprise you."

"And you have. Thank you, Sean." I threw my arms around his neck and pulled his head down so that I could kiss his lips. I did not try to contain my happiness, because not sharing joy is wasting joy.

"I have a good deal to be thankful for this year, Solace. When I saw the holiday on the calendar, I decided to find out what it was all about. We don't really have an equivalent, but I love the idea. I researched it. I called your Mum and got some recipes."

"You called my mother?" I was shocked.

"It was a risk," he admitted. "Anyway, it's all planned and in preparation, and we have a little time to ourselves. Come away from the kitchen." He took both of my hands and, facing me, backed into the lounge, leading me with graceful steps. "I told you that there are many things for which I am grateful, and I want to express my thanks to God and to you, Solace Murphy. I am thankful that Tim is recovering. I am thankful that, at last, my house is becoming my home. I am thankful that my daughters are turning into lovely young women, and that my parents are still healthy. Mostly, I am thankful that I have finally gotten to know you. I love you so very much. You are intelligent, kind, strong, funny, and the most beautiful woman I can imagine."

I lowered my gaze as he sank to one knee, still holding both of my hands, but not using me for support. In fact, I felt as if he were supporting me. I was melting even before he spoke again.

"I am thankful that I know you, that you are a part of my life. The girls and I love you. Will you be my wife?" His poem ended, and he asked simply, "Will you marry me, Solace?"

I dropped to my knees too, and touching my nose to his, I said, "Yes." I wanted to kiss him, but he was looking down blocking me from giving him even the barest of an Eskimo kiss. When he looked up he released my hands, and I threw my arms around him. He responded in kind, and our lips came together.

For once in my life, I was completely sure that I was making the right decision. Every minute I had spent with Sean had been worthwhile. He had helped me find strength, confidence, and purpose. He brought a family with him, but that no longer frightened me. In fact, I found it reassuring.

We kissed, laughed, and cried for a while, celebrating our moment. Then after some five or ten minutes of intense but restrained contact, he asked, "Solace, aren't you even going to look at your ring?"

"What?" I sputtered. Amid all the excitement and my impatience to throw myself at him, it had not registered that he had been holding my hands and looking down in order to slip a ring on my finger. Once he drew my attention to it I lifted my left hand and looked at it, gasping with awe and delight. I had never pictured anything this lovely on my finger. Though I felt the ring was of lesser importance than the agreement we had just made, I knew that Sean would have spent more time selecting it than me. To him this was a way of proving his financial ability to support me.

"Do you like it?" he asked eagerly. "I'll get you whatever you want, if it isn't just right. You're hesitating."

I was. "It's perfect, Sean. It's…so nice," I said slowly. "Can you really afford to spend this much?"

He laughed. "You know I can."

"But," I began, not knowing what else I intended to say.

"I wanted to get you a ring with stones I could see without my glasses," he explained with a wink. "It's not that I think a man must present a ring at the moment of the proposal." He made a face that belied his comment to some degree. "I am right, aren't I, that you would have chosen something, um, petite?"

I nodded. "I didn't think I could wear something like this."

He lifted my hand and turned it gently this way and that to examine the ring. "It seems you were wrong."

"I take it the girls knew about this?"

"Yeah. They insisted upon being included. I pretty much had to force them to go to school today."

"You practiced?"

"A little." He blushed.

"It seemed spontaneous, but you were very smooth, very well timed. You have got a lot of style, Sean Donovan, I grant you that." I shivered with delight.

"You've found your calling: drama critic." He laughed and started to rise.

I rose too. "I take it the decorator thing was a ruse."

"All made up," he acknowledged with a nod. "I really wanted to give you a nice surprise. By the way, your boss is coming to dinner. I wanted corporate cooperation."

"No wonder he told me not to come back to work." Suddenly I laughed. "Did he know you were planning to propose too?"

"Where do you think I got the money to buy your ring?" He replied without missing a beat. I stopped suddenly. "Geez, Solace," he cried. "That was too easy. No. I did not tell him I was planning to propose to you. I only told the jeweler and my daughters."

I snooped around on the stove with him standing behind me, rubbing against me. I could feel his excitement and arousal. "It was silly of me to invite a crowd over, now wasn't it?"

"Who is coming?" I asked.

"The usual friends and family. I invited my in-laws. I hope you don't find that inappropriate."

"They are a part of your family."

He kissed my cheek, still holding me from behind. "So, when do you want to get married?"

"Tomorrow." I stepped aside so that he could open the oven door.

He pulled out the rack and began to baste an enormous turkey. "Okay."

"Sometime next year."

"Probably more practical. We have to see the priest and everything. That takes some time."

"Are you sure you don't want to get married in your family's church, Sean?"

"Doubt they'd let us. You're divorced, remember? They rather frown upon such things."

"Would they recognize my Protestant, American wedding?"

"Count on it." He pushed the turkey back inside the oven chamber, closed the door, and stood. He picked up his list and looked at the clock.

"Anything else for the oven, Bionic Bloke?" I asked.

"Not for another half hour. Do you know how to do gravy?"

"Aye, Sir."

"I might ask you to make it. Reen always gets stuck."

"I can't believe Rina didn't let something slip." I moved in next to him so that I could see the list too.

"I suspect her whole school knows." He wrapped his arm around my waist.

"Sure we don't need to do something?"

"Want to get married on the beach?"

"No. I don't want to have to shout over the roar of the surf or get blown apart by the wind. I want to look pretty at my wedding."

"You always look pretty."

"If you want to do it outdoors, how about a flower garden?"

"You always have a better idea. No sand. I like it. What about the Botanical Gardens?"

"Maybe. You are so romantic. I just assumed we'd get married in a church."

"Do you want to get married at your church in Virginia?"

"I'd rather get married here." I started to peek under the foil of one of the casseroles, but stopped when I heard voices from the front of the house.

We went to the door together. Tanya had picked the girls up from school, and she trailed behind them up to the porch looking at her younger brother as expectantly as they did. No one spoke. They smiled at us, and with our entire beings we smiled at each other. I saw their eyes move from his face to mine and back again.

"Coming in?" he asked.

"I really can't stay, Sean," Tanya said. "I just wanted to make sure the girls got in and that everything is on track."

"Everything is very much on track," he said, his voice cracking slightly.

The girls screamed with joy and jumped all over him, hugging him, and loudly crying, "She said yes!" over and over again.

Tanya walked around them to where I stood watching their celebration and touched my arm. I looked into her teary, sky-blue eyes. She threw her arms around me in a bear hug and kissed my cheeks. "Bless you, Solace, my sister," she said warmly. "You are wholly welcome into our family."

Sean had planned to announce our engagement at the table after he finished leading the blessing, but word spread before we began to put food on the table. I was hugged and kissed and welcomed by most of his family members who were present. George shook our hands with polite restraint, while Olga embraced me and kissed my cheeks. "Our blessings on you both! I was certain this would come: the two of you." She shook her head. Her eyes were damp. "I only ask, Solace, though I know you can't promise, that you not take him too far away."

I just looked down shyly at my hands. Sean said, "Mum, she's happy here," and he wrapped his free arm around me. Her face relaxed.

I wasn't sure it was a good idea to announce our engagement in front of Megan's mother, but my concerns were unnecessary. She seemed pleased. She kissed my cheek and offered to do some of the things that my mother, so far away, would be unable to do to help with the wedding plans before she turned to congratulate her granddaughters warmly on their gain.

The person I should have worried about was Mike. He stayed in the background until the main course was cleared. Then he squatted by my chair for a whispered conversation. "Gee, Solace, you're going to get married twice before I do it once. You ought to be pickier." He smiled, teasing me, unable to hide the loneliness I knew he was feeling very keenly at this moment.

"I was this time, Mike. Otherwise, I'd have married you a long time ago."

"My loss too, Solace. You're a wonderful woman, and I would never have felt that I deserved you."

"Then you would never have been happy. It's better to be alone than with the wrong person, Mike."

"Masturbation beats getting Herpes," he said with his unique style of optimism. "Now, you and Sean, you're being careful, right."

"That's none of your fucking business, Mike," I said smiling.

"Shit, that's what you always say. No fair bragging." He stood up suddenly and so quickly that he had to grab the back of my chair for a moment.

"What's wrong, Mike?"

"Nothing. I'm happy for you."

"You could have fooled me, but then you're never happy unless you have something to complain about."

"Damn straight. Like right now. They've sent the pies on past my seat," he said, turning away from me. "I've got to rescue my dessert."

Chapter Fifteen

The next couple of weeks passed too quickly. Sean and the girls moved to the house before the end of November, and before I adjusted to their being out of the building they left the country. Suddenly I couldn't put off thinking about the trial any longer. I tried to focus on the trip that came afterwards, but honestly I just wanted it all over so that we could go on with our normal lives.

I prepared for my extended absence by working long hours and for testifying with some coaching by the prosecutor. Knowing that I would be lonely and anxious, my friends tried hard to include me in their activities. Cindy and Melissa persuaded me to eat with them several times during the first week. Then on the first evening I planned to stay home, Mike insisted that I go out with him. He took me to the Royal Carollonian for dessert. He finally admitted that he was dating Cara Reilly, who had recently taken a position at the hotel and moved back to Williamsport. Mike segued his uncharacteristic talk of happiness into expressing his concerns for mine. More than assuring me that I would be alright, he reminded me that I didn't need to make myself sick with worry. "I'll go with you."

"I don't want anyone to go with me."

"Come on," he urged, not believing me.

"Cindy doesn't believe me either."

"Well, duh, of course not. Don't be stupid, Solace."

I raised an eyebrow. "I got into this on my own. I need to finish it alone."

"That's bullshit," he responded calmly. He was still assessing me, which made me feel jumpier. He sighed. "Let me and Cindy help you."

Of all the people I knew, Tim was the one who came closest to missing Sean as much as I did. So instead of going straight home after a trip to Sean's house I took the bus to Tim's nursing home near Little Russia. He was sitting idly on his bed when I first looked into the room. His roommate was on the side with the windows, and the curtain was drawn across the room, as it had been every time I'd visited. I wondered if Tim was ever able to see outside from his bed. I cleared my throat. "Sean says hi."

He turned. Pale and bone thin, he still looked very much like my fiancé. Seeming sincere, he greeted me, "I'm thrilled as hell to see you."

"I heard a rumor you got to go home for Christmas." I dropped into the visitor's chair.

"Yeah. Just for the day. But the time is coming for me to check out of this four star facility. Maybe I'll mooch off Mum and Dad for a while," he said with a nervous smile. He held up his hand to display his crossed fingers. "Touch wood, I'll be bunking with my baby brothers again soon."

"That ought to be interesting."

"You bet. Have to get the parents away for a night so I can give a party like the old days." He lowered his voice. "Just because I can't drink doesn't mean I can't tap a keg for my guests. I owe, like, everyone."

"You always got too much air in the beer."

"Just for you, heh: extra foamy. I heard American girls liked head. On their beer."

"I'm not a Marine groupie anymore, so keep your conversation clean, my dear future younger brother."

"Shit," he drawled, testing me. "Don't play prissy with me. I know enough about the real Solace Murphy."

I rolled my eyes. "Well, don't bother trying blackmail. I don't have enough money, and I'm writing a tell-all confession book anyway. It simply won't work."

He laughed. "You'll use an assumed name to publish it, but I bet it will be juicy. I understand you missed us so much that you mended your ways when we went off to the no-porno zone." He fidgeted. I'd never seen him have excess energy before. "But Sean sure is happy, my girl. I love you for that."

My eyes welled with tears. I nodded. "I'm happy too."

Tim offered me his hand, and I stood briefly to shake it. His behavior was remarkably pleasant. "This last week has been so long. No one can keep a conversation going quite like good, old, dependable Sean."

I nodded in agreement. "Sean made me throw a pottery mug against a brick wall on our first outing." I don't know why that seemed an appropriate thing to say.

"Kinky," he commented. "There's a leftover med bag on the hook up there you can toss, if you like." We both laughed.

"I don't feel like celebrating today."

"Got some Russian in you somewhere?" he asked with a wry smile. It was like seeing Sean's cloudy day shadow.

"I don't think so."

"You don't. You worried about breaking that mug," he nodded decisively. "Sean didn't tell me; I just know. You didn't carry on too wildly at those social gatherings either. I'll wager you didn't go to bed with any of my mates, but we all liked to think you would. Not now, of course, 'cause you're my big sister-in-law-to-be and I'm on so many drugs that I couldn't get a hard-on if I tried." A quick smile.

"But not forever?"

"Sure hope not!" He stared at his knees. "But you're the last person I expected to take that comment head on." During his silence, I realized that I was staring at him. His hair looked dull and brittle. Then I made myself look away to give him privacy. When he was ready for more conversation, he joked bitterly, "Maybe I'll become a priest."

I pretended I thought he was serious. "It would make your parents very proud, but if that is your choice then you should make it because of what you can do, not because of what you can't."

"Yeah, well, I don't always have the guts for all this crap."

"Why do you think Sean visits you almost every day? He doesn't want you to pull your own plug. Damn it."

Tim laughed. "Nice punctuation."

"Only now, you aren't on life support anymore. You would have to actively kill yourself, and that *would* damn you, wouldn't it? Your parents couldn't even bury you properly, could they?"

"You are a surprise," he said with a droll smile, rolling his eyes.

"I saw some pretty nurses. Any of them tickle your fancy?"

"Yeah, they've got a few lookers here," he said with more energy.

"You are well enough to notice. That's good."

"You've been tossed around a bit yourself. Did your ex-husband beat you?"

"No. It was all emotional."

"And that Rosie prick?" he continued, studying my face.

"I don't want to hear another suggestion that your brother, who you've known all your life, would intend any harm to me."

"Oh, we are defensive!"

"You know better."

"Yeah, he's a good guy. He's done everything he could to make sure I didn't give up, 'cause there have been times.... That's probably why I'm still around to piss you off." He was ready to change the subject.

"Yeah, I came to see you because I was running out of things to complain about." I made a sour face, which got a chuckle out of him. "You know, Tim, it really is time you stopped feeling sorry for yourself." He choked on the last of his laughter. He seemed to like it when I scolded him, but I may have said too much. I continued in a more compassionate tone. "I know it'll be difficult."

"I'm not running out of things to bitch about," he insisted.

"When you get out of here there won't be as much. And you'll have to watch what you say and how much you say. You're going to be with your family all the time. They'll have to do things for you that they may not know how to do. You'll have to help them learn how to help you, and you'll need to show your appreciation."

He lay back against his pillows and closed his eyes.

Apologetically, "Would you like to go outside?"

In a flat voice, he accepted, "Yes, thanks." I stood up to help him with the walker, but he waved away my assistance. "I can do it myself."

"Need an update on what's hot in the States?"

"Definitely. I'll need a whole new wardrobe when I go home. What's the latest in men's fashions? Please tell me skinny and pale are in and what movie star's haircut I should borrow." He became livelier as he concentrated on walking and chattered on this easier topic.

I did my best to give him useful advice and offered to bring him a fashion magazine, which he found extremely amusing. I still couldn't say that I liked Tim. His resemblance to Sean was like a crude stick figured copy of an artistic masterpiece. He cared too much what I thought of him; he cared too much what Sean thought of him. Yet I would visit him again, if only to nag at him not to add to Sean's burdens. Sean might be angry with me, but I loved him enough to risk it.

I talked to Sean and the girls late into many nights, and I often went to their house to cut flowers and harvest vegetables, which I shared with Cindy and Melissa. I took some of the flowers home to enjoy and delivered the rest to Tim on my second visit.

"Did you leave any for the bees?"

Ignoring his question, I spun down into the visitor's chair and asked, "Got permission for your furlough yet?"

"Christmas Eve. I think." He grinned, beaming. "Maybe overnight."

"Really? Oh, how wonderful. Can I tell Sean?"

"Sure. Have you told him yet that you've been coming to bitch at me?"

"Not exactly." The visits were too intimate and unpleasant to bring up on our short telephone trysts.

"Good. He'd be upset. He'd like to think we all love each other and get along."

"He's a parent. What do you expect?"

He laughed. "You're alright, Solace. You've given me some pretty big, hard kicks in the ass, but I needed them. I admit it now. I know I must have seemed a nasty, old fart the first time you came."

"Only the first time?"

"I'm just trying to say that I'm glad you bothered to come back. Have I improved at all?"

"Well, I wouldn't say that hanging out with you is pleasant, but we seem to have developed something functional."

"I told my shrink about you. He agreed that you were a nosy bitch."

"My, well, that's a very professional assessment," I drawled with dismay.

"Yeah." He turned and swung his legs over the side of the bed, preparing to rise. "Those were my words, not his. He just kind of nodded."

"I thought they always did that nodding thing."

"Yeah, but this was actual agreement. He asked me what I thought about what you said. He asked it the way he does when he thinks I've said something meaningful." I stopped fidgeting and gave Tim my full attention. "Well, I admitted you might be right. He jumped on that, man, with a 'how do you feel?' *and* a 'what do you think you will do?' I said I felt bad, but I didn't know what to do." Then Tim looked up at me, evaluating me and whether he should continue speaking. He was no longer kidding around, and when he spoke again, his tone was sincere. "Solace, do you know how to change the way you get along with someone? You know, like to fix things? I mean, when two people are the way they are with each other for so long, how do you remix it and make things fairer?"

"No. I don't know how to do that. I have wished I could sometimes." I walked beside him out of the room into the corridor.

"You just left, didn't you? When things got bent too wrong. That's been your solution?"

"Yes, I suppose that is what I have always done."

"What about you and Sean? Is your relationship gonna get fucked up while he's away?" He genuinely seemed to care, so I didn't take offense.

"I don't think so. It's just a short trip, and I'm going to go too. Remember? It should be good for us." I held the exterior door open. So much better, I reckoned, to be a doorstop than a doormat.

He nodded. "Good. I wouldn't want this stupid ass stunt of his to ruin what obviously seems like such a good thing for both of you."

"You want to change things between you and Sean, right?"

"Yeah," he answered glumly. We walked past the first bench.

"Has he called you?"

"Nyet."

"So, perhaps his going away will help. When he gets back, just treat him the way that you feel he deserves to be treated, and then you two will find your new balance. You love each other and you didn't have a fight; you just have, well, seen some things from a fresh perspective."

He stopped at the third bench along the walk. "Yeah. That's what I'll do." He worked his way down onto the bench unaided. "So, how about you? Are you ready for your day in court?"

"I'm not sure," I stammered.

He laughed. "You've got to handle him better than that! Remember two things, Solace. First, this was his doing, not yours. And second, that you'll never have to see him again. You can burn your bridges. You were the victim. Don't let that asshole into your mind."

"I hate being the victim," I said stiffly. I felt tired.

He stared at me silently with a look I did not recognize. "Yeah, me too." After a long spell of silence, he reached over and put his hand on mine. He patted it in a fatherly manner. "You'll do fine. You're strong. You can keep it together."

I grimaced, "I'll try."

Wednesday was to be my last day of work for the year 1993. By the time I had completed all of my work, I was hungry. It was late, already dark, so I stopped at the Hunan Bouquet, the place Peter had introduced me to last year, for some takeaway. When I entered I set the bells clanging against the glass door. The cashier glanced up and nodded a greeting while still attending to the order she was taking from the man facing her. He turned automatically, looking to see what was happening behind him, but I had already recognized him. I felt my mood lift, and a smile came to my lips.

It was Peter. He swiveled his head a couple of times between the cashier and me while he made sure that he could trust his vision. His poise returned, and smiling, he stepped toward me, calling my name and offering me an affectionate hug. He walked me to the counter, his arm still loosely flung over my shoulders. "I was just ordering. Will you join me?"

"Sure."

"What would you like?"

"Is this the same order?" the cashier asked.

"No," I said, and Peter said, "Yes." We laughed, the poor girl's eyes darting between our faces. "Yes," he repeated, and I didn't argue.

"I'd like some pork fried rice and tea," I told her.

"Let's wait outside," he suggested. "So we can start catching up." There were two benches facing each other at the opening of what had been an alley before the restaurant building was erected. Red lanterns were strung overhead. During the day this spot would be hot, but it was pleasant in the evening.

"How've you been?" I had seen Peter a few times in the past few months, but our meetings had always been in passing and in public, giving us no opportunity for a real conversation. We weren't nervous, just uncertain how to start.

"Good, and better for seeing you. Imagine this!" He looked up and met my eyes. "You look thin. You haven't been unwell?"

"Oh, no, I'm fine."

"Still with your landlord?"

I nodded, smiling and feeling calmer at the mention of Sean.

"Doesn't he like Chinese food?"

I laughed. "Actually, he loves this place. Right now, he's in the U.S. with his girls."

"Really?" He didn't look pleased.

"It's okay. I kind of drove him away. It's time for me to finish up dealing with Ken Williams. The trial starts tomorrow, and I didn't want to involve Sean. I handle things better alone. But half my friends have offered to go to court with me."

"What a nuisance. You are such a one, heh, to live on the edge," he teased. We were interrupted by the cashier bringing our supper to us in a tall paper bag. Rising, Peter asked, "Do you want to eat inside, Solace, or go somewhere?"

"We could go back to my place and eat on the balcony?"

"Would that be alright?"

I knew he was concerned about what Sean might think. "I don't see why not."

"Why don't we use the University Pavilion? It's closer, and I'd like to eat while my supper is hot." It was a neutral setting.

"Is it open at night?"

"It has lights," was his answer. "How long is your Sean going to be gone?"

"It's okay, Peter, really," I defended my beloved. "It's easier for me when I don't have to see him worrying about me. I know that he's busy and having a good time, and he's keeping the girls distracted. When I'm done, I'm going to meet him to have Christmas with my family."

Immediately understanding the implications of this news, Peter glanced at my left hand. A wistful smile came over his face. "You're engaged." He lifted my hand to his lips and kissed it. "My dear Solace, bless you and your landlord. God bless you both."

I touched his cheek. I didn't know what to say.

When we settled at a table in the pavilion with our food, I let him talk about the trips he had taken. He'd gone to London on business several times and had done a lot of sightseeing while he was there. He'd also taken an Incan study tour of Peru. I enjoyed listening. It was all very interesting, and I was a little envious of his adventurousness. Yet I felt sorry for him too, because I couldn't help thinking how much fun I would have taking trips like that with Sean.

When he turned the conversation back to me, he pretended to search the food bag for something. "Tell me about your plans. When's the wedding?"

"June. That will give my relatives time to make travel arrangements."

"Big wedding then?" He pulled his hand out of his bag, a mustard packet in his fist. He fussed with the mustard and an egg roll for a while, giving me an opportunity to dig into my rice.

"I'm not sure. I think it will be small by Carollonian standards, but huge by American."

He laughed. "So you're only going to invite half of the village?"

I nodded, laughing. "Sean eloped the first time. He feels he owes everyone a big party."

"I wish I'd known about your engagement, Solace. I'd like to offer you something better in the way of a celebration."

"Oh, no, Peter. This is perfect," I effused.

He poured fresh tea into our paper cups. "A toast then, shall we? Best wishes to you, my dear Solace." We lifted our cups in salute. After we drank we sat them back on the table.

After a little more conversation, I excused myself to go to the restroom, which was in a separate building down the hill. As I hurried along the dimly lit path toward the river I recognized a stronger call than I had realized while I was sitting.

I stepped inside the restroom and flipped the switch to no result. When the door shut behind me, I stood in utter blackness. The trees around the building blocked most of the light from outside before it came in through the window openings. I put my hands out to feel my way, debating if I could do what I needed to do. The hairs on the back of my neck rose. I imagined that another person was there with me. I turned to feel my way back to the door, which should have been only a couple of steps behind me, but I couldn't even see an outline of light. I became disoriented. My hand touched porcelain; it must have been the sink. A hand slapped over my mouth cutting off my scream before it reached my throat. I was pulled backward, a strong arm binding me to the form of a large man.

His voice confirmed what my nose, skin, and instincts had told me. It was Ken. "You're with that Carly Adonis again, Solace," he whispered hoarsely. His whiskers abraded my cheek. Everything about him was rough. I struggled to breathe and to understand how and why he had trapped me. My mind was snagged upon this curiosity, and so I was slow even to begin squirming.

He grunted, and his arms clamped onto me even tighter. "You lying, cheating, whiny bitch, you've turned the whole world against me. Everywhere I go people stare at me and point, and they act like

I'm a monster. Every lousy minute there's someone watching me."
He made a low scoffing sound. "But they're idiots." He moved his
hand from my mouth across my cheek and ear, into my hair, which
was down loose. His lips were at my ear. "It won't work, Solace, all
these lies and games; I won't take you back."

"What?" As confused as I was I could see that he had lost his
perspective, perhaps even his sanity.

He became rigidly alert, rasping, "Hush." He tightened his arm
around my middle, restricting my breath. I felt lightheaded. He let
go of my head long enough to open the door. "Adonis is coming to
look for you. I'll break your neck if you make even a peep. Got it?"

I nodded with as small a motion as I could manage. Like a rag
doll, I dangled in front of him, the tips of my toes barely touching the
ground as he moved us into the brush. I had to work at remaining
limp and not reacting when Peter called my name. I didn't know
whether I should hope that Ken would make some kind of noise,
scatter some stones or crack a stick under his foot, because he was
likely to blame me for alerting Peter even if it was his own fault.
However, if Peter were able to reach us before Ken crushed my
windpipe, I was sure that he could rescue me. Ken was gymnasium
strong, but Peter was more fit and he had been practicing tae kwon do
since he was a boy.

Peter knocked on the restroom door, and when there was no
answer, he opened it. "Solace?" he said when he found the lights
weren't working. He started back toward the pavilion, and then
reversed, continuing on the path toward the university, as I would
have presumably done when I couldn't use the restroom. I heard him
call my name several more times.

Soundlessly Ken directed me the other way along the path that
led to the river, stopping and starting in a way that told me he did not
have a plan. I guessed that he had improvised my capture and that he
didn't quite know what to do next. If I could only speak to him, I
thought, I might be able to reason with him, but I didn't have a
chance until he stopped at the turn in the walk where he had to decide
if we were going to cross the river on the pedestrian bridge, take the
stairs down to the bike path, or turn back toward the university.

Ken froze, debating which way to go. Through the heavy sound
of his breathing I heard the river's movement and the mantras of the
insects. He changed his hold on me, uncovering my face so that he

could clamp his hands on my shoulders, and swung me around, forcing me to look into his anger-swollen face.

"Let me go, Ken," I begged, gasping for breath. "It's time to say good night and go home."

"I say when it's time to go. And it isn't time to go anywhere 'til I'm sure you won't testify against me." He seemed to be waiting for me to respond, becoming impatient, as he tightened his hold on me.

I didn't know how to reply. By nature I am more honest than wise, and I have never convincingly lied to anyone other than myself. Ken would not have believed an untruth coming from me, even with his distorted mind, even if I had been able to think of something to say that might appease him. At length I managed to steady my voice, and I said, "I have a subpoena, Ken. I have to testify."

He made a noise deep in his throat that confirmed he had no intention of allowing me to appear in court.

"Listen to me, Ken," I began, determined to stand up to him, and hoping hard that my will was as strong as his thick arms. "What you're doing now will just get you into deeper trouble." His grip on me tightened, and I decided that I should say nothing more that he might construe as a threat. "I know that you were just angry, Ken, and you lost control. Lots of people do things they regret when they lose their temper. I will explain that to the jury, Ken. They will understand that you didn't mean to injure me."

He sniffed loudly, showing his distrust. "You set the dogs on me, Solace. You've ruined my life."

"No, Ken. I didn't, really, I didn't. I trusted you to leave me alone."

"Shut up!" He looked around frantically. The passage of time and the increased risk of discovery were leading him to a state of panic. My fear level rose as a result. I tried to back away from him, but he had me completely in his power. He spat something unintelligible and pushed his face into mine. With one hand he grabbed my cheeks to keep my eyes on his drastically altered visage. There was nothing left of the man I had thought attractive when I met him a year earlier except the bully who had demanded that I accept his constant attention, thorns and all. He jolted me several times then tossed my face away. "Shut up," he spluttered. "You're ignoring me."

The instant he let go of me, I turned and ran as fast as I could toward the lights across the river. I didn't get more than a third of the way across the bridge before he caught up with me. I was jerked to a sudden stop, my balance thrown off when he grabbed my upper arm. While my feet still scrambled to gain solid footing, he pushed me away, sending me reeling toward the railing. My head and shoulders were flung forward as my ribs and abdomen slammed into the barrier. Doubled over and panting, I reminded him of the restraining order.

He snorted defiantly, his indecisiveness having been ended by my attempt to escape. His presence seemed to grow in stature and malevolence. He lifted me to standing again, compressing my arms so tightly that my hands became numb. He began to shake me with such force that it seemed my teeth were being jack-hammered into my sinuses. When some blood from my nose splattered his shirt, he froze, staring at the spots, still holding me up so that only the tips of my toes could reach the pavement.

Nauseous, dizzy, and contorted by powerful muscle spasms in my legs and abdomen, I was pressed with my belly against the railing of the bridge by Ken's heavy body. Shallow as the panting breaths I took were, each one stabbed me. My inner thighs were warm and wet. For the moment, he seemed to be catching his breath too, following the exertion of ramming me into the railing countless times. While he rested, I could finally think, but I could see no way to escape the next set of blows.

From my place in the darkness I tried to focus my blurry vision on the glints of reflected light on the water's surface—tiny specks like the stars, like the shining eyes belonging to each soul who would feel the loss of my life, which had only recently truly become worth living. I was overwhelmed with sorrow for those I was leaving behind, especially Sean and the girls, whose lives would be rent again. I thought about Sean's promise to rescue me from drowning in this very river. I had always believed he would be there to save me, yet now when I needed his help, he was gone and I was not in the water, but high above it. Staring at the inverted heavens, I realized that Sean had already given me the power to save myself when he told me to place my trust in God. I found that it really was the easiest thing to do. And when I did it, the vertical distance from the bridge to the water became negligible. The probability that my body would be broken on the riverbed or swept downstream by the current no longer caused me fear. The river could take me away from my tormentor, and death would free me of my mortal concerns. With absolute faith, I decided to end my life by my own choice just as I had tried, and mostly failed, to live it.

I found strength in certainty.

I thrust the small, hard tip of the heel of my remaining shoe into the soft place near Ken's ankle. He stepped back instinctively, cursing, giving me some room to maneuver. I kicked my legs high against his body, pushed off once my feet were above the rail, and let go with my hands. I tumbled over the railing.

A sliver of the moon smiled upon me as I fell, and I heard my name. My suffering ended the instant my body impacted against the water's surface.

Chapter Sixteen

My faith was justified.

My connection to the Earth was severed.

I went under the water's surface only to be raised again, supported by the arms of an angel. The agony of coughing water from my lungs was the first clue I had that I was still alive.

Cradled in the arms of my burly and very human smelling rescuer, I felt strangely safe. I was aware of little else.

He helped me to sit with my back against a tree while he went to get some things from the trailer on his bicycle. I only knew that he took me in his arms again and covered us both with some heavy, rough cloth so that we could share our body heat. Then my angel made an emergency call on his two-way radio. He held me, protecting me from worse things than cold and wet, until the ambulance arrived, and when it did, he carried me up the stairs to it and laid me on the stretcher. He took the silver crucifix from around his neck and looped the chain over my wrist to secure it in place before he laid the cross in my palm and closed my fingers around it.

Peter came running when he heard the sirens. Sobbing my name, he promised to stay with me. He held my hand, the one clutching Christ, until he was asked to release it during my treatment at the hospital.

Because the pain in my mind and body were too great to bear, numbness overtook me, allowing me to endure. I shivered with cold, yet my belly burned. Dawnless, the understanding of my loss grew in my mind until I could grasp nothing else. Though I was distanced from the reality of the moment, I was centered upon the most important fact of it. I wept without sound, sob, or convulsion for the life inside of me that I had been unable to protect from the blows that had stolen my breath and broken my ribs. Though the death I had sensed was not my own, a part of me had been destroyed, and I was left nearly too weak to mourn the life within me I had never had the courage to confirm or celebrate.

I was beyond caring what was done to me; it could be no worse than what had already been done. Some medication they gave me increased the vagueness of my sensations. I knew that Peter was there, and that Cindy joined us sometime later. I was recovering in an overnight room when I shifted from sedated to regular sleep, and another hand held mine. Finding particular comfort in this new presence, I cradled the hand against my cheek.

I slept soundly until morning when I woke enough to become curious about the identity of my consoler. My eyes moved up the length of her arm to the sleeping face of Olga Donovan where it lay, facing me, on my bed. She slept so lightly, as the mother of a sick child will, that she was roused by my glance. Her head jolted upright, and her eyes flew open wide, meeting mine. "Solace, dear. Oh, you're awake. That's grand." She leaned over and kissed my forehead. Then she pressed the call button on my bed.

George Donovan appeared behind her, leaning toward me timidly. "There, there," he said sweetly. "We rang Sean, my dear, and he'll be on his way."

My head seemed clear. I began to wonder about the extent of my injuries. In a surprisingly detached way, I took roll of my extremities, finding that every piece of me was achingly present.

When the nurse arrived, she surveyed me visually. "You're coming along nicely," she said as if I were a roast in her oven. "All your meds are coming through the I.V. on your right arm. The left is broken." She tapped her pen against the plaster cast. "Your lower ribs are broken. You've got some internal bruising. You'll need a few weeks to rest and heal." What she told me seemed superficial, as if she didn't want to mention the worst damage.

I tried to speak. I think my mouth moved, but no sound came out. The nurse nodded, showing me that she understood my concern. She went on. "All of your cuts and scrapes have been cleaned. You didn't need any stitches." She looked astonished. "All your fingers and toes are accounted for. I'm very sorry about your baby."

Olga's eyes filled with tears. "We didn't know, Solace," she began, patting my hand to reassure me, not only for the loss of my unborn child, but also in acceptance of my pregnancy.

"The doctor said you should heal completely." The nurse lifted my wrist to take my pulse, but instead she said, "The police are eager to speak with you." She came back later to tell us when to expect them and promised the hospital chaplain would stay with me if I wished. I accepted the offer with a nod. Olga and George passed the day with me. It was mostly quiet, except for short visits from Mike and Cindy.

The chaplain was the first to arrive. "My name is Steve." He offered me his hand and nodded to George and Olga. "Why don't you go get some lunch? I'll stay with Solace."

They looked at each other, and I said, "I'll be okay." But they didn't leave until a few minutes later when the police arrived and ordered them out of the room. I was relieved not to have them fussing over me while the police interviewed me about such private matters. Father Steve sat in the chair beside my bed. The police stood. They began by asking me what had happened.

I stared down the long lump my body made on the bed, not wanting to speak. Knowing I must, I blinked while I tried to find my voice. The officers waited. Slowly and almost coherently, I did my best to answer their questions. "Where is he now?" I asked.

"Mr. Williams is in custody." Then he realized I needed to know more. "You are safe here, Miss Murphy."

"Who saved me?"

"Oh, yes, you were quite lucky, heh, weren't you? His name is Seamus Petrov, a plumber who was on a late, emergency call. He was on the bike path, and saw you fall from the bridge as he was approaching it. Dived right in and pulled you out. Knew just what to do for you. Couldn't have a happier ending there."

"Yes," I said in a tired voice. "I never expected that kind of good fortune." Thinking of the life that had ended, my tone was hardly grateful.

Seeing my fatigue, the officers soon concluded the meeting. Before they did, they confirmed what I instinctively knew: that my baby had died before I plunged into the river. They also explained that Cindy and Peter had authorized them to photograph my injuries, a procedure I was glad not to remember.

After the police left, Father Steve sat with me. He only spoke once. I appreciated the silence then almost as much as later I appreciated his words. I rested, as I needed to after the stress of the interview. He waited until I seemed calm to offer comfort.

"Solace, your name is a prayer. I hope that you may find peace in knowing that this is not your fault. No one deserves to be mistreated the way that you have been. You need not share this guilt."

I tried to believe him.

The next day Olga spent only part of the morning with me. In the afternoon her daughters Tanya and Lucy helped me wash and begin to feel human again. They tried to block my view of the mirror, but I still suffered a strong wave of nausea when I caught a glimpse of my swollen, discolored reflection. Helpless under their ministrations, I didn't question Lucy's confidence in my swift recovery, even when she declared that I would have no scars. Soon I was dressed in a clean gown and tucked into my freshly remade bed. They whispered, "Sweet dreams," and I fell asleep intending to thank them.

Lucy came again the following morning to help me get up and wash. She stayed through my breakfast, then seeming pleased with my progress, she left me with an, "I'll see you if you're still here tomorrow." I leaned back into my pillow, just relaxing, for once not sleepy. I sat this way until my lunch tray arrived, followed soon after by Olga bearing some flower arrangements. She placed one of them on the rolling table beside my untouched meal, and I realized it was the same bunch of flowers, now faded and wilting, I had given to Tim. There was a square of yellow paper sticking to the side of the vase, and I pulled it off to read Tim's note. "You need these more than I do. I'll race you to get paroled."

After I ate, Olga helped me walk around the wing of the hospital, and left me to rest until supper. I reread Tim's note, smiling at his sentiments as I drifted to sleep.

I must have shifted my position, because I was awakened by stabs of agony, though the dull aching seemed to have faded. In a way, it was an improvement. I felt more alive, and for the first time, I felt hunger. I shifted and tried to reach the controls for my bed.

"Let me help you with that, Solace," a melodic voice offered.

"Sean!" I gasped, and turning too quickly, I winced from pain as he moved into my field of vision. I tried to lift my heavy, plastered arm to embrace him.

He ducked down beneath it and brushed a damp kiss across my lips. His face was lit with joy, but his cheeks were pale, his eyes and nose telltale pink. "Hullo, Solace. I have missed you something awful." He had to work to hold his smile steady.

"Me too."

After the bed was raised, he leaned over and kissed my lips. "What's this?" he asked, pointing to the yellow notepaper stuck on my fingertip. I poked my finger toward him and he removed it.

"I think you'll win."

I lifted my hand to his cheek and, feeling incredibly sentimental, said, "My dear Artificial Boy is home."

"I got here as fast as I could." He squatted beside my bed, unwilling to go as far away as a chair. "I left the girls at home this time, much to their displeasure. So I told them to start putting up Christmas decorations. You got your wish: Christmas in the Carollons surrounded by Donovans. What won't you do to get your way?"

"Are they okay?" I asked, my voice breaking with emotion.

"Yeah," he nodded. "I'm mean, they're upset, of course, but they've been covering it." He laughed a little, uncomfortable laugh. "They're worried about you, glad to be home, and eager to fix up the guestroom for your convalescence. And, no, you have to stay with someone for at least a few weeks."

"I'm in no position to protest."

He stood, looked down at me, evaluating my condition, and decided he could be a little braver. "God, it's good to see you! Even when you look like this. Can you talk about it? I've been so worried."

"It's hard to talk about. The police came. The doctor said I'll be okay. I mean...."

"I've talked with Dr. Patel." That was his way of telling me he knew everything. "Would you rather hear about us?"

I nodded. "Yeah. I know what happened to me is important, and that I have to be able to discuss it, but it's an aberration."

"We had just gotten back to the ski lodge after dinner when my mother called. I was terrified when I heard her voice. There I was thinking that Tim or Baba had died, and she said you'd been attacked and thrown off a bridge. That you'd lost the baby. I didn't even know..." His voice broke. "All I could think was how I'd promised to be there for you. I thought you were safe." He shook his head, still chastising himself.

"I jumped, Sean," I said. He stared at me, shocked, not believing his faulty ears had heard me correctly. "Well, I mean, I kind of pushed off and over. To get away. That yoga thing I do, when I walk my feet up a wall. With Ken as the wall. The important thing is,

Sean, that I trusted God to protect me. You *were* with me. That helped me to have the faith to get away to the safety of a better death. Only I was rescued, which is even better."

Unable to take anything more in through his senses, he closed his eyes and prayed. After he crossed himself, he began telling his story again. "No one had called your parents yet. They knew I would want to do that. I got on the phone right away to reschedule our flights. Stopped in Virginia to tell them in person. It didn't delay our arrival here. It wasn't the best way to meet your family, I can tell you." He looked weary. "They appreciated it though, that we came in person. Of course, they wanted to fly here with us, but I persuaded them that it would be better if they waited. That you might need more help later. I thought that's what you'd want."

Delivering this news to my family in person was Sean's way, even if it had meant delaying our reunion. I nodded and whispered my thanks. "Did you tell them everything?"

"Yes."

"I'm sorry you had to do that, Sean."

He gazed into my face with a tender expression. He was too gentle to ask me why I hadn't told him that I might have been pregnant this soon after the loss. He needed reassurance before he could move forward. I reached out my hand to him, and he took it in his, folding it around his fingers with his other hand.

"Sit beside me. Hold me, if you can figure out how."

He slid onto the bed and folded himself over me as gently as he could, putting his head on my shoulder and an arm around my middle. It was awkward and uncomfortable, but I had no sense that he was harming me. I could smell his fear, and I felt the gentle movement of his silent sobs. I wished I knew how to console him. Slowly, he lifted his tear-streaked face and looked into my eyes. His tears were more rending than my own. That the man I loved was suffering because I was hurt only added to my pain. I did not feel guilt for causing him pain, but I felt some responsibility for it.

I remembered the hospital chaplain's words. I still needed some convincing, so disciplined was I to accept responsibility for the results of my actions that I even tried to accept responsibility for actions of others toward me. I did make a good victim. I would share the blame with those who would harm me. Up to a point. Beyond that point, I would stand up for myself and for justice and even, perhaps, seek retribution.

When he raised his head he saw me wince. "Did I hurt you?" He moved his hands to the mattress on either side of my body, and he raised himself without causing me any more pain. "I'm sorry."

"I'm alright, Sean," I said. "I liked holding you. I'm just kind of tender. Everywhere."

"I need to be strong for you."

"I'm strong enough," I said very softly. He read my lips.

"I know you are, but I want to help you. I always want to help you. I want to make things easier for you. I hate for you to suffer."

"Oh, well, yeah, me too." I tried to smile. "I feel pretty crummy, to be honest with you. The drugs have mostly worn off, and every time the bed moves, I feel it somewhere." He put his hand on my belly, and a sad expression came over his face again. I lifted my hand to cradle his cheek. "I missed you, did you know?"

"I knew," he said. "My mother has your belongings, and I'll get them for you. And I'll bring you anything you want the next time I come. Now, should I let you get some more sleep?"

"I just woke up." I yawned. "I need to talk to my parents soon, but I'm afraid. I know they will say that I should have come home to live after the last time and that I should be more careful and," I stopped, not wanting to think of the things they would say. They were the ones who taught me to be so responsible, never guessing that I would encounter experiences so beyond my making.

"You don't need to think about that now." He was trying to soothe me, but it had the reverse effect. I sat up straighter and opened my eyes wider. "Solace Murphy! You are so contrary."

"They will give me the birth control lecture."

"Hush."

"They will say it is probably for the best that I lost this baby."

"Trust me, they won't. Don't think such things." He put a finger to my lips to silence me. He took my hand. "Let your mind rest. I can sing for you. I'll close my eyes, and I won't know what you're saying."

I started to laugh, and continued even though it hurt. He kissed my cheek, closed his eyes, and began to sing so quietly that I had to concentrate on listening to him.

The following morning, Dr. Patel told me I was ready to go home. I could have argued with him had I the energy, but I agreed that I would improve more rapidly once I left the hospital. Before I was discharged, the prosecutor dropped by to update me on the changes in the case against Ken. "Obviously," concluded Colin Wu, "while new charges are being processed, the trial is suspended. I can't tell you when it will resume."

As much as I wished this whole thing was finished, I accepted this delay as necessary. Other matters seemed more urgent. "Can you tell me a couple of things, Colin?"

"I hope I can."

"Was he still there when they arrested him?"

"On the bridge?" He nodded. "Yes. Standing there, leaning over the rail and blubbering."

"Blubbering?" My stomach turned.

"Yes. He seemed," he paused to hunt for the right word, "conflicted about your injuries and your having escaped further suffering at his hands." Colin straightened his posture, apparently as disgusted as I was. "Well, anyway, your friend explained about your history. So the police took him into custody."

"Why did Ken come after me? Did he really think he could stop me from testifying?"

"He nearly did," Colin replied sadly. "I haven't been able to learn much from Williams. He hasn't said much that makes sense."

"It makes me wonder," I began. All those months when I thought I'd been safe I could have been leading Ken all over town. He might have found my new home. He might have found Sean's. He could have tried to hurt the girls. "Has he been prowling around the city all of this time?"

Colin shrugged, adding nothing to my confidence until he said, "If he was, he won't be able to do it anymore. He won't be free to wander streets in the Carollons again."

Those words worked some calming magic on me. "How could I have been so blind?"

"You weren't alone, Solace. I thought the same as you, that what he did to you before was caused by anger and embarrassment, and that it wasn't something he would normally have done."

"I guess you know now that I wouldn't make a very good character witness."

He laughed. "I'll keep that in mind. Perhaps we won't have to put you on the stand now. Williams should plead guilty."

The girls had raided my apartment to prepare the first floor guestroom for me with my own things. From the bed I could look out through the usually open french doors into the flower garden. As moving about became easier, I found myself ever more frequently sitting amongst the flowers, benefiting from their beauty as well as the fresh air and sunshine. Sean watched over me, making sure I paced myself during my recovery. He understood that I needed solitude, but he intruded enough to ensure that I did not pull too far inside myself.

I only went out once in the first two weeks, and that was to see the doctor. I didn't miss being out and about, and never had the chance to be lonely. Most of my friends allowed Sean to meter their visits. Cindy came by daily, bringing solid support and doing her best to ease Sean's burdens by slipping away to do some item of housework each time she came. Bridget stopped by several evenings, always calm, always sending the girls into the backyard to run around with Patrick. Mike telephoned me daily and came when he could.

Another frequent visitor was Rev. Green, the pastor of St. Anne's Church. Sean and I both looked forward to our meetings, at which we discussed our renewed gratitude for life, my growing faith, and our wedding plans. Rev. Green welcomed me to his congregation. He also asked us if we wanted to schedule our nuptials for February, when my parents would be in Williamsport.

"I don't think I'll be ready," I answered. Sean took my hand supportively.

The attack itself, however, more than the results of it made me want to wait. I was healing well. The bruises were fading, my broken bones were knitting, and my breaths came more easily. Sean and I took longer walks, venturing ever further from his beautiful home. I wasn't afraid to leave the house, even alone. But I knew that my mind had not yet been opened to the worst of my suffering.

As Christmas approached, Maureen and Irina filled the house with every delicious odor except that of the natural Christmas tree. Because they must be imported to the Carollons, few people chose to afford the expense. Sean's shiny, red tree was a polar opposite of the Fraser fir I had enjoyed at my parents' house the previous year, yet its cheeriness made it just as perfect. Summer was beginning, and Christmas in the Carollons is a time for bright colors and outdoor gatherings. I managed to attend a few, and our first Christmas together was a bittersweet, but special time.

We spent much of Christmas Eve at George and Olga's, where for the first time in several years their entire family was able to gather at once. Tim was allowed to stay overnight, and we two convalescents sat together in a corner receiving kind encouragement to rest and enjoy. Judging by the level of activity in the crowded room, it was a good thing there were not two more able bodies moving about and helping.

Sean took care of everything at my apartment. He cleaned, threw out food, and brought me things I wanted. The first time I went with him, we tried to make an event of it. He did most of the little work that needed to be done. It was less difficult than I expected to see my personal space looking so impersonal and unused. Walking back into the empty living room, I said, "It looks like you've taken care of everything. Thank you."

"You're welcome. Always aim to please." He put his arms around me and began to kiss me in the most tempting way.

"And you succeed," I giggled. "You've done so much."

"Not really. The place was clean. There wasn't much to do."

"Okay, well, then I guess I'm just grateful that you didn't move me out and re-let the apartment while I've been out of circulation."

"I know better. You'd probably break off our engagement if I took such a liberty."

My fingers crawled up his shoulder and across his chest. "Well, I guess you know me well enough to marry me."

"You still had doubts?"

"No."

"Why don't you just stay on with me? It would be nice."

I smiled then shook my head. "It's too soon. I need to move back here when I'm better."

"I'm going to miss you."

"Me too, but there are things I need to finish. Besides, I've never liked the idea of living together before marriage. I don't know how to explain it," I continued weakly. I looked up into the soft blue of his eyes, but though he was close enough to touch, I felt like I was beyond his reach. "Sometimes I feel like there's a barrier between me and the world, Sean. I don't know if I am capable of making the necessary emotional commitments."

He pulled me to him, so that even with my dullness, I could feel the warmth of his body. "I know," he whispered into my hair. "It will come back to you."

I lifted my head from his chest. "I—I'm," I began. My gaze dropped.

"Solace, you don't need to apologize or explain. If it's important to you to move back here, that's all I need to know. I've never really liked the idea of living together either, except that now that you are living with us I don't want you to leave. I like having you there. That's why I want to marry you."

I smiled shyly, feeling better for his support.

He nodded gravely. "It was very difficult to actually, finally move to the house. I would have liked to wait for you, but the timing wasn't right. We'll be sad when you leave us."

"It's the right thing to do. You and your daughters have been planning to live in that house for so long. You should be there without me for a while. Plus I still have a few things I need to work out. I've gotten sidetracked, and sometimes I don't remember what I have to do that is so important." I laughed at myself.

He smiled too. "When do you want to move back then?"

"Definitely before my parents get here!"

"Goes without saying."

"Yeah, I've got to prove that I can take care of myself."

"You know, you are allowed to be proud of your accomplishments. You've grown so much in these last few years, and your folks, especially your mum, haven't had the opportunity to see it. So, strut a little."

"They'll hardly be seeing me at my best, but maybe I can show them how...durable I am." I stepped back, supporting all of my weight on my own two feet.

He leaned forward and placed a big, wet kiss on my lips. "I'm proud of you. You've learned to admit you have faults without denigrating yourself."

I shook my head, still unconvinced that my self-esteem was in any way linked to the way I described myself. "You do it at times," I murmured into his shirt.

"Not in the same way. I may joke about my foibles, but I don't punish myself for having them."

"I don't deserve," I stopped suddenly, laughed at my mistake and corrected myself, "Sometimes it seems like you know me better than

I know myself." His smile warmed me. "You just might be right. Again." I rose to my tip-toes and kissed his cheek. "And I will come, Sean. You didn't lose me."

As I was locking the door, which was the only useful thing I did while I was there, he told me that he had another errand. Hoping to surprise the girls, he had secretly arranged to see a woman about adopting a kitten.

The girls spied us coming through the back gate, shoulder to shoulder, with our heads bent over the sleeping bundle in my arms. They ran to meet us. "It looks like you're bringing a baby home from the hospital!" Irina called out laughing.

"Shush!" Maureen cried sharply, reprimanding her sister and flinging her arm out to the side, striking Irina across the belly with enough force that she doubled over and released a loud huff of air. "How could you say such a thing?"

Sean jumped forward, quickly evaluated Irina's wellbeing, and yanked Maureen away by the arm. She was quicker to recognize his anger than to understand that her blow was not only worse than Irina's comment but delivered too late to protect us from any harm it might have caused.

Irina fell against me, covering her face and sobbing over and again, "I'm sorry!" As much as her sister's blow had hurt her, I knew she was more upset to think she had said something that might have hurt me. My shoulder was wet with her tears.

"It's alright, Irina," I said, hoping to soothe her. The cat grew nervous. "Look at your kitty."

Still punishing herself for the hurt she had neither intended nor delivered, she tried to meet my eyes. "It's so c-c-cute," she hiccoughed. "I'm so sorry, Solace. I didn't think. I'm so sorry."

"I'm okay, Irina. You didn't do anything wrong. Do you want to hold the kitten? It's hard for me with this cast."

Irina took the kitten, and in an instant her tears faded. "We'll have to get her something to eat, won't we?"

I looked over my shoulder at Sean and Maureen. She looked miserable and ready to bolt off to her room, but he made her wait until we went inside. Irina took the kitten off to explore on the carpet, and I waited for Sean in the kitchen.

There was still a quiet conversation going on as they entered the house. "She gets me so frustrated sometimes, Dad. Why won't she think about what she says before she says it?"

"You're blaming Irina?" He stopped her again. "I would have hoped that what happened to Solace would have convinced you that violence is wrong. How could you think hitting your sister would make Solace feel better?"

"But after…." She didn't finish. She did not want to say the kind of thing she had punished her sister for saying. "It just seemed cruel."

He held her by the shoulder with one hand. She gulped and looked for her sister. "I'm sorry, Rina."

Irina wasn't quite ready to accept her apology, so she just nodded and continued playing with the cat.

Then Maureen turned to me. "Mr. Wu phoned while you were out. He wants you to ring him back. He said it was important."

I had already been tired. Now it seemed more than I could do to walk to the telephone. Maureen was gone before I started dialing, but Sean fussed around near me, ostensibly making a shopping list for pet supplies, but mostly he listened to my part of the conversation, which was much less than half, because Colin did most of the talking. When I hung up, I announced in a shaking voice, "Ken has agreed to plead guilty. Now he will be taken for a psychological evaluation."

"That is good news," he decreed. "It should make things much easier for you. Maybe you won't need to testify. Did he say how long a prison term Ken could receive?"

"No," I answered with a quick shake of my head. "I didn't ask."

He put his arm around me and kissed the top of my head. "It's coming to an end, Solace."

"Yeah," I said with a wry smile. "It's about time." Close to collapse, I leaned my cheek against his chest. I fell asleep before he and Maureen left to go to the pet store. Irina had been given the first offer, but she wanted to stay home with the kitten. At some point during my sleep, Irina crawled onto the bed beside me. I don't think she expected to sleep, but she did, with the baby cat snuggled up against her neck, nestled in her auburn hair.

Chapter Seventeen

The first time I went out on my own, I took the bus downtown to my office to arrange returning to work. I would start off at three hours a day and add time as my stamina increased. The temporary worker who had been filling in for me would stay to help me, while she prepared to take over for another employee who would soon be going on maternity leave.

After saying hello to my officemates, I took the bus back to mid-town to go to my apartment. I got off at an earlier stop and began to walk. I thought I would wander toward home, maybe window shop or stop at Higgie's for a snack. I ended up walking past the chinese restaurant, and then tracing the route Peter and I had taken the night Ken attacked me.

As I healed I had thought little about Ken or the attack. There wasn't room inside me to really feel anything deeply, and for the time being my deepest wells held more gratitude than anything else. There was love and faith, but sorrow, anger, and hatred floated at the surface. I was tempted to skim them off, but that hadn't worked very well when my marriage ended; I was sure I would bring myself more long-term pain if I dismissed those feelings before I learned to handle them.

There were at least a dozen people visiting, studying, and eating early lunches in the pavilion. I saw a girl who had been in one of my classes last year. When I waved to her, she reddened and waved back slowly, so I knew that she knew what had happened to me—at least part of it. I didn't stop. Farther along I noticed that the brush had been cleared away from the restroom building and a couple of street lamps had been added along the way. I didn't stop. I followed the path Ken had dragged me along with his hands at my throat. When I reached the top of the stairs, I looked down, picking out the tree I had leaned against while my angel radioed for help. I turned and walked back toward campus, my curiosity at an end for the moment.

Away from the river, the walks became more formal. The campus was built on squares. I walked the width of it, past the gym, and out the other side to Gordon Street. Looking at shop windows, I walked slowly toward Higgie's. A few shops from the café, I noticed Cara Reilly selecting produce at a sidewalk market.

She saw me before I said anything and rushed over to hug me. "Solace! Oh my God, I can't believe you're out on your own, but you look great, I mean, considering what happened. How are you?"

"Pretty well, considering what happened. I feel better every day. I'm having a bit of a celebration day."

"That's wonderful. Where are you going? Do you have time to chat over a cuppa?"

"If you do! I'd love to visit. I was going up to Higgie's anyway."

"Perfect. I'll catch up with you, Solace. I just need to pay for these." She was at my side a few minutes later, and took my arm, which I appreciated after so much walking. "It's my day off. And I didn't make any plans."

"I've been busy. I went to my office this morning to arrange going back. I think I'm still in shock," I joked. "But I'm so glad I ran into you. We've never gotten a chance to talk without a hundred people around."

"We'll have to find our ways," she chimed. "So, how is Sean? Is he ready to kill that Rosie bloke?"

"He's okay," I said thoughtfully. Sean had never let me see his anger, but of course he must feel it. "He is more concerned with me. He knows there is no point in interfering with the judicial process."

"True enough."

"We have enough going on anyway. I'm probably going to move back to my apartment in the next week."

"Really? Will you be able to fix dinner and stuff?"

"Maybe."

We stayed at the café for about forty-five minutes, getting to know each other better. "Your family has been kind to me," I said as we got up to leave.

Her face grew serious. "We know a bit about the delicate nature of life, Solace," she said in an instructive manner. "There is no point in hoarding our vitality or our kindness. Joy must be a part of as many moments of our existence as it can possibly be."

"I admire that view, but how does Mike get by?"

She laughed. "Oh, Mike! Mike can't be happy unless he has something to gripe about."

"I can relate to that too," I admitted.

"Well, you are kindred spirits, whether you like it or not."

"In many of our faults," I responded. "I love Mike, Cara. He and I tend to kind of twist our optimism."

"Glass half empty doesn't bother you?"

"I like my glasses washed and put away."

She laughed again. "Oh, Solace! You're a delight. No wonder Mike is so comfortable with you. You're my sister already. I can tell."

I telephoned Sean as soon as I arrived at my apartment. Pleased to learn that they weren't all hovering over the phone, anxious for my safety, I left a message that after I did a few things at my place I would take a taxi home in time to eat lunch with them, given they were home for lunch. There was nothing for me to do, so I went out on the balcony to enjoy the fresh air and the view of the ocean in the distance.

As soon as I sat I began to melt into my chair. My eyes lost focus and my head tilted to the side. I jumped to my feet, suddenly awake, when I heard a noise behind me. Wobbling at first, I turned to see Sean coming in through the living room and calling softly, "Solace?"

"I'm out here," I said, going inside.

"Hallo, sweetie, I got your message. I hope you don't mind me coming down. Thought you might prefer my taxi." He walked to me with an arm out ready to embrace me. "Can I take you out for lunch, or are you too tired?"

"I'm glad you weren't worried about me." I stretched up to kiss his lips. "I thought I wanted some time alone, but look, I fell asleep. Must be the company."

"What did you expect?" he replied with a chuckle. "So what have you been doing? Go shopping or something?"

I hesitated to tell him the whole truth. "I took the bus, but I got off near Hunan Bouquet." I watched his face pale. "I walked up to where Peter and I ate that night."

"Solace," he moaned.

"I started down toward the bridge, but I didn't go that far. They've added lights and cleared out some of the brush."

"How did you feel?"

"I was okay. I thought I might be terrified, but I wasn't. I saw enough. Now I know I'm not afraid to go back down there." I don't think he quite believed me. "I ran into Cara, and we had tea at

Higgie's. It was nice. She had the day off and didn't seem to know what to do with it."

"Leah must be at work." He ran his eyes over me. I was surprised to find that his evaluation stimulated me. "So, should I leave you to sleep?"

"Not on a deck chair." I twisted my body around to loosen some of the kinks.

"Your bed?"

"Then don't leave me."

He took me into his arms, and we kissed like new lovers, with caution and passion, reigniting the fire that my injuries had forced us to bank. I moved awkwardly, and I know that I was far from sexy, but it didn't matter. We found our way. For a long time he sought only my mouth. It was wonderful. I never wanted him to move his mouth from mine, because I wanted him to do other things so very badly. I could barely feel his touch, and yet it thrilled me. Just as lovemaking had always been with Sean, it flowed joyfully, generously, and naturally out of the emotional love we felt for each other.

For a split second I drifted, exhausted and satisfied, until Sean nuzzled his nose against my ear and neck, luring me back to wakefulness. I wasn't ready to move yet, but he sat up, saying, "I'm starving, heh. Let's go get lunch. Shall we go to O'Brien's?"

"Okay," I yawned. I began to push myself into an upright position.

"Let's celebrate."

"I thought we just did."

"Indeed. However, I'd like to please a few more of our senses."

"I'm a lucky girl, Sean Donovan. It took me a while to figure it out, but I know it now."

"It took you about ten seconds to change your mind about me once you knew I wasn't married." He collected clothing from the floor. "That is hardly a long time."

"Was it that long? I guess I was standing there with my mouth hanging open for a while, wasn't I?"

"I like knowing a woman has a healthy mouth."

"Oh, that's what you were doing, Mr. Green Hair, evaluating my teeth and gums?"

He handed me a bundle of cloth. "Hardly." He pulled on his trousers. "I was looking down your shirt."

"That sounds more like the Sean Donovan I know." I started dressing.

Sean helped me move back to my apartment the following weekend. Though we both had mixed feelings, we agreed I needed to do it. The girls didn't understand why I was leaving so I didn't ask them to help me pack. After I was resettled, we met Mike and Cara at a seafood shack and spent the afternoon hanging out with them. It helped to take my mind off the fact that I wouldn't be sleeping beside Sean as I had been since I'd been able to go upstairs without help.

It was a false kind of independence, because I needed help to do many things. Cindy popped in frequently to do me two-handed favors. "You're getting the knack of this one-handed thing, eh, Solace."

"I have it mastered. I evoke pity and get other people to take care of me." I rinsed the soap off of the measuring cup I had just washed. "It's all kind of weird."

She and I had made a stretchable supper, most of which was portioned and put in the freezer. As I washed what I could, she leaned against the counter waiting to scrub the rest. "You could have just stayed with Sean."

"That would be too easy."

"There's nothing wrong with doing things the easy way."

"I'd feel like I was cheating, Cindy. Don't get me wrong; I was happy at Sean's. But I wasn't supposed to be there yet. I felt like I was getting ahead of things. I wouldn't have been there if Ken hadn't attacked me." I rinsed my hands and turned away from the sink. "Well, I suppose the pregnancy might have gotten us to move everything forward." I turned my back to her while I dried my hands. "I miss Sean and the girls terribly, but I need to be on my own again. I, we need to come together on our own terms. Not because I need his help, or because it's convenient to be together, or because Ken Williams hurt me, just as I don't need to move back here to prove anything to my parents, although, I admit that might be part of my motivation."

"That's okay. You deserve a chance to show off for them." She ran steaming water over the pan she had just scoured. "And Sean understands?"

"Yes," I said, nodding.

"You've had a big blow, Solace." She dried her hands and set one on my shoulder in a comforting manner. "You've got to have a zillion things going through your mind now. And you must be so angry that it's hard to concentrate. Hell, I'd like to take an axe to that bastard. Beats you up and tries to drown you like some unwanted cat. I get angry when people drown cats!" She tugged at the bottom of her shirt, straightening it and quieting her anger in one movement. "I never liked him."

"I know, but why didn't you say something sooner?"

"Would you have listened?"

"I like to think I would have, but even when I was given the sketch—and I knew it was a warning—I still didn't want to believe that I could be making that kind of mistake again."

"See? Besides, I wasn't sure. I was kind of angry at men then, so I didn't trust myself."

"Cindy, you sound like me. My head says one thing and my heart another, and I keep thinking that my brain ought to be smarter than my gut."

Crinkling her nose, she asked, "Does your brain love Sean? Or your heart?"

"Oh, both," I cried giggling. "Head, heart, gut, genitals, and toenails too, I think."

"Hoo! Hoo!" she cried. "Go, Sean! Now, him I've always liked." She assessed my emotional stability. "Even though you're stumbling a bit right now, eh, you aren't feeling less for Sean, are you?"

I shook my head. "He's wonderful. I'm glad I have him." For a moment I thought I might cry. "Very glad I have him."

"You okay, girly girl?" She lifted my chin, forcing me to meet her steady green eyes.

"Not really, but I'm coming along."

She shook her head sympathetically. "It's terrible to have joy and anticipation torn away from you. You were afraid of being pregnant, and yet I know you wanted it too. We could tell you were scared. Did you know we'd guessed you were pregnant? I bet you were more afraid of attaching yourself to the idea of having a baby for fear that something would go wrong than you were of having one."

"Sean says I shouldn't worry about bad things happening; that sometimes worrying about them makes them happen," I said. I remembered how kind she and Melissa had been to me while Sean was away. I hadn't suspected they knew what I hadn't dared to consider. "Of course, he still worries."

"He is wise, Solace. It would be great if we could control our worries so that we didn't stress about things, yet still have enough concern for the future that we don't behave like a bunch of grasshoppers."

"There are always lots of grasshoppers. Their methods can't be all wrong."

"When you have, like, a million babies at a time, the odds are some of them will grow up."

"Babies," I said wistfully. "We really do need them."

"I suppose that's why my lifestyle is condemned. The oldest, most sacred rules are there to make sure the species survives. Melissa and I cannot make a baby." She sighed. "I wish I could have children." Her eyes filled with tears. "There you go, Solace. You almost make me wish Melissa was a man!"

"I know it must be hard for you to be torn between the right relationship and some of the things that you have always wanted and expected from your life," I said. She nodded. "If you were with a man, there would still be no guarantee that you would have children. Even if you both wanted them."

She nodded again and brightened. "That's true, Solace. I might keep trying, and wondering, and go to special doctors, and all that just to find out why I wasn't getting pregnant. Could go through a lot of pain, eh? But Melissa and I know what to expect in that way. Maybe it is easier."

My parents arrived a few days later. My father had a list of things he wanted to do, and while my mother made it clear that she only went with him because I had to work, she made no complaints about climbing the volcano on Pentecost Island or spending two nights at the St. Mary's Bay resort on St. Joseph's. I thought that breaking up the visit made it more successful than it might otherwise have been, because we never sat too long rehashing events or previous conversations.

Though I was still supposed to use the sling on my arm most of the time, I was cleared to drive. I borrowed Sean's van to take my parents to the ferry from their hotel. When I returned it to him, I found him slouching into the cushions of his soft, old couch. He didn't respond to my entrance until I leaned over the back of the couch and kissed his cheek. I rested my chin on one shoulder and a hand on the other and asked as a way of prodding him out of his lethargy, "What's the matter? Is the creative atmosphere wrong here? You haven't painted at all since you moved."

"I think I'm just too, I don't know, something to work," he said shaking his head.

"Preoccupied? Miserable? Lonely? Horny?"

He chuckled. "Horny usually makes me work better." He turned to me, evaluating the moment. Apparently having decided it was not the right time for a sexual advance, he continued in a serious tone, "Preoccupied, miserable, and lonely."

"Solace withdrawal?" I walked around to sit beside him.

"Cocky, aren't you?" He raised an eyebrow. "Yeah, that's part of it." He looked down to hide his face. "God, we miss you."

"Should I come back and take care of you? I'm holding up pretty well."

"Naw," he answered, back in control. "You need to do what you're doing, and we need to do what we're doing."

"Were you putting on a cheery façade for my benefit while I was here?"

"Maybe a little bit. Taking care of you gave all three of us some purpose that we don't have since you moved out." He turned to face me. "Now that they don't see you every day, the girls are starting to move on. But they miss you. There's a lot they don't understand."

"I know. And you?"

"I worry about you quite a lot. I know this hasn't really hit you yet. You're kind of insulated from your emotions. And, Solace," he added, gently addressing my unstated fears, "don't worry about us growing apart." He reached over to comb my hair with his splayed fingers. "I am glad you are protected from the worst of your pain." His voice cracked. His head dropped over, his neck unable to support the weight of his thoughts. "I don't feel less for you because your eyes are dry."

"Should we postpone the wedding?" I asked. I was afraid that this might be the right thing to do.

"I don't want to." He paused, collecting himself. "I want to be with you more than ever, but I can wait. We've been changed. It's my hope that helping each other through all this will bring us closer and make us stronger." He ran his fingertips along the line of my jaw, his forefinger lingering under my chin, raising my face, demanding I meet his eyes, reassuring me. "God will guide us, Solace." I leaned forward and kissed his forehead. "I stay busy. Keeps me from moping." He rubbed his nose on my cheek, warming me. "I've had conferences with the guidance counselors at the school about the girls and the things we've gone through. And I've been at the church a good deal. I've been getting a little private counseling with Rev. Green, and I've been helping Marcia with organizing the children's music programs."

I kissed the tip of his nose and then broke his delicate hold on me. "Have you painted anything?"

"I've done some sketching, but I'd botch the painting if I touched it now. I do know what I want to do with it. I just need to pause and think about how to complete it."

I dared to ask, "You haven't lost your inspiration?"

"Not at all." His voice brightened, and his eyes, even his skin, seemed to glow with the creative energy I had seen in him when his work was going well. "It's in my head now, Solace. It will come back to my hands."

"So, you're not stuck?"

"Not in a technical sense. It is still happening. It's just redirecting itself now, so I can catch up with the changes in the subject." Then seeing the look of concern on my face, he added, "She's more mature now, Solace. She's stronger."

"Oh. Okay. And you think I am?"

"You're stronger than you think. Think how much you have on your plate now. You are recovering from serious injuries, easing back into work, planning a wedding, catching up on your social life, taking care of your home with one arm in a sling, hosting company, and soon you'll be going back to school too." He took a big breath. "You are also grieving, whether you recognize it through your shock or not. All of those things are protecting you from some of the pain, but they are also dulling your senses and tiring you, just as a narcotic would. Thinking about it, you probably should take the next semester off from school."

"Wow," I said dully, sinking into the cushions. "No pep talk?"

He smiled mechanically. "Not today." He patted my lap.

"Should I analyze you too?"

"You don't need to," he said. "I've already done it. I took too long a break from my painting, but I'm glad we took our trip. The girls love you and are so happy about our plans to marry and everything, but it was good for us to have that little time alone together, because from now on, *you* will always be part of *us*." He looked up, and I nodded to let him know that I understood. "Then you were hurt and I couldn't think about anything as superficial as art." He shrugged.

"I agree so far."

"Then you moved out." He took a deep breath. "It gave me a break of sorts since I didn't have to be strong all the time. And now I'm settling into a new kind of normal, I guess. With summer winding down, I've had to do more for the kids. Maureen's joined the cross-country team at the high school. I try to help my folks with Tim."

"I *have* missed a lot, Bionic Bloke."

"And much of it damned well worth missing." He laughed and brushed a kiss on my cheek as he rose. He offered me a hand. "I must confess: I'm a bit more Artificial Boy than Bionic Bloke, no matter what you believe."

"It doesn't matter. I love them both." I followed him out to the garden. "Is it helping to talk to Rev. Green?"

"Yes." He examined his plants, deciding what was ready to pick. "We have lots of history. I'm one of his test cases, heh, one of the lambs who can't quite stay in the fold no matter how hard I believe."

"You just like to stretch the boundaries." When he bent to pick some beans, I tapped his bottom with my pointed toes. He turned to give me a sweet smile. "I like living on the edge with you, Sean Donovan. I used to believe I had to stay inside the fence too, but I've learned that sometimes the grass really is greener on the other side. Why not stray a little and try it?"

Two days later Sean and I collected my parents at the ferry, took them back to the hotel, and accompanied them to their new room. Sean started back to the elevator while I was still arranging to pick them up for dinner later. As I turned to go, my father went into the bathroom, and my mother put her hand on my arm to stop me. "Solace, are you and Sean getting along? He's moody."

"We're fine."

"Is he always like this?"

"No."

"What's his problem?" She persisted.

"What do you think?"

"He isn't still upset about your accident, is he? You're okay now. Why hasn't he moved on?"

"It was not an accident," I stated. "I'm not okay now, and Sean knows that I haven't really even begun to grapple with it. It was all a big shock."

"But you weren't that far along, Solace. I know having a miscarriage is difficult, but it often happens early in pregnancy. You need to move on. Try again *after* you get married."

"I didn't have a miscarriage," I corrected her firmly. "I was beaten and driven to suicide. It is a very different thing. If I'd had a miscarriage, I might be able to console myself by thinking that there was a problem with the baby—that it was sick or malformed and would have had a miserable life—but I don't have even that cold comfort. My child was murdered before it had a chance to live." I started to cry. "Sean and I never even got to rejoice over its creation."

She was taken aback, but still tried to soothe me. "You didn't have an emotional attachment. Don't cry, Sweetie."

"Don't try to stop me from crying!" I snapped, throwing her hand off my arm.

"Why are you so defensive? What can I do to help you?"

"Nothing. You can't do anything and you shouldn't do anything. You cannot make this right. You cannot make it easier for me. Your being here is enough."

"You are awfully busy feeling sorry for yourself. You need to get on with your life, Solace. You have so much to look forward to. You are about to marry the man you love. You are going to move into a beautiful home, and your new family seems very kind. You can have other babies. You need to look forward, not behind. It could be so much worse than it is."

"Right. I could have died too," I monotoned.

I didn't notice that my father had returned until he spoke. "What's wrong?"

"She's making things harder on herself."

Dad cracked a smile wrought by knowledge. He put a comforting arm around her then turned to me. "How's your arm?"

"It's getting stronger and moving better." I swung it around to demonstrate.

"Good," he nodded. "You'll be able to help Sean with the bags on your honeymoon."

I shook my head. "Not likely. He was brought up right. He'll always insist on carrying the bags."

"He's alright," Dad announced. "You kids have both been through things your mother and I can barely imagine. It's tough, but your experiences seem to be making you a better person. You're stronger, and kinder, and somehow getting hurt hasn't taken away your innocence. Now, go on," he said indicating the open door. The confidence in his eyes soothed me. "We shouldn't push your boyfriend's patience much longer. We'll see you at four-thirty."

As soon as we knew that my parents' visit would coincide with the beginning of Lent, the girls began planning a Shrove Tuesday pancake dinner for various family and friends. They transformed the lounge into a banquet hall, with tables, mostly boards on sawhorses covered with table cloths, arranged throughout the large, open room. Flowers had been brought in from the gardens and placed everywhere. The sun was fast disappearing, but there was plenty of light in the room from lamps and candles. Through closed doors, we could hear an in-progress piano lesson.

Noting the low level of the music, my father observed, "The walls are good and solid in this house." While he was never fond of listening to amateur musicians, he did like the house. "You feel like this is your home already, don't you, Solace?"

"Almost," I said with a smile.

"Will Sean be willing to decorate?" my mother asked, looking around at the bare walls and old furniture that had been pushed into a conversational corner. "You'd think an artist would be interested in that."

"He's a guy," I said with a shrug.

The student started his piece over again. It was something by Grieg that sounded very difficult to me, and it sounded better on the second attempt. My mother remarked upon that. Maureen headed down the hall to answer the door for the day's final student. I snooped over the countertops.

"I guess you won't need to do much cooking," my father observed as he surveyed the array of borrowed electric griddles that would allow us to cook dozens of pancakes at once.

"The girls are great with big events and baking, but I think that Sean and I will do most of the everyday cooking." I pulled out glasses and began to arrange them for easy pouring.

"He's done a good job with them."

I agreed. "He's a good father."

Mike and Cara came in through the back door. A few minutes later, Bridget entered through the front, followed by Cindy and Melissa swinging Patrick between them as they walked. "Sean's folks are pulling up." Mike hurried to the front of the house. The music started up again. This student had obviously been practicing. My mother listened, enjoying. Rob and the two youngest Donovan brothers strolled in gloomily, their feelings hurt because Tim had chosen to lean on his former comrade-in-arms. Gabe and Baz half-wrestled their way down the hall belching some rude complaints through their fists. Both boys were on their worst adolescent behavior as they tried to prove their maturity.

We had our own pancake races in the backyard before dinner, but most of our guests still opted to depart for the festivities downtown before eight o'clock. Except for my mother, who kept glancing over at the mess, the rest of us were settled with our feet up, ignoring of the stacks of dirty dishes in the kitchen. To distract her, I asked, "When do you want me to take you back to the hotel?"

"Oh, whenever. We don't want to get mixed up in the carnival. Can I help you clean up or are we holding you back?"

"No to both. We'll get to it. As long as we clear away all the food, the wash-up can wait until the morning," Sean answered for me in a voice saturated with indolence. Irina was snuggled against him, half asleep. Maureen sat on the floor in front of me, leaning her head against my knees. "I feel my second wind coming, and since I hardly helped get things ready, I will head the clean-up."

"Great," Maureen grumbled, knowing her father would delegate the work.

"You'll help me, won't you, Leah?"

"Sure, Mate. I'll throw all the dishes away and buy you new ones."

"I like these dishes, and they don't make them anymore, so you can't replace them."

"Geez, Donny, you're just way too domestic." Mike flashed a smile at me, "Do you like the dishes? They aren't your style."

"He's got fifty-two place settings, Mike. I don't care what they look like. They go in the dishwasher and we can feed most of the Donovans without scrounging. What could be better?"

"Fifty-two place settings?"

"Clearance sale, Mate. I bought them out. Two fifty each for a box of four. I counted it up and figured it would be enough for most occasions."

"You bought them new? Wow! Didn't think you had it in you."

In response to Mike's continued harassment Sean discretely displayed one finger to him in such a way that only Mike and Cara could see. Mike stopped his verbal play and stood up. "If we are going to help, we ought to get to it. We both have to be up earlier than the rest of you slugs."

We all rose then, except the cat, my father, who cooked but did not clean, and Tim, who was staying the night. They conversed while the rest of us wound things down to a stack of rinsed dishes, most of which would take a turn in the dishwasher the next morning.

I spent the remainder of their visit alone with my parents. I waited with them at the airport on Saturday, and they concluded their visit by expressing their satisfaction with my circumstances. As we exchanged our last kisses, my mother smiled and said, "It's hard for me to remember sometimes that what is good for me is not necessarily going to be good for you. Because I would never have wanted to be a second wife or a stepmother, I assumed it would overwhelm you. I see now, it's not a matter of strength, but of your finding your place. You've made decisions that suit you, Solace."

Chapter Eighteen

I should have been elated by my mother's comments. And I was. Briefly. Then I got out of the taxi and went upstairs to my apartment. The moment I walked through my door, a second emotion, triggered by the euphoria, overwhelmed me. I staggered to the telephone and somehow dialed Sean's number. Sobbing and not listening, I sank to the floor, dropped the handset, and curled into a tight ball.

Days later or just minutes, Sean was there, holding me, stroking my back, lending me strength. He kept us in physical contact. I wasn't up to understanding much beyond touch and tone of voice. I felt as empty as I had in the river, yet full of fury and sorrow. Gradually I began to comprehend his words, and even to respond with more than incoherent weeping. I began to reawaken. I agreed to let him call my counselor, who I had seen a couple of times in the weeks since I left the hospital. He made an appointment for me to see her the following morning. I knew therapy would help, but all I wanted was to be alone with Sean until I was calm enough for useful discussion. There was a war going on inside my mind, and Sean understood that well enough to watch me to make sure that it did not escalate.

He stayed close. We barely parted during all those hours before he took me to my appointment. I could almost function. My fragile calm held until my counselor looked at me. Then I crumbled again.

Sean waited outside. When I was done, I leaned on him. We went to the house and picked up the girls to go to church together. Sean and I were both quiet. The girls tried to be lively as they avoided serious conversation of any sort, which they did for many of the following days.

The next day, I found them loitering in the hall near my door when I got home. They frolicked into my kitchen with a new recipe they wanted to try, much as they had when we were new friends. "Dad couldn't come," Maureen explained. But he had sent them to watch over me. "He has to give some make up lessons." I was free to watch, listen, and hopefully absorb some part of their buoyant spirits.

Counseling was helpful and difficult. At first, I cried so much that it was a wonder my counselor could understand me. When I didn't know what to do, she guided me and when I doubted myself, she reassured me that the grief and anger I felt were normal and necessary and that my inability to concentrate was merely my brain's reaction to the internal bombardment it was trying to survive, similar to shutting off a valve to prevent an explosion. After a few sessions, I began to reconnect with the world and the people around me. And I began dreading to go, because during our sessions I reopened the wounds I had managed to keep closed in between. Yet after each session, I had worked through things well enough that I could lay my pain aside for another span of time.

During this time when I was so vulnerable, it was especially important to me to have my home graced, acknowledged, and sanctified by guests. Social visits proved that it was not just a place for me to rest in privacy. Even a ten minute visit forced me to rise and offer a proper welcome. I credit Cindy with passing the word to my other friends, and they went out of their way for me as she continued to do with or without Melissa.

Well, not Sean, because we had always seen so much of each other. Things didn't change much with Mike either. He and I had always found impromptu ways to see each other often, but usually at a restaurant or the beach instead of our homes ever since I'd moved out of the house.

But Bridget came by when she was doing her regular shopping, and usually invited me to join her or offered to pick things up for me. Karen or Steve usually collected me before we went to Rob's script workshops for his latest play, *The Tea House*. Olga visited me, sometimes with one of her daughters and sometimes with Maggie Reilly to work on wedding plans. If they hadn't come, I, feeling undeserving, would have postponed making preparations.

As I lived through them, the weeks after my crash felt static. It seemed to take me forever to do anything, as if I had more to do than I could handle, and that the hours crept by. Like pages of an oft read book that have become stuck together, the contents could be neatly summarized. I moved forward, knowing the pain, but not having to live through it each time I thought about it. I have few distinct memories. It feels, now, like I was a spectator.

In fact, it was a busy time. I was healing and rebuilding, and I was helping Sean to some lesser degree than he was helping me. Our needs were as different as our strengths, and we each benefited by sharing more than we ever had before. With a level of sensitivity added to our already intuitive relationship, our partnership solidified.

My mind eased. He regained his vigor. The ever-present tingling in my limbs subsided. He completed a few small paintings, and spent less time in the garden and more at his piano. What was normal for us had been permanently changed. I became resigned to a feeling of overflowing emptiness, and in accepting that my soul began to refill. Almost without realizing I had come out from behind the barricades, I was on my way to my marvelous future.

Easter arrived. We were up early for church and met the rest of the Donovan family at George and Olga's for a picnic lunch and the grand egg hunt that Tim planned. He'd gotten Sean and his younger brothers to hide eggs all over the yard for the youngest of the next generation to find. I was drafted, as the official family accountant, to help him count and award the prizes.

It was a pretty, sunny day. I wasn't sure that I wanted to spend that much time sitting next to Tim, but there was no avoiding my assignment. It was the first time that I would be alone with him since he'd come home, and I didn't know what type of behavior to expect from him. My trepidation lessened when I saw how cheerfully he waved me over to the lawn chair beside his, under a big tree. Sean was dispatched on an errand. Tim showed me the prizes, in a box placed between our chairs, and explained how he wished to distribute them.

"You're looking like yourself again," he observed.

"Thanks. I still don't always feel like myself."

"That's because you let that bastard into your brain. I told you not to do that."

I scoffed. "You said that about going to court, not being beaten."

"I wasn't specific about when." He shifted in his chair. "You shouldn't blame yourself. I mean, I kind of understand why you do, but none of this shit was your fault. You told that bastard to leave you alone."

"Please, Tim," I moaned, pouting. "I don't want to talk—"

"Then just listen," he instructed. I obeyed. "Most of the bad stuff that happened to you happened after you told him to go away. You never revoked that; you didn't ask him back. And you were very clear. You told him to stay away from you forever. He didn't. Everything that happened after that was his fault. Not yours."

A few people heard him and stared. I turned toward the tree to hide my face.

"When I was really sick, I could barely think an hour ahead. By the time I got moved to the hospital here, I used to just think ahead to the next visitor that was coming to see me, looking forward to seeing their eager hope and planning how to piss them off good."

I offered him a conciliatory smile. "I guess you have to figure out what your talents are."

"Exactly." One of the tots came over with a basket of plastic eggs for me to count. Tim awarded him a little prize, and he bounded away to continue the search. "I'm irritating. I know it. I might as well embrace it."

"Perhaps you'll find a way to make a career out of it."

"I've been thinking about that." He sorted through the prizes, admiring the selection. "Now, you are good at lots of things. It's no wonder you've had trouble figuring out what you want to do with your life."

"Yeah?" I braced for another round. After the way I'd treated him when he was in the nursing home I didn't have grounds to complain, but I still didn't like it.

"The thing about you, Solace, is that you're always punishing yourself for the things you've gotten wrong. No, Solace, listen," when I opened my mouth. "I'm onto something. You have made some mistakes, and some of them have cost you. And you've gotten hurt sometimes by things you couldn't control. You're willing to forgive everyone but yourself. And yet, you've done a lot of good things and you've found a lot of happiness. Haven't you?"

I nodded in agreement. "Even now, Tim, I'm happy. I've just got this sorrow clinging to me."

"Of course you do. Events have changed you, are changing you. And I hope that you won't let your losses take away from who you are. You can gain or lose from tragedies. It's your choice, at least partly, and I hope that you'll choose to be the woman my brother believes you are. The woman he needs."

I swallowed. In my pain, sometimes I forgot Sean's. On the bridge, I had known that losing me would be a tremendous blow for him. That was one reason that my faith had guided me to risk jumping.

"You should trust yourself. You've made more good decisions than bad ones by a long shot. And you followed up the bad ones with good ones. Like marrying that dude that put you down all the time. You left him. But you still kind of believe what he had to say about you. You know he was wrong, but it still niggles at you."

I opened my mouth, thinking I would object, but nothing came out until I said, "Yes." I remained composed, and that was a bit disconcerting. I would have thought that I would have collapsed into tears by now. Only there was something that kept me alert. I saw more of Sean in Tim than I ever had. Except that Sean would have been gentler and more patient. In fact, Sean might have waited too long, trying to protect me. But Tim wasn't patient. He'd already wasted a lot of his life, and he wasn't waiting around anymore. And he wasn't about to let me do it either.

"Can you extend the trust that you have in your friends, people like me and Leah who have grown so much because of you, to accept what we think: that you're a super person who has the right to be the snobby bitch I thought you were when I met you?"

My hands, steepled as if in prayer, came to my lips. I recognized genuine, honest praise. And. I couldn't argue with him.

He reached his hand over to pat my shoulder. "I'm sorry I upset you, Solace. I'm sorry, but I hate to see you punishing yourself. I mean, you're, like, the most innocent person I've ever met, and it's just wrong. The biggest mistake you've ever made is believing the bad stuff jealous people have said about you."

"Tim?"

He retracted his hand. "Sorry." I lowered my hands, and he saw the smile on my lips. "Lent is over. It's Easter."

"Time to stop eating locusts?"

"Sister, it was *never* time to eat locusts." A couple of the children came over to collect prizes, and he began to count their eggs himself. "You know, I think I can handle this. I think Sean would like to kiss you."

"Thanks," I said, jumping up and planting a kiss on the top of his head. His hair was thicker and shinier, but I forgot to notice. I rushed across the yard to find my beloved.

"What's been going on over there?" Sean asked gently.

I took his arm and led him to the front yard for privacy. "Your brother is in a weird mood. He's being nice."

"You okay?"

"Yeah. He was just pushing me a little. Gave me some things to think about."

"Is he on a new self-destructive binge?"

"No," I shook my head and squeezed his arm. "He's doing fine. And I think maybe I should do the same."

He leaned down and kissed my lips. "I like the sound of that."

Mike would already be in the water, so I hurried downstairs to the pool to meet him. I wasn't sure that I was prepared for an afternoon at the pool. Since my fall I had only been in the water to bathe or wade at the shore's edge. At first my injuries kept me dry; now my emotions did. I wore my swimsuit with no intention of getting wet, though I suspected Mike might try to convince me to at least dangle my feet over the edge.

Mike, still dripping from his last plunge, was on the diving board. I stood in the doorway to the women's shower room watching him. At thirty-four, he was at last at ease with himself. His outdoor work suited him. He looked healthier than he had since he had gone to the war. Though he had matured into a very different person, he again resembled the fellow I had met just after moving to the islands. The maturity sat upon him well. The trained Marine's posture had returned, but he was no longer a puppet standing straight because it was demanded by his unit sergeant. His skinny body had developed a few muscular curves, his face was fuller, and his sinewy limbs bulged slightly—changes so subtle that I had hardly noticed them as they had occurred. When he saw me he made a goofy face, bounced on the board to spring high into the air, flailed his arms humorously, and turned a perfect pike into the water.

I laid my things on a lounge chair and walked to the side of the pool. He pulled himself up, crossed his arms on the rim, and rested his chin on his wrists. "Glad to see you, Solace," he called to me. "Good thing Donny didn't have you booked today."

"Do you and Sean have some kind of secret you're keeping from me that you always pretend you aren't the best of mates?"

"You're my best mate, Solace." He hoisted himself out of the water, and sat on the edge of the pool for a moment before he stood. Then we walked toward the lounge chairs. As he rubbed himself with his towel, he began again, "I need to talk with you about something important." He dropped the towel onto the seat and sat down next to it.

I laid my towel out over the chair, and stretched out on it, pretending to be relaxed, "What's up, Mike?"

"How do you know when it's right to get married?"

I blinked. It was still Mike sitting in front of me. "Perhaps you should ask someone with a successful marriage under his belt, Mike."

"You're trying again. You've told me about how your ex-husband mistreated you. Now, I know Sean's a better man, but if you were so unhappy before, how do you know that it won't go wrong this time too?"

"Are we talking about me? Or you?"

"Me, but first let's talk about you."

"Okay, well then, the answer would be that Sean is a better man."

"That's it. You are just sure that he's right and you go in again?"

"Pretty much," I said with a confident, little sigh. There was something about Mike that boosted my ego, at least in relation to his. "The future is never certain. All we can do is make the decisions that seem most likely to work for us. I love Sean, and I love being with him. He helps me to feel good about myself, while my ex only took from me. There's nothing wrong with marriage itself. I liked being married. It was nice to have someone to come home to, to share plans and dreams with, and to take care of. I left because I realized that I had grown to be grateful for the time we spent apart. And I felt worse than lonely when he was with me."

"But shouldn't we marry for more than just having someone to do things with?"

"Yes. It's more than that. You need to find someone you belong with."

"I suppose," he said slowly and thoughtfully.

"You don't need to rush. Enjoy what you have now. Then take the next step when you're ready."

"Cara's pregnant," he blurted out quickly. Then more slowly, more seriously, he added, "I want to do the right thing."

I smiled and started to cry. None of my multiple emotional reactions to Mike's news completely registered in my mind.

"I wanted to tell you quietly, off by ourselves like this. I know it's got to be hard for you to hear about babies," he said apologetically.

I waved my arm in a way that told him it was alright, despite my red nose and quivering chin. "Life hasn't stopped going on around me." I swallowed. "It's right that it does, and it helps too, even when it hurts."

He took my hand. "I think that Cara should be my best friend before I marry her, Solace," he began, "but how can she be, when I already have you?"

I paused and thought about my feelings for Mike and Sean. "You can have two different kinds of best friends, Mike, as long as each one respects the other friendship." I sat up and put my feet on the concrete so that I could face him directly. "Do you feel that you can or will be able to share everything with Cara? Will you be able to show her the true you?" He nodded, his eyes fixed upon my face. "I don't know, Mike. I had one bad marriage. It was empty of sharing. No," I corrected myself, "the sharing was one-sided. It all came from me, so I didn't realize that it was missing for too long. I revealed all and had it turned against me. Can you trust Cara? With everything? Does she want to marry you? What do you think would be best for the baby? Doing what is right is not the same for everyone."

Overwhelmed, he threw his towel over his shoulders and huddled under it like he was cold. "I don't know."

"How long have you known about the pregnancy?"

"A few days. We've been kind of afraid to talk about it."

I thought about how, certain as I was about my future with Sean, I had not dared to question if my missed menstrual period could have been caused by anything other than the immense stress I felt about the upcoming trial.

In a breaking voice, Mike whispered, "I love her, Solace. She has done something to me."

Agreeing, I said, "And it suits you."

"So you think we should—"

I didn't let him finish his question. "Mike, as much as I am honored by your wish to talk to me about this, as much as I want to try to help you, you should be discussing this with Cara. She's got to be frightened now. Go to her. Comfort her and give her the assurances that she needs. Marriage is a big step, but I think you can handle it. I think you would be a wonderful father and husband, but I'm not the one whose opinion matters. You need to work some of this out on your own, and then you need to work the rest of it out with Cara."

He was silent, head down. He started playing with the drawstring on his swimming trunks. Still hiding his eyes, he asked, "Won't I hurt her if I say the wrong thing?"

I struggled against the urge to take his hand and tell him exactly what I thought he should do, but I managed to limit my response to letting him know that I understood his reaction. "You will hurt her more if you say nothing." He looked up then as he waited for me to say more. "Be fair to her. Speak to her openly about your concerns. Your fears are more centered on your own ability to handle the situation than anything negative about her, am I not right?" I looked into his melting eyes. "Well, then, let her know that. You don't want to be a bad husband and father, so you're rightfully frightened at the challenge you may be facing if you try to tackle learning both of those jobs at once. She probably has as many concerns about her own abilities as you have about yours. Only she is carrying the child inside of her, and that feels very different than it does to be her partner."

"Oh, God, Solace," he cried in a choking voice, "I do want to be her partner. For real, through thick and thin."

"Then make sure Cara understands that."

Mike's news was wonderful and difficult. After talking to him I felt more hopeful than I had in what seemed a very long time. That he had risked hurting me to confide in me and ask for advice, as he had done in the old days when I was stronger than he, meant a good deal to me. I wanted to live up to his confidence in me. So far, I felt I had done well.

At last I was ready to look into my legal options as the victim of a violent crime. Sean encouraged me in this, thinking as I did, that it might help me put events into perspective as well as the past. His brother Greg worked as a paralegal, and he referred us to a capable attorney, who helped me to assert my rights.

In the meantime, I wanted to express my gratitude to my rescuer, so I contacted Seamus Petrov, the plumber who pulled me from the river. I thanked him, and with a shaking hand I returned his silver crucifix. He protested its return until I showed him the dainty, golden cross Sean had given me. I longed to tell him of my plan to donate a portion of any monetary settlement I received from Ken to the victim's services program run by the St. Agnes Catholic Church. I was certain that it would please him, but as he was a potential witness, my news had to wait until a settlement was reached out of court several months later.

Chapter Nineteen

Our wedding preparations were in full swing. Flowers were ordered. We were already addressing invitations. Dresses were begun for me and for my two lovely bridesmaids. Rushing out to meet them for a fitting, I threw open my door and found Sean with his hand raised, ready to knock.

My greeting was less than cordial. "Why are you here?" I asked in an impatient tone, looking around him for his daughters. He knew my plans did not include him.

"I thought you might like a ride to the shop. I already dropped Reen and Rina off there," he replied. "Besides, we have plans you don't know about." I still had not invited him in, so he stepped around me. "We don't have to leave this instant, Solace, so come in for a minute," he said, reversing our roles. "Now, let me see you." Awkwardly, I turned around, in a sense reentering my home. His eyes moved up and down, evaluating me with a critical eye. "You need to change."

"What?" My mouth had been hanging open, and I barely closed it enough to utter that one syllable.

He smiled. He leaned toward me, lifted my chin with one gentle finger, and kissed me on the lips. I managed to keep my jaws together, so he risked another kiss, and that one got my attention. It had been a while since we had fully engaged in a heated, nonverbal exchange. When he pulled away, I was more welcoming. Seeing that, he said, "Should I have called you?"

"No. It's okay." I smiled a little, closed-lip smile. "What's going on?"

"Mmmm," he mused. "I can't tell you yet." He turned around and leaned out of my door. "But I brought you this to wear." He displayed a garment bag bearing the name of my dressmaker's shop. That was when I finally noticed that he was all properly turned out in a suit, looking like something out of a fashion magazine, only manlier. He had even shaved, that afternoon, and he looked very trimmed and debonair.

"You look very nice," I said weakly.

He smiled the way he usually did when he had been making some sort of practical joke and shrugged. "I hope it fits." He turned down the hall toward my bedroom.

I followed him. "Can I see it?"

He laid the bag out on my bed and unzipped it to display an elegant, pale yellow dress.

"You had this made for me?" I asked, frightened and delighted by the concept.

He nodded. "She knew exactly what you would want." He smiled. "I hope."

"It—it's beautiful." Awed, I shyly reached out to touch it. I closed my eyes, feeling the smooth silk. I looked into his watery, sky blue eyes.

"I hope you'll like wearing it." His voice was warm.

"Do I need to hurry?" I bustled over to my dresser. "I need to change everything."

"May I watch?" he uttered, sounding rather helpless. "Oh, I like that bra. Need help with it?"

"Thanks. The hooks are difficult. Okay, fine you hold it up to my breasts, and I'll do the hooks."

"You should let me help you more often," he said with the excitement of a teenager. I smiled. "You seem happy, Solace. I promise you today will only get better."

I laughed. "You like this, don't you?"

"Love it! Ha!" he sang happily. "Knickers too? Those *are* nice."

I slipped the dress over my head, and turned to look at myself in the mirror before I began to button it. It was gorgeous, and it suited me perfectly. I have always loved to wear yellow, but most of my clothes were blue or purple. This dress was the result of good planning, or I should say scheming, on the part of my fiancé and my dressmaker.

After I was dressed, I touched up my hair and makeup, changed my jewelry, and picked out another pair of shoes. I was still flustered from the surprise and full of questions I knew he wouldn't answer. I just needed to go along and enjoy.

The girls were pinned into their bridesmaid dresses when we arrived at the shop. They were bursting with excitement, but they kept their secret. When we got into Sean's well-used minivan, which seemed completely unfit for the four of us in our best attire, I was still in the dark about our next destination, but Williamsport is not such a large city that the secret could be kept much longer. We were over the Williamsport Bridge and heading north within minutes of leaving the shop. Soon we were pulling up in front of Queen of Heaven Catholic Church.

Eyes wide with wonder, I asked, "Who is getting married?" He shot me a mischievous smile. "Mike?" I screeched. "He didn't tell me!" I felt like crying because I was so happy for Mike, because I had been left out of the planning, and just because I cried so easily those days.

"He knew you had a lot on your plate just now, Solace," he explained. "Just thought it would be fun to surprise you. I tried to take care of everything."

"Did we get them a gift?" I took his responding guffaw to mean we had not yet done so.

Ed and Laura Leahy stood in the shaded portico greeting guests as they arrived. Sean kissed my cheek and handed me off to Mrs. Leahy who led me away from the noisy chatter and laughter. "Michael wants to see you before the wedding, Solace," she explained. We passed the church office, and she stopped to knock at the next door. "I'll leave you here."

Jimmy opened the door, but beyond him I could see Mike happily rambling away with some friends. He stopped when he saw me, and shouted, "Solace! Dear girl, come in." He pushed past his inert brother a little roughly, grabbed my hands, and pulled me inside. "Hey, you look sharp," he said before he threw his arms around me and gave me a big kiss. He smelled of liquor.

"Why the secret, Mike?" I asked.

"Oh, we just thought it would be fun to surprise you, since this was all put together so quick. Fool that I am, I waited until Cara got back from that seminar in New York to actually propose." Watching me, he slowed and quieted his voice. "Are you happy for me?" he asked with genuine concern.

Looking at him bubbling over with giddy bliss, there was no way that I could be anything less than thrilled for him. "I am very happy for you, Mike."

"Will you be my best man? My best woman? Whatever the fuck—the best of the bunch?"

"Seriously?" I asked with an intake of breath.

"Otherwise, it might have to be Jimmy," he whispered. He shrugged and tilted his head toward his brother.

"Now, don't ask me to do it out of pity, Mike," I whispered back.

"Come on. Stand by me in my terror."

"Consider me your comrade then, Mate."

"Oh, thank you, Solace! Thank you! Thank you! I love you," and he kissed me again.

"Are you sober enough to get married?" I asked.

"You bet! We only had a couple of drinks, celebrating! Want one?"

"Thanks, but I think I'll wait for the reception. You *are* having a party after, aren't you?" I was still on medications that restricted my alcohol consumption, but Mike didn't need to know that.

"Hell, yes, but this one is at a nice place, not the bloody hellhole where I usually host them."

"Oh, where?"

"That fancy Russian place, 1812."

"*Nice.*" That was way out of our budget. "But you and Cara will be living in that bloody hellhole?"

"Yeah," he giggled, "but she's already shopping for furniture."

"It could use a feminine touch," I commented.

"Damn straight. We've got to have a nice home for our baby, our beautiful little alien creature. Did I show you the sonogram picture?" As I was saying that I had not seen it, he pulled out his wallet and produced a black and white blur. "There is it. It looks human and everything."

I felt a lump in my throat. "Your baby," I whispered. I blinked back tears. "It's so wonderful, Mike. You and Cara and the baby will be so happy, I just know it."

He squeezed me around my shoulders, careful not to muss my hair or make up. "I don't know why it took me so long to make up my mind."

"Did it really?" I asked. "I think you knew what you wanted to do from the start, but you had to make sure you weren't missing some option. It's like that with big decisions that come easily."

The priest poked his head in, saying, "It's almost time. You gentlemen might want to take your seats. Michael, are you ready?"

"Yes, Father," he said. He clasped my hand in his and we walked to the door. "Father Joe, this is Solace Murphy, my best friend person."

"Hello, Miss Murphy," the priest said with a friendly smile. We shook hands. As we walked toward the sanctuary he briefed me on the wedding procedures, since I had missed the rehearsal. "There will be a full mass."

I snickered at the look on Mike's face. "You planned that just for me, didn't you? You know how I love kneeling," I teased.

We entered the sanctuary through the chancel, which allowed us a good view of the crowded pews. The front row of both sides was still empty, except for Grace Reilly waiting for her parents. Mike's brothers and their families were in the second row, directly behind us. Sean and the girls sat in the second row, behind Grace, with her brothers, Tom and Ryan and their families. Behind them, were many of the neighbors I had met during my time of dating Sean, including George, Olga, and most of their offspring.

"How's Cara doing? She must be exhausted. Where are you going for your honeymoon?"

"She's okay. She's not been sick much," he said cheerfully. "I think she was more certain of me than I was."

"Yeah," I said to say something. We took our positions.

"We can't get off work for a honeymoon now. We'll plan something soon, though, it probably won't be too fancy. We're both more interested in fixing things up for the baby. Did I tell you that, if it's a girl, we want to name her Megan? Do you think Donny'll be okay with that?"

Tears came to my eyes. "I think that he would. As long as you both like the name as well as the sentiment."

"Yeah, actually, we both think Megan Leahy sounds really pretty."

"It does."

"Will it bother you, Solace? I wouldn't want to step on your toes. No matter what."

I thought for a moment. Should it bother me? I couldn't think of a reason why it should. I'd always gotten along with Megan Reilly Donovan. Perhaps, like moving her picture from bedside to dresser, having her namesake as a niece might help to keep her memory at the proper distance. "I don't think so," I said at length. "I can't imagine anyone would object, except maybe Cara's mom, since she's so high-strung."

He shrugged. "I care more about how you feel, Solace. Just let us know sometime in the next few months." He looked up, alert. "This is the last song!"

I turned. "Your Mom is coming in."

"She's today's hero, let me tell you." He dropped his head again and spoke in a low voice. "She took care of everything. You know, Cara's been planning her wedding since Megan eloped. Swore she'd never have a quiet, little ceremony. I proposed to her twenty-two days ago. I think we're supposed to have about two fifty—three hundred coming."

I shook my head with amazement. Sean and I had had a relatively easy time putting our wedding together, but we still couldn't have managed all the preparations in three weeks.

"Mum just told Maggie and Kevin she would handle all the calls. This late in the game it turns out there are cancellations, plenty of them, and as long as we were willing to jump into the openings, we could do pretty much whatever we wanted. All the people we dealt with were happy to make up for the lost business."

The bridal procession began with a flower girl, Ryan's daughter, and two bridesmaids in matching long, blue dresses and carrying flowing bouquets. I was grateful to be a groom's woman with my lovely, reusable dress and free hands. Mesmerized, Mike watched Cara approach, floating on her father's arm with her face framed by her dark red curls and a veil of lace.

I managed to deliver the toast Sean helped me compose en route well enough to receive a whispered self-congratulation in my ear from Rob about the stage training he was giving me. We all danced and ate and had a wonderful time. Then when the party was over, we went to the Reillys' house for part of the evening.

Wedding gifts were stacked in a corner of the girls' bedroom where Megan, Grace, and Cara had slept together growing up. Grace and Cara had stripped the room of everything that had belonged to them, but there were still some things Megan had left behind when she married Sean. The girls felt a special attachment to their mother when they slept in her old room, and they played on their grandparents' sentiments by asking if they could stay the night. They kept a few things there, so there was no need for them to go home and pack a bag. Sean gave me a meaningful look, making me wonder if he had put them up to inviting themselves to stay.

On the way to my apartment, I leaned back into my seat, thinking. We didn't try to talk. It was never easy for Sean to hear in the noisy van while he drove, but in the dark it was nearly impossible. He put a hand on my thigh at a stoplight, and just said, "Tired?" but I didn't have time to answer before he turned his eyes back to the road and began to move the van again with the green light. I was a little tired, but mostly I was just lost in my thoughts.

I had no doubt that Mike and Cara would be happy together. Since he had started seeing her, his outlook had brightened. She seemed happy. I thought about how being with Sean had changed me; all of the changes had been positive. He was good for me. I hoped that I was half as good for him. I loved being with him, even if we were doing nothing. As a matter of fact, he was one of the few people with whom I could contentedly do nothing.

I admired Mike and Cara for trying to have the wedding of her dreams despite the quick nature of their alliance, though the wedding itself often seems to get a disproportionate amount of attention compared to the marriage. They were both social creatures with lots of friends, and I was happy for them that they were not embarrassed by her pregnancy as I might have been. I was a bit jealous. They had known each other in passing for years, but had only come to know each other well in these last few months. And now they were married.

Our long afternoon and evening caught up with us after we returned to my place. We settled at the kitchen table each with a glass of milk and some carrots on the cutting board between us. I was pensive and uncommunicative. Except for the crunching of carrots, we were silent. It wasn't as late it felt. I drained my glass. Sean watched me as I doodled on the cutting board with the juice from the carrots, orange on white. I assumed that he was ruminative too, though he was probably only trying to figure out what was going on with me. He took my hand in his.

I let go of my carrot stylus. I didn't look at him. "Mike told me that they want to name the baby Megan, if it's a girl."

"Really?" There was a smile in his voice.

"I told him you would like it!"

"And you?"

"I." I began to say I thought it was nice, but I never spoke the words. I brought his hand to my lips and slavered onto his fingers briefly before I let go of it. I stood and walked out into the living room with no intention. I sunk to my knees and picked up one of the pillows that were strewn in the corner near my television. I hugged it to my chest. Sean knelt with me, holding me. I felt so safe and so lost and so angry. I squeezed the pillow and clamped my teeth onto the roping around its edge.

Protected by Sean, I envisioned our child, a fuzzy blur like Mike and Cara's, on the screen of an ultrasound monitor. Sean sat with me, holding my hand, his eager face aglow with joy. I would have been wearing maternity clothes for quite some time. The girls would hold regular conversations with my rounded belly. Instead of wondering if we needed to postpone the wedding because we were still too deep in mourning, we would have moved our wedding plans forward.

I hiccoughed a little cry.

"What is it, Solace?" He held me without restraining me.

"We will never know our child," I said in what must have sounded like a terribly pathetic tone. "It's not fair," I stammered.

His muscles tightened. His hand trembled slightly until he steadied it again. "No, it's not." His words were slow and solemn. "We will miss a lifetime of experiences."

"I wish I could have seen our baby, Sean. I wish I could have held it, even just once," I whispered. Sean clicked his tongue soothingly as he pulled me closer. I curled my body around the pillow. "Am I losing my mind? Am I losing my grip on reality?"

Sean barked a laugh, but he answered me without bitterness. "No. You've had too much reality. You need a break from it for a while. Go ahead. Pound your fists into the pillows."

"Pounding fists is what got me into all this trouble!"

"Not yours. It's okay to hit a pillow." He nestled against me. Seeing that I was still hugging the pillow, he said, "You're so sweet."

"No, I'm not," I declared. "I'm going to squeeze every God-damned penny out of that bastard!" I squished the pillow even harder, pulling, twisting, and contorting it, still holding it against my bosom.

"Here, get his Mum and Dad's money too," Sean said picking up some more pillows. "I'll help. Maybe he's got some ruffian cousins. Would you be upset if we ruined your pillows?"

I laughed suddenly, the tension broken. "I do kind of like them."
I shrugged, the violent mood beginning to pass. "But no, I think it
would be okay." We ended up lying close to one another on the
floor. I rolled over and put my head on the pillow I had been
gnawing. "I hope our children have your eyes."

"I hope they have your hair," he crooned back to me. He turned
on his side to face me and ran his hand down the contour of my body.
"And if they have my eyes, I hope they work as well as yours. I
would not wish my myopia on anyone." He wrapped some of my
hair around his hand and wrist.

I smiled. "It's your hearing we should worry about."

"Naw...my hearing was fine before...well." Sean had told me
that he'd blown out some of his hearing during his garage band days,
long before the war.

"How important do you think it is for me to see that Rosie is
punished?"

He looked serious again. "I don't know. It depends on you."

"What about you? You've been hurt by this too, even though I
don't think Rosie has any idea you exist."

"What? You didn't tell him about your stalker?"

"God, no. I think I knew that would be dangerous. Even before
I had proof. Of course, you might have been able to give him back
worse than he gave."

"Could be." He leaned back with his hand on his forehead,
fingers in his hair. "I've thought about vengeance, but, you know,
it's not worth it. We have too much to lose to risk it. Even if I didn't
end up in jail too, it would still damage us. And I don't want to do
that. I must be content with whatever the law decides to do with
him."

"Even if he were sentenced to time served?"

"It will have to suffice. We have to accept it. I think that
society's affirmation of his wrongdoing is more important than his
punishment."

I bowed my head indicating agreement. "Should I forgive him?"

"Of course you should, but it's not something you can just
decide to do. It's too complicated. And you can't do it until you are
fully ready. But it might help you to move on if you acted in a
forgiving way."

"That might work, as long as I don't end up convincing myself
that I'm as bad as he is."

"You won't do that. You've changed, Solace. You still need to be coaxed a little, but I think you really do believe in yourself."

I hung my head. "I guess, like everything else, it's a matter of balancing my feelings and allowing time to give me perspective."

Sean lifted my chin and met my eyes. "Yes," he mouthed, and then he kissed me. All of the passion we felt earlier as anger and hurt came forward now, again as love for each other. We drew closer, until our bodies were pressed against each other.

"My darling man."

Later, we showered together. I hogged the water, and Sean looked a bit blue before I stepped out to dry. Then he luxuriated under the steamy stream for a few minutes. I ran to the bed to wait for him, but I drifted even before his warm, still damp body slipped in beside me. I rolled over to embrace him, and he pulled me to him. We interlocked, and I felt a serenity I had not felt in a long time. I closed my eyes and held the image of his dear face on my eyelids. His arms encircled me, his lips touched my ear, and I was surrounded with his warmth and love.

Our sleep was peaceful, spooned in the same position, close together all night. I awoke once, heard his soft breathing, a quiet, reassuring little snore every few breaths, closed my eyes, and returned to sleep until the room was flooded with light. Sean was still sound asleep. I wanted to let him rest, so I lay beside him quietly.

When he woke, he rubbed a somewhat scratchy cheek against mine in a nearly automatic caress that was as natural to him as stretching or yawning. I thought it said many good things about him that his first semi-conscious act of each day was loving. I turned my head to see his face, puffy with sleep, next to my own, so close that it took a moment to focus my eyes upon it. He smiled at my movement. He was still mostly asleep, and he pulled me in closer, inviting me back to the oblivion of slumber. "Sean?" I whispered. He nuzzled my cheek with his long nose. He couldn't hear me, of course, so I would have to wait. I closed my eyes and rested.

I had something important to tell him.

In the months since I was attacked, I had pushed myself to be independent, and I had succeeded, though it meant more suffering on my part than may have been necessary. Loose ends and unfinished premarital goals no longer hung over me as bridges I must cross before I could begin the next phase of my life.

Later, when we were awake and playing at making the bed, I stopped him with my hand. "I need to ask you something important, Sean," I said in as serious a voice as I could summon.

"What, darling?" he asked, a sudden concern coming over his face.

"Would it be possible for me to break my lease?"

His eyebrows rose. "Break your lease? But, Solace, you're already—" The instant he understood my question he stopped and allowed me to explain. It was the last step I needed to take alone.

"Sean, I've proven I can be independent. I've fulfilled whatever it was I needed to fulfill, accomplished what I needed to accomplish. I want to come home. I want to be with you."

Yesterday he might have asked if I was sure. Not today. His expression changed as he moved from carefully searching me, pondering my motivation and evaluating my certainty, to a silent celebration. His eyes glistened. He knew I was sure. He lifted my hand in his, holding it in front of his lips briefly before kissing it to seal our bargain.

He shook his head, watching me, wonderment in his eyes. "By God, Solace, I love you. I want you to come home too."

Chapter Twenty

My final move took only a few hours. When we told the girls of our decision, they urged me to move immediately, so Sean dropped us off to start packing while he rounded up a truck and the muscle power of his two youngest brothers. Since a professional crew would clean the place before a new tenant moved in, I didn't even need to clean before I left. I liked knowing that this first home of my own would still belong to me.

By evening, I was well settled, rocking gently in time with Sean's shower concert. The girls were in bed, and the house was otherwise quiet. I put aside thoughts of informing the world about my move until the morning. It wasn't like I was going to forget that I had done it. So what if I didn't cancel my telephone or newspaper for a few days?

I looked around our room. It needed my touch, beginning with curtains and more color to go along with the furniture I had brought with me. Through one of the open doors, I could see the back of Sean's easel in the room we referred to as the nursery. Sean had offered to move his art studio to one of the empty rooms, but I said I'd rather put any babies we might have into another room instead. Then we wouldn't have to move the child when it was older, and I wouldn't feel guilty for keeping my own creative spot, a small study we could reach from the door on the other end of our room.

Never feeling the need to suppress his music, Sean kept singing when he turned off the water. He came out of the bathroom naked except for the towel with which he was drying his hair. I looked up and sighed contentedly. He sat cross-legged on the floor at my feet and let the towel fall over his shoulder. "Happy?"

I nodded and lifted my foot to touch him with a pointed toe. "I feel like I've accomplished something."

"You have accomplished a good deal."

"I love you."

"I love you too."

"I hope I show it well enough."

"You do." He leaned his head forward for a moment. His glasses slipped down his nose, so I pushed them up with my toe. He smiled. "Gentle toes."

My answer was to run my pointed toes down the side of his face. Then I slid forward off my seat and knelt with him on the floor, wrapping my arms around him and bringing my lips to his. Still kissing, we reclined on the floor. His hands made their way inside my nightgown. When next our lips parted, Sean's head dove under too, and he moved his mouth from one breast to the other while one of his hands moved up the side of my leg.

He looked up, wrinkling his forehead. "Why do you always wear things with so many buttons?"

I trailed my fingertips along his jaw line. "To fill your love life with stimulating challenges."

"I don't see the relationship between buttons and stimulation, but you, well, you are always stimulating."

"Thank you. But the buttons are for the challenge part."

"I'll just bite them off."

"You can sew them back on again then, Artificial Boy."

"Is this what it's going to be like when we're married?"

"Wouldn't want you getting bored. I like undressing slowly. Sometimes my clothes just fall off too fast."

He chuckled, and shaking his head, he replied, "I'm getting a bad feeling about tonight." With the care and caution necessary to diffuse a bomb, he slowly slipped the buttons through their slits, his head drawing closer as his hands moved lower. His concentration was complete, and I watched with fascination until his hair began to tickle my neck.

I began to giggle and confessed, "You know, I could have just taken it off over my head."

"Why didn't you say so sooner?"

"You were having so much fun." I pressed one finger into his chest and pushed him away. While he feigned a protest, I lifted my nightgown off over my head.

"Oh!" he cried, staring at my chest as I lowered my arms. His mouth hung open slightly. "Oh my God, Solace! You are so lovely." He reached out to feel the contour of one of my breasts. Then with resolve he whispered, "I've got to paint tonight."

"Not before we make love," I insisted.

"I should, but I couldn't." Still there was an increased sense of urgency, our passion propelled by his inspiration to paint. "Not until you are sound asleep and dreaming of our pleasures." We were kissing again, touching and demanding more of each other. He carried me to the bed when it was time for me to sleep. I rolled onto my side, my eyes already shutting, I heard him ask, "Now how am I going to paint?"

"With inspiration," I mumbled.

"Sleep well, Solace." He kissed my face in several places, caressed my cheek, and pulled the covers over me. I was asleep before he stepped away from the bed to find some clothing.

Sean never came to bed that night, but he did stop painting before I awoke. I found him in the kitchen creating breakfast, moving briskly and seeming chipper. He greeted me with a huge smile and proudly asked, "Did you see what I did last night?"

"No. I didn't dare peek, beyond seeing that you weren't in there. Did it go well? Did you sleep at all yet?"

"Go look. You decide how it went," he answered in a way that told me that he was very pleased with his overnight work.

"I will." I kissed him and asked, "Are you going to sleep after we leave?"

"Probably."

I returned upstairs and ran into the girls, who were bustling between the bathroom and their bedroom getting ready for school. I greeted them, and they hugged me. "It's so good to have you back, Mum," Irina said.

"We missed you," added Maureen.

"I missed you too," I said, returning their hugs. I went around through the study, through our bedroom, to the nursery to view the painting in privacy. Sean would tell the girls when he was ready to show it to them.

The painting was turned so that it could only be viewed from one corner of the room, and I stood motionless and hidden by the easel as I gazed into the mostly familiar underwater scene. The only changes Sean had made were to the mermaid. He had softened the shadings and contours of her body and tailfin, making her appear more fragile, yet strong enough, as she risked her life to save the man who had ventured into her world. Nude, her hair swirled around in the water, hiding and revealing her. More than resembling me, she was Sean's image of me. Her features were mine without the imperfections of heredity and harm.

I stood long, stunned and staring. I had never thought that I was so beautiful, yet I knew that this was how Sean saw me. Only when

Sean joined me could I look away, though I had to focus through flowing tears. His visage fell forward humbly when he saw my face.

"Oh my God, Sean," I said softly. "I just didn't know...."

When he looked up, he smiled with damp eyes. He was still energized by his creative burst. "Breakfast is ready."

With its central figure done, the painting was soon completed. He called the piece "Salvation."

I was very proud of Sean. His work was moving forward artistically. This was his strongest piece yet. For the first time in my life, I found that I could stare at one painting indefinitely, wishing to continue gazing at it, and gaining from the experience. This piece met every criteria of my personal definition of art. Boris agreed. He and Sean arranged for the painting to be shipped to London for sale at the gallery where the original of the volcano and some other pieces of Sean's best work had been sold.

Irina's school play was staged the weekend after I moved. The children and their teacher did a wonderful job on the production; the many long hours of preparation paid off. After the final show, there was a party for cast, crew, and families.

Later that night, while we were getting ready for bed, I asked, "What were you talking to Irina's teacher about for all that time?"

"Hmm? He thinks she's quite talented."

"She's a natural performer." I brushed my hair and began to braid it. "She's so comfortable in front of a crowd, and she's got such a lovely voice. A few acting lessons, and she would be happier on stage than off, I should think."

"Yeah," he said. While I knew he was proud of her, he did not seem terribly pleased. He was probably thinking about how much trouble our talented Rob Murphy had earning a living or even of his own small paychecks when he was playing in a band. "She'd like having someone else write down what she's supposed to say. Then Reen wouldn't smack her."

"That's a lovely way to put it," I said sarcastically.

"Well, it's true."

"Still, somehow it doesn't seem like your way of saying it. Is something bothering you?"

"I've just been thinking, Solace," he said. Then he was quiet again. He pulled out his toothbrush and topped it with paste without looking at me.

"Not ready to talk?" I asked. I twisted an elastic band around the bottom of my braid.

He kissed my cheek and went into the bedroom. I climbed into bed next to him a few minutes later. The light was still on, and I didn't turn it off in case he had decided that he wanted to talk. He touched my cheek when I leaned over to kiss him. I decided to say, "I've always thought you should try to go back to teaching."

"I know." He swallowed.

"I suppose seeing a student production makes you feel like you're missing out."

He sighed. "He wanted me to know that Nina Brewer is pregnant."

"Who is she?"

"The one who replaced me. She and Quinn are friends. They'll be looking for a long-term sub, but he hinted that she wants to stay home with the baby."

"I like Mr. Quinn." I settled in next to Sean with my head on his shoulder. "Wouldn't it be nice to go back in time to your old job?"

"I'd prefer staying in the present, with you, and going back to my old job. I'll look into it, Solace. You won't be too disappointed if it doesn't happen?"

"I'm not the one to worry about."

He grimaced. "I've taken bigger risks. I can be brave enough." There was doubt in his voice. He yawned and lifted his hand to my cheek. I could feel him falling asleep. I thought I should turn off the lamp, but I didn't want to disturb him. I wrapped my leg around his as I nestled against him. I felt so contented with all that warm skin touching that I was asleep before I had another thought.

It was only a few busy weeks later when, following our wedding rehearsal, Olga and George hosted a suppertime picnic in their backyard. While the Murphys and Donovans tried to find common ground for conversation, George, usually so quiet, held most of the children and American men rapt with stories from his years of working as a heavy equipment operator. Whispering to Sean that I enjoyed seeing his father so full of animation, I remarked, "I'd love to hear his version of raising eleven children."

"He never really does it, heh. Always gets sidetracked. It reminds him too much of the war, and then he starts in on telling war stories. That is, he used to before Tim and I went to the Gulf."

"It must be more difficult to send your children off to war than to go yourself."

He nodded and turned away from me and this too-tender subject. Now that I had come so far in my recovery, I increasingly understood that my injuries and the loss of our child had in many ways been harder on him than they had been on me. While my part would simply have ended, he would have had to go on, and he knew what it was to survive such a loss.

We walked to the gate with some of his cousins, who were beginning to depart now that the food was running low. After we wished them well, he turned to me brightly, happy to have found another subject to discuss. "Did you hear what your mother told me?"

"I guess you know I didn't." I settled into a spot along the fence near the gate, inserting one foot into a chain link diamond.

Sean flashed his teeth. "She told me that she was glad that you had moved in with me and that we hadn't waited to get married to be together."

"My mother?" I stopped suddenly. "Were your batteries dead, Bionic Bloke?"

"No." He was amused. "I heard her correctly. She trusts me." He threw back his shoulders.

"Well," I replied, still skeptical. "So do I."

"It feels like tomorrow is still an age away. It'll be a hell of a night."

"I don't think I'll sleep. I hope you'll still love me with dark circles under my eyes."

"I've seen you look a fair bit worse than that, Solace, and it never affected how much I cared about you."

"I'll miss you tonight," I whispered. "I hope your best man won't take you off for too much drinking."

"Rob? Not likely. Besides, I know my limits, and I promise I will barely exceed them tonight."

"You'll have fun with your mates. Mike promised you'd make it to the church tomorrow."

"He'll keep me safe for you." He drew me close against him so we could say good-bye while we had a little privacy. "At least you get to go to your very own, comfortable bed at a reasonable hour tonight. I'll probably need an extra drink just to get to sleep on the Murphy's couch, so enjoy having the bed to yourself. We'll make up for our night apart tomorrow. You packed?"

"Yes. Somehow."

I didn't have the bed to myself. In fact, I barely managed to get into it. Too excited to sleep, the girls and I stayed up late playing Hearts on the floor of my bedroom, and after that we played Yahtzee for a couple more hours, until the cat chased a die way underneath the bed. Right on cue, Irina yawned and curled up on the floor. She was barely conscious when I kissed her, but she whispered, "Love you, Mum," to me, filling my heart with a joy that would last all through the next day and beyond. Maureen had the wherewithal to set the alarm before she bundled into the bed beside me.

Perhaps I should have gone to bed earlier and alone, but I wouldn't have traded that night for any other. I was glad I had the girls to myself during those special hours. I had thought they might need some last-minute reassurances. Though they didn't seem to, I could tell that they appreciated my efforts. There had never been a time when they made me feel that I did not belong in their family.

The wedding was scheduled for ten o'clock. We left the house by taxi before eight. Olga was already at the church with the florist and the wedding coordinator. Once the girls were dressed, their grandmother began to weave flowers and ribbons into their auburn waves. I sneaked around the church to see the flowers in the sanctuary and the caterers setting up the luncheon in the social hall. Before anyone else arrived, I was back in the changing room where Bridget surprised me by bringing a friend from Rob's theatre to help me with my hair and make-up.

My family arrived about half an hour before the service, and they crowded into the parlor for photographs. When it was time, I walked with my parents behind Maureen and Irina as they danced down the corridor, pretty as fairies. My mother waited beside Olga near the sanctuary door while George pinned a flower on Tim's lapel. Olga was escorted to her seat by Tim, and my mother followed with Greg.

My father and I waited, back out of view, as the girls began the walk toward the altar, side-by-side. He was feeling sentimental. He knew that this would be the last time he walked one of his daughters into her new life, and he hung back a moment too long. It was all as I hoped it would be. The music, the flowers, our friends, and our emotions, every bit of it was beautiful. I treasure and hold close those moments of our union.

We both trembled with happiness as we turned to walk up the aisle together toward the sunlit foyer after the service. We had only a few moments to celebrate alone, but we lingered in that moment as long as we could.

The party spread out over the church lawn for the hour before our luncheon began. After the meal, most of us went outside again for the music and dancing. I danced with Sean, my father, Sean's father, all of our brothers, and even my "extra father-in-law," Kevin Reilly. The girls followed suit, dancing with their father and all three of their grandfathers. They were having the time of their lives. In a quieter way, so were Sean and I.

Once my bouquet was tossed, we gathered around Rob as he made a proper and fitting toast to which we responded by draining our glasses and hurling them against a brick wall. We had one last dance together after cutting the cake. Sean whispered, "Are you ready to go?"

"Do we have to? Oh, I guess we should."

"Which is it?" He smiled persuasively.

"Let's change our clothes."

"Together?"

"We'd better not. This crowd might expect you to come out waving a bloody sheet or something."

He chuckled. "I think they know it wouldn't be bloody."

"Great," I pouted. "Not an ounce of illusion left."

Cindy came to help me out of my gown and collect the things I'd asked her to take home for me. While I unbuttoned my sleeves, she opened all of the fasteners on the back of the gown. "Did Sean tell you where you're going for your honeymoon yet, girlie girl?"

"Italy."

"Oh my God! That is so romantic. You are going to have so much fun."

"I know!" I threw my arms around her. "Cindy, you're an angel. You've always been so good to me. I doubt I would have stuck around here long enough to like Sean Donovan if it weren't for you. Thank you."

She backed away, crying a little, but mostly laughing. "Careful or I'll get makeup all over your wedding dress!"

Mike plowed a path through the crowd toward the waiting taxi. Behind us, our friends came together again, propelling us forward when they did not impede our movement with the delivery of Russian bear hugs and Irish blessings. When we reached Cara, I kissed Mike's cheek and pushed him toward her. My family waited near the car. I embraced everyone and wished them all a safe trip home. Rob and Bridget stood with their distant American cousins. She was the last to embrace me and whisper a blessing before we reached our ride.

At the open car door were Maureen and Irina. "Can't we come too?" Irina pleaded.

"No," answered Sean firmly. As he kissed them farewell, he added, "Mind your Aunt Tanya, and don't do half the stuff I would have done when I was your age."

After sharing sweet hugs and kisses with me, they turned to their father again with exuberant cries of, "Love you, Dad!" Roughhousing, they mussed his hair and clothing. Baz and Gabe passed them colorful plastic spray foam and bright green hair mousse, which the girls massaged into Sean's hair, creating multiple spikes with amazing skill upon their uncooperative, dodging victim. Irina giggled, winding a final curlicue on top. Then they both shouted a happy, "Bon voyage!"

Good naturedly, Sean pulled some foam off and tossed it back at them before he ducked into the car. I was still staring, amazed that I hadn't been touched, when Sean yanked on my elbow, saying, "Let's get out of here." He looked a horrible, happy, worn wreck, and I snuggled up next to him cautiously. Instead of necking, as we otherwise might have desired, we remarked on the wisdom of changing out of our fancy clothes. Once we were safely away from our guests, the driver reached over the back of the seat to offer Sean a box of tissues.

Sean's van was parked on some anonymous side street. We transferred everything to it and drove out of the city, passing through farmlands and into the rainforest for about twenty kilometers before turning onto the coast hugging highway that went all the way around

James Island. We passed through several villages before we stopped at an isolated cottage situated on the border between the forest and the beach. It was a primitive place, with running water from a cistern and a minimum of cooking facilities. Sean had stocked food for the two meals we would consume there. A fresh breeze blew the curtains while we made love, then we had a cold chicken picnic on the beach for our supper.

The next morning we flew from Williamsport to Brazil and on to Rome. Once we were there, we followed Sean's flexible agenda, which was heavy on sampling the tastes of Italy. Our hotels had been chosen for their proximity to the places we wanted to visit, so some of our rooms were cramped and shabby, while one was not even terribly clean. I was able to cast aside my fastidiousness and found them all charming.

On our feet, we explored the cities, the neighborhoods, and the historic areas. Off our feet, we ate and drank at sidewalk cafes and made love in our hotel beds. We rarely looked at a clock. We had enough purpose each day to get out and going, but not so much that we couldn't stop and rest or change our plans if we wanted. We took off our shoes, put our feet into fountains, and watched people going about their daily business. Sean brought sketching materials with him everywhere we went. He frequently pulled them out, quickly catching the spirit of each place and the spirit of me in each place.

He was having fun with his art, and I was happy to see him enjoying it, so I played along by posing for him. He never drew me as he saw me, but placed me, nude, among the ancient and modern sights. Most of his drawings were serious however, and he carefully marked the correct colors so that he could use the sketches for reference if he were to do a painting later.

I watched people, but mostly I just enjoyed being with him. His creative spirit passed along to me, and I walked atop stone walls rehearsing my lines from *The Tea House*, the play Rob had cast me in for his first production at the new community theatre he founded, or more often singing. In Florence, Sean laid his baseball cap on the pavement and people began to toss in small coins as they meandered past. Sean wouldn't let me touch the money, but he claimed it was enough for him to purchase our supper and a silver charm of Michelangelo's David as a companion for the mermaid he gave me on our first official date.

After the cap incident, I forced myself to contain my creative enthusiasm, so I commandeered his spare sketchbook. While he drew, I wrote, and we spent less time seeing the sights. That was fine. We were there to have fun, sex, and good food, and that was enough for us.

Perhaps because the lines were absent from the pages providing me with an unstructured place to restructure my thoughts, I was able to dive headlong into the kind of story I had always feared writing. The place, the occasion, and the clearing of my mind of worries all had a part in allowing me to begin it, but mostly, I believe it was the man. I was capable of doing things with Sean at my side that I would never have dared to try if I had not known him. Knowing he was there for me changed everything.

Chapter Twenty-One

The girls were waiting for us at home. They had even shopped for our supper. Maureen didn't know how to ask us about our trip, and Irina was so excited about getting a role in a new school play that she hardly asked us how we were. She was disappointed not to have been assigned the lead again, but we managed to reassure her that playing the comic relief was potentially a greater challenge. Maureen caught me alone later to ask if she could go out with a new boy from school. I was honored to receive the inquiry, which would have only been given to Sean two weeks before.

Thrown off by our long flight, we went to bed earlier than the girls that first night. They were downstairs watching a movie on television, and we talked quietly in bed while we allowed our fatigue to turn over into sleepiness. After being cramped on the plane, we both needed to stretch and straighten before we could cuddle together the way we normally did. He kissed my bare shoulder. "Only two more days of vacation for you."

"They won't be play days. We have a lot of catching up to do."

"Lots of gifts to open."

"That'll be fun. Did you see the stack Irina was building?"

"Where?"

"The living room. She was using the stepstool." I flipped over onto my stomach and leaned on my elbows. "We've gotten lots of checks. I know you want a piano, but is there anything else you want?"

"Not really. You?" He slid his arm under my body and rolled over so that his body was leaning against mine. "You have ideas for the money?"

"Plenty. There's the college fund and furniture. At least the house is perfect. Thank you."

"Welcome."

"I guess we should just save it for someday."

"Do you want to quit work and stay home?"

"We haven't gotten that much money," I joked. "No. Someday I'd like to stay home, especially if we have children, but I like doing what I'm doing. I like my job, and the people, and the place. I'm content. Have I thanked you for giving me the impetus to change careers?"

"Not recently," he chuckled.

"Well, then I must, and heartily." I arched my back and kissed his lips. "Now that we're a family, it isn't all going to change, is it?"

"All? No. Some things will," he said with a philosophic air. "Soon you'll be pestering me to do all sorts of things. You'll probably want me to plant grass over the vegetable patch or something."

"I was thinking about asking you to do that."

"What? No way!" He bristled.

"And you don't think that eating all that organic produce is just a bit too natural for my Artificial Boy?"

He let forth one loud burst of laughter. "Oh, Solace!" he drawled, smiling. His eyes were shining. "How did I survive those years when I couldn't talk to you?"

"Better than I did, Sean Donovan." I slipped my hands up to his ears to remove his hearing aids gently and carefully. He threw them around at times, so I knew they were somewhat durable, but I was not going to be the one to break them. I placed them on the bedside table. I was going to take his glasses too, but I decided that the conversation was not over yet. "I appreciate everything you've done for me."

"I know you do, but I don't want you to feel that you owe me anything."

"I don't. I've done a few good turns for you too."

"That's what I wasn't sure you understood, Solace. I'm glad you do," he said watching me contentedly.

We faced each other, lying on our sides, talking a little, kissing and touching in a slow, comfortable way, allowing passion to build. Love needs to be allowed its own pace.

"I wish we'd taken a few more photographs on our trip. Our friends, especially the people at the office are going to ask what we did. Honesty might not be the best policy."

"What about my drawings?"

"Not appropriate."

With a decisive nod, he added, "I'll get them ready to sell."

"You do that." I moved my fingertips along his chest, up over his Adam's apple, and touched his lips. "When are we getting a hot tub for the backyard?"

"Oh, now that's an idea! I'm glad you keep reminding me why I want to be with you. Let's make sure we never just settle in so that we have to think about it."

"I like to think about it, Sean," I whispered. I took his glasses off and dropped them an arm's length away onto whatever surface was there to catch them. His eyes were closed. The conversation was over. I kissed his lips, he wrapped his arms around me, and there was nothing else in the world but the two of us.

We were soon in what could be called a normal routine. Three days a week I walked to Uplands High School after dinner for rehearsals of *The Tea House.* I enjoyed working on the play far more than I had expected to when Rob insisted that I take on my small role. Though I had few lines, I was on stage for at least half of the production.

"Got some news I wanted to share with you first." Sean took my hand as he let the door to the school dropped behind us. He usually walked me home, as there were not many people about by the time rehearsals were done. It was a good time for us to talk about our plans, even if one or both of the girls came with us. "I got the job!"

I jumped up and threw my arms around him. "That's terrific. Sean, are you happy?"

"Yes, but I think this might make me even happier." His pale eyes reflected the light of a nearly full moon. "I'll have a couple of weeks of orientation stuff, and then I'll start in the classroom at the start of the new semester. I'll probably work with Nina a bit to make the transition go smoothly."

"Congratulations."

"Thank you."

"And I promise I'll start doing more around the house. Especially after the play ends."

"Don't worry about it." He swung our arms in time with some internal melody. There was always a tune guiding his steps. "After the play, you'll have more time to write. You do enough."

"You don't need me!" I moaned.

With a patient sigh, he said, "We're all happy. Don't let that bother you. Life really can be this good."

I stopped and looked up at the sky. I put my hand on his shoulder and let my head fall against it. He accepted my invitation to put his arm around me. He knew me so well. "I've got to remember not to disturb the calm waters."

"You do need your own personal lifeguard, don't you?" Then he whispered, "I can tell when you write about sex. I like it."

"Me too," I giggled, blushing.

"Will you let me read what you've been working on?"

The bright moonlight made it easy for him to see to converse. We had a view of the city with the dark ocean beyond. "You'd badger me for unwritten chapters, or I'd be upset that you weren't."

"I'm already badgering you."

"It's different when you know nothing about it."

He was silent, seeming to understand my point of view. "I love being able to look up at the sky and see the stars so clearly. You'd think the lights from town would drown them, but they don't up here." He ran his fingers through the Milky Way. "Do you know your southern constellations, Solace?"

"I don't know many of the northern ones," I admitted. "We should get a book from the library, and bring the girls out for a night of stargazing."

"We should," he agreed. As if this excused him from his celestial studies, he brought his gaze back to the ground, turned, and took my hand so that we could go home. He talked more about the new job, excited and full of ideas he'd been storing away for the last three years.

The girls were already in bed when we got in. I went up and wished them "sweet dreams" while he lingered downstairs locking doors and shutting off lights. I waited near their door to share their pleasure in his good news, which meant extra hugs and kisses all around.

I slipped away before he did, and started undressing. He joined me in the shower, which meant neither of us got enough hot water, so we were both chilled before we stepped out to warm each other with our towels and run to the bed. Winter in the Carollons is never very cold, but the breeze on our wet skin from the open windows seemed icy to us, and we cuddled up close under the covers. It was a night for sleep and skin to skin contact, and we soon drifted off.

Sometimes there is nothing more sensual than being held with calm, trusting love. His warmth, my warmth. His breath, my breath. His hand of its own volition, during sleep, cupping my breast, literally warming my heart. My head moving just so, so that his cheek could rest against mine. His dreams seeping out through his ears and nostrils, projecting onto my third eye. With a mental tie, we woke early, kissing before we were fully awake, as if our lovemaking were an extension of our dreams. I don't remember turning to face him, and I don't remember bringing our lips together. When my eyes opened fully, he was struggling to do the same.

"Did you want to wake up yet?" he asked in a whisper.

"It seems so. I had such lovely dreams."

"Me too." We brought our mouths together again, and we kissed more aggressively. We were awake now, and there was no going back. We were cuddled back into each other's arms before my alarm went off.

"Guess I'd better get moving, Bionic Boy. You getting up?"

"Might as well start getting used to it."

"That's right. You will be on a regular schedule soon."

"Right." He sounded mournful.

I touched his hand. "It will be alright."

The next few weeks breezed by. I had to attend rehearsal every night. Despite the presence of Sean, Cindy, and Bridget backstage building sets, I spent my time between scenes writing. Once the sets were ready, Sean settled into a kind of restless boredom. He had already transferred many of his students to other teachers and he didn't know what to do with so many quiet evenings.

He was sitting at the bench of our new-to-us upright piano playing scales. He had meant to get one as soon as he moved to the house, where the walls weren't shared with neighbors, but had been distracted until now by all of the excitement of the last few months. He kissed the air between us when he saw me.

"Did you have it tuned?"

"No. I'm just learning a few more secrets. It's a living thing, an acoustic instrument." He put his arms out and placed his hands on the sides of the case, hugging it. He winked at me and kissed the top of the music stand.

"Too bad we can't claim it as a dependent on our taxes." I leaned on the top. "When you're done petting your new mistress, your wife might like some attention."

He laughed. "That's not quite the nature of our relationship."

"I see. Anyway, if you're looking for another distraction." I let it dangle. I knew I had his full attention, and that knowledge gave me the boost of confidence I needed. I turned to leave the room and ran up the stairs. I headed to my study.

"I always like your distractions!" His footsteps pounded up the stairs, and then it was quiet as he moved through the carpeted nursery. My husband was, in my opinion, as ready for high school as any boy had ever been.

He was sitting on the edge of our bed, looking very eager, by the time I entered the room. I know that he expected me to attempt some kind of seductive gesture, but he showed no sign of disappointment when I arrived carrying a bundle of papers.

"It's my story," I managed. My throat was constricted and dry from nerves. I had poured so much of myself into this story that I was afraid even to show it to the person I trusted the most. Still, I knew that it was time for me to share it. "I finished the first draft."

He gulped and leaned away slightly, as if it was a snake charmer's basket that might contain a venomous cobra. Slowly, he raised his hands to take the book from me. His eyes were locked with mine.

I nodded to force some moisture into my mouth. "Please read it. It might help us both. I hope it will distract you—I think it is good. But it would be nice to get some feedback from someone whose judgment I trust."

He put the book down, and he held out his arms. I allowed him to enfold me. "I am honored."

"I'm sure it needs a lot of work," I explained anti-climactically. "It's just that—hell, I don't know."

I stood in his embrace, his cheek to my belly, united in body and outlook. It was a truly serene moment when I had expected a frantic one. Maybe I had changed. Maybe I had grown up. Somewhere along the way, I had curbed my anger and learned to coexist with my fears. I had never again felt the uncontrolled and impotent rage I felt when I thought Sean had betrayed his wife by asking me to go out with him at the beginning of our acquaintance, not even toward Ken Williams at the very worst moment. I was learning to turn that energy toward building my strength and my trust in the people I loved.

"I won't talk about it with anyone but you, Solace," he promised.

"I know you won't." I bent over to touch the tip of my nose to the tip of his. "I trust you with my very soul."

Sean was so secretive about reading my story that I don't think the girls even knew I had given it to him. Always the teacher, he wanted me to learn to wait for feedback. He asked no questions, expecting the story to stand on its own without my commentary or explanations. I had no choice but to restrain my curiosity until he was ready to tell me what he thought.

I had had lunch with Mike, and he'd told me an off-color joke I wanted to share privately with Sean. I was trying to remember just how it went when I saw Maureen and Irina waiting for me along the walk. Before I said anything, Maureen began to explain why they hadn't stayed after school. "Coach is sick, so practice was cancelled. And Rina asked to be excused too, since I was coming home. We need to plan something for Dad."

"Since he's going back to work," Irina specified.

"Right," agreed Maureen. They were both aglow. "A special dinner."

I admired them; they never missed an occasion to celebrate, yet their celebrations never grew stale. "Right. I should have thought of it."

"You would have, but your imagination is stuck in bed these days," Irina said.

"What?" I cried defensively. "Actually, I'm spoiled because you always think of it first." We stopped to wait for a car before we crossed the next road. "What shall we make?"

"We all loved that American food," Maureen said. "Could we make Cheshire pink shrimps and chips?"

"Chesapeake? Spiced, steamed shrimp." It took me a minute to interpret her request. "You want to do it on his first day of work, right?" I looked from one to the other, confirming, "I take it you've already planned something for dessert?"

Sean and I rose early on his first day in the classroom so that we could breakfast together without the girls. He needed to leave almost an hour ahead of them. Because we would have much less time together from now on, we would make this effort even on the days when I did not go to work. I wondered over the toaster what it would be like to have the house to myself each Friday. "Will I feel single again?" I thought aloud.

"I beg your pardon?" Sean asked leaning over to look into the toaster, as if he expected to see a little person standing in one of the slots. He put a hand on my shoulder and quietly said, "I certainly hope you won't feel single again. You can't be entertaining a brigade of Marines when you have gardens to weed and shops to conquer."

"A brigade of Marines?" I asked, stunned by the suggestion. The toast popped up, and I pulled it out and dropped it on our plates.

As we walked to the table, he explained himself. "You kissed a lot of them."

Flustered, I just stared at him. With a skeptical squint, I asked, "Are you referring to that piece of fiction I lent to you?" I dropped the plates with a thump onto the table and sat. He sat too, and I started to put butter on my toast. "Well?" I asked.

He nodded gravely, drained his juice, and placed the glass down firmly on the table as punctuation. "I've read it." He looked at my expectant face.

"And?"

He smiled again and took a breath. "I like it. I cared about the characters. I made some notes you might use when you edit it. And even though I technically don't need a distraction any more, I hope you'll include me through the whole process. I have to make sure you don't decide to kill off my favorite character or something."

I smiled, keeping my eyes on my untouched breakfast. I was too elated to carry on the conversation I longed to have, so I smoothed my napkin and abruptly changed the subject. "I shouldn't keep you. Can't be late for your first day of school." He glanced at the clock and ate the last of his toast. "Thank you," I said, touching his hand across the table. He lifted mine and kissed it. His eyes lingered on my face for a moment before he rose, gracefully letting go of my hand by sliding his away from mine. Our fingertips touched just a little longer than was necessary. I tapped his middle finger with mine, as a farewell, and I turned my hand over, as if to keep the moment, his touch cupped in my palm.

I daydreamed at the table, my toast grown cold, while he was upstairs. He was back in moments, brushing a kiss over my cheek as he moved his lips to mine. "I love you, Solace Donovan. And I am very proud of you," he said.

"I'm proud of you too." Sensing that he wanted to linger, I urged him to go. "Now get along. You want to impress the headmaster, right?"

"Yes, but before I go, Solace, I just want you to know that I will be right by your side to support you in everything. That's my job, you know."

"I might be more than you bargained for, Bionic Bloke," I said.

"You are, absolutely, more than I could have ever expected you to be."

"That's not the way I meant it."

"I know, but I mean it the way I said it. I swear." He crossed his hands into the now-familiar X over his heart gesture.

I touched his cheek with my cupped palm, and he rubbed against it before he patted his pocket to make sure he had a spare set of batteries and turned to go. I could hear him whistling as he went through the door. I would miss our old ways, but I was so happy for him, taking this step, that it more than made up for it.

The End